LOOK AWAY, BEULAH LAND

LOOK AWAY, BEULAH LAND

a novel

Lonnie Coleman

DOUBLEDAY & COMPANY, INC.
Garden City, New York

To my sister
Mary Cecil Rogers

LOOK AWAY, BEULAH LAND

Part One

1864-1865

"Hell is empty, and all the devils are here."
The Tempest

1.

A stranger passing would almost certainly have stopped to ask himself or his companion: "What is that place? Who lives there?"

From the public road a narrower one led through an orchard of fruit trees into an avenue of oak and cedar to the columned gray house that was the heart of the plantation known as Beulah Land. At a distance it looked much as it had in former days. It had never been beautiful except to those who loved it, but even four years of war had not robbed it of its air of authority. Once the gray exterior had been kept fresh with paint. Now that there was no paint, nor the hands needed to apply it, the graying was left to Georgia's blistering summers and cold, wet winters.

It was the field slaves who first walked away in the night, to find roads to seaports, for word had spread among them that ships lay in every harbor laden with gold that was theirs for the asking. From slavery they were to be catapulted to a heaven on earth of leisure and riches and consequence. The stories were infinite in their variations, but always alike in essentials.

When they started to go, Edna Davis, the octogenarian mistress of the neighboring plantation, Oaks, said to Sarah Kendrick, "They're just the field workers; they don't love us like our house servants—" But the house slaves began to slip away too, a wife to join a husband who had been conscripted to work on roads or to dredge the harbor at Savannah, a restless maid or gardener hoping to collect the silk dresses and gold watches the rumors promised.

Seeing her world changed and knowing that more change was to come, Sarah did not like to leave Beulah Land even for an hour, but she went directly to Oaks on the afternoon she had word that Edna was ill. She took a back way through woods, crossing a corner of the farm that separated the two plantations.

Arriving at Oaks, she entered without asking for her daughter Rachel or her granddaughter Jane and marched through the house to Edna's room. "What ails you?" she said when Edna opened her eyes and saw her standing beside the bed. Although thirty years younger, Sarah knew no ceremony with her friend.

"Old and worn out."

"They said it was rheumatism."

"It eases their minds if I give them a word," Edna said. "I'm figuring to die before Sherman gets here. Don't you think that's a good idea?"

Sarah relaxed, assured that there was nothing really wrong with Edna. "Not as good as some you've had."

"He'll be here directly, now he's got Atlanta."

"How do you know Atlanta won't pacify him for a while?"

Edna grunted. "They say half our officers are drunk."

"They say a lot of things. People are quite agreeable to inventing bad news. If he does come, he may miss us by ten miles and never look this way. You'll have died in vain when all of us need you."

"Nobody needs me. The harvest is so mere I could gather it with my own two hands. Most of the stock's been sold or given away. No, ma'am. There's nothing to do but wait for Mr. Sherman, and I'm not a waiter. I wish somebody'd take me out and shoot me. I'm like the old mule they hitch up to the pole that turns the sugarcane grinder. Walks round and round, not thinking. That's all my life has become."

"Will you try to sit up if I get some more pillows?"

"No."

Sarah looked around the room with irritation. "Where is everybody?"

"I make them leave me alone. Doreen fidgets unless she's out doing. She'll be with her chickens, or walking the land with her pa, or riding Pharaoh."

"Benjamin with her, I expect. He treats Doreen more like his mama than Rachel."

"She pays him more attention. The trouble with Rachel is she won't forget James for a minute. She won't learn that keeping busy is the best way."

"I'll talk to her again," Sarah said. "Maybe get her to come over and spend the day with me."

"She won't go. Afraid she'll miss an hour of James if he comes home sudden."

"Where's my Jane?"

"She was in, but I sent her out. She made me nervous."

"A servant ought to sit with you in case you need anything."

"Few enough for the real work. I don't want an old granny watching me with her hands folded, hoping I'll die so she can tell everybody she saw me do it."

Sarah almost smiled. "You don't sound like dying to me."

Edna looked at her challengingly. "How many house servants do you have left?"

Sarah considered before making an answer. "More than I care to feed."

Edna nodded. "The ones who stay are too old to work or too ignorant to understand there's nobody to fetch them back if they go."

They were silent for a little while until Sarah said, "Do you hurt anywhere?"

"No," Edna said.

Sarah turned to pull a chair to the bedside and sit down. When she looked again, Edna's eyes were closed and her rutted cheeks were wet with tears. Sarah took her hand and held it until Edna slept.

2.

It was dusk as Sarah, after her visit with Edna, left the woods path and walked across a field toward the big house. She knew the scene in every season and at every time of day and night. Dusk had once been a favorite time for her to pause and look around. Its work done, the plantation found another rhythm, that of night coming and a seeking of shelter and home comfort. People exchanged news of the day. Fires were lighted, indoors and out. Dogs trotted about singly making thoughtful last inspections of the grounds, or stood together and barked a challenge to darkness from pure insolence. A cow complained, a mule brayed and was quiet. Laughter, high and gleeful, pierced the air for a moment and died. The smell of cooking food was everywhere.

Now, though, it was a stiller scene. Smoke came from fewer chimneys, for many of the cabins stood empty, just as most of the bedrooms of the main house were now unoccupied. Once, a dozen had been required for family members and visiting friends, each wanting the furniture placed in a certain way and the windows opened so; but now only Sarah and Nell took candles up the stairs at night.

Although arrowheads and pieces of Indian pottery were still turned up occasionally by a plow, Beulah Land had been a working plantation since Leon Kendrick's grandfather settled it in 1783. He'd built a house with cooking rooms separate at the back, but when the house was later enlarged, the two parts had been connected by a covered breezeway. Yet in spite of the hundreds of slaves and masters who had lived out their days at Beulah Land, there was only one grave on its sixteen hundred acres. That held the dust of Ezra, who was born a slave and died free. Ezra and his family had been more to the Kendricks, some said, than the Kendricks had been to each other. Ezra was the blacksmith, but had often acted as doctor to men and beasts. His wife Lovey was housekeeper for Beulah Land, chosen for the work by Leon's mother Deborah, when Deborah was a new bride and Lovey little more than a girl. Deborah was long dead, and Lovey, at eighty-four, nearly blind. Her daughter Pauline had been the life companion of Deborah's daughter Selma; and her son Floyd, Leon's closest friend. It had been Floyd, indeed, who found Leon and cut him down when he hanged himself in one of the barns at the beginning of the war.

Sarah went past the cabins and was about to step into the deeper dusk of the trees near the house when she saw a figure seated on Ezra's gravestone. "Lovey?" she called.

The figure drew erect, turning its head.

"Is it you, Lovey?"

"Who else?" the old woman answered.

"I couldn't make out. It's getting dark."

"Little difference to me," Lovey said without self-pity.

"There's a chill tonight."

"I don't feel it," Lovey said.

"Come along to the kitchen. Lotus is cooking supper. Smell it? You can sit and have a cup of coffee."

The old woman pushed her lips out disdainfully. "Coffee made of peanuts. I never thought I'd live to see—"

"It'll be hot and sweet."

Together they went in. Lotus was a stout woman in her mid-

dle thirties. With her twin Otis, she had been an early pupil of the school Sarah kept until Deborah died and Sarah became mistress of Beulah Land.

"What is it you're cooking?" Sarah asked. "I smelled it a long way away."

"Stewing rabbit and onions. Otis snared two. Weren't that lucky?"

"Tell him much obliged for me," Sarah said, drawing a chair nearer the cooking stove for Lovey and guiding her to it.

Lovey jerked free and found her own way. "Don't have to do me like a child," she said.

"Floyd's waiting in the office," Lotus said.

Sarah glanced at her with surprise, for Floyd always came to the office at this time, to go over the day's work and the next day's prospects. It was an hour she looked forward to, one during which she needed no guard but could think and speak common truth without fear of being misunderstood.

She went through the breezeway into the wide central hallway that ran the length of the house. Before entering the office she paused, hearing what she took to be voices from the drawing room; but when she stepped into it, she found Nell sitting alone. She was rocking herself in a low chair, her feet treading air when she pumped the chair backwards.

"I thought I heard talking," Sarah said.

"I was singing. I was lonesome."

"I've been over at Oaks," Sarah said. "Edna's gone to bed."

"What for?"

"Says she's old and worn out."

"Fiddle," Nell said. "She's only two years older than I am, and I'm not worn out. Maybe she needs a dose of sulphur."

"She says she's planning to die before Sherman gets here."

"Not me," Nell said. "If he's coming, I want to meet him at the door to slap his face. Lotus is cooking rabbit. I love a good stew with a lot of onions and sage."

"I'd better go talk to Floyd before supper. Lotus seemed to think there was something in particular—"

"Oh, there is!" Nell stopped her chair and giggled.

"What?"

"Sometimes you don't see what's right under your nose!"

"Well, since everybody knows but me, I'll go find out," Sarah said agreeably.

Floyd glanced up when she came into the office; then his eyes went back to the ledger opened flat on the table before him. "Here's where we left off," he said, forefinger pointing to a line of figures on the page. Sarah looked over his shoulder until she found and understood his reference, and then sat down at the side of the table.

"Things are so bad I've stopped worrying," she said.

"Going to get worse before they get better."

"Do you think there'll ever be a 'better'?"

"Oh, yes." Floyd was the only Negro overseer in the county. They had worked together more than half their lives. They had shared trouble, and they trusted one another. When together they tended to think alike, because they felt the same way about Beulah Land. It was his home as much as hers, and as he had pointed out to her one time, had been his home longer. At fifty-eight Floyd was still a powerful man, but his hair, which he kept short, was more gray than black, and the lines of his face and at the back of his neck were deep. They saw each other so regularly they seldom looked closely; but as she studied him, she saw that he was growing old and remembered her own age. She laughed. Floyd was writing in the ledger. Without raising his eyes he said, "What?"

"God knows I have no reason to laugh. I just remembered I'm fifty-three."

"Are you?" he said mildly, as if she had given him some minor workaday fact.

"You know I am."

"I never think about it."

"Nor I," she said. "That's why it seems strange when I do. I don't feel any different from the way I did thirty years ago."

"Well, you'd better start," he said with good-natured irony. "We got a lot to think about."

"But nothing much to do," Sarah said. "The only thing we can do is to hold on and hold out until something changes."

"That's no little job."

"If only we can keep the hands we have through the winter and plant a crop."

"I shift them from the fields to the sawmill to the cotton gin so fast they won't think about taking off. They're too tired."

"Lordy," Sarah said. "I used to think everything would come right one day."

"They were right for a long time."

"I have the feeling that nothing I do matters any more." She told him of going to see Edna that afternoon and finished by saying, "The only old ones left are Edna and your mama and Aunt Nell. When they go, *we'll* be the older generation. Floyd, I don't believe it! I'm not ready to be old yet."

Floyd's smile was not quite true. "Maybe that's why I've decided to get married."

Sarah heard, but understanding did not penetrate at once. "What have you decided?"

Floyd looked at the open pages before him, sighed once, and closed the ledger. "I'm going to marry Lotus tomorrow morning before I go to the sawmill."

Sarah looked at him and saw that he meant it. "Lotus said you had something on your mind. Why? I mean, after all these years, why Lotus?"

"She's going to have a baby. It'll be mine, and I want to claim it."

She held her head so steady it began to tremble. "I'll give her 'free papers.' —But Mr. Lincoln has anticipated me there, hasn't he?"

It was his turn to study her, and feeling him do so, she would not let her eyes meet his. "Well! That's something definite. That's something good we can all look forward to, no matter what else happens." She stopped, unable to say more, and when she looked at him, he continued to study her.

"What do you truly feel about it?" he asked.

The silence between them was long before she said, "I wish the child were going to be mine."

His face relaxed. He smiled, and then he laughed. "You've always taken in the children of others!"

"Only Leon's." She began to laugh with him. "You make me sound like a hen stealing another's nest and sitting on her eggs. Yet, oh, what I'd have missed if I hadn't taken Roman and Rachel."

"And what they'd have missed." He studied her again. When he spoke, his voice mocked her and himself. "I used to wait, hoping you'd get old and I'd stop caring about you."

"Well, I'm old."

They rarely touched each other, but now their hands met and held briefly over the ledger on the table.

3.

Sarah had dispensed with being served at mealtimes unless there
was someone there besides Nell and herself. Lotus put the food
on the table, and Sarah and Nell helped themselves and each
other. Nell had always been fond of her victuals, and the close
attention she gave to the act of feeding made her a dull table
companion. Ordinarily, Sarah did not mind, even enjoyed the
freedom it gave her to pursue her own thoughts. That night,
however, she would have welcomed conversation, even prattle.

Because of Floyd's announcement of his intention to marry,
they had not bothered to discuss the business of Beulah Land,
which usually dominated their hour together at the end of the
working day. Instead, they had drunk a glass of peach brandy
and talked a little of the past. When they separated in the hall
outside the office, Floyd went to the kitchen to Lotus and Lovey.
Sarah joined Nell in the drawing room until Lotus rang the supper bell a quarter of an hour later. Nell obliged with a smug
smile when Sarah said that Floyd and Lotus would be marrying,
but she was not interested in dwelling on the match since she'd
known about it before Sarah had. Her thoughts were on rabbit
stew, which she could smell, and when Sarah began to speak of
her sister Lauretta, Nell's head was cocked in the listening attitude of one who hears a heavenly music and does not register ordinary words.

In the course of her fifty-five years Lauretta had married and
lost, one way or another, three bigamists, but had occasionally
been employed as a professional actress. Now and again she had
come to Beulah Land to visit. The first time she came she stayed
to bear her and Leon's child, named Rachel by Sarah, who
claimed her as her own, before eloping with Bonard Davis, who
was married to Selma, who had no use for him anyway.

In 1853 when her third marriage turned out to be no such
thing, Lauretta came again to ask asylum and to be made condi-
tionally welcome. That time she had set her middle-aged cap for

Bruce Davis, Bonard's surviving brother and master of Oaks plantation, but Edna had put a stop to it. She had come again to Beulah Land when the war deprived her of her living as an actress in the North. The war had provided another kind of activity for her in the nearby town of Highboro: preparing bandages, watching cavalry units drill, superintending punch bowls at soirees—but few opportunities of a personal kind. Lauretta was, alas, no longer young, and most of the soldiers and their officers were. So, fretting finally at the confinement of war and seeing months turn into years that would not come again, Lauretta wrote letters to such of her old professional acquaintances as might put her in the way of acting jobs. Luck was with her, and she was invited to join a company resident in Atlanta to perform various roles calling for a "character woman." She played stern mothers and witty, conniving widows. Often she carried a folding fan which she learned to use skillfully to punctuate lines of dialogue or to keep audience attention when the author had provided her with no lines. She opened scenes but never closed them, that being the opportunity of leading players; and when the entire cast came out to take their bows, Lauretta made hers from a position on one of the sides, never stage center. Yet she smiled and curtseyed for all the world as if she were Sarah Siddons, so long, that is, as the eyes of the leading players did not catch her.

She had not written often to Sarah, but now that Atlanta had fallen, Sarah wondered about her. She wondered merely, did not yet worry, for Lauretta had in the past shown a gift for survival second only to her gift for romantic self-deception.

When they were called to the supper table and served themselves with the rabbit, Sarah returned to the subject of Lauretta, not so much from genuine concern as to avoid her own thoughts. Nell had been waving her old face over her plate of stew, appreciating its vapors before attacking it with the fork she held ready. She looked up with surprise. "Oh, I assure you, Lauretta will be quite safe. She's a fool, but she can take care of herself."

"I hope you are right," Sarah said, "but it would relieve me to hear directly."

Nell broke off a piece of corn bread from the hoecake and crumbled it into her plate. Then she began to eat, not greedily, but with a relishing absorption that would have made interruption unprofitable.

The doors were open, for it was still September, and Sarah could hear Lotus's voice all the way from the kitchen. She caught no words, only the high, excited tone of it. Floyd had told her something of his talk with Sarah; that much was evident from the bashful laughter with which she had greeted the arrival of Sarah and Nell in the dining room before suddenly throwing her apron over her face and retreating to the kitchen. Lovey would be happy too, or as happy as she could be nowadays, for she had despaired of Floyd's ever marrying and giving her a grandchild. Briefly, Sarah felt herself a part of the celebration in the kitchen and was happy with them until the barren loneliness of her own position closed over her again.

Slowly she began to eat, knowing the food good but not tasting it, hearing with envy the voices from the kitchen. Nell finished every morsel on her plate and set down her fork, not as one who abandons it, but merely intends to give it a rest. She untied and retied the sash at her waist, her eyes on the covered bowl of stew. She would have more, but seeing that Sarah's appetite was no threat, paused.

"Where—are—you!"

The plaintive wail came to them from the front of the hallway. Sarah and Nell looked at each other in wonder until it was repeated.

"*Where are you all?*"

Sarah's face lit up with recognition even as Nell scowled. "Speak of the devil!" Nell said. "She came back once before when we were sitting down at our victuals."

Sarah pushed her chair back and went running. Nell lifted the lid of the large bowl and heaped her plate again with rabbit stew. There was no knowing how hungry Lauretta would be.

4.

As Sarah came to her in the hallway, Lauretta was apparently overcome by emotion, for she broke into a storm of weeping. Whatever control and discretion she was used to exercising on the stage was forgotten. The character woman, player of feed and filler roles, took stage center. "Home! Home again!" she announced through her tears. "Thank God! I shall never more leave it!"

Sarah was gentle with her and murmured soothingly, letting Lauretta play her scene. If she responded less fully than her sister's pitch seemed to invite, it was not because she was an unfeeling woman, but only that she knew Lauretta. At last the storm diminished enough for them to make themselves comfortable in the drawing room. Sarah maneuvered them so that each sat in a chair, avoiding the sofa as offering too much scope for Lauretta's histrionic bent. From past homecomings, Sarah had learned that Lauretta's calms were sometimes shattered by a renewal of storm, and she had no intention of being clutched and wetted with tears more than she had already allowed.

The arrangement proved satisfactory, and perhaps the brandy Sarah poured for her had a further quieting effect on Lauretta's troubled heart, for she soon began to talk sensibly and informatively.

"We had known they would come. Indeed, no one had spoken of anything else for weeks. Yet like all cataclysms, it was none the less shocking for having been foreseen. Many fled. Some even managed to hire boxcars and have their entire household effects carried to safety—if there can be safety in this war! As panic spread, anything with wheels served to haul trunks of clothes and stores, bedsteads, chairs—whatever could be snatched from the path of the invader. There was a scarcity of horses and mules. I saw men and women pulling carts and even wagons. I wanted to leave, but there was no way, for I had put it off too long. The company had disbanded when nobody came to see us, and I was working with the wounded." She paused and drank deeply from her glass. Sarah filled it again to the brim. "I know now something of what your Roman must have endured working in the hospital in Washington. Is he still there?"

"I've had no letter for months," Sarah said.

"They do say, however, that women our age make the best nurses. I saw younger ones faint, and some men also. It was very horrible, of course."

Having finished her supper, Nell was drawn by curiosity more than courtesy to join them. As she entered the room, Lauretta sprang to her feet, remembering an event that had transpired since her departure from Beulah Land a year and a half ago. Nell, who had always abhorred being touched, avoided Lauretta's embrace by popping herself into the little velvet rocking chair that was hers by custom.

Lauretta cried, "Poor Aunt Pea, dead these many months!"

From the safety of her chair Nell said, "She was most certainly dead or we shouldn't have buried her."

"Ah, ma'am, these are grievous days we live through," Lauretta moaned, resuming her seat and taking glass in hand again. "What released her from our earthly sorrows?"

Sarah answered. "Everything seems to end in pneumonia. But she suffered a gradual decline in health and spirits before that."

"No stamina," Nell said firmly. Then facing her chair squarely toward Lauretta, she asked, "And how did you find life in Atlanta when you grew tired of us and left? Plenty of good things to eat, I suppose?"

"Oh, there was food to be had, but at such prices a nabob would have needed all his riches. Ten dollars for a chicken and as much again for a pound or two of beefsteak. Gingham at five and eight dollars a yard—*gingham*, mind you, ma'am! And on the very last day before the Yankees came I saw an old gentleman offer five thousand dollars for any horse at all—and there was no one willing or able to oblige him!"

Sarah said temperately to Nell, "Lauretta has been telling me that she nursed the wounded."

"I should not have liked that. Surely no nice woman—"

"I promise you, ma'am, every hand was needed. It would have broken your heart to see them. So many of them young, and all of them brave. I saw a boy—he was no more than a boy, though war had forced him to take a man's part and play soldier—quietly eating a biscuit minutes after the doctor had amputated his left leg."

Nell nodded approval. "Good appetite is a blessed thing. If Penelope had eaten more and wept less over the past, she would be sitting in this room tonight. And what were you expected to do for the wounded? Entertain them?"

"I did read to them sometimes—"

"Read to them!"

"Poems and scenes from plays—"

"How vastly peculiar!" Nell laughed. "And did they like that?"

"I assure you they did," Lauretta said coldly.

"I shouldn't have thanked you for playing Juliet to me if I'd just had my gizzard cut out!"

"I do not recall your ever cherishing a regard for literature, ma'am; but it can be a great comfort to those in distress of body and soul. I wrote letters for them also, to mothers and wives and sisters. And helped them with food and drink if they could not help themselves. Many a gallon of tea, and spirits too, have I spooned into their poor mouths!"

"Was it ever necessary for you to assist the surgeons?" Sarah asked quietly.

"Oh yes. I grew quite used to it, although the first time I stood by during an operation, I could not watch; and when I turned my head again, I discovered that I was holding only the poor man's arm in my hands, it having been removed as I kept my eyes averted."

"I beg you—" Nell murmured.

"That was nothing, ma'am," Lauretta continued. "I later became accustomed to seeing stacks of severed limbs, and often dead bodies too awaiting removal."

Sarah said quickly, "You have been very good and useful. How did you manage to get away, after all?"

"Now that is a story!" Lauretta declared.

"One we shall no doubt hear," Nell observed testily. "What a way you have of dodging thunderbolts!"

"Thank God," Sarah said.

"Are you hungry?" Nell asked in a voice more curious than encouraging.

"I am," Lauretta admitted.

Sarah stood. "Forgive me, dear Lauretta. Come now and eat. We were at supper when you arrived and called out to us."

"And you stayed to finish yours," Lauretta said to Nell. "I suppose you've had food aplenty?"

"None to spare," Nell said.

"We've done very well," Sarah assured her. "Come."

Sarah had taken up the single candle and moved to the door when Lauretta's voice made her halt. "Stay a moment. There is something I must tell you without delay." Leaving her chair, Nell moved closer, for Lauretta's tone promised a revelation. "I have not come alone."

"Ah-ha!" Nell exclaimed. "Married again, are you?"

"I cannot appreciate your levity on the present occasion, ma'am."

Sarah said, "Tell us, please. Where is—? Who—?"

"A young soldier waits on the porch."

"Then ask him to come in," Sarah said.

"I'll fetch him," Nell said.

"Before you do, you must know—he is not one of ours."

"A Yankee!" Nell screamed. "She's led the enemy to our door!"

Sarah went into the hallway with her candle and to the front door of the house, which stood open to catch the night breeze. Lauretta and Nell followed on her heels. "Sir!" Sarah called, unable to see beyond a foot or two. "Are you there?"

There was movement in the dark, and a tall, thin young man came to show himself in the candlelight. He did not speak. His eyes, staring out of deep sockets, revealed an agony of anxiety, not daring to claim the acquaintance even of Lauretta. Sarah thought she had never seen a face so bony. At jaw and forehead only skin hid the skull. He looked not merely hungry, but starved.

"Who are you, young man?" Sarah asked.

He continued to stare at her. His mouth opened but made no sound.

At last Lauretta found her tongue. "Daniel Todd is his name. He brought me all the way, helped me to the very door, and as you value my survival you must make him welcome."

"Come into the house," Sarah said.

The soldier obeyed as she stood aside, and Lauretta closed the door quickly after them. The man wore no uniform, only shirt and trousers and cracked soldier shoes.

"May we eat now?" Lauretta begged. "For I am about to perish! Later I shall tell you everything."

Sarah said to the soldier, "You are welcome to come and eat with us."

"I thank you, ma'am, for I am surely hungry."

"Heavenly Father!" Nell said. "He truly is a Yankee. Listen to his twang!"

"Aunt Nell, will you ask Lotus to bring plates and whatever food she can get ready in a hurry? Simply tell her that we have two guests, suddenly arrived. Take my candle. I'll light another."

"I don't think I should leave you alone with this—"

"Please make haste," Sarah cut her off, stepping into her office and returning immediately with another candle. She proceeded to the dining room, and Lauretta and the soldier followed her without further invitation. Lotus had cleared the table, but Sarah bade them sit. They did so, Lauretta in tired relief, the soldier awkwardly, as if he had forgotten how to use a chair, having known only the ground for so long. They continued silent, waiting for the food.

Nell entered first with plates and cutlery. Lotus followed with a pot in each hand. One contained boiled potatoes, which she proceeded to heap onto the plates when Nell set them down; from the other she ladled the remains of the rabbit stew, mostly gravy, to which she had added a jar of butter beans and a jar of tomatoes she had put up in July for their winter store. Her promptness in providing food indicated that Nell had made clear the urgency of the occasion, whatever else she might have told her.

Only when Lotus had served them did she greet Lauretta, whom she had known long, although neither held the other in particular regard. Her eyes rarely left the soldier. So strong was her curiosity he might have been no fellow creature at all but a wild beast from a foreign land she had never before observed.

"Is there no corn bread?" Sarah asked sharply, not so much to reprimand as to penetrate the spell Lotus appeared to move under.

"Cooking it now. Right back." She hurried out.

Lauretta attacked the food on her plate without pause or comment. After a moment's gulping shyness, the soldier found a spoon and kept his mouth full for as long as the food lasted.

Lotus returned with corn bread and a pitcher of buttermilk, which she poured out for them. She emptied what remained in the two pots onto their plates. When her eyes went to Sarah for further instructions, Sarah nodded approval and dismissal, and Lotus went out to give her report to Floyd and Lovey in the kitchen.

Although entertained by the adventure of Lauretta's return, Nell watched the disappearance of the last of the stew with regret. Usually there was a little left, and Lotus warmed it and spooned it over her grits at breakfast the next morning, knowing her to be partial to the flavor of game.

When they finished eating, Lauretta looked actually fatter than she had when she sat down. There was no such illusion in the soldier's appearance, but he no longer had the starving, staring look Sarah had earlier noted. She asked Nell to escort them to the office and said that she would join them presently. Going to the kitchen, she told Lotus to have one of the house girls put clean sheets on beds in two of the unused rooms and said to Floyd that she would be obliged if he could come to the office for a little while before he went to his quarters for the night.

In the office she found Nell in a chair she had drawn up near the big working table, like a spectator who arrives early at a theater to be sure of his seat for the performance. The soldier sat on a straight chair in the shadows, eyes closed. Lauretta idled on the working side of the table, flipping through pages of a ledger without curiosity or understanding, only to pass the time.

"Now," Sarah said, taking the ledger from Lauretta and closing it. She sat down and asked Lauretta to take a chair. "You were going to tell us about it."

"Yes, dear Sarah." Lauretta did not take a chair, tired though she was, her actress instinct telling her she could make their eyes follow her if she were free to walk about. She faced the soldier briefly, reviewing his features. Frowning, he opened his eyes, as if he felt hers upon him.

"Daniel here was brought in wounded." She turned and moved a step toward Sarah. "You understand there was confusion at the time, and when two men were found bleeding and brought to the nursing station, nobody asked who they were. One might be a Confederate and the other a Yankee. Impossible to know with so few wearing recognizable whole uniforms. Daniel's wounds were dressed, a bullet having entered his knee and another the calf of his leg. But shock and hunger made him appear worse off than he was. What had weakened him so, what was most the matter was a long siege of dysentery. He said little more than a word at a time, so no one thought of his being a Yankee. But I suspected, with my quick ear and years on the stage with actors from everywhere. When I was tolerably certain, I said nothing. It was like a little joke I kept in reserve. But Daniel could see I knew and begged me most earnestly not to tell others. He was scared, you see, they'd send him to Andersonville."

"What's wrong with Andersonville?" Nell asked resentfully.

"He meant the prison, not the town," Lauretta said. "It's understood among the Yankees to be a most terrible place."

"I didn't know that," Sarah said.

Nell raised both hands in the air. "I'm glad to hear something about us scares them! Coming down to Georgia and going on a rampage where they've got no business to be at all. Hooray for Andersonville!" The soldier looked at her wonderingly when she turned to glare at him.

"Please proceed," Sarah said to Lauretta.

Lauretta said, "All soldiers have dysentery. I heard a doctor in Atlanta say it's lost more battles than generals have won."

"Do stop talking about dysentery," Nell said.

"I took to bringing food to Daniel from my boardinghouse, first a tidbit or two, then regular meals, which were better than he was getting at the nursing station, although nothing to brag about either. I was busy all the time, I can tell you, ma'am." She smiled coolly at the older woman. "Not simply reading to the men, which so unaccountably amused you—writing their letters if they had no hands or education to write for themselves. I brought them tobacco and candy. I held their poor heads when they had to vomit. I even bathed them when there was no male orderly available."

"Had you no shame?" Nell said.

"None to weigh against the needs of crippled soldiers. It would have grieved even your heart to see and hear them, ma'am. The smell of pus and corruption was indescribable—"

"I'm thankful for that!" Nell said.

"But the severest strain was in trying to comfort the perishing. Many a young man in his valedictory moment would cry out, 'Kiss me, Mother, for I am dying!' —Shall I ever forget it?" Lauretta turned her back to her listeners, to check her emotion.

"And did you?" Nell asked.

Facing her again, Lauretta asked, "Did I do what, ma'am?"

"Did you kiss them?"

"Countless dozens," Lauretta said.

"Total strangers!" Nell was outraged. "I certainly could never have brought myself to do such a thing."

"Nor, ma'am, are they likely to have begged such benediction, had *you* stood in my place."

"Well, you are bold!" Nell declared.

"Please go on," Sarah said.

"Daniel gained in strength. But the flood tide was swirling around us by then, and we knew it was only a matter of days before Atlanta was lost. They began to move out the less seriously wounded. Daniel was still afraid of being sent to Andersonville if he was found out to be a Yankee. Sometimes he pretended to be asleep, or hurting too much to be moved. They left the dying, for what good was there in saving corpses? There were so very many to see to, they hardly paused to look at Daniel if he groaned that he was dying, but went on to another. One morning when I arrived at the nursing depot, everybody had left. I can't tell you what a feeling that was. As I stood among the dead bodies wondering what to do, I could hear the battle cannon. The air was not fit to breathe with its reek of blood and scorch of gunpowder. Then Daniel came. He'd slipped away the night before and hidden himself in a shed to wait for the Yankees to find him. But he grew worried about me, you see, and so he came back. I asked him if he would help me get to Beulah Land, for I was at the end of my rope."

When Lauretta turned her head to look at the soldier, so too did Sarah and Nell.

"I was sick of the war," he said as if he had been talking to himself in his head and now spoke this thought aloud.

Lauretta continued. "Nobody noticed us, although we had a story ready I had made up, about Daniel's being commissioned by a certain captain to give me safe escort to Savannah. However, that does not signify. It was like everybody had his hands full thinking about his own self and just keeping out of each other's way. The roads were choked with people and carts and wheelbarrows and wagons—anything with wheels to carry a few pitiful goods. And when people had nothing that would roll, they tied up whatever was most precious in a sheet and slung it on their backs. We were pulled with the tide leaving the city. The first day it was all walking, but God points the way to the weary—"

Nell said, "I'm surprised to hear you needed directions from Him."

"Would you credit it, ma'am?" Lauretta leaned to poke a finger into Nell's shoulder. "I let them think I was *enceinte!*"

"Nothing you do surprises me," Nell assured her.

"My first ride was on a wagon, but it broke a wheel around midday. Then I just rolled up my cloak and stuffed it under my dress in front, and a woman helped me into another wagon without my having said a word. When that wagon turned in a direction we didn't want to go, I got off and begged another ride.

Poor Daniel had to walk every step of the way. Food was hard
to hustle. I ate anything. Folks had stopped sharing, and who
could blame them with all of us so hungry? What Daniel could
lay his hands on he put into mine."

"I wasn't wanting anything," the soldier said, "my guts being—" He caught Nell's eyes on him. "The sickness had come back
on me."

"So here you are," Sarah said, and added more to herself than
to the others, "What are we to do now?"

Lauretta yawned, and yawned again, and yawned a third time
as they studied the question. "I'm too tired to think beyond bed,"
she said. "I want to sleep until the war's over." She drifted to the
door. "Is my old room ready for me?"

Sarah said, "One of the girls is making the beds."

"Wait a minute!" Nell commanded. "I'm going up myself,
though I'll never get to sleep after all the horrors you've told us,
and probably more to come. Sarah, you'd best come now too."

"Not for a while."

"Good night," Lauretta said, and went out.

Nell followed her, but paused at the door to call to the soldier,
"If you have rape and plunder in your heart, I give you warning:
I sleep with a loaded pistol on top of my bedside Bible. —Lau-
retta! You just tarry for me."

As if he had been waiting, Floyd knocked and entered. His
eyes found the soldier, and the two men looked at each other.
Sarah gave them a moment for scrutiny before saying to Floyd,
"His name is Daniel Todd. He's a Northern soldier. He was
wounded at Atlanta, and my sister nursed him. When Atlanta
was taken, they made their way here." To the soldier she said,
"This is Floyd Kendrick. He sees to all the work at Beulah Land,
as well as our sawmill and cotton gin."

"A nigger slave in charge?"

"He's as free as you," Sarah said sharply.

"Not by Mr. Lincoln's Proclamation," Floyd said. He went and
sat down in the chair Nell had used, shifting it so that, although
he faced Sarah across the desk, he kept the soldier in his line of
vision.

"You understand what it means?" Sarah said.

"Yes," Floyd said. "A big mess."

"What can we do?"

"You can't keep a Yankee soldier," Floyd said. "You'll have to report him."

"No!" the soldier said harshly, but his next words to Sarah were pleading ones. "Please, ma'am, don't do that!"

Sarah shook her head. "He may have saved Lauretta's life."

"Then she's in his debt," Floyd said. "You are not."

"You know how she is, never follows a thing through in her mind. Though, to be fair, she hadn't much choice in what she did this time."

"Doesn't she always say that?" Floyd said.

Sarah smiled briefly. "She calls it Fate."

"You'll have to report him," Floyd insisted. "You've never wanted to be involved in the war more than you could help, but you can't have the whole county calling you a traitor."

"I never cared what the county thought, and who will tell them anyway?"

"They couldn't have come here tonight without being seen and your sister being recognized."

"Did people see you, soldier, before you turned in here?"

"Yes, ma'am."

"Did you speak to them?"

"No'm. I didn't."

"Did my sister?"

"Not to say talked to anybody. Waved or nodded a time or two."

"Did people appear to pay you particular attention?"

He hesitated before admitting. "Some stared like."

"You see," Floyd said to Sarah.

She sat frowning at nothing. Without knowing she did it, she touched a forefinger to the side of the melting tallow candle. "As you say, I've had as little to do with this war as I could. It's what killed Leon, or made him kill himself. I've let them take our men for working parties, and I've sold and given them more horses and mules than we could spare. But I have never let the war rule my private conduct, and I won't now. If I give the man up to them, it'll mean taking part in a way I never have done."

"This time you've no choice."

"Ma'am!" The soldier left the straight chair so abruptly it fell on its side, and he did not set it right. "Ma'am, I can't sit and have my life decided by a nigger, free or slave!"

Sarah stood too. "You will pick up that chair and sit down and be quiet. You have no say-so in what happens to you now. You will do as you are told, or I *will* turn you over to them. I am the mistress of Beulah Land, and I make the decisions here."

Floyd stared at her with as much surprise as did the soldier, and she did not comment upon it. The soldier moved awkwardly to the chair, righted it, and sat down. Sarah remained standing. The men waited. She left the desk and walked back and forth between them.

To Floyd she said, "He will have to stay, at least for a while. Lovey and Lotus know he's here, but none of the others."

Floyd said, "The children see everything, and they'd have told their mothers by now."

Again Sarah walked, rubbing her hands together as if they were cold. "We'll tell them he is a cousin—wounded in the war, and Lauretta found him at the nursing station and asked him to bring her here. Close enough to the truth."

"Except the cousin and his being a Yankee," Floyd said drily.

"Ma'am," the soldier begged, "just let me go. I'll fend."

"The first word you said, they'd know you for a Yankee."

"I'll travel by night."

"The country is full of soldiers," Floyd said. "Confederate soldiers. They travel by night sometimes too."

"What would you say to them?" Sarah asked.

"I could manage."

"They'd kill you when they saw you were a stranger and knew nothing of the country."

"Even if he goes now," Floyd said, "we'd have to explain who he is and what happened to him."

Sarah went back to her chair. For a moment she glared at it as if she hated it, and then sat down. "What can we say about the way he talks?"

Floyd thought about it. "Say he's from a place nobody here has been? A cousin from away, but still a Southerner."

"What is such a place?" After a minute she said, "Missouri."

"I don't know anybody around here who's been there," Floyd said. "Do you?"

She shook her head. Facing the soldier, she said, "You'll be from Missouri."

"I won't give up my own name," he said.

"You don't have to be a Kendrick cousin," Sarah said. "Keep your name and be a cousin of my sister's. We were Penningtons.

All you have to remember is that your mother was a Pennington and came from Savannah before you were born. Can you remember that and say it to anybody asks you?"

"I reckon so."

"He'll live in the house," she said to Floyd, "being a cousin. I'll tell Lauretta and Aunt Nell what to say, and you must make it clear to Lovey and Lotus. If they say it, everybody else will believe it."

"Or pretend to."

Sarah said to the soldier, "You understand that you'll have to work. We've no place for the idle."

"I've worked all my life," Daniel Todd said. "I was born on a farm."

"Where?"

"Vermont. Me and Pa did the work between us. No slaves."

"You cannot write to them, or anybody, even to say you're alive."

"They don't care."

"Later you can write."

"I'm done with them. Ma didn't even cry when I went, and Pa made money on me."

"How do you mean?" Sarah said.

"I wasn't old enough to have to go. Pa took me to Rutland, where he got two hundred dollars for me. I went in place of a rich man's son. That's the most money Pa ever held in his hand at one time in his life."

"A slave sells for more than two hundred dollars," Floyd said.

The two men had avoided looking at each other, but they did so now. The soldier nodded his head. "I won't call you a liar because what you say is true." He asked Sarah, "Will I work for him or you?"

"For Beulah Land. However, you'll take working orders from Floyd Kendrick."

"I won't have him lording over me."

"He will never tell you to do anything that isn't right," Sarah said. "You can take my word for that."

"I take your word for it. Just the same, I don't like darkies. Though it was Pa sent me to war, I've heard men talk, and I figure the war is on account of them. If it hadn't been for them, the South wouldn't have tried to break up the Union. And if the

South hadn't, there wouldn't have been war. I pure-and-T despise the darkies."

Sarah said, "You've never known any. —It's the end of a long day and I'm tired. We'll all go to bed."

"Where is he to sleep?" Floyd said.

"There are plenty of empty rooms upstairs."

"Ma'am—" The soldier stood, embarrassed. "I don't think I'd better do that. I'll sleep on the porch—"

"You can forget what Aunt Nell said. She's old and takes fancies."

"I don't mean that, ma'am. I mean I can't sleep in your clean bed."

"Whyever not?"

"I've got things," he said so low Sarah strained first to hear and then to understand.

She turned to Floyd. "What does he mean?"

Floyd said to the soldier, "Bugs?"

The soldier nodded.

Floyd said, "I'll take him to the barn where he can wash. Lotus will heat water and I'll see he's clean before he comes back."

"Burn his clothes. That would be wise anyway. What can he wear?"

"There are some things of Roman's he left."

"Was he a darky? I won't wear clothes a darky's worn."

Sarah and Floyd exchanged looks. "His father," she said, "was the master of Beulah Land."

5.

At Oaks, with most of the small harvest taken, they lived in a kind of waiting confusion. The house servants were largely undirected. When something went undone, Doreen said, "I thought Rachel—" while Rachel said, "I supposed that Doreen—" So long had Edna ruled there, no one realized all she did until she stopped doing it. Suddenly meals were no longer on time, and when they were put on the table, there was no sense or balance in them. The family dogs trotted unreprimanded in and out of the undusted living rooms of the main floor, and beds upstairs waited to be made until afternoon, and sometimes were not made at all.

No one except Sarah took Edna's going to bed seriously, since there was no common affliction. —She was old. It was a crotchet. She would be up in a day or two, and then house and servants would come to order. It was not that Edna had given many orders on the running of the house in recent years, but her presence had been enough to assure a continuation of old standards of care. The number of house servants had fallen to three, and none of these would have been allowed to cook or superintend other servants in former years. The Davises had never been fastidious about the way their house was kept, it being merely the place they had to be when they were not outdoors, a shelter from heat or cold or rain or night; but they had taken for granted its cleanliness and rough comfort as long as Edna managed it. Now no one did.

Doreen was most often busy outside, but Rachel kept mainly to the large room she and James had shared during their marriage, until James went to war. How she filled and passed the hours, she herself could not have said. She waited for James. Every few months he had managed to spend some days at home, but she had not seen him now since March, and she had had no letter for three weeks, when he told her his company was being sent into Florida. And so, she waited. Having no maid, she kept the room herself; and since that did not take very much of her time, she created a multitude of small tasks. Where once all of her pins and buttons and ribbons had been tumbled together in a drawer of the wardrobe, she now separated them into categories, assigning each a place: a glass cup, a china lady's slipper, a little basket woven of pine needles. She graded her clothes by age, material, and fashion; and then sorted them into those James had said he liked and those he had never commented upon. She no longer allowed herself to dwell on cracks and lines of the walls and ceiling. That way, she had decided, lay torpor or madness. Sometimes she sewed. Sometimes she read a book or looked out her windows, imagining that she would presently see

James riding his horse along the carriageway to the front entrance. Last Christmas, when he had returned for less than a
week, he had brought her a guitar to pass her time, and she had
learnt to play it a little in a simple fashion. Many times she did
no more than sit in her chair, a piece of clothing James had worn
on her lap as she thought of him.

Doreen counted her chickens, before and after they were
hatched. She monitored the feeding of pigs and the milking of
cows. She looked for evidence of rats in the barns now that every
stored morsel had its value, and she set the fiercest cats in the
storage rooms that showed evidence of the worst marauding.
And she too longed for James's homecoming, for had she not loved
her brother before Rachel, and as tenderly? Her one indulgence
was riding. Seeing the horse Pharaoh at a stock sale five years
ago, she had asked her father to buy him. Of the things she had
wanted in her life and been able to get, Pharaoh was the one
that had meant most to her. He understood her as no other living
creature ever had. She had only to murmur a word or give the
slightest physical indication of what she wanted him to do for
him to do it. No one rode him except her. As his reputation for
intelligence and obedience grew in the county, he became an object of attempted bargaining, but there was never a question of
her letting him go to anyone else. There were hints when the war
lengthened that such a remarkable animal belonged in the service of the Confederacy, and Doreen's married sister Annabel
noisily insisted that it was an act of disloyalty to think of keeping
him. Doreen was unmoved. Pharaoh was hers.

Since Jane's birth she and her mother Rachel had been rivals
for James's love and attention. He knew it and they knew it, although her strongest love had been for her grandfather Leon.
His death had left her lonely in a way she had not grown out of.
Her best friend now, and the only woman she really cared about,
was Sarah.

Her brother Benjamin had become Doreen's substitute for
James when James went to war, but in the last year—he was
now more than ten and fourteen months older than Jane—he
had turned increasingly to his grandfather for companionship,
and Bruce Davis responded gratefully. They spent much of
every day together. It hardly mattered what they did, although
they usually gave it the name of 'inspecting'—that is: walking

the plantation and observing its activities and the condition of its livestock and structures.

Today, though, the two were fishing. They had set poles at a bend of the creek near a clump of cypresses growing in the water. Arriving at the spot, Bruce had said, "Saw an old pike the other day right about there, long as your arm. He was lying just under the surface to catch the sun, unconcerned as an alligator. Must be somewhere around. Wouldn't surprise me if there's fish under that stump yonder too. How much you bet me?" They made bets frequently, wagering extravagant sums of money they did not have. It was a way to feel rich now that they had to live poor.

Benjamin broke a long silence with a question. "Grandpa. Why didn't Aunt Doreen get married?"

"She's got us and Oaks. Not everybody gets married."

"Most women do if anyone asks them."

"You can be sure she had chances, and will have more if she wants them."

"She's thirty-three. Jesus died then, didn't he?"

"The circumstances were different," Bruce said.

Thinking about it, Benjamin began to giggle and continued until Bruce laughed too. They got up from the bankside where they had been sitting waiting for the fish to bite. Taking up their poles, they checked the bait. The worms on both were intact.

"He's seen it, I bet you a hundred dollars," Bruce said. "Foxy old fellow, studying how to get it off the hook but not get hooked himself. What made you think about people getting married?"

Benjamin did not answer his grandfather, but offered another comment. "At least she doesn't sit and wait like Mama does."

Bruce gave him a sharp look. "You are my son's son. I am your father's father. That doesn't make it any easier for us to talk about certain things."

"Grandpa, what's going to happen to Grandma?"

"She's not your grandma, she's your great-grandma. She'll be up and around before the week's out, telling us what to do again."

They swung fishing poles simultaneously in gentle arcs, watched as the sinkers settled the lines under water, and then dug the ends of the bamboo poles into the soft moss and earth of the creek bank.

"What else is going to happen, Grandpa?" Benjamin asked lazily a few minutes later.

"It's going to rain. Look."

Bruce nodded toward the water. The usual coppery color of the creek had turned slate gray. No bug disturbed the surface. One raindrop started circles and then another. The dense leafiness of the creek bank was such that they'd had no warning of the rain's coming. A single cloud over the sun was enough to shadow the place. They made no move to go, and presently the raindrops ceased. The man closed his eyes. The boy examined a spider's web over his head that joined a thin branch to a thicker one. Looking farther upward, he saw a leaf at the moment the wind detached it from its twig. It fell and was caught and held by leaves below, fell again, was caught again, and finally came to rest miraculously on the back of Benjamin's hand. "Grandpa—"

As Bruce opened his eyes, there was a clap of thunder that sounded very near, echoed by another clap more distant that rumbled away yonder in the heavens. "It's going to rain," Bruce repeated. "We better go." As they scrambled for their poles, aware suddenly that they had waited too long, Benjamin overturned the jar of earthworms he had dug earlier from their bait bed near the kitchen door. At first the rain was only the sound it made in the leaves above them, but then it began to reach and wet them, and they looked around for shelter. They saw a tree with heavier foliage than those crowding the creek bank and ran for it, trailing their poles after them.

Thunder rolled and stopped, sounded again, then thinned to a distant mumble. A sudden bolt of lightning found its target in a tall pine tree close by, splitting the trunk and sending chunks of hard bark through the air, one of them striking Benjamin on the neck. The earth shook with the accompanying thunder, and before it could mumble itself away, another streak of lightning found a victim nearby, although not so near as the first.

The tree under which they stood no longer provided shelter. Rain poured through the leaves and branches upon them, drenching their clothes, making soggy the straw hats they had worn against the sun when they left home, and filling their shoes. Shoes were not easy come by, and Bruce ordered Benjamin, "Take off your shoes," as he removed his own.

Benjamin obeyed, understanding the reason behind the command. But when they stood shielding their shoes in their arms, they saw it was not enough to save them.

"Take off your clothes and wrap the shoes!"

Man and boy quickly removed shirts and trousers—they wore no jackets—and squeezed the garments as dry as they could before winding them around shoes.

"It's getting worse, Grandpa!"

There was hardly a pause now in the sound of thunder, and the lightning changed only from quivering bright to blinding. They were used to thunderstorms, and even found some exhilarating, but this one was a killer.

"Home! Go home!" Bruce had to shout to be heard. "Leave the poles!"

The boy nodded. They began to run, barefoot and wearing nothing but their drawers, knowing the tall trees attracting the thunderbolts were even more dangerous than open fields. Leaving the woods after a few minutes, they continued to run, although they could hardly get wetter than they were already, their haste now sparked by the animal terror of fire and noise. Panting hard, they came at last to the outermost barn and took shelter. A few chickens were there before them and cackled in alarm when the man and boy joined them.

Gradually, as they watched the storm and waited for it to be over, they breathed more normally, losing some of their primitive fear; so that presently when they saw a horse and rider leap and clear a fence, they shouted with delight. It was Doreen on Pharaoh; they had been caught in the rain too.

Jane was in the kitchen buttering her hands to pull syrup candy. She would save four pieces to take as a gift to her grandmother Sarah in the morning. In her room Edna slept and did not dream. In hers, Rachel dreamed in her chair awake, waiting for the storm to pass. She wished James were there and that they were in each other's arms. Presently, her ears telling her the storm had slackened, she took the guitar on her lap and picked at its strings, humming the tune of "Oh, for Wings to Soar."

6.

"Yankees coming! Yankees coming!"

It began as a children's game, a cry of alarm to fool and frighten each other and gullible adults. Black and white played it, in town and country. At first their elders tried to stop them, but the children persisted even after the surprise was gone. Neither Benjamin nor Jane played the game, but the slave children never tired of it; and who was to hush them now that so few of their mothers and fathers remained to do the work?

"Yankees coming!"

In her room Edna heard them, and although she knew it to be child's play, she was prompted to repeat to herself: "Hurry, Edna."

Her dying in the first week of October was an act of will, although Dr. Platt called it pneumonia. Whereas none except Sarah had considered her going to bed important, they now declared that they were not surprised, and that it was to be expected, for after all she had been eighty-four. Little time is required for people to resign themselves to the death of old relatives. She had been widely respected but narrowly loved, because she was a principled and outspoken woman; and it was doubtful that any would really miss her other than Sarah. Theirs had been true friendship, the like of which neither had known with another woman. For a long time Sarah would see daily events partly through Edna's eyes and mind, and even hear her voice commenting on them, as one does when such a friend has died.

Because Rachel continued remote and withdrawn, Edna's death seeming hardly to touch her, Jane offered herself more often as Sarah's companion. Doreen had taken charge of the household, but no one at Oaks cared how Jane used her time, so she spent much of it with Sarah. It was natural then that it was she, not Doreen or Rachel, Sarah chose to go with her one day to tend the family graves in the cemetery at Highboro. It was a task

Sarah and Edna had shared twice a year. They might have had the work done by servants, but liked doing it as an act of family regard. It had also provided the occasion of forgetting for a day the responsibilities of being plantation mistress and of relaxing in simple companionship. They had been jealous of sharing those days with others.

On the morning she had settled for the excursion Sarah was putting fried apple tarts into a hamper when Jane arrived with Bruce and Benjamin. She was to spend the night, and had brought with her a doll's trunk which was her favorite possession, because her grandfather Leon Kendrick had given it to her. Too old for dolls now, Jane used the trunk to store her treasures: a cameo, a hand mirror backed in tortoise shell which her father had given her when she was a baby, a miniature painting of Leon copied from the portrait of him by Casey Troy that hung in the drawing room at Beulah Land, and a lock of Leon's hair that had been clipped before his coffin was closed by Floyd. Over these, which never left the doll's trunk for more than a few minutes, she had folded a nightgown and a dress and a handkerchief, locking the trunk, which had a tiny perfect lock, and carrying the key on a string about her neck. She had held the trunk on her lap in the buggy, ignoring the camaraderie of her grandfather Bruce and her brother Benjamin. She liked them well enough, but she did not love them very much, and she had decided that their eternal betting and joking were childish.

Bruce and Benjamin had their own plans for the day.

"Decided to drive around the farms and talk to people," Bruce explained. "Not much chance when everybody's busy working the harvest, though we can't say *that* took much time this year."

Sarah and Bruce walked out into the side yards together when Benjamin and Jane darted into the house to pay their respects to Nell and Lauretta and to "say howdy" to the servants.

Nodding toward it, she said, "I haven't seen that old buggy of yours for years surely. I thought you gave it away."

"The Army borrowed the others."

Sarah said, "You've given them the coach and the rockaway too. You'd give them everything if Doreen didn't watch you."

"This was no use to the Army, but me and Benjamin got it to roll again." Uncomfortable with the subject, Bruce touched the toe of his shoe to the base of the sundial they paused beside. "Used to be ivy round the bottom of that," he remembered.

"It got so thick it looked snaky," Sarah said. "I chopped it out myself."

He said, not unhappily, "I can't get used to the idea of Mama's being dead."

"I doubt that I ever shall."

"She was something, wasn't she? Said she was going to die and went to bed and did it. —You remember what she used to want more than anything? You for a daughter-in-law. Not you for *my wife* particularly, but you for her daughter-in-law!" They laughed.

Sarah said, "It didn't matter to her that I had a husband?"

"Not one bit."

"Well, it's too late now."

They walked on to the shade and sat on a wooden bench that had been built around the trunk of an oak tree. "Why don't we, Sarah?"

"Do you know I haven't had a proposal for a week or more, or is it a century? I'm much obliged to you."

"You shouldn't take it for a joke."

"You've got a houseful of women."

"There can't be too many. You've nobody here now but yourself and your sister and your Aunt Nell. Why don't all of you move over?"

"You just want us to make a circle around you and save you from the Yankees if they come." They laughed. "There was a time a few years back I'd have sworn you were taking a shine to Lauretta."

Bruce blushed. "I don't deny it. *Mama* stopped that! It was after Bonard was killed in California and Lauretta came home again. Everybody felt so sorry for her."

"I have never," Sarah said firmly, "felt sorry for Lauretta."

Recovering his good humor, he said, "What about it, Sarah? Why don't we surprise everybody?"

"I don't know what's got into you old boys," she said. "First Floyd and now you." Shaking her head, she added, "You've surely made me feel good this morning, but I wouldn't marry a man just because his mama told him to ask me."

Bruce picked at a piece of bark until it came loose in his hand and threw it like a boy at a rose bed that was still showing late loose bloom. "I suppose I always minded her and did what she told me. Do you reckon that was weak?"

"It might have been in another; not you."

"How's your new hand working out?" She looked at him quickly. "This sudden cousin I never heard of before he came."

"I told you we'd forgot all about that branch of Daddy's family after they went to Missouri. He's doing fine. Chafed at first at having Floyd tell him how we do things, but now they get along pretty politely. I told him when he came he'd have to work, cousin or not, with us short-handed. Anyway, he'd rather do that than sit with the women and rock all day." She rose. "We're late leaving. Your proposal has made me forget the time! Edna and I would have done an hour's work by now." Walking quickly toward the house, she called in a carrying voice, not knowing where they were, "Jane! Benjamin! Time to go!" Then standing still, she clapped her hands until they came running.

7.

The two shabby buggies rattled down the carriageway one behind the other, parting when they came to the main road. Bruce and Benjamin turned to go into the country, while Sarah and Jane headed for town with broom, shears, shovel, and rake, to work in the Kendrick and Davis plots of the cemetery. Sarah held the reins loose in her lap, the fingers of one hand curled over them. The mule Jonah walked. He would never run and seldom trot, but at least he did not stop stock-still in the road as some mules did, refusing to go forward.

Progress being slow, Jane observed the shadow of the buggy. She allowed herself the whim of surprise that the shadow slid smoothly over all obstructions, seeming to lag when the road bent one way only to jump ahead when it bent another. They passed an open field where soldiers had bivouacked the night before. Stopping the mule, Sarah called, "Good morning!" to an officer who was crossing the road and asked who they were. He told her they were a company of newly recruited riflemen from South Georgia on their way north, to Augusta maybe, or somewhere else, he wasn't just sure. Jane called, "Sir, have you seen, do you know, Captain James Davis?"

"No, ma'am, I do not. I never saw or heard of him."

"He is my father," she explained.

"Then I'm sorry I cannot give you news of him," the officer said, as Sarah shook the reins and Jonah pulled the buggy away.

The next bend in the road revealed a rickety wagon coming toward them. Drawn by one scabby mule, it held a few sticks of furniture and so many children Sarah could not count them until the bearded man walking beside the mule tugged it to a halt. With a cringing smile he doffed a straw hat almost black with sweat stain and greeted her. "Morning, ma'am! Morning to you!"

"Good morning," Sarah answered. To excuse Jane's staring she added, "A fine lot of children you have!"

"Eleven, ma'am, eleven. The poor man's blessing, so they say. Eleven above ground and six below."

Sarah then saw a gaunt woman wearing a sunbonnet that hid her face, and assumed she was the wife and mother of the party. She sat motionless in a hide-bottomed chair at the back of the wagon and neither spoke nor gave a sign that she was aware of their stopping.

"Where are you heading?" Sarah asked.

"Nowhere, anywhere," the man said. "Name of Lowry. Lost our farm. Yankees come and taken everything, burnt house and barn. We're just a-traveling, depending on the Lord to lead the way to good people who will help us. Yes, ma'am. We ain't got nothing, and the littlest one nussing the cat, she's Charlotte and been so poorly all week we thought to lose her—"

Sarah easily picked out the thin girl in rags clutching a dirty black and white cat in her arms, so listless she might been been asleep with her eyes open. "I can't turn back, I'm going to Highboro," Sarah said, "but if you keep on about a mile and a half by this road, you'll see a big gray house through an orchard on your left. You stop and say Mrs. Kendrick sent you and they're to give you what they can spare to eat. If that'll help any."

"Lord bless you, ma'am, Lord bless you!"

"Go along now," Sarah ordered, and slapped the reins on Jonah's flanks.

Half an hour later they passed the first houses and were in the town proper. Shade trees, mostly oak, were thick with dusty foliage. Sarah greeted some of those they saw on the wooden sidewalk or pausing at their front gates hoping for a chat with passers-by. In front of the bank and post office were the usual loungers, old men in the main with nothing better to do than gather to exchange gossip about the war. Coming out of the post office, a well-dressed Negro man and boy stared at the passing buggy, but no greeting was made on either side. The man was Roscoe Elk, known as Junior Elk in spite of his forty-two years to distinguish him from his father and son, since the three shared the same name. The father had been a free Negro, overseer at Beulah Land until he accumulated property, which by now had been expanded into acreage greater than that of Beulah Land, although in separate pieces. The first Roscoe Elk was dead, but he had passed on the hatred he felt for the Kendrick family to Junior. Junior was not as bold a businessman as his father had been, but he had consolidated his gains. The thing his father had wanted most of all was Beulah Land. Junior thought about that often. Maybe a way would open. The times were on his side, and he knew it.

"You turned to stone?" he said to his son, who was tall for his twelve years but ungainly with fat and early adolescence.

"No, sir," the boy mumbled.

Junior frowned. The boy Roscoe took after his mother, a woman of weak character whom Junior had married to suit his father. Her father had been a white banker in Savannah, and old Roscoe had seen the marriage as a business connection.

"Why don't they ever speak to us, Papa?"

"You know why," Junior said impatiently.

"Yes, sir," the boy said evenly, "but they see us same as they do everybody else."

"You got no judgment? No memory? I've told you: all Kendricks are against us and we against them."

"She's not a Kendrick."

"That's enough."

"She's a Davis," Roscoe said stubbornly.

"Her grandfather was Leon Kendrick, *your* grandpapa's boss man."

"That was a great long time ago, and she's just about the sweetest-looking girl I ever saw."

Junior swung his hand and slapped Roscoe powerfully on the side of the head. When Roscoe caught his balance, both stood trembling for a minute as people stepped around them with quick, curious glances.

"Come on," Junior commanded. They progressed to a less crowded row of storefronts and he said, "Wipe your nose. Can't you feel it running? Don't let me see you cry, and don't ever use words like that about any white female. Don't even think them."

Beyond the business district Sarah stopped the buggy at a house almost hidden by a hedge of japonica that grew to the size of small trees. Taking from the hamper on the floorboard a jar that held fresh butter, she gave it to Jane and said, "Tell Pauline this is from Lovey, churned this morning; and tell your Aunt Selma we're all well, and in a big hurry and can't stop because we were late getting off; and ask her if she wants to come for Sunday dinner."

Waiting, her mind went back to Junior Elk, and then to her old enemy, his father, dead now four years. The day of his funeral, she remembered, was marked also by one of Lauretta's returnings-home, that time from Philadelphia, where she had been jeered off the stage, suspected of being a spy for the Confederacy. Before Roscoe died he had gone to see Leon one day in the office at Beulah Land, a room in which they had so often confronted each other. She had never known what passed between them, but she knew it had something to do with Leon's suicide. So much of the past she knew, and more she would never know. Since Edna's death she thought often of how little is known and remembered of what we do and are, until knowledge thins to speculation and finally all is forgotten as though it had never been. "What?"

She was aware that Jane had returned with the girl Lilac who had once been pupil-protégée of Selma and Pauline and now helped them in their teaching. Lilac was smiling. "Miss Selma says please to step down and come in, for she has just brewed *real* coffee, only you're not to ask her where she got it!"

"Oh!" To be polite, Sarah pretended to hesitate. "I wish we could, but we're late this morning and have to go on. You tell her much obliged, Lilac; and are we to expect her for Sunday dinner?"

"Yes'm," Lilac said. "All of us coming. Miss Selma and Miss Pauline and me, all three."

Sarah laughed. "Well!" Jane was beside her again on the buggy seat, and Sarah slapped the reins to make Jonah move.

"Come back and see us!" Lilac invited as they waved goodbye to her.

"They spoil her," Sarah said.

"They say she's smart and a big help."

"Whatever she does for them is easier than the field work she did before they took her up."

Again they exchanged greetings with people they passed on the sidewalks, or sitting on their front porches, the women often with vegetables on their laps they were preparing for noon dinner. "Get out and come sit a while!" one invited, and Sarah answered, "Can't this morning!" shaking her head as if with regret.

"It's my unlucky day!" Sarah declared when they arrived at the church and found a place for the buggy under an oak tree in the grove. A dozen or so townswomen were talking in groups on the church porch, evidently arrived for a meeting. "Dear God, there's your Aunt Annabel! I'd rather run into the devil himself this morning."

Jane giggled as they got down from the seat of the buggy and Sarah began to loosen the mule's harness. Detaching herself from her friends on the porch, Annabel Saxon came over. Annabel had been a pretty girl and was a handsome woman. She might have been beautiful except that vanity made a kind of gross simper of her smile and a determination to lead had given hardness to her eyes.

"Why, Auntie Sarah!" she exclaimed. "If you don't look like some old farm woman stepping in from the fields to put on a pot of collard greens!"

Sarah said, "We *are* country folk, you know, and don't try to compete with you fashionable town ladies."

"What! This old thing? Sukie has made it over twice; you surely remember it?" She asked Jane how everyone was at Oaks, and was told. "Well, I don't know why Doreen didn't send me something, a chicken at least or a cup of butter. Everything's so hard to get in Highboro now. You tell her that quart of blackberry jam she gave me tasted burnt, but we made ourselves eat it anyway."

Sarah asked what she heard from her husband. "Blair's somewhere around Savannah with his company, and that's all I know." Sarah asked about her sons, Blair and Bonard. "If I weren't so young myself I'd be embarrassed to say they're mine —biggest things you ever saw for fifteen and seventeen! Grown

men nearly! If this war goes on another year, I won't try to hold
them back from the Army, they're so raring to go. And handsome! All the girls in town are crazy about one or the other. I
swanee!" She laughed noisily. "Boys are so much more rewarding
than girls." She looked straight at Jane as she said it, and Jane
looked back at her without blinking. "But I can't stand talking, I
have to get back to my meeting. Why don't you come in for a
while and see what we're up to? They won't care how you're
dressed. You're always so aloof from us. We're deciding what to
do if the Yankees get to Highboro. I'm for resisting to the last
drop of our blood, you may be sure."

"Yes," Sarah said. "We've work over in the cemetery and better get to it." She and Jane took up the tools they had tied to the
hay box at the back of the buggy.

Margaret-Ella Singletary called from the porch, "Come *on*,
Annabel! We're waiting for you, and we want to *start!*" She and
her sister Ann-Elizabeth Dupree had long resigned themselves to
being lieutenants to Annabel's command of the townswomen's
war activities.

Annabel ignored the call, waiting to walk with Sarah and Jane.
"When you going to bring your new cousin to church, Auntie
Sarah? Everybody's just dying to meet him."

"We stay so busy." Sarah smiled discouragingly.

"Now what is his name? I've heard it but I—"

"Daniel Todd."

"You know what everybody says?"

"No, and I don't think I'll concern myself with it."

"That he's run away from something. That he's a *fugitive* from
somewhere and you've taken him in. Is it true? You can tell me.
Some even claim he's a Yankee!"

"What nonsense!"

"You act so secret, you can't blame us if we wonder. And it's
not as if Beulah Land hasn't furnished plenty to wonder about
before now!"

"You tell everybody they can wonder all they please!"

"They will without your permission, thank you. We hear he
works with the Nigras—"

"We need his help, and he offered."

"It looks funny him not going back to fight."

"He was wounded and ill. That's why they let him come home
with Lauretta."

"Not too sick to work at Beulah Land."

They had come to the church porch and before Sarah could move away, Margaret-Ella said, "Which are you for, Miss Sarah? Resistance to the last or giving up when they come?"

"I'll decide that if they do come."

Other women sidled over.

Ann-Elizabeth said, "Mama says she just can't see them enter this town and go on living."

Sarah said, "Well, I intend to go on living just as long as I can."

A skinny woman named Helen Carpenter said, "I had a letter from my cousins up in Marietta. They've been raided, oh, any number of times. What they call 'bummers' come along after the Army stealing and burning, and Sherman's own men are devils in human form. Before that, when there was real fighting, they used her piazza to operate. It was like a charnel house. They couldn't step out their own front door without stepping over dead men. That's what they wrote me. I'm telling you they've been through *everything!*" She looked around her with satisfaction. "In Marietta they say General Sherman has vowed to bring every Southern woman to the washtub!"

Sarah listened, shaking her head now and then patiently, knowing that Annabel could not long resist the temptation of command and would presently break up the group.

"Come along, all. We've lots to get settled."

Leading the way into the cemetery, Jane said, "I hate Aunt Annabel."

"Don't ever say such a thing to anyone else; but you can say it to me as often as you like."

In the cemetery they went directly to the plots of the Kendricks and Davises, which were separated, as were the family plantations, by a patch of ground that belonged to others. Jane dropped the tools she carried and went to Leon's grave. Edna's grave had no stone yet, and the red-orange of its clay mound was ugly to Sarah. She made a brief inspection of the graves of both families to see what needed doing before going to stand beside Jane at her husband's grave. The stone read, "Leon Kendrick. Born December 24, 1805. Died April 12, 1861."

Sarah did not touch the child but after a moment said, "You see how that brick border is working loose? The rain does it. Set it straight and press the brick ends into the ground as far as you

can. Then you come help me weed. We don't want to see anything growing around our graves we didn't put there. That will
take us right up to dinnertime. Lotus made some good things for
our basket, and you can have a sip of my peach brandy. You
won't like it now, but you will later."

8.

To Nell's horrified disapproval Sarah had lent one of Leon's
sporting guns to Daniel soon after he arrived at Beulah Land
and observed that the woods were full of wild turkeys and other
game. Nell's disapproval subsided when Daniel began to go
hunting alone before daybreak and return with a mess of quail
or squirrels before joining Floyd's working plans for the day.
Knowing that Jane would be there for supper, he had gone out
early that morning and shot two turkeys, fat on autumn acorns.
They were roasting in Lotus's ovens, and their scent followed
Nell when she took her cane and started her short daily walk in
the grounds. It was her only exercise, to propel her fat little body
along the side of the carriageway to the point just before it
joined the main road. A stone bench had been set there so that
she could rest before returning to the main house. It provided
her with recreation, she said, and assured her of a healthy appetite.

So it was Nell who saw the sorry mule pulling the creaking
wagon from the main road into the carriageway. She stared at
the wagon with its human freight and at the scrawny man who
walked beside it. "You there!" she called.

The man peered about until he found Nell, then called,
"Whoa!" to the mule, who was glad enough to halt. The man
took off his hat. "Morning, ma'am!"

"Who are you?"

"Lowry's our name, my wife and me and eleven children."

"Eleven! Lord Almighty!"

"Yes, ma'am. The poor man's blessing, so they say."

"Why have you turned in here?"

"Well, ma'am, we lost our farm and got nothing but what you see. We're hungry, and my little girl there's sick. Raise your hand to show her you're the sick one, honey." The child named Charlotte, still holding the black and white cat in her arms, lifted a hand feebly and let it fall.

"Never mind that," Nell said. "The poor man's blessing is the curse of those you ask to feed them."

"Ma'am, that's a cruel way to put it—"

"It's the truth. You can just turn that wagon right around."

"But, ma'am! We was told to come! Met a kind lady down the road, said her name was Mrs. Kendrick and we was to come along here and they'd feed us—"

Nell thought of the turkeys, and her voice rose in volume. "You've come to the wrong place!"

"But I turned just where she told me."

"I reckon she meant the next place. You'll see a house in an oak grove. That's the place, surely. Now you-all just get away from here."

"Mrs. Kendrick was so positive—"

"If you don't go, I'll call the dogs!"

"We'll go, ma'am." Neither the woman sitting on the chair nor the children tumbled about her had made a sound during the exchange; nor did they show any reaction when the man took the mule's bridle and led him in a clumsy circle that almost over-turned the wagon.

Nell continued to sit for a quarter of an hour after the wagon disappeared with the Lowry family. She felt no shame at sending them away, only vexation that Sarah had told them to come. Let the Davises deal with them as they would. Doreen was not so softhearted as Sarah. Anyway, she'd saved the turkeys from the hungry mouths of strangers.

It was Rachel who spied the Lowry wagon approaching the main house at Oaks, Rachel at her window watching the long carriageway and hoping to see James come riding home. She observed the tedious approach mystified, but before she could make out faces, indeed before she could see more than that the wagon carried what looked to be a dozen souls, the man stopped. She expected him to come on again, but he held the wagon where he was with the diffidence of the unwelcome wait-ing to be noticed. Frowning, Rachel leaned out the window and called, "Who are you? What do you want?"

The man replied, "Poor folks, ma'am, with a sick child. We was told to come—"

"Told by whom?"

"Mrs. Kendrick!"

Rachel left the window, threw a shawl about her shoulders, and hurried from the room and down the stairs and outdoors where the strangers waited. When she came to them, she asked, "You say Mrs. Kendrick sent you here?"

"We met her on the road driving her buggy with a beautiful little girl beside her. I 'spect it was because of her she took pity on our own sick little girl, as any tenderhearted lady might."

"I suppose she sent you here instead of Beulah Land because she was to be away all day."

"That must be the way of it, ma'am." The man paused, thinking. "We was drove off our farm by Yankees. Lost it all and had to move on, hoping for a better place and asking God's blessing on them that kindly help us on our way. I can see you're not one to harden your heart against a sick child, ma'am."

Rachel hesitated. "The child you saw with Mrs. Kendrick was my own."

The woman, who had not moved from her chair all morning, now rose and stepping heavily over several of her brood who were in the way, pushed the child Charlotte toward the edge of the wagon.

"Have you had anything to eat today?" Rachel asked.

"No'm," the man said quickly. "Nor yesterday. Nothing in us but a cup of water that was all we could beg of a hard man down the road."

"You can have a meal here." She paused. "I don't know where to say to put your wagon—"

The man said eagerly, "We'll just pull off the road here, ma'am, lest we be in somebody's path. We're not asking to come no further!" He smiled accommodatingly and bowed his head.

The woman in the wagon pushed Charlotte toward Rachel.

Rachel had little use for her own children and none for those of others, but the sight of the sick girl both repelled and fascinated her. "You're her mother?" Rachel said.

The head in the sunbonnet nodded once, as if the woman was too weak to do more.

Rachel stared at the child, registering the dull misery on her face, and touched a hand to her cheek, withdrawing it instantly.

"She's burning with fever!" Again the woman nudged the child toward her, and Rachel caught her in her arms, for she would otherwise have fallen. "I'll take her indoors. She must be put into bed. I'll send someone to give you food and water, and hay for that poor mule."

"Bless you, ma'am! God bless you, ma'am! Oh, the Lord has led us to you! Your goodness surely will be known in Heaven, ma'am! We'll love you and pray for you evermore!"

Walking with the child in her arms, Rachel hardly heard the words the man cried after her. Charlotte whimpered once when the cat leapt down and made a beeline for the back yards, disappearing through the open door of the first outbuilding she saw, which happened to be a corncrib.

Entering the house, Rachel called, "Flossie! Flossie!" and when the old Negro woman shuffled down the hallway, explained that she was taking a sick child upstairs to her room, that they were to send to town for Dr. Platt, and to please find Miss Doreen, wherever she was, and ask her to feed all those hungry people in the wagon in the carriageway.

Doreen was found and came to Rachel's room, but cut short her questions when she saw Rachel busy attending a child who was so obviously ill. The sight of such activity on Rachel's part was so surprising she felt strangely embarrassed. She went to the kitchen and told the cook to make a lot of corn bread and fry a batch of fatback to feed the family she had seen in the wagon. The black and white cat had found a party of rats in the corncrib and was ending her long fast.

9.

"It's like a party," Lauretta said. "Just like a party."

Sarah and Jane had returned to Beulah Land late in the afternoon tired and dirty, but feeling the satisfaction of having done worthy physical labor. They bathed in the old tin tub that was shaped like a big hat, and they used the same water to save the kitchen girl work, although Nancy would not have minded filling the tub twice. She was thirteen and had only recently been shifted from field to kitchen; and she was eager to learn the ways of life in the big house. She was an open, merry creature, sometimes rude from ignorance, but Lotus was teaching her.

Downstairs they found Bruce and Benjamin in the drawing room with Nell and Lauretta. Lauretta was at the piano playing a love song by Stephen Foster and singing a phrase here and there with theatrically sweet feeling. Sarah smiled as she observed that it was Benjamin who stood at the piano watching her, while Bruce contented himself with sitting beside Nell and listening from a distance.

Finishing the song, Lauretta left the piano, she and Benjamin joining the others to share the exchanges of news they had gathered during the day. Bruce finished a brief review of his country tour by saying to Sarah, "And since we had to pass you to get home again, we stopped for a quarter of an hour—"

"But I," Lauretta said, taking the words from him, "persuaded them to stay for supper."

"It wasn't hard work," Nell said, and they laughed at the gloomy way she said it.

"Such smells I never did smell!" Benjamin declared.

Bruce winked at Sarah. "Your Lotus is a better cook than our old Marie, who gives us whatever's handy without bothering how it tastes."

Nell nodded her head in quick, positive jerks. "When I saw we were to have company, I asked Lotus to make a couple of pecan pies. She wasn't sure the pecans were dry enough but I felt them and told her they were."

"We're all perishing!" Benjamin said, and looked at his grandfather. "We shared noon dinner at the Rayfords, and I must have drunk a quart of buttermilk to fill up."

"You ate your share of pot-dodgers too. I bet you a dollar Mrs. Rayford doubled the amount when we said yes to her offer of dinner."

Sarah said, "We saw Annabel at the church."

Jane said, "She told us how good-looking Blair and Bonard are getting to be and how all the girls run after them!" She and Benjamin laughed together rudely; they and their cousins were old enemies.

"That's enough," Sarah said mildly. "Annabel asked after all of you at Oaks. She was holding a meeting of town women to decide—something or other. They're all full of Sherman talk."

"So are the farmers and their wives. They've even started hiding things, the little silver and gold and jewelry they have. They talk more about Sherman than crops and weather."

Benjamin said, "Crops next year will depend a lot on what he does, won't they, Grandpa?" It was not his own thought, but one he'd heard expressed variously that day.

"So they say; yes, so they say."

There was a knock at the door, although the door was open. "Come in, Daniel!" Sarah called, guessing who it was. Although she had told him he was welcome to use the living rooms as they did, he shied from joining them until just before meals. Roman's left-over clothes had served him well enough when he first arrived, and he still used them for work, but the weeks at Beulah Land had already put weight on him. He no longer appeared the starving boy he had when he came, and was beginning to look a credible member of the family. Seeing this, Sarah gave him some of Leon's clothes that had been packed away in trunks after his death. Daniel never asked whose they were, but he guessed, having heard the manner of Leon's dying from the slaves. Except for Sundays, supper was the only meal at which he sat with the family. He ate his breakfast in the kitchen with Floyd and his noon meal wherever the day's work found him. Ordinarily, he appeared for supper in plain shirt and trousers, but tonight he wore a jacket too, just as he did Sundays, in Jane's honor.

Entering, he discovered the group and blushed. "I didn't know there was such company," he said, turning to the door. "I'll wait in the dining room."

Sarah said, "Come and sit by me, Daniel," in a tone that commanded as much as it invited. He obeyed. "You know who everybody is."

Bruce watched him with interest. Lauretta shifted irritably in her chair, but smiled to deny any resentment of Sarah. Daniel had, after all, brought her back to Beulah Land, and everyone knew that she had a special claim on his regard.

Bruce said to him, "Have you and Floyd been at the sawmill today?"

"No, sir," Daniel answered. "Today we split the men. Floyd took the biggest number to work the mill, and I took a few hands to the gin."

"I thought the cotton was about played out," Bruce observed.

"Yes, sir, that's right; but a wagonload still pulls up now and then. Late, scattered cotton. We ginned four bales today, but mostly we've begun to clean up from the summer's work and take stock."

Lauretta beamed generously. "Daniel is being such a big help, a real credit to me for bringing him to Beulah Land."

Seeing his discomfort, Sarah said briskly, "We've him to thank for the turkeys you'll see on the table."

"Aunt Nell told us," Benjamin said.

"Give the devil his due," Nell said judiciously.

Benjamin said, "You must be a real good shot, Daniel, after being in the war. You killed a lot of Yankees, I expect?"

Daniel shook his head hastily even as he appeared encouraged by the boy's friendliness. Until tonight they had exchanged no more than a nod or a word of formal greeting. "Big lazy things just standing there like they was waiting for somebody. Could have run them down almost, without bothering to use the gun!"

Nancy appeared. It was not for her to knock. She marched straight into the room and spoke. "Lotus say come on, everybody. Things is all on the table, and don't they look good! Never in my life see the like of it!"

Sarah led the way with Bruce and Nell. Lauretta took Daniel's arm, which made him blush and shy like a nervous horse. Once she had fed him with a spoon from a bowl and changed the dressings on his battle wounds, and he had submitted humbly, but now that he was well and they were both dressed up, his shyness made him lean away from her.

Behind them Benjamin pointed to Daniel and Lauretta and smirked at Jane, although his amusement was really at his Great-aunt Lauretta. Jane, who pitied Daniel, glared at Benjamin, and he, feeling that he had been misunderstood, stuck his thumbs in his ears and waggled his fingers at her. She poked her tongue out at him angrily, and Nancy, who waited at the door for the party to pass, laughed delightedly. Their dignity returned instantly, for they were old enough to resent being caught behaving like children.

It was when they all had entered the dining room and taken seats at the table that Lauretta said, "It's like a party. Just like a party!"

"There used to be such grand parties," Bruce said. "I've often seen fifty standing up to dance in the hall—"

"And another fifty sitting on the sides to watch them," Nell added.

"Would you believe it, Daniel?" Lauretta said gaily. "We used never to sit down for a meal in this room fewer than eight or a dozen!"

"We lived well," Nell said, "before you—before the Yankees brought this terrible war down on us!"

Sarah said, "There hasn't been a party here since before the war."

"They were so common then, nobody bothered to call them parties," Lauretta said.

"'Before the war, before the war,'" Benjamin teased. "Everything good was before the war! I don't remember it all that way, do you, Jane?"

Sarah said, "That only proves what a baby you still were."

"Who wants sweet milk with their victuals? Who wants buttermilk? Who wants tea? Who wants coffee?" Nancy stood at the sideboard waiting for them to settle themselves so that she could pour. Lotus had told her to hurry up with it when they sat down and then come help her bring the turkeys from the kitchen. Everything else was on the table, ready.

"I should warn you," Sarah said, "that the 'tea' is probably stewed holly leaves and the 'coffee' may be anything from peanuts to corn husks! Lovey refuses to drink it."

Daniel swallowed, staring at the table. "I never saw such a thing in my life."

"Didn't I tell y'all?" Nancy crowed.

None of them was used any longer to seeing a table so loaded with food, and they followed Daniel's example, staring and marveling with him.

Nell recited the inventory with the satisfaction of a Midas counting his gold. "Rice and gravy. Boiled Irish potatoes. Baked sweet potatoes. Creamed onions. Turnip greens. Stewed tomatoes. Mashed turnip root. Beet pickle. Cucumber pickle. Watermelon rind preserves. Deviled eggs. Potato salad. Corn and bell pepper relish."

"And salt and pepper!" Benjamin finished, laughing.

"Hush, little silly," Nell reprimanded him.

Nancy was laughing with pleasure as she poured glasses of milk for everyone whether they indicated acceptance or not. Lotus entered with a huge platter on which sat the two roasted turkeys. "Go to the kitchen," she told Nancy, "and bring that biggest bowl of dressing and the biscuits! Make haste! I want everything to be hot!" She set the turkeys down before Sarah.

Sarah looked at them and looked at the faces around the table. All were focused on the turkeys. She was surprised by emotion. Tears sprang to her eyes, and she gripped her face with both hands to stop them. Managing a quick laugh, she stood to use the carving knife Lotus had earlier set, newly sharpened, at her place. "It's only my amazement," she said lightly, making deft cuts at the breast of one of the birds. "Amazement at what a feast Lotus has managed for us." The concern on the others' faces changed to relief, and their eyes glowed with frank, cheerful greed.

Returning from the kitchen bearing a bowl of corn bread dressing in one hand and a platter of hot biscuits in the other, Nancy assured them gleefully, "There's pecan pie after all this if anybody's got any room left! I picked out the pecans myself!"

"You get back to the kitchen," Lotus ordered her, "and start whipping that cream before I skin you alive!"

Plates were filled and passed. They ate and laughed, repeating Nancy's words. Lips shone with grease, eyes with pleasure and satisfaction. The thought that had brought Sarah so suddenly to tears was: "and the condemned ate a hearty meal."

After supper Sarah found Floyd in the office and closed the door. He knew the Davises were waiting for her and went through the day's business quickly. They exchanged no personal remarks. Sometimes they did; as often they did not. They had known each other long, and every word and look was personal in the way of revealing more to the other than anyone else would have gleaned. When he rose from his chair to go, he was not surprised to hear her say, "Something is on your mind."

"It can wait."

"Then why does it show in your face when you're talking about something else?"

"I'm glad Lotus doesn't know me as well as you do. One woman reading my mind is enough."

"Tell me. It obviously concerns both of us."

"Tomorrow will do as well."

"For you maybe; but if I wake at three o'clock, and I often do, I'll wonder about it."

"It's too much to talk about tonight. We've touched on it a hundred times anyway. We don't consider anything without grazing it."

She sighed, her feelings a mixture of resignation, concern, and contempt. "Sherman."

He sat again, but only on the arm of the chair. "What happens to everything?"

"That won't be for us to say."

"Not if we do nothing. Have you thought about it? You hear all the talk. You must. I do."

She nodded. "Yes, everywhere."

"We mustn't just wait. We ought to make a plan of how to manage things if we know he's on the way here."

"*You've* thought about it." It was both statement and question.

"We can't do anything about Beulah Land. You can't hide sixteen hundred acres or the people who work it."

"Some of *them,* are you thinking?"

He shook his head. "I wouldn't know who to trust, and I've known them all my life. They're hearing things too—but different things from what you hear or even I. They don't talk to me any more because they don't trust me, and that tells me I can't trust them."

She tried to accept what he was saying. "We can't hide the cotton gin any more than we can hide the fields."

"We might dismantle some of it," he said, "but I think we'd better leave it the way it is. What I do want to think of dismantling and hiding is the sawmill."

"Why?"

"As long as the war lasts things will be destroyed, but when the war is over, everybody will have to build again. The lumber we cut and sell may be our only way of making a living."

"When the war's over, we'll plant and harvest the way we used to, and the cotton gin will run full force from August through October."

"If they don't burn it. Who's to plant the big crops? You won't have the hands. More than half are gone now, and they won't come back—or only the no-account will. Others will leave, or if they agree to stay, they'll have to be paid cash. Whatever happens, slavery is done."

"I can't argue. You say dismantle the sawmill. Can you do that?"

"We move it wherever the best timber is to be taken now."

"Where would you hide the parts? Who can you trust to help you?"

"I don't know yet. You see? I wasn't ready to talk about it. You have company. I'll leave you."

"Lotus did us proud at supper."

Floyd nodded with a faint smile. There was a knock at the door. Sarah said, "Come in."

It was Daniel. To Floyd he said, "I thought you'd be gone. I came to borrow a book."

"We're done," Floyd said. "You've energy to read after the day's work?" he said with an edge. "Well, good night to you too. The turkey was good."

Daniel said, "I'll be up as early as you in the morning. The cotton gin again?"

Floyd nodded. "Take the same men if they worked all right."

"They did."

"Somebody ought to be there through this week." Floyd nodded to Sarah and went out, leaving the door open.

"What kind of book?" Sarah said.

"A story book, something easy. There's a Bible in my room Miss Nell gave me and told me to read, but I can't read the Bible, I go to sleep."

Sarah looked along a shelf that held a jumble of ledgers and old school books she and Roman had used when she started the school for slave children. There were a few books of English poetry too, Byron and Wordsworth mostly, and some novels and books of sermons and history. "Here's something," she said. *"The Vicar of Wakefield.* But before you go upstairs, come with me to the others for a little while. It will seem strange to the Davises if a cousin simply disappears after supper."

"I walked around the grounds some."

Together they went into the drawing room and found Nell at the piano playing a lively waltz in a ragged fashion, to which the others danced. Lauretta was teaching Benjamin, and Jane had coaxed her grandfather to the floor.

Nell stopped playing when she saw Sarah. "How nice you all look!" Sarah said. "Go on playing, Aunt Nell; it's good to hear you."

Nell hesitated. "It *is* like old times, a little. I never liked to be danced with myself, but I don't mind playing for others."

"Then play some more. I want to dance."

"I claim you as my partner!" Bruce said.

Sarah made a quick, jokey curtsey. "Honored."

"Aunt Lauretta is a good teacher," Benjamin said handsomely, to make up for his occasional funmaking at her expense.

Sarah said, "Jane, you dance with Daniel then."

"I don't dance!" Daniel held his book more tightly, as if it were threatened.

"Neither do I," Jane said, "but Grandpa was showing me, and I'll teach you what I know."

Nell had begun to play. Her choice this time was the jolly, jiggish "Camptown Races," and she played it as approximately as she had the waltz before it. When the others began to dance, Daniel set his book down on a table and let Jane show him a simple, bouncing step. Shortly after, the clock struck nine, and Bruce said that he and Benjamin must go home.

10.

Bruce returned to Beulah Land next morning to find them still at breakfast, although Sarah and Jane had risen much earlier and made a morning tour of the yards and barns to gather eggs, before joining Nell and Lauretta in the dining room for hominy and turkey hash.

Everyone but Nell stopped eating when he came in unannounced and said, "Lotus said you all were in here. I'm on my way to town and stopped to tell you we've got a little trouble at Oaks—"

"Rachel!" Sarah pushed her chair back.

"Now, no! Don't jump at things. Rachel is all right, just all tired out and dispirited after what happened."

He told them what he had been able to put together from the incomplete accounts Doreen and Rachel and the servants had given him of the arrival yesterday of the Lowry family at Oaks. So much was agreed: the large family had been fed but refused to leave their wagon when Rachel took the sick child Charlotte to her room, putting her to bed and tending her.

"She says she asked the servants to send for the doctor, but it turned out nobody sent or went. Flossie's head is getting as woolly inside as out. She doesn't hear half what we say to her, or do the other half." He paused. "Well, when me and Benjamin got home last night, we found Doreen in Rachel's room trying to persuade her to lie down somewhere else to sleep. Rachel was just sitting there and wouldn't budge or hardly answer, like she didn't hear us." He hesitated again. "Rachel wouldn't admit the child was dead. —Sarah! Wait!" He caught her as she reached the door.

"I'm going to Rachel," she said.

"No, you mustn't. I've come to ask you not to!"

"Do you forget Rachel's had yellow fever? —Was it the fever the child died of?"

"I just don't know. It's doubtful. Dr. Platt—oh, he finally came but only after I'd sent for him most urgently, and then he didn't get there until two o'clock this morning. Dr. Platt can't or won't say what the girl had. He gave orders to use lye on everything she touched and we've done that. He dosed Rachel with laudanum and sent her to bed."

"I'll go to her."

"Sarah, now sit back down and let me explain it all."

Lauretta had left her place at the table and was there to help him guide Sarah out of the dining room and along the hallway to the office. Without thinking about it, they took her there as the place that always seemed to suit her best. When Jane rose to follow them, Nell stopped her, saying, "Stay here, child. Always keep out of people's way when they're distracted. Push that bowl of gravy to me, and take another biscuit for yourself. Eat some fig preserves. Your Grandpa Leon was partial to them. The worst thing you can do is neglect your victuals. Did you ever hear that when your grandpa was a baby, they used to pack him and Floyd in pillowcases like papooses and let them swing in the wind from a limb of that old fig tree near the kitchen door?"

In the office Sarah was saying, "I don't understand," but she was calmer; she was no longer insisting that she go to Oaks immediately. "Lowry is the family I met on the road yesterday when Jane and I were driving the buggy into Highboro. I told them to come here, not to go to Oaks."

"Then they got it wrong. You know how people are."

"I remember saying to that man: 'Go about a mile and a half' —I met him just beyond that field where the soldiers spend the night on their way north—I told the man he'd see a big gray house through an orchard on the left and to turn in there."

"He came on to us."

"Then it's my fault, I wasn't clear—"

"Nobody's fault. The girl would have died whatever turn was taken. They'd neglected her too long."

"You're certain Rachel isn't ill?"

"Only tired and resting. If you went over, you'd upset her."

"Why are you on your way to Highboro?"

"To buy a coffin for the child."

Sarah nodded. "Her father said he had nothing."

"Her father's disappeared."

"What?"

"They've gone. The whole family. Before I got home last night. Nobody saw them go, they just vanished like Indians. My guess is they decided the girl was better off left with us."

"Her mother—"

"Has ten others."

"But to leave her and not know—"

"Better perhaps than knowing what's happened now."

"Aren't you going to send after them to tell them?"

Bruce shook his head. "I'll see the child buried and put her name and age on a marker in case they come back this way. Families like that are on the road nowadays, and we'll be seeing more like them. People who've been burnt off their land because it was in front of a marching army. —Damn the Yankees."

"You might as well damn the war," Sarah said. "It's our war as much as theirs."

"No. They started it. They brought it on us, and they are determined to kill, or starve and humiliate, all of us before it's over. We have no army left in Georgia to hold them back. —Will you do what I ask? Take care of Jane and Benjamin. Doreen and I can manage things at Oaks if they're here with you."

Sarah said, "You know I'm glad to have them, but first I'm going to see Rachel and decide if—"

"Rachel wants you to keep them, and she doesn't want you to come to her," Bruce declared. "Before she had the laudanum she told me to bring them to you in case that child *did* have something they might take from her being there, in spite of our scouring with lye."

"But what of Rachel herself?"

"Dr. Platt promised to come again at noon."

"She should have someone in the room with her every minute. Doreen is too busy. So are the servants, not that I'd trust them—"

"I'll go stay with her." It was Lauretta who spoke, for the first time beyond murmurs calculated to soothe her sister. "I'm not the kind to catch anything. I was never healthier than when I was nursing sick and wounded soldiers."

Bruce said, "I left Doreen packing clothes for Jane and Benjamin, and I told one of the men to hitch up a wagon and bring him with their trunks later this morning."

"I'll go back in the wagon with my trunk," Lauretta said.

"I must see Rachel!" Sarah begged. "She's my child." There was no contradiction in the look Lauretta gave her, but Bruce's embarrassment reminded her that Rachel was also Lauretta's. "It's good of you, Lauretta. Forgive me. And I can see that it's wise to get the children away. I should be here, of course. Floyd and I have a lot of business. But when you get there, feel her head; and if there's the least sign of fever, send for me, you hear?"

"Yes."

"If she cries, if she can't sleep, let me know and I'll come."

"All right."

"Send word the minute she turns better or worse—or if she stays the same. Don't leave me to wonder."

"No," Lauretta said.

Bruce looked from one to the other and decided that no more questions or assurances were necessary between them. "I'll go to town then."

Lauretta said, "I'll be ready when the wagon comes with Benjamin and their clothes."

Bruce and Lauretta went out of the room together, and Sarah heard them whispering in the hallway and did not blame them.

Her thoughts were with Rachel; but reflecting on the last half hour, she was not pleased with herself. They had been sensible; she had not. Of course she must look after Jane and Benjamin and leave Rachel alone with Lauretta until she was certain there was nothing that could be passed on to the children.

11.

Lauretta was true to her word. The first few days she sent a servant every two hours with a report of Rachel's physical condition and state of mind. And every messenger returned from Beulah Land with a note of loving concern to be given directly at Rachel's door. Jane and Benjamin, neither of whom had ever felt a particularly strong attachment to their mother, briefly enjoyed playing the part of dutiful children. They picked a few late, ragged zinnias to go with Sarah's notes, and one afternoon Lotus allowed Jane and Nancy to make divinity candy with pecan centers, six pieces of which found their way to the invalid's room, where they were eaten by Lauretta. Dr. Platt called daily at Oaks for a week, stopping at Beulah Land on his way back into town, as he had been charged to do, and furnishing Sarah with a firsthand account of his patient's condition. It seemed to him much ado about nothing, but doctors seldom say so to the powerful of their parishes. Bruce came to Beulah Land every day, but as much to see Benjamin, whose company he missed, as to reassure Sarah.

And Sarah was reassured as the days went by, only anxious to see Rachel herself. On the fourth day she slipped alone through the fields and woods, taking the back way to Oaks. She found Rachel asleep in her bed—Dr. Platt was liberal in his use of laudanum, and the patient's nerves had continued unsettled— and Lauretta sitting reading by the window that overlooked the carriageway. Lauretta put her finger to her lips importantly and led Sarah out of the room into the hallway, where she kissed her on the cheek and covered her clenched hands comfortingly with her own.

"I never leave her—or only for a little while now and then, with Doreen taking the vigil. No, never just a servant! Dear Bruce insists that I need a breath of air and walks with me for five minutes to see that I have daily exercise. Otherwise, I assure you I leave her not at all."

"You are good," Sarah declared gratefully. "How does she seem to you who see her constantly and must be sensitive to the smallest variation in her condition?"

Lauretta allowed herself a moment's consideration. "She sleeps much of the day. Dr. Platt says that is helpful. There is no fever."

"Thank God!"

"Her skin is dry and cool."

"Not cold?"

Lauretta shook her head. "But not warm either. She will eat little but enjoys a greater than normal thirst. Dr. Platt says that is because of the laudanum."

"Is there *no* change?" Sarah pressed her.

"Little that I can see."

"Does she talk to you?"

"Only a word when necessary. She is perfectly sensible but uninterested in what goes on around her. On the day I came I told her why I was here and she replied that yes, she understood."

"Do you think she is getting any *better?*" Sarah insisted.

"I can only assure you that she is no worse. The doctor seems certain now that there is no awful disease."

"That's as he tells me, thank God."

"But for a continuing lowness of spirits and lack of regard for what goes on, I should say she is not especially unwell."

"Does she never show a spark?"

"Only when she sleeps will she stir, restless with dreams, and call to James in a tearful voice—"

"Poor child! But we must not leave her for so long."

They tiptoed back into Rachel's room but found her as they had left her. When Sarah made as if to go close and touch her, Lauretta shook her head and stopped her for no reason other than to show her authority. Sarah submitted, only whispering, "Tell her I was here," as she departed.

That night at supper, after Sarah had related news of her Oaks visit, Jane said, "I'm nearly ten years old."

"You're not," Benjamin said. "I'm nearer eleven than you are ten. I'll be eleven in April and you won't be ten until June. How old are you, Aunt Nell?"

"One hundred and thirty-five," Nell said.

"Oh, you're not."

"Sixteen then," she said.

"I don't believe you," Benjamin said.

"Then why did you ask me? It doesn't matter how old I am."

Daniel looked at the others as they spoke, although he seldom offered a comment of his own. At first he'd thought the whole family a little crazy in the way they talked. His own family had been as poor in words as money, keeping themselves to necessary questions and plain answers. He had never heard idle conversation before coming to Beulah Land.

Observing him and guessing his reaction to what had passed, Sarah said, "I believe today was the last day you were to keep the gin operating."

"Yes, ma'am." It took Daniel a moment to realize that this was part of "conversation" too. She knew as well as he did that today was the last day for the cotton gin to work that fall. Nevertheless, she had encouraged him to make an independent remark. "There was a peculiar man came around. Not to gin any cotton. Just stood watching for a while."

"What sort of man?" Benjamin wanted to know.

"Well, to begin: colored."

Sarah said, "That wouldn't make him peculiar, would it?"

"He was dressed up, not working, and didn't belong to anybody."

"There are a few F.P.C.'s in Highboro besides Floyd's family." Sarah saw that he did not understand. "Free persons of color."

"Oh."

"What made him peculiar?" Benjamin took up the question.

Daniel glanced at the boy but directed his answer to Sarah. "He talked some to one of your men. The one they call Zebra, with the birthmarks."

"What did they talk about?" Sarah asked when he volunteered no more.

"Zebra wouldn't say much after the man left other than he'd wanted to know all about who I was."

"Zebra told him, of course."

Daniel hesitated. "Said I was yours and Miss Lauretta's cousin from Missouri."

Jane said, "Was there a boy with the man?"

"That's right," Daniel said. "Stout-looking boy, and not as dark as the man."

Jane and Sarah looked at each other. Sarah said, "It was Junior Elk and his son Roscoe. Junior's father was overseer at Beulah Land for many years."

"Him." Daniel had heard about the first Roscoe Elk.

"What's Missouri like, Daniel?" said Benjamin, who had been studying him.

Daniel was caught by surprise. "Like any other place, I guess."

Benjamin looked disappointed, but then Nancy brought in a tray holding a jug of milk and a big bowl with a stack of smaller bowls. "Rice pud'n," she explained, setting the tray down before Sarah. "Them specks is cinnamon, Lotus says, not from flies."

12.

Time condones and sometimes ennobles old scandal. The fact that Lauretta and Leon, neither innocents, had a brief love affair after his marriage to Sarah that resulted in the birth of Rachel was shocking when it happened. But to most of those who knew and remembered now, it seemed only gently romantic to reflect that Lauretta's main concern in her fifty-fifth year was the well-being of the daughter whose care she had formerly left to her sister. To think of it as her main concern, as Bruce Davis did, was not, however, to see the matter quite right. Bruce had always looked at women sentimentally, although there was not one who had seen him so, including his wife, mother, and two daughters. They had used him when they could to suit their own purposes. That he survived their maneuverings was due less to his own cleverness than to the fact that they had sometimes saved him from each other.

Once upon a time, before Rachel married James Davis and became mistress-apparent to Oaks, Lauretta thought to capture

Bruce, thereby becoming mistress of Oaks herself. Her mistake
was in underestimating Edna, who saw what she was up to and
told Bruce simply that she would not have it. But now Edna was
dead, Rachel merely waiting for James to return, and Doreen a
spinster with no apparent aptitude or appetite for command.
Lauretta looked at herself in the glass and knew that she was
past youth and beauty, but she understood Bruce's weakness for
womanliness, and set about to win him again. When he was present, she stirred herself busily, knowing what comfort men take
in the sight of women at domestic chores. If she sat quietly, she
held sewing on her lap. She never appeared idle before him. As
an actress she had learned the ways of using voice and face, and
it was only a little time before Bruce was once again thinking of
her as a most appealing and worthy woman. She was careful
with flattery and subtle in the ways she encouraged him to move
from courtesy to courtliness.

On the same day Sarah paid her first visit to the ailing Rachel
at Oaks, Lauretta made up her mind that she could indeed have
Bruce Davis and his plantation. To pass the afternoon after
Sarah left, she examined Rachel's personal belongings. Nothing
was locked away. All was orderly, since Rachel herself had
recently learned the uses of small domestic chores. Having examined clothes and jewelry, Lauretta opened another drawer of
the wardrobe to find it full of letters. She saw from reading one
and glancing at the handwriting of others that they were all
from James.

"What are you doing?"

Stage experience had taught her never to appear startled unless she had calculated the effect herself as part of a performance. Lauretta turned easily toward the hall door where Doreen
stood, her expression interested, not suspicious. "I heard such a
noise from this drawer I decided a mouse must have trapped
himself. I opened it"—she clapped her hands together lightly—
"and sure enough, away he scampered! I wonder he did not run
past you in the hall."

Doreen laughed. "No. Is she all right?" Lauretta nodded without glancing at the bed, as one who knows every minute the condition of a patient even when she may not appear to be on
watch. "Would you like me to sit a while so that you may have a
stretch outdoors?" Lauretta shook her head. "Then I think I'll

give Pharaoh an hour. I haven't ridden today, and he gets temperish if I don't take him out."

"It's good for your nerves too." Lauretta smiled sympathetically.

"Do you need anything from the servants?"

"I think not."

"Well then." Doreen turned.

Lauretta said, "You might ask Flossie to have some water put in my wash pitcher. If you see her or Marie."

Doreen said she would and left.

Lauretta heard a whimper from the bed. Rachel was waking and finding it unpleasant. She had discovered the solace of sleep and dreams as one who had found consciousness too hard to endure alone. Lauretta closed the drawer on the letters. But she returned to them half an hour later when Rachel slept again. Restless and unhappy, Rachel had asked for a drink of water and then laudanum, which Lauretta had given her with no hesitation. It was considered harmless enough to administer to children, and Dr. Platt had more than one adult patient who relied on it. Knowing Rachel would sleep deeply for a while, Lauretta read right through the letters. As she did so, her astonishment increased. There was little in them concerning James's own activities and only the customary inquiries about family and conditions at Oaks. Their main concern was his love and his need of her. In expressing these he called up the most graphic and detailed descriptions of hours they had spent together, descriptions such as Lauretta had never seen committed to paper before. Her neck and cheeks flamed and her loins tingled. No stranger to passion herself, she was nonetheless thunderstruck at discovering the violent nature of the love between James and Rachel. It was obvious from the letters that Rachel was no mere acquiescent wife but an intense and knowledgeable mistress to her husband.

"Well!" thought Lauretta. "Well, well—she is truly my daughter after all!"

Finally she returned the letters to the drawer just as she had found them and stood beside the bed looking down at the sleeping woman who had inspired them. No wonder her life was torture without James. Pity stirred in Lauretta, the only genuine feeling she ever had experienced for her daughter. Years before on one of her visits to Beulah Land, she had tried to establish intimacy with Rachel, who had snubbed her firmly. There wasn't very much, Lauretta decided, that she could do for her except to help make her waiting easier. She was obviously not ill, only pining in the most desperate way. The death of that abandoned child had simply furnished the occasion of her succumbing to her private despair. Well, if laudanum made it easier for her to bear James's absence, Lauretta would see that she had it. And she herself would continue at Oaks, just now in the line of duty, eventually perhaps as lady to its lord.

She went through the doorway that connected Rachel's room to her own. Opening the wardrobe there, she studied the dresses carefully, finally choosing a pink organdy with ruffles at the neck and sleeves and a hooped shirt. Flossie had not sent the water up. She took the empty pitcher from her washstand to the kitchen, where Marie filled it from a kettle she kept on the cooking stove. In her room again, Lauretta removed her clothes and bathed carefully from the washbowl, using sponge and cloth. She would be fresh and pretty tonight when she joined Bruce for supper, and she would ask Doreen to sit with Rachel afterwards while she and Bruce walked through the grounds.

13.

Benjamin and Jane liked each other about as little and as much as brother and sister generally do at their ages. Father at war, mother withdrawn, their situation isolating them from other children, each had chosen a grandparent as friend. But Sarah was busier than usual, and Bruce, although a frequent visitor to Beulah Land, was no longer casually available to Benjamin as he had been at Oaks. He and Jane therefore became occasional companions. Each would have stood by the other if attacked by enemies; indeed they had fought side by side against Annabel's sons. And either would desert the other instantly if a more likely friend appeared.

Both were happy to be at Beulah Land. It was a livelier place than Oaks, and the food was better. A particular interest made them allies and, in a way, rivals: Daniel Todd. They rejected the explanation that he was a cousin. Without baiting him, they questioned him about the past and saw his vague answers for what they were, a hedge to hide the truth, which they could only guess at. Their grandmother knew all about Daniel, they were certain, and so must Aunt Nell and Aunt Lauretta; but they would never let on. In fact, they had begun halfway to believe the story they put about, as people will when they invent to accommodate the demands of circumstance.

Benjamin suggested that he was a deserting Yankee, or possibly a spy, until common sense canceled the latter conjecture, for what was there to spy on at Beulah Land? Jane was inclined to accept him as a Southerner because she wanted to, accounting for his unusual accent by his having come from Missouri, which she knew from maps to be remote. She imagined him a Gypsy, or part Indian, or an adventurer who had lost his memory, but Daniel's homely features and direct manner, except when she touched him about the past, made her reluctantly discard such fancies.

When the cotton gin was closed down, Floyd did not shift Daniel to the sawmill, where most of the other men were working, but left him to perform caretaking jobs at the plantation, hoping thus to stay comment and speculation on his identity. Daniel showed himself to be capable and after the first day required no supervision. He saw what needed doing and did it. But the work was seldom solitary, for Jane or Benjamin, and often both, followed where he went, helping when he allowed them to, and keeping still and out of the way when he would not. He was doing jobs they had seen others do all their lives without interest. What held them was, at the beginning, Daniel's mystery, and then Daniel himself.

He quickly lost his shyness with them. At eighteen he was not so very much older than they were. He'd had no brother or sister and had made no friend during two years at war. The others in his company, coming mainly from large towns, made fun of his innocence and country ways. For the first time in his life he found himself accepted as he was.

While admitting Floyd's fair dealing and abilities, he continued to resent taking orders from him. He distrusted the Negro men he worked with, as they did him, largely because their ways were strange to each other. He was getting used to Nell and even beginning to enjoy, in a wry way he never let anyone see, her greedy appreciation of the results of his hunting. Sarah he remained shy with, because he found himself wanting her good opinion. He had never before sought to please anybody, and the new desire puzzled him.

Another thing puzzled him: the feeling he was beginning to have for Beulah Land itself. The home farm in Vermont had been an unyielding, rocky adversary, but these fields gave under his feet when he walked them and smelled alive even in autumn fallowness. They were fields that would give back more, not less, than a man put into them. When Daniel paused in his work to look up and over the land, his heart stirred with warmer feelings than he could explain. He saw the illogic. He had come as an un-welcome and dangerous guest. He was a stranger in the country of those his own people called Foe. But there were times when he felt easy and at home in his own skin in ways he never had before.

"Daniel, what are you thinking about?" Benjamin asked. Jane was not there that afternoon, but with Sarah in the sewing room. After the noon dinner they had whispered together. Seeing him watching, Jane had assumed a maddening air of female secrecy and Sarah, laughing, had let herself be piloted to the sewing room, the door of which Jane slammed after them with the satis-faction an empress might have shown signaling the execution of a false lover. Too proud to admit to himself his need of com-pany, Benjamin had read twenty pages of *The Last of the Mohicans* before going in search of Daniel and finding him in one of the barns.

"Why would I be thinking about anything?" Daniel replied.

"Well, you looked like it. You sure you don't have any brothers or sisters?"

"I've said so. Wouldn't I be the one to know?"

"You said it, but somehow I don't think of you by yourself. You seem a whole lot of people."

Without understanding what Benjamin meant any more than Benjamin did, Daniel felt complimented. He took up the stiff straw broom again and finished sweeping the dried muck out of the cow stall. Then he fetched an armful of fresh hay and scat-tered it thinly on the ground of the stall.

Benjamin said, "Are you glad we're cousins?"

"Not anything to be glad or sorry about, is it? Kin is something that is or isn't."

"Well, *I'm* glad we're cousins. It helps make up for some I don't like. Blair and Bonard Saxon. They're my Aunt Annabel's boys and older than me. I hate their stinking guts."

"You do?" Daniel said with plain surprise.

"I sure do. They're low-down churls." Daniel laughed. "I just thought," Benjamin continued. "If they're my cousins and you're my cousin, then they're your cousins too, and you don't even know them yet!"

"You don't make me eager to," Daniel said.

Frowning, Benjamin's face broke into disappointment. "No, they're not. You're on Grandma Sarah's side, and Aunt Annabel was a Davis, no kin to all the Penningtons. Unless you want to claim her. You can. Everybody's polite about that kind of thing down here."

"I'll let it go the way you say," Daniel said.

"Does your mama look like Grandma or Aunt Lauretta?" Benjamin said.

Daniel thought of the gnarled little woman he had last seen standing dry-eyed in the doorway watching him leave, an old woman at forty. "Not a whole lot," he admitted. "She's not as—" He shrugged.

"Grandma and Jane are sewing."

"Women do."

Benjamin nodded. "What are you going to do next?"

"I'm about done for the day. I figure to finish up this other stall and go down to the creek for a wash."

"Can I come with you?"

"All right, but it's too late in the year for you to go in."

"I went in last year as late as November and nobody cared. Today's like summer anyway." Without asking if he could, he began to help Daniel, singing, "Shoo, fly, don't light on me—"

"What's that?" Benjamin sang right through the ditty. Daniel laughed. "It's a crazy song. Why is it funny?"

To Benjamin's satisfaction Jane appeared as they finished work in the stall and were starting off. "Where are you going?" she asked.

"None of your bee's wax," Benjamin said.

"To the woods," Daniel answered.

"You can't come," Benjamin said.

"Why can't I?"

"Because we're going in the water in our bare butts!" Benjamin jeered.

"I'll tell Grandma you said that!"

"No, you won't. The only good thing about you is you don't carry tales."

She tossed her head and skipped away unconcerned, disappearing into the kitchen wing of the house. But twenty minutes later she had discovered them. She knew where they would go; it was where all the men of the plantation had gone to swim since there was a Beulah Land. No storm or flood had ever changed the outline of the circular pool made as the creek turned, its banks widening for a distance of thirty feet. Keeping herself concealed, she watched them. Benjamin was swimming. Standing in the shallows, Daniel tore a wad of moss from the branch of a cypress overhead and began to scrub himself. She studied his nakedness thoughtfully but with no special interest. She'd once seen Benjamin's thing on a day five years ago they had never mentioned to anyone, or referred to again to each other, when Benjamin made a suggestion that most children are fated to make: "I'll show you mine if you show me yours." It had seemed a fair bargain.

14.

The days passed, and it was November. Rachel stayed the same, as did Lauretta's answer to questions about her progress. "She is tolerable. No better, no worse that we can see. Only weak from being so long in bed, and little inclined for any company except mine, which she is so used to she hardly notices—"

Sarah came regularly, but the visits were shorter than she had made early on, for she often found Rachel asleep. Lauretta explained it by saying that she needed rest during the day to make up for the hours on end she lay awake at night. Whether this was so, Lauretta couldn't have known, since she herself slept soundly the night through. Having discovered, as she thought, the secret of Rachel's true malaise, which had nothing to do with ordinary illness, she did not hesitate to leave Rachel's supply of laudanum within reach, retiring to her room next door as soon as the others in the house had gone to theirs.

Dr. Platt came less frequently. Indeed, he seldom stopped at Oaks unless sent for, or unless a visit to another patient in the neighborhood made it convenient for him to appear attentive. He made no fuss about giving laudanum in substantial quantities. He assumed the other ladies of the household, as well as Rachel Davis, used it to settle their nerves.

When Sarah found Rachel awake, she tried to persuade her to come for a week or two to Beulah Land, hoping thereby to offer distraction, and when she was stronger, occupation. But Rachel responded without enthusiasm. "When I am better perhaps," she murmured. "Why do I not have a letter from James? Can he be ill, as I am?"

"No, no; or someone would have written for him."

Rachel started up from her pillow. "He may be dead! Sometimes I think he must be! —And then I hear him riding up the carriageway!"

"You mustn't agitate yourself," Lauretta usually said at such a juncture, suggesting with a nod or smile that Rachel would rest more quietly if Sarah left them. If Sarah persisted, Rachel wept and accused her of hardness, which sent her away silenced and saddened.

Rachel had become completely self-absorbed. If she thought of James constantly, it was of her need for him. She did not think about her children, or Sarah, or Bruce, or Doreen. To her father privately, Doreen allowed that Rachel had no more consideration for others than a cat.

At Beulah Land, Sarah vowed to deal with Rachel more firmly the next time she saw her, and at Oaks she continued to give way. She was haunted by Edna's taking to her bed and dying. She had told herself she must be, would be, patient. The cases were different. But she was sorely troubled. There were, however, many problems at Beulah Land to worry her too, most of them demanding more immediate decisions than Rachel's.

Lauretta too cautioned herself to patience, for there were times she wanted to take Bruce by the shoulders and shake him. It wasn't that he failed to notice her, but that his notice carried no special response. He was a man who had lived all his life with women, one who declared that he liked it so. He had not said it

to flatter Sarah that there could never be too many at Oaks to
suit him. But having proposed to Sarah, which Lauretta did not
know, he evidently felt that he had done his courting for the
year. He paid compliments to Lauretta on her appearance, her
character, and her conversation; but so he did too with all
women visitors to Oaks, and with Doreen, and even with the female servants.

One evening as she sat with him after supper, a piece of embroidery on her lap and a pleasant smile on her face, she was
thinking thunderously: "If I danced before him in my drawers,
he would say no more than 'How charming you look tonight,
Miss Lauretta.'" Still, she was there, and there she was determined to remain. He was getting used to her, and that counted
so much with tame men. She let her thoughts go to his brother
Bonard and the years they had lived together until he allowed
himself to be murdered in a gambling quarrel in California.
They had called themselves married, although they could not be
because Bonard already had a wife, Leon's sister Selma, who had
left him after their wedding night. There, indeed, had been a
man. He had neither liked nor understood women, but he had
needed them. That need could make him beg or ravish. There
had been times she despised him, feared him, and distrusted
him, but with Bonard she had known the power and the glory of
being a woman. She thought now of the times they had lain together, no reticence of any kind between them. He had kissed
and bitten and penetrated her everywhere his mouth and penis
could explore. He had made her scream with rage as well as passion. But she had never, never had to woo him.

"What are you thinking, Miss Lauretta?" Bruce asked.

Her hands tightened on the embroidery hoops. "I'm afraid that
I—"

"You were in a study. So charming sitting there, your smile
soft and happy as if you were remembering the innocent days of
childhood. Am I not right? Tell me."

"I fear you would not believe me, sir, if I spoke the truth."

"Try me and see."

She sighed. "I was thinking of you."

"Of me!"

"You must not affect surprise. My thoughts are often of you.
You are so kind, so understanding. For an instance: although you
know as well as anyone my special relationship to—" She lifted

her eyes briefly to indicate Rachel's room over their heads, where Doreen now sat with the invalid. "Yet you have never spoken a word of it, respecting, even seeming to honor, my private feelings."

He blushed. "Miss Lauretta!"

To steer him from thoughts of her motherhood to the inception of it, she continued gravely, "I cared deeply for her father." She did not specify who the father was, and Bruce was left to assume him to be the actor Douglas Savage, whose name she had carried when she came to Beulah Land to have her child, although he had deserted her some years before. "He was a weak man, but I loved him. I daresay that was weak of me, but women are seldom wise in giving their hearts. I wonder that you have not married again. Your wife died young. You are still young."

"Mm. I was devoted to her, of course." He believed it as he said it, although he remembered her features only vaguely. "And there were the children. Four of them."

"Ah." Lauretta gave a brief maternal croon, following it with a look that was questioning, almost provocative. "How many ladies you must have disappointed by your fidelity to a dead love!"

"Well, well. I don't know about that."

"I am certain of it. True then." She caught her breath. "True now perhaps? I never saw a man appear so modestly unaware of the way he flutters hearts. Yet I wonder that you have not sought the consolations that may only be had from a loving wife." Lauretta had not spent so many of her years on the stage without learning how to keep her eyes down during the first part of her speech and to lift them suddenly to his as she gave intimate weight and meaning to the last two words.

"Miss Lauretta!" Bruce's voice was clotty with the mood she had conjured.

When he did not speak further, she decided to chance all. "I would not deny that I, even with my thoughts so entirely with that poor girl of mine upstairs—have not been immune to the force, I might even say the thrust of your strong presence."

"My presence?"

"Even in these days I think you might set a candle inside the entrance and another in the hallway!"

It was Annabel talking as she sailed briskly into the room, taking off her bonnet to shake it, and beating her hands lightly against her skirts when she had dropped the bonnet to a table. "Well, here you are at last, and I've come all this way to let you know! I hitched the buggy and drove myself, for I had to tell you tonight, Papa. Ah, evening, Miss— I heard you were here to take care of Rachel, although I'm sure there's nothing wrong with her a little hard work on my committees wouldn't cure. Now I forget what we call you. 'Miss Lauretta' or 'Cousin.' Though, in fact, you are neither, are you? However, where the country is unmapped, they say 'Cousin' opens many odd doors—" She turned to her father then, ignoring Lauretta. "*Why?*" she demanded. "Why in heaven did Hood go hoop-de-ha off into Tennessee leaving us all at the mercy of that monster? Can you tell me?" Briefly she pondered the military mind. "I say it was jealousy that made Jeff Davis put Hood in General Johnston's place. What other reason can there be?" She planted herself firmly in a chair, shifting it to face her father, not noticing or caring that it had the effect of cutting Lauretta off from them. "There was no one to see to my horse and buggy. I simply left them at the door. Well, nothing will happen to them. How far will a horse wander at night?" She laughed. "He'll want a rest after the way I whipped him along!"

Lauretta addressed herself to Bruce. "Would you like me to withdraw? Your daughter appears to have much to say to you, and I should see to my own."

"Please stay, Miss Lauretta," he said to atone for Annabel's rudeness.

"Law yes, stay if you like, or go if duty calls, for what I have to say is nothing private." She stared again at her father. "You have not heard?"

"I cannot know until you say it."

"Sherman has left Atlanta. After the election up in Lincolndom, without warning, he pulled a force of troops from the city, and they are said to be rampaging all over Georgia!"

"Indeed?"

"Yes *indeed!*" Annabel affirmed with quick nods of the head. "His army is on the march again, and none of us are safe in our beds." She glanced about the room. "Where is Doreen?"

"Upstairs with Rachel."

"I thought that was your job, ma'am. What is wrong with Rachel?" she said impatiently. "She has an unsteady character.

Bad blood from somewhere I've always felt. Else why would she take to bed like poor old Granny? They say it's James. —Who could pine for James? He's as dull as lard."

Unwilling to be ignored if she sat with them, Lauretta said, "I understand from your sister, who relieves my vigil now and then in the sickroom, that you busy yourself untiringly for the noble cause."

"Did Auntie Sarah tell you that, or Doreen? It sounds more like Auntie Sarah. She says things with a mocking edge sometimes, as if I care what she thinks. She's so out of things the way she keeps her nose in Beulah Land she's hardly aware we're at war. However—" She reached out and gripped her father's arm. "What are we to do?"

"What can we do except wait?"

"Wait for them to plunder and burn and murder? I declare, sir, I hoped you would have something better to say than 'wait.'"

"Then you must tell me what to do." If she caught the rebuff in his voice, she ignored it.

"Organize resistance to the invader! Ride this night to every farm you can reach and rally the farmers!"

"Only the old and weak are left," he said.

"Is any man too old to defend his home and womenfolk? If that is so, then I as one of those women vow that I shall challenge the enemy every step of his way, dispute every ditch, and die if I must a martyr to the South but never a craven coward!"

"You forget yourself, Miss Annabel!" Lauretta exclaimed, rising from her chair.

Annabel rose too and looked at her squarely. "By what leave, ma'am, do you presume to comment on my conduct?"

"I plead concern for your father's feelings only—"

"I trust you do not misread a long sporadic acquaintance for intimacy—"

"Now, Annabel," Bruce tempered, getting to his feet. "You must not let your—"

She turned to face him again. "And do you, sir, plead concern for the feelings of the lady? Oh Lord! Can it be that you still cherish some ill-considered regard for the creature? I well remember when you were ready enough to have her until Granny got wind of her schemes and put an end to them. Oh yes, Doreen was listening that day and told me every word that was exchanged between you. At least then you had the excuse of being somewhat younger, but now both of you are so old I should have thought you beyond such fooleries."

"I assure you," Bruce said, "although you are behaving rudely and impertinently, that there is nothing but honorable friendship between Miss Lauretta and me."

"Do you swear it?"

"Madam," Lauretta said, "how dare *you* presume to extract such a promise!"

Annabel shrugged. "Ah, well, what matter a few antique grunts and hand pats! —I have let you distract me. The important concern tonight is that we are to be besieged by savages and must make plans. What are we to do?"

"I can hardly put my mind to it the way you jump around."

"I beg you most earnestly to attend to the matter with all the wisdom and courage you can summon. You will surely agree that we must resist them."

"It would avail nothing," Bruce said. "It would hardly delay them an hour. They are an army. We are a few defenseless souls living on the land."

"We have guns and swords, and while we have them, it would be shameful not to use them! I know well enough you have done all in your power for our army, giving horses and hay and equipment—"

"No need to speak of that. But having served our forces as well as we could, the time now comes when we must think of survival. We stand to lose all if we try to resist without our army. It is impossible that we could do so effectively. But if we are passive, we may be able to salvage a little of what we still hold."

"And what is that?" Annabel challenged him.

"The land itself. With the land we can begin again."

"Nothing has ended unless we submit!"

"You will not understand!" he declared helplessly.

"Come, sir. I do not flatter myself when I remind you that I have worked long and hard in our cause and that I pride myself on knowing exactly how the scales tip. If Davis hears we are not bowing to the foe, he will send help."

"What help? From where?"

"You give me nothing but questions and doubts. If but one of us raises his fist—"

"That man will be struck down. Your fine words will count for nothing against Sherman's determination to crush us."

"I never thought to hear my father counsel tail-tucking. Am I to believe, sir, that you have resigned yourself to our defeat?"

"I know that it is upon us, if the news you bring is true. Resignation is necessary, however bitter it may be."

Annabel tapped a foot rapidly on a wooden space between carpets. As the three stood unspeaking together, the air was split by no ordinary cry, but a scream of such horror as could only announce tragedy. They ran directly into the hallway to see Doreen rushing down the stairs wailing like a soul in hell. Reaching them, she thrust a hand toward the front door. "Go!—See!"

As Lauretta hurried upstairs, Doreen found more breath. "Not in her room—out there!" Bruce waited for no more, and the women followed him out of the house. "It happened so quickly. Sleeping. Suddenly started up like a madwoman. Cried, 'James! James! James is coming! I hear him!' Before I reached her, she sprang from her bed, ran to the window, and threw herself out!"

Bruce found her. She had fallen to the patch of pavement just below the main entrance steps. When he took her up in his arms, he knew her neck was broken.

15.

Rachel Davis was buried beside her father, Leon Kendrick. Her funeral was lightly attended, for she had been curiously little known in the county. The mystery about her birth had never been entirely forgotten, and she had not made friends in Highboro. Her acquaintance as well as her life was almost entirely restricted to Beulah Land and Oaks. As a child she had been the darling of Sarah and Leon. Two or three of the house servants had been fond of her and she of them. She had fallen in love with Adam Davis when she was still a girl, and when he died of yellow fever shortly before they were to be married, she had been surprised into marrying Adam's brother James and subsequently had fallen in love with him. The feeling the two had for each other increased, with the effect that she centered her whole attention on him. That was why not even her children felt very close to her. The intensity of that love finally doomed her. On the night of her death, Doreen wrote to James, Lauretta supplying the address in Florida from which he had last written to Rachel.

Standing beside the grave as it was filled with earth, Sarah held tightly to a hand of Jane's and a hand of Benjamin's. She thought of how Rachel had loved the place when she was a little girl, running to it every time they came to church. Someone—was it Nell?—had once said, laughing, "Rachel dearly loves a funeral." No, it had not been Nell who said it but Penelope. She could hear her voice; it had been the day of the funeral of old Dr. Chester Porterfield's wife Mamie. Sarah's eyes found a lone ant hurrying haphazardly, evidently confused by the freshly dug earth, and she moved the toe of her shoe and crushed it, taking a small satisfaction in its death because she had been offended by its show of life. Although the day was cool when the wind stirred, the crepe covering her head was caught too close at the neck; she had begun to sweat. She could not watch any longer as the earth fell on Rachel. Her eyes wandered to her Aunt Penelope's grave a few yards away. She remembered the first time she had come here, when she was a visitor at Beulah Land with Penelope, before she married Leon Kendrick. She had looked at some of the names on the graves, strangers then to her. Now she knew them all. She had reached an age when she seemed to know more of the dead than the living. The thought made her hold tighter to the hands of her grandchildren until both glanced at her to see what was the matter.

When the coffin was covered, Sarah turned away from the grave, the boy and girl with her and others following. Only Bruce stayed to watch the job finished. Sarah saw Lauretta talking to Doreen as they were joined by Selma and Pauline. Selma and Pauline would have walked from their houses in town, for they kept no horse and buggy, and the distance was short. Lauretta had come in Bruce's buggy. Sarah did not stop to speak to anyone but went into the grove of trees, where she found Floyd waiting. He had not wanted to go into the cemetery, although he had sat with Sarah and the others in church for the funeral. Negroes did not come to the church for ordinary services, but they were usually assigned a separate place for such events as weddings and funerals to which they had some special tie. They were free to come if their "families" brought them, and in any case the Kendricks had long been a law unto themselves. Floyd helped Sarah into the buggy. She took the reins and drove them home, Jane and Floyd on the seat with her and Benjamin perched alone on the hay box at the back.

Arriving at Beulah Land, Sarah went into her office and shut the door, although it was the middle of the afternoon. Half an hour later though, there was a knock and when she called, "Come in!" Lauretta entered. "Oh." She had not expected her sister and did not welcome her. They had not talked since Rachel's death. "Did Bruce and Doreen bring you?"

Lauretta nodded. "They're outside with Jane and Benjamin. They've all gone to the barns to look over the stock—the sort of exercise generally reserved for the men on Sundays. I never cared much how the stock looked, and I never know what to say when somebody asks me if that isn't a fine cow. May I sit down?" Sarah shrugged and opened a ledger on the desk. It was understood that no one came to the office unless asked, and she made no effort at courtesy. "I know that you blame me." Sarah did not deny it, but she closed the ledger, fixing her eyes dully on its rough cover. "Did you ever discuss the matter of her parentage with Rachel?"

"No!" Sarah said with surprise.

Lauretta looked thoughtful, as if making up her mind to something. "I did."

"After you promised you would not? She was about to be married the time you came back from California, and you wanted to claim her. I told you I wouldn't have you here unless you agreed never to speak of it."

"I am not much of one for promises, you know." Lauretta spread a handkerchief on her lap and looked at it critically. Then she pinched it at the center, shook it out and tucked it into a sleeve. "I told her she was my daughter, and Leon's."

"How dared you, even you?"

"I think I was jealous of everyone that day. I must have been out of sorts for some reason and decided to poke a stick into a hornet's nest to see what would happen."

"And what *did* happen?" Sarah asked, curious in spite of herself.

"She denied that I was her mother," Lauretta said calmly. "Oh, she agreed readily enough that I had borne her. It seemed that Selma had told her years before. So you see, although I broke my promise to you, I did not, as it happened, get much from the hornet's nest. She told me in no uncertain terms that she was *your* daughter and declared that I had merely borne her for you as an act of sisterly convenience, because you could not. She scored me roundly for my presumption."

Sarah's shock shattered suddenly into laughter. "Is what you say really so?"

"I assure you it is, for I remember it very well. I sometimes forget my age and invent whatever pleases me at the moment, but I shall never forget that half hour."

"I wish I had known!" Sarah said.

"I'm glad it pleases you," Lauretta said without rancor. "It makes you seem a little more human to me. You don't realize how I have always feared and hated your everlasting 'goodness'!"

"Oh, I am human enough." Sarah checked her laughter. Suddenly serious, she said, "Did you ever feel sorry that you had given her to me?"

"Not once," Lauretta said without needing to consider the question. "The mother part was left out of me. I think you must have got my share. —The way you raised Roman too, as if he was yours. And then starting the school here for the other children."

"Well," Sarah said, "both Roman and Rachel *were* Leon's children, you'll remember."

"Mm. I suppose I meant no more to Leon than that darky who was Roman's mother! Not a flattering thought, is it? Were you ever jealous of me and Leon?"

"I was certainly angry when I found out," Sarah said. "I suppose that had something to do with jealousy."

"He didn't love me. I am not somehow a woman who inspires love in men. I have never understood that."

"Why are you saying all this to me?" Sarah wanted to know.

Lauretta said, "You'll admit it's made you feel better. And I am going away again." Seeing Sarah's surprise and judging correctly that it included no regret, she continued a little maliciously, "Oh, not very far. We shall see each other constantly, I assure you. Only I shall not be living at Beulah Land."

Sarah thought about it. "Bruce Davis has asked you to marry him!"

"No!" Lauretta cried in what sounded like rage.

"Well, you don't have to bite my head off. There was a time I certainly thought— Now tell me."

"Selma has suggested that I move into town and help her with her school."

"*You* teach?"

"Why not? Reading and elocution. Lord knows, the pickaninnies need someone to teach them how to speak the language instead of that gibberish they jabber at one another. And the number in Selma's school is growing. When the slaves up and run off, they don't always take their brats along, knowing someone will take care of them, and perhaps uncertain what the future holds. They may even plan to send for them when the war is over. The way things are going, Selma no longer has to pretend that she takes them merely for religious instruction. She says the town is finally glad to have her and her school."

"Where will you live?"

"With her and Pauline. Who knows? She and I may even one day get around to comparing notes on Bonard!"

Sarah found herself laughing. "Pauline would murder you!"

"Do you think they ever—? I don't mean now, but when they were younger. Well, what *do* women do with each other?"

"You are a disgrace!" Sarah declared.

"My dear, that is not original of you." Lauretta said it with a certain pride.

Sarah pushed her chair back. "Come. Let's go and see what the others are doing. I mustn't seem to shut myself away to mourn."

Following, Lauretta touched her on the shoulder. "Do you hate me?" she asked curiously.

Sarah turned and studied her face. "I do sometimes."

Lauretta shrugged. "That's the way with sisters, I expect. At least you're not namby-pamby about it. If I could learn that you had ever deceived Leon with another man when he was alive, I might almost like you."

"Oh, but I did," Sarah said mildly.

"When?"

"You weren't here at the time."

"Who was it?"

"You never met him. Casey Troy."

"The painter who did all of your portraits! Well, I do declare! Did you love him and did he make you dreadfully unhappy?"

"He made me happy, and I still love him a little when I think of him, which isn't often."

Lauretta was outraged. "You leave me nothing!"

Laughing, they went into the hallway and entered the drawing room with their arms about each other's waist. Looking up at them ironically from her rocking chair, Nell said, "Will wonders never cease? Bruce and Doreen are staying for supper. I told Lotus to kill another chicken, and Daniel's digging us some sweet potatoes for a pie. How was the funeral?"

Nell had declared when Penelope died that hers was the last funeral she would attend, except her own.

16.

Lotus's pregnancy was beginning to show; and she told Sarah without embarrassment that the baby was in its fifth month, although she and Floyd had been married only two. Lotus was happy. Even-tempered by nature, she let nothing trouble her now. Everyone else complained almost as a matter of course. Flour was in short supply and coffee not to be found, but otherwise she managed her kitchen well enough, using what she had the best she could, and putting three meals on the table every day that no cook would be ashamed of. She and Floyd were companionable, neither asking more than the other was willing to give.

Lovey was not easy, but then she never had been during her sixty-five years at Beulah Land, most of them spent as she often bragged as "mistress of Beulah Land after the Mistress." She had

been there a year when Deborah came as the bride of Arnold
Kendrick in 1800. She had known it during all its high years of
glory, and it was no wonder that she hated being witness to its
decline. Lotus understood this and treated the old woman with
patience and kindness, but never to the point of provoking her
resentment. Floyd was less careful of her feelings. He knew her
faults as well as her worth. He made mild fun of her sometimes
to keep from treating her more roughly, for she was in truth a
difficult woman. In his heart he agreed with her frequent bellig-
erent statement that she would be better off dead.

But Lotus appeared undisturbed by her fits of temper, even
when she found her abusing Nancy, whose help and loyalty
Lotus needed and wanted to keep.

"When *I* was running this house," Lovey quavered angrily at
the girl, "you wouldn't have been allowed to empty slop jars!"

"My! You are a terrible old lady!" Nancy mocked her.

Lovey stamped both feet in a tantrum.

"Nancy, you are not showing respect," Lotus would say. "You
tell Miss Lovey you're sorry for whatever it was."

"I won't do it!" Nancy protested. "She say mean things to me
all the day long. Didn't you hear?"

"You are a worthless! ignorant! Geechee gal!" Lovey told her.

"Now tell her you're sorry," Lotus coaxed the girl.

Nancy looked as though she wouldn't mind doing so but had
her pride.

"Make peace in a time of trouble," Lotus reasoned.

Lovey waited until the girl muttered an apology, and when
she did, went into another foot-stamping tirade. "Don't *let* her say
she's sorry! Sassy, twitchy-tail slut! Thirteen years old and already the devil's daughter!"

"I take it back! I ain't sorry!" Nancy screeched.

"Lord God, what a punishment to me to live my last days with
ignorant Geechees!" Lovey lamented.

Patiently Lotus talked them into better tempers. They often
marked renewed amity by sharing a pot of sassafras tea and a
johnnycake.

"Good" was a word used often, but discriminatingly, to describe various qualities having to do with character as well as
physical skill, its particular meaning at any given instance being
perfectly well understood by all from the context and inflection.

Lotus was often said to be "good." Floyd had known many women, but there had never been one before he would have wanted to bear him a child. He had known her ever since she was born and seen her gradually become the woman she was now.

They saw each other early in the morning but not again usually until suppertime during those days, for Floyd was busy both at the plantation and at the sawmill. The fields waited for whatever future next year would bring, and Floyd had been thorough and shrewd in the way he secured the cotton gin for the winter. It was a large building but not such as to attract attention now that it was closed. Consisting as it did of big pieces of machinery shrouded in old sacking, he hoped it would not invite destruction by the invaders, as he feared the sawmill would. A single reflective look at the sharp-toothed circular blades and the trolleys to carry the logs was enough to tell anyone what the sawmill could produce and therefore how valuable it would be to the defeated or to the conqueror. Of all the assets of the Kendricks, the sawmill, Floyd decided, was the likeliest to insure Beulah Land's survival after whatever was to come had come. He studied it and finally knew how to save it.

He could not do it alone. He would need at least two men to help him dismantle the mill's key equipment and hide it in separate places, none of it at Beulah Land. He and Sarah talked about it. She suggested that Daniel be one of the men to help him.

"When they come," Floyd said, "won't he join them?"

"I don't think he wants to," she said in surprise, for she had observed Daniel's gradual adaptation to their life. "I'll ask him."

"*Ask* him?"

"Certainly."

"Would you trust his answer?"

"I don't think he would lie to me."

After supper that evening, while Floyd worked on the ledgers in the office, Sarah managed a few minutes alone with Daniel in the drawing room. "You know what everyone's concerned about and talking about, Daniel—Sherman, and when his men will come." Daniel looked at her and waited. "It seemed at first that he intended to miss our part of the state, but now he's changed directions, and even I must admit that he may ride up one day. If he does, will you tell him who you are and join his men?"

"I couldn't!" Daniel protested. "I deserted, as much as."

She pitched her voice to encouragement. "You could make up something and be believed. —That you had been captured in the fighting near Atlanta and brought here as part of a work gang, then managed to escape when you heard they were coming."

Daniel looked doubtful but turned over in his mind what she had said. His frown become a scowl. He glanced at her quickly now and then as if hoping to catch a sign of her own preference in the matter. He assumed that she had decided what she wanted him to do and was trying to lead him to it politely. "I don't love them any more than I love Rebels," he said stiffly.

"They're your people. We're not."

He looked at her helplessly. "You want to get rid of me."

"I want to know, and know now, what you might do."

After a pause he said, "Would you let me stay?"

"It would be easier for you to do the other thing."

"You don't want me to stay," he said soberly enough, but his voice carried something of a child's hurt feelings, and she remembered how young he was.

"We're in for some hard days, whatever happens," Sarah said. "The time for you to go if you're going is when the Yankees first come. If you wait and then decide to tell them, you'll have to explain why you waited, and they might not believe you."

Although steady work and food were beginning to give him the body of a man, he had never looked so young to her. "I like it here," he said in an uncertain voice. "Do you mind if I stay?"

"They'll treat you like one of us—whether you 'love' us or not."

"Yes, ma'am."

"If anybody recognizes you, that would mean trouble for you —and us."

"I never got close to any of them I soldiered with. They thought I was common and young."

For the first time her voice softened. "You're not common, Daniel, and it's a good thing to be young."

"I never felt young in my life."

She knew he spoke the simple truth. "You've been a help to us since you came. If you want to stay, you're welcome. Just be sure."

For Daniel this was not merely permission to remain at Beulah Land but acceptance of him by the one person he wanted to please. "I'm as sure as I am that God's got clean fingernails."

She laughed as much with relief as surprise at what he had said.

"That was a saying around home," he explained.

Nell called over to Sarah, "Why are you-all laughing?"

"Daniel said something funny."

"He never said anything funny to me."

"That's because he's afraid of you," Sarah called back.

"Good." Nell rocked herself gently, her own baby, her own nurse.

Daniel said to Sarah, "You'll have to tell the Federals I'm a Southerner."

"We won't push you forward so they'll wonder at the way you speak. But if they ask— I've lied about you to my own people; I'm not likely to stutter over the same lie to Yankees."

Sarah reported her conclusions from this encounter to Floyd.

Floyd said, "You believe I can trust him."

"Yes. You said you'd need two to help. Who will the other be?"

"Lotus's brother."

"Otis! Of course."

"We won't hide the mill pieces until just before they get here."

"Why wait for them to come?"

"Nobody will be watching us then; they'll be hopping around worrying about their own hides. Junior Elk was at the cotton gin asking questions not long ago."

"Daniel told me."

"He's been around the sawmill too. There's nothing to stop him. We'll have to work at night to get things ready to move in a hurry."

"You think Junior will side with the Yankees when they get here?"

"I know it. It's what he's been waiting four years for. He's a man of property, though a Negro. It's one time being caught in the middle is the best place to be. When we've hidden the machinery pieces, I'll leave Otis in a shack in the swamp, not at, but near, the main hiding place. Daniel and I will bring the mules back."

She smiled faintly. "You've thought it all out."

"Only that far," he said.

17.

Lauretta moved into Selma's house and declared herself delighted with its history. For many years it had been lived in by a "family" of whores, who called themselves the Bixby sisters. When the war started, they left. One day they were there, the next day gone—people said to Atlanta or Savannah. Nobody knew, but they assumed that the women had migrated to one of the big centers where they would find more custom than Highboro promised, with its men away fighting. The house stood empty until Selma and Pauline thought of opening their school in town and decided it would do for them. No one wanted it, so Selma was able to buy it cheap from the bank which Annabel Saxon's father-in-law owned.

It was screened from the road by high hedges that gave it an air of seclusion. It had an excellent artesian well, and there was a quarter acre to make a kitchen garden. It was small enough to run with a pair of servants and large enough to provide separation of classrooms for the pupils. Lilac took the younger children; Selma and Pauline taught the older ones. No one lived in except Selma, Pauline, Lilac, and the servants, and now Lauretta. Her room was just off the top of the stairs, and she amused herself with speculating on the men she had known (Leon? Bonard certainly. Even Bruce perhaps?) who might have climbed those stairs puffing and puffed with lust. She declared that she sometimes laughed so much at her own imaginings she could hardly get to sleep at night.

At Oaks the Davis family was reduced to two. They did not mourn Rachel except in occasional conventional words, but both were concerned for James and possessed of a dreadful anticipation as to how he would respond to his loss of Rachel. Bruce acted as his own overseer and assigned daily jobs to his men, checking on their performance now and then but not as strictly as an overseer whose main duty it was. He found plenty of time to visit Beulah Land and to call on other neighbors. There had

been talk of Jane and Benjamin's returning to Oaks, but everyone was content to let them stay with Sarah. Doreen was neither
energetic nor skilled as a housekeeper, but she did her best, and
she and her father did not care very much that things were always a little out of order. Both valued personal freedom more
than order that had to be closely supervised. Doreen spent several hours each day with Pharaoh. She gave him a variety of exercise, and she was as careful of his grooming as a trainer would
have been. In return he trusted her completely and quickly
obeyed her few necessary words and gestures of control. In addition, she talked to the horse in a social way, not fancifully, but
simply as an extension of her thinking.

She had never made friends other than those who came naturally into her range. She and Annabel had not been intimate
when they were growing up, and were direct with each other
now only when their special interests coincided or collided. Her
grandmother Edna had been Doreen's closest friend when she
was younger, as she had been Benjamin's closest friend when he
was younger and still a little awed by his grandfather Bruce.
James was the one Doreen loved most dearly, but she had lost
him to Rachel. He loved her too, but without the passion her
love for him included.

After the Lowry family had come and gone, others like them
followed. Their wagons were often to be seen on the roads, a reminder that not far away guns sounded and fires burned, and
those who had dispossessed the wanderers would come after
them. Some of the families found their way to Oaks to beg food.
Doreen never let them stay for more than an hour, giving them
little and sending them on. For the most part she avoided them,
leaving it for the servants to turn them away, for there was nothing to spare, no one knowing how long present supplies must
last. She seldom used the roads around Oaks that others used,
but kept Pharaoh to the back paths of the plantation's fields
where no strange wagon ever came.

Annabel returned to Oaks more often than she used to, but her
stops were generally said to be on her way to see someone, or on
her way home, never admitted as intentional since her father's
rebuff. However, she lectured Doreen firmly on the need to hide
valuable possessions. Doreen listened and agreed, but was slow
to act on her sister's suggestions. She gave a few things into Annabel's keeping such as rings and brooches, necklaces, a bracelet

or two—family jewelry which she did not, in any case, wear her-self, and which Annabel had not already managed to take away. Annabel urged her to bury the silver, and she did, substituting iron cutlery at the table until Bruce, who noticed few household arrangements, complained; whereupon she dug some of it up again. In truth, they kept little at Oaks anyone other than them-selves would consider valuable.

After setting his men to work one day, Bruce walked over to Beulah Land, and he and Benjamin became engrossed in a race they were trying to make four toad-frogs run. A considerable time was taken by the race, and more before they could agree that Benjamin's favorite had won and that Bruce now owed him altogether a total of one hundred and thirty-four million, three hundred and eighty-seven thousand, two hundred and fifty dol-lars. They never bet in lower denominations than fifty dollars. Bruce waved a hand. "I can wipe out the whole debt with a lucky week," he said. By then it was time for noon dinner, and Sarah asked him to sit down and eat with them.

Doreen spent the morning in the woods looking for a place that was suitable to hide Pharaoh, if that precaution ever seemed necessary. She returned before noon and after unsaddling the horse was making her way toward the house when Flossie came out of the kitchen to meet her. Her eyes rolling tragically, the old woman gripped the younger one by both shoulders, seeming un-able to speak until Doreen guessed her message.

"My brother has come home!"

"Yes'm!"

Doreen tore free, but before she reached the back steps, Flos-sie's voice stopped her. "He can't *see*, Miss Doreen—*he can't see nothing!* Walks with a cane. Man brought him right up to the door and left him. —Miss Doreen, wait and listen to what I'm telling you!"

Doreen raced into the house and through all the downstairs rooms. Not finding him, she hurried upstairs but stopped, afraid, outside the door of the room that had been his and Rachel's. Without knocking, she turned the knob, and the door swung open. The room had acquired a musty smell since Rachel's death for want of airing and cleaning. James was seated in a chair by the window where she had sat so often to watch for him. He turned his head at the sound of the door's opening. "Rachel?"

She stood speechless a long moment and finally broke silence with a sob.

"Doreen! I know Rachel is not here. —Where are you?"

In a rush she was before him kneeling. He held her head in his lap, and together they wept. He did not know that her tears were from happiness, which was as well.

Later, when Marie finally dared to ring the dinner bell, they went to the dining room, eating with little appetite the indifferent meal set for them. It was then that news was fully exchanged. Doreen elaborated on what he had learned from her letter, and he told her why he had not written for so long a time. He had been blinded not in any brave action but from an accident with explosives at the camp in Florida. His hands had been burned as well as his eyes, and he had been afraid, knowing Rachel's constant apprehensions for his safety, that she would fear him dead if she received a letter not written by him telling of his condition. The accident had been unnecessary, and he might have missed it but for a careless error a recruit had made. For weeks he had lain in the hospital not knowing how to tell her what had happened, and even wondering if he might not wait until he recovered and went home.

When they left the table, James allowed Doreen to walk him about the grounds and in and out of the barns. He was awkward, and she sometimes forgot to warn and guide him, but with the familiar smells he appeared to gain some confidence. James had always been a serious man; he had no lightness. But by the time they turned back to the house she thought him a little more his old self, and she had never been so happy.

18.

There were usually two major hog killings during the winter, and the first was done at Beulah Land and Oaks just as November ended, the weather coming suddenly right: icicles on the hoods of the water wells and sheaths of ice on the ground where puddles had been yesterday. When the freeze held the second day, fires were lighted before daybreak. The chosen hogs were stunned with ax blows on the head as they fed from troughs of slops; their throats were cut, and when they had bled, the bristles scraped from their fat bodies after being softened by boiling water. The air was at one moment pungent with the smell of burning pine and the next heavy with that of fresh blood and entrails.

Work proceeded as smoothly as it customarily did, only this year it lacked the usual sense of festival, for none of those taking part in it, from Sarah to the merest third helper on the sausage making, was certain whether the meat would eventually feed them or strangers. Nell took a lively interest in all that went on, and was beside Lotus as she drained the first cracklings from the lard-making tub, happily burning her fingers to sample the greasy, succulent morsels. Annabel paid a visit to Oaks that morning, returning to Highboro triumphantly with a handsome share of fresh meat in her buggy. Selma and Pauline borrowed a wagon and made a similarly rewarding afternoon trip to Beulah Land.

Sarah seemed to be everywhere at once: the butchering barn, kitchen, smokehouse; wearing against the cold an old brown shawl which Nell asserted was as big as a quilt and as old as the moon. Sometimes she forgot it, and it slipped from her shoulders, but Jane, who followed her grandmother around all that day, was there to catch it. She had stayed on at Beulah Land after James came home, although Benjamin, at Bruce's urging, had returned to Oaks. They were, however, back and forth so much it hardly signified where they said they "lived."

The largest portion of the kill, that not to be consumed as fresh meat by the families of Beulah Land, went into the smokehouse as hams and salted fatback and ropes of sage-scented sausage. Daniel observed how things were done and how the ways differed from the same jobs he had done on the farm in Vermont. Nancy too was everywhere that day, treating the occasion like a party given in her honor. She was looked upon with fresh interest by the younger men of the plantation because of her recent elevation from field to kitchen. She flirted and laughed with all of them, happily immune to Lovey's dark mutterings. Lovey hovered, but kept herself out of the way. Her eyes were not strong enough for her to take any useful part in the work.

A week before this, Floyd had found his hiding place for the sawmill machinery. The most nearly permanent location of the mill—although, as he reminded Sarah, it had been moved several times to accommodate a particular fine stand of trees—was a piece of woodland the Kendricks owned a few miles from High-boro. Behind the mill with its stacks of lumber and pyramids of sawdust a wagon trail wandered crookedly through the back-woods for several miles, often hardly discernible, but a thread of it continuing and eventually crossing a branch of the creek to an isolated island set in the wide main stretch of the creek and covered in densely tangled palmetto. Floyd knew it was there, but he had never seen it before. On it he found a derelict shack with brick walls, its wooden roof rotted away. He and Otis gave it a new roof. Satisfied with the result, he forgot his earlier no-tion of separate hiding places for the machinery. So lost was the island it was unlikely that anything less than a determined, lucky search would find it.

They called it simply the Shelter, for that is what it would be for Floyd and Otis and Daniel. To the Shelter they brought a supply of smoked meat, cornmeal, dried peas, rice, and lard. There were fish in the creek and there was game in the woods. From the main house they also brought guns for hunting. Al-though not many miles lay between the Shelter and Beulah Land, the best part of a day was required to get from one to the other. Not knowing how things would go beyond the simple plan they had made, Sarah and Floyd chose the man called Zebra to act as messenger between them.

Although he was noticeable and easily identifiable because of the violent birthmarking that had given him his nickname, Floyd had observed that he was a man people glanced at only briefly before looking away. He had no wife, therefore no one to share his secret. He was pleased to be picked for the responsibility, and without Sarah's knowing it, he was grateful to her, because she looked into his face when she had anything to say to him, not at the ground or the sky.

Word traveled rapidly from one town to the next on the prog-ress of the Union soldiers. The Confederate patrols they were all used to seeing suddenly disappeared, and for a day it was said that Yankee scouts were in the neighborhood. By noon the day after, everyone claimed to know someone who had seen a Yan-

kee, and the children's cry was no longer "Yankees coming!" but
"Yankees here!"

Three of the first to enter the district saw the big gray house
off the main road and trotted their horses through the bare orchard along the carriageway. They were hungry. Dismounting with
guns held ready, they let the horses follow them around the
house to the door of the kitchen.

Nancy was the first to see and recognize them as Union soldiers from their faded blue jackets. It was afternoon and she had
been left alone in the kitchen to finish the dinner dishes. Dropping a heavy bowl, which bounced on the floor without breaking, she cried, "Mercy! Mercy on us! Mercy!"

The three men looked down at her curiously as she fell to her
knees to retrieve the bowl. One by one they stepped inside the
kitchen doorway, whereupon Nancy commenced screaming in
earnest. Her cries brought Sarah running from the office and
Lotus from the storerooms beyond the kitchen, where she had
gone for an hour's rest on a cot they kept there.

"Who are you?" Sarah demanded, although she knew well
enough. "Why are you here?"

The leader, a short man with pale eyes in a hard, blond-
bristled face, wiped his mouth with the back of his hand. "Sergeant Haigh." He shrugged one shoulder to include the other
men. "Scouts for Sherman's army."

Sarah said, "I understand the General's orders specifically forbid his men's entering our dwellings." The sergeant blinked at
her and did not deny it. "That being so, I will talk to you outside." Nancy ran to Lotus, and they took each other's hands. The
sergeant hesitated, then looked at the two men and grinned. As
the three sidled into the yard to stand beside the fig tree, Sarah
followed them.

"Have you got whiskey?" the sergeant asked her.

"No."

"Chewing tobacco?"

"You're chewing now."

He emptied his mouth into his hand and held it for her to see
before he threw it away. "Piece of tar I picked up on the bridge.
It's better to chew something than nothing."

"I don't have any tobacco."

"We're hungry. You have to feed us."

"I don't know what there is—"

"Whatever, it's better than the hardtack we been making out on."

"Wait here." Sarah stepped into the kitchen and spoke to Lotus, returning to the soldiers. "I've told her to fill three plates with what is ready. I won't let you come inside to eat it."

"We're used to eating outdoors," the man said. The other two snickered and began to look around them, casually appraising.

"How many live here?" the spokesman said.

"I. My aunt, who is old. A young girl, my granddaughter."

"No menfolks?"

"My husband is dead."

"Sons in the Army?"

"I have no children."

"How do you have a granddaughter?"

"Her mother was my daughter. She is dead."

"No men at all?" He peered at her quizzically.

"No," she said, denying Daniel's existence without having planned to do so. "There are a good many men who work the place of course."

He nodded. "How many niggers you got?"

"I don't know exactly. There are fifty or sixty, I imagine."

The sergeant turned to his men. "She imagines."

"Some of them have gone away," Sarah explained.

"You got horses."

Sarah hesitated. "Only a few necessary for the work. We use mules mostly, and two or three oxen."

"How many horses and mules you got?"

"I'd have to find out from the overseer."

"You told me no white men were here—"

"He's a Negro."

"Where is he?"

"Off in the fields with a gang of workers."

The sergeant looked at the men again, but they exchanged no words or laughter, merely speculative looks. Lotus and Nancy came out with the common heavy plates. The food heaped on them was to have been their supper. The men promptly propped their rifles against the fig tree and ate standing. The three women watched them without speaking. When the men finished the food, they held out the plates. Lotus and Nancy took them back into the kitchen, Lotus then coming to stand in the doorway behind Sarah, with Nancy behind her.

"We're looking over things," the sergeant said to Sarah. "Getting the lay of the land, you might say. We'll be back when we've further business." With that he and his companions claimed their guns, mounted the waiting horses, and rode away.

Sarah thought she was calm, but her legs turned weak as she entered the kitchen again. However, it was over, the first meeting. Except for lying about Daniel, which she regretted, she felt that she had not handled the men badly. It was something to build on the next time they came. She felt a little burst of relief, which she realized immediately was unjustified, for they would certainly return.

"Lord, Miss Sarah," Lotus said.

"Wasn't you scared, Missy?" Nancy asked. "I was so scared myself I like to have wet my drawers when that man took the plate from my hands. And when I took it back empty, I was sure he was going to throw me on the ground and do the worst on me —declare I was!"

On the way to the office Sarah looked into the drawing room to find Nell asleep in her little rocking chair, nothing having disturbed her. Jane had walked over to Oaks after noon dinner to visit her father, but she would return before night. Sarah went into the office and sat down at her desk, only then realizing how tired the encounter with the men had left her.

News of the event spread quickly over the plantation. —Five had come. No, thirty. Miss Sarah had ordered them to leave, and they had obeyed. The Negroes were half cheered, half disappointed.

As soon as he heard the news, Floyd went to the main house. "We'll move the sawmill tonight," he said to Sarah.

"They asked me what men lived here. I mean besides you-all. I told them none. I don't know why, but I couldn't mention Daniel."

"We'll explain him when we have to. I'd better leave him with Otis at the Shelter. At least till we know how they're going to act."

"All right." After a moment she said, "It's here, Floyd. What everybody's been talking about so long."

After supper Otis hitched their strongest mule, whose name was Bartholomew, to a wagon and left the plantation by a back road. The sides of the wagon were built up by linked boards to a height of four feet, a little more than half the height used to carry a load of loose cotton to be ginned, twelve or fifteen hundred pounds of which could be expected to make a four- to five-hundred-pound bale of ginned cotton. The wagon, which had been used most recently to haul cotton, smelled of cottonseed. On its floor, lying quietly beside each other, were Floyd and Daniel. An hour and a half later when they arrived at the sawmill, they made no light but sat in the dark a few minutes to make sure they had not been followed. Floyd had no expectation of being surprised by Yankee soldiers, but he wanted to be certain that Junior Elk had set no spies on the mill. To this end he left Daniel and Otis in the wagon and went over the immediate area. Returning to the wagon, he let Otis light the lantern they had brought along, which they moved from one spot to another as they loaded the machinery. When they were ready to move, he told Otis and Daniel to get back on the wagon. Taking the lantern in one hand and the bridle in the other, he slapped the mule's side. Bartholomew strained forward. The wagon moved, but slowly. Without needing to be told, Otis and Daniel hopped to the ground. Otis took the bridle, and Floyd led the way with the lantern. Daniel said he would follow to make sure none of their cargo slipped or bumped out. They began the slow long way on the back trail into the deep woods.

It was a cold night, but not freezing as it had been during the time of the hog killing. They were forced to stop often by obstructions that Floyd had not noted as such in the daytime but which presented problems at night with a heavy-loaded wagon. They had to tie branches of dead trees into bundles and set them under the body of the wagon to float it when they came to the wide creek. Even so the wagon came near to foundering during the crossing and its contents were flooded before Floyd, struggling alongside the exhausted mule, managed to bring them to the bank of the island. It was midmorning when they had finally unloaded and dried and greased the machine parts that might have rusted otherwise. By then they had consumed all the cold biscuits and fried meat Lotus had packed for them. Before he settled himself to rest for an hour or so on the ground, Otis fed Bartholomew and left him to wander free. The other two men were already asleep.

19.

The people of Highboro hardly knew what they had expected until it failed to happen. They had waited for an army with solid ranks of marching men, flags flying, drums and bugle calls. They needed the perverse satisfaction of witnessing forces superior to their own, of seeing the strength of the victor in order to accept defeat. They might then have said to each other, "That is how it was. Our men could not withstand such might."

But what dignity, let alone nobility, could they find in bowing to a ragtail mob? The men who came were, in the main, as ignorant as they were arrogant. They hated all Southerners, black and white, blaming them equally for the war and grudging them any peace to come. They could be simple to the point of savagery. They considered few things as funny as a fart, and the man who could most accurately aim tobacco spit was that day's hero and winner of wagers.

These conquerors came in straggling lines on foot, or jostling each other to rest their rumps on overloaded wagons. They came in strung-out groups of horsemen who acted as scouting and foraging parties as commanded, and sometimes as not. No one seemed to own an entire uniform but all seemed to be clothed in whatever rag had come to hand. There was, to be sure, an occasional burst of gaiety, for their job was easy. They were meeting no organized resistance, and they found plenty of food and whiskey. After a diet of salt pork and weevil-infested hardtack—they joked that it was best to eat it in the dark—they were glad to gorge on fresh meat and corn bread and sweet potatoes. If whiskey and food were the first things they sought, their next demands were men's clothes and watches and women's jewelry.

There was supposed to be no looting, but the common attitude of the officers was: 'Do it but don't let me see you do it,' when they did not actively join in the stealing themselves. They occupied the train depot and took over stores to serve as various kinds of headquarters. The conquered were required to give up arms ānd all their supplies, and then draw back daily rations as allowed.

Annabel Saxon did not know what to make of it. Her first reaction was astonishment; she could hardly bother to sneer. But she did parade through the center of town each morning, often with her big sons in tow, one on either side managing to look both fierce and uncertain. Her female troops had deserted her. They kept to their own houses as much as they were able, to protect them, they said, and were unmoved when Annabel sought to shame them into braver action. The severest blow came to Annabel when both her old friends, Margaret-Ella Singletary and Ann-Elizabeth Dupree, admitted Union officers to their dining rooms as boarders in exchange for favored treatment. The other townspeople might look on such behavior with frowns, although they too had begun to feel that they must make the best of things, but Annabel vowed never to forgive them. Strangers may be forgiven anything; friends, nothing.

Annabel felt that she could bear whatever the invaders inflicted except being ignored, so she set out to provoke them. Meeting acquaintances on her daily forays into the town center, she would speak clearly and insultingly of the town's new rulers, but her attacks had no apparent effect on those rulers, who continued to treat her like everyone else.

One morning she hung a Confederate flag from a window, and finally, some hours later, two soldiers came and told her to take it down. She refused, whereupon they entered the house, found the window from which the flag hung limply, and pulled it up, one of them making a great wad of it and tucking it under his arm. When she spread-eagled herself against the front door and demanded that he hand back the noble cloth, he blew his nose on it, and the other soldier pushed her aside.

"Sir!" she cried. "Would you have your wife or mother treated so?"

The men looked at each other ānd roared with laughter. As they went out, she followed them. "You will see! My sons, though they have not yet come to man's estate, will find you and settle with you!"

The older of the two soldiers looked thoughtful as he shifted his chewing tobacco from one side of his jaw to the other. "Listen, ma'am. You just keep them shit-ass younguns of yours at home if you know what's good for 'em. Don't set 'em up to no more mischief, or I for one am going to slap them cock-eyed."

Trembling with frustration when they had gone, Annabel swore to avenge the humiliation. Bonard and Blair were with Rector Stewart Throckmorton of St. Thomas's; he tutored them three mornings a week in Latin and ancient history. Otherwise, she told herself, they would have— What would they have done? Nothing, unless she directed them, and Annabel craved a more fervid and spontaneous action than that would have provided. They had no weapons, and the soldier had threatened actually to lay hands on them if they were got up to any more "mischief." Remembering his words, Annabel set her lips grimly. They *had* noticed her and her sons; they *were* aware of her as an unkneeling spirit. She vowed to make them more aware.

After that morning she added to the verbal insults with which she peppered her public conversation a strong element of family bragging. She spoke of her husband, Colonel Blair Saxon, as one who had led his men into battle on a dozen occasions to slaughter the foe and who at that very hour stood ready to do so again. Her brother James Davis became in her telling one of the fiercest of Southern warriors, blinded as he led a charge against the men—yes, of this very army of *Mister* Sherman's! Her father Bruce Davis was a great patriot who had eagerly given the best his plantation afforded in food and horses to the Confederate Army. And let them beware—he would be heard of again. In future he might decide to assume a more active role in the Cause for which he had already done so much. She had heard him say —but she "would not repeat it here on the street where anyone might overhear."

Some of her acquaintances thought her brave; some, an embarrassment and a nuisance. Others considered her a fool, and a few said to themselves that she was worse than a fool to suggest things that were not so and might carry a potential threat for all of them. But they did not contradict her. A lady's word was not disputed, however wide of the truth.

Annabel did not know it, but her campaign of provocation was strengthened by an unlikely ally. Junior Elk had quickly made himself known to the Union commander, Captain Abel Ponder. He owned large properties both in town and the surrounding county which he must now protect and which, if the chance offered, he would like to expand. Because of his name the commander was called behind his back "Captain Cain" and "Captain Plunder," although in fact he was not very wicked and only moderately piratical. He was a solemn man of little imagination and no gift for understanding people. He had led his company capably enough, but he possessed few talents as an administrator. Since he would like, if he could, to return to his home in Ohio richer than when he left it, he turned a willing ear to the opinions of a man of so substantial a fortune as Junior Elk.

When Annabel Saxon's tales were brought to him, it was natural for him to ask Junior for information and comment. Junior's answers were careful. Yes, he believed that most of what Mrs. Saxon said was true. Her husband was a colonel in the forces of the Confederacy, and Junior "heard reliably" that he had led his troops into battles that had inflicted heavy loss of life on the Union. It was true too that her brother James Davis had recently returned home blinded from war service. Junior did not, he said, know the details but was himself satisfied that James Davis was a bitter and unreconciled man. As for Bruce Davis—well, he was the owner of Oaks, which was one of the two richest plantations in the county, the other being Beulah Land; and all knew he had responded overgenerously to the needs of the Rebel cause.

Although Beulah Land had a mistress instead of a master, Junior described Sarah Kendrick as an arrogant woman who had always gone her own way, disregarding law as well as convention when it suited her to do so. She might pretend, he said, to have taken little personal part in the war, but "it was known" that much of the support Bruce Davis had given to the Confederacy's military effort had come from Beulah Land. Both Sarah Kendrick and Bruce Davis were people to watch. They were so often secretive in what they did.

Junior pointed out that the Kendricks owned a sawmill as well as the plantation and the cotton gin and warehouse; and where had the machinery of the sawmill gone? It was no longer at its old location. Junior had wondered about this, he said, because his father before him had acquired a thousand acres of good timberland; and he, like his father, had not touched it, but he was thinking now of doing so. There would be a great demand for prime timber to rebuild after the war, which, they had agreed, must soon come to an end.

Then there was the recent appearance of a strange white man at Beulah Land who was said to be a cousin, discharged from the Confederate Army because of wounds and illness, although no one before had heard of such a cousin. Until recently he had been observed working on the plantation, or at the cotton gin or sawmill. Where was he? He had disappeared about the time the sawmill vanished. Some said he was no Kendrick kin at all. Some guessed him to be a Union soldier who had deserted and been taken in at Beulah Land as a reward for treason. Junior did not know, but confessed to having doubts which the Kendrick secrecy did nothing to remove.

Unlike Captain Ponder, Junior Elk was sensitive to others when he wanted to understand and use them, and he read correctly as greed the stillness of Captain Ponder's face as he talked of the riches of Oaks and Beulah Land. Of the free families of Highboro, white and black, Junior Elk's was the only one that had been allowed to keep its property and goods intact. No one bothered them. Word had been passed by Captain Ponder the morning after the first evening he went for supper to the Elk house.

The house was another of the properties that had been accumulated by Junior's father. At one time it had been the Highboro home of Nell and Felix Kendrick. Nell's husband was a lawyer and businessman prominent in the affairs of the county until a few years before his death in 1853, when illness sent him back to Beulah Land to finish out his life in its shelter.

The house was now well kept by a woman named Geraldine, who acted as general housekeeper as well as mistress to Junior, offices she had performed for his father, and before him for his brother Alonzo until Alonzo's murder. Junior's wife Dorothy cared little how the house was run, as long as he left her alone. Junior had never loved her, nor she him. She had been the indulged child of a white Savannah banker and a Negro woman, and old Roscoe Elk had arranged the marriage hoping for a business advantage. Dorothy was nearly beautiful, missing the full condition only from lack of energy and intelligence. Her vanity was all-consuming. She could spend hours contentedly before her mirror with a handful of pins and combs and a row of jars and bottles. Her skin was exactly the color of a magnolia blossom the hour it begins to darken and fade. She sometimes, when she remembered her, regretted the death of her first child in its first year. A daughter might have given her something to do and think about, another face to mold and play with. She could not care for her son because he was ugly.

That son, the last of the household and the least considered, was coming into an age of self-awareness. He had loved his grandfather because he was loved by the old man. His father and mother disliked him because he reminded them of each other; and his resentment of this and of them increased. He was discovering that they were not the world. When he stared at them, his blue eyes made them wish he had never been born.

On the second occasion of Captain Ponder's supping at the house, Junior decided that the white man's awkward courtesy and reserve with Dorothy were not shyness but a mask to hide his attraction to her. He then noted Dorothy's awareness of her appeal, and was certain. No woman is so dull that she does not instantly sense admiration in others. She might prove a business asset after all, as old Roscoe had said. The idea afforded Junior a moment of rare amusement.

20.

A dozen parties of horsemen had ridden up to the plantation since the visit of the three scouts, but Sarah had a way of meeting them, firm but unbelligerent, that so far had kept them out of the main house, although not out of the barns and the smokehouse and the kitchen. From these they took what they wanted: the best of the remaining horses (they left the older ones), the pick of the cured meats, and what they found on the stove or in the pantries that struck their fancy. They could not, it seemed, have enough whiskey or syrup, taking all they found in the smokehouse and demanding to know where more was stored.

Sarah, like others in the area, had thought that whatever was to happen would happen and be over, but that was not the way of it. Party after party came, seeing the big house through the orchard off the road, none admitting to knowing about the others who had been there. Nothing they did was formal or organized. By keeping watch and keeping her wits, and making sure that she was always the first to meet them, Sarah managed to keep Beulah Land going. She tried not to show emotion, especially anger and fear. She made herself appear ordinary, never proud, or cold, or disdainful. After the soldiers, and sometimes even mingled in their raiding parties, came the scavengers, called "bummers" by those they lived on. It was not easy to tell them from the soldiers, and every stranger who approached was looked on with suspicion and dread.

A fence in the way was something to kick down. Any evidence of order invited destruction. They were sometimes sober; they were often drunk. All, though, were greedy—not hungry any more, simply desirous of getting what they wanted and spoiling what they did not. One party collected all the chickens they could catch, tied their feet together, and hitched an ox to the old barouche they found in the barn to carry them away. It was the vehicle that had most often been used to take the Kendricks to church, or for group attendance at weddings and balls and funerals. The same men killed six of Lotus's geese and then, deciding they would be too much trouble, left them bleeding on the ground.

After their first experiences Sarah and Lotus and Jane and Nancy began to divide their supplies, storing them in separate locations so that all of any one thing would not be found together, and some part of everything had a chance of surviving. Seed for next year's crops was stored in bags and jugs and hidden in the near woods, or carried to the farther Shelter by Floyd or Zebra on one of their regular night trips to Otis and Daniel. More and more, the Shelter became the repository of whatever hope there was for the future of Beulah Land.

Sarah gave orders to the Negroes remaining on the plantation to try to avoid the raiding parties, but not to run away if they were seen. They were to answer questions however they could, but she asked them not to reveal more than was necessary about the hiding places of food supplies, which all of them must depend upon through the winter. She warned them to make no attempt at resistance. Lotus and Nancy were to stay in the kitchen. Lovey was to be kept out of sight, for she could not be made to understand what was happening, or why such rude intrusions were allowed. She was growing deaf as well as blind, and unless shouted at, she heard little except what spoke to her in her own mind.

But she was sometimes in the kitchen sitting in her cane chair by the cooking stove when they came. Seeing her age and infirmity, they usually ignored her, but one day one of the men—they had all grown clever at guessing the simple hiding places—found an old kettle, set aside because of an unmended leak, with eggs stored in it. When he grabbed it, Lovey tried to take it away from him. In their brief struggle the kettle was dropped and the eggs broke. Another group discovered three sacks of newly ground cornmeal that had just come from the mill. Lotus and Nancy had had no time to move them to safer places than the pantry. Nell was in the kitchen, as she often was, to observe the cooking, and as the last sack was carried by her, she said, "Please leave us one sack. That is all we have."

The soldier paused and opened the sack. Taking a double handful, he scattered it on the kitchen floor. "There's some for you to lick up when you get hungry."

"Do you want us to starve?" Nell said.

"Root, hog, or die." He grinned at her. "You're a damned old Rebel, and if you don't get out of my way, I'll shoot your brains out."

During this time Nancy was eager with gossip and tales of how others met and bested the invaders. How news came to her, no one could say, because she never left the plantation; but people will always manage to pass word on somehow, without their ways ever being explained.

"When they come to steal clothes, what you s'posed to do is tell them: 'Go right ahead and take them all. They're dead folks' clothes anyway.' —Then they don't touch nothing!

"One girl I hear of, when they tell her she got to go with them and be their cook, she hop into bed and pull the covers up and moan: 'Glad to come with y'all soon as I gits over the yellow fever!' "

At one noon dinner, when Jane had excused herself and Sarah and Nell sat on a few minutes at the table, Sarah told Nancy that she might clear without waiting for them to leave. Nell was complaining in a companionable way about how hard times were and saying she didn't know how she could face another raiding party, when Nancy, listening and bursting with new-heard advice said, "Miss Nell, one thing you don't have to worry, for I have the answer. This girl told me what to do. When they try to rape you, say, 'Oh, mustn't do that, sir, for I have got the pussy pox.' —That's what I'm going to say, and I advise you to do the same!"

After the smallest pause Nell said, "Thank you, Nancy. I'll try to remember that."

A country church was burned, to make a signal fire from one company to another, it was said; but no private dwelling had been destroyed in the neighborhood of farms, although stories were told of fires set in other parts of the county. Negroes as well as whites were robbed by the soldiers and the bummers, and they were whipped when did not obey orders. The name of Captain Abel Ponder was known to all as the district commander, though he was never in the raiding parties. It was assumed that he received a share of whatever was taken, by an agreement with his men. Aside from his, only one name gained currency, that of a Sergeant Billy Smede, said to be ruthless and thought to execute orders only directly from Captain Ponder.

But for all the trouble and loss, Sarah and Floyd had no reason to suppose Beulah Land singled out for particular attention. Floyd made at least two trips a week to the Shelter, because he did not dare carry very much at a time. He was never easy in his mind about leaving Beulah Land; but as the days passed, he began to feel that Sarah and Lotus could handle the raiding parties as well as he could, even perhaps better for being women whose appearance suggested no resistance.

One night in the second week of December there was a new kind of raid. After supper Floyd had taken Lovey to her cabin and then gone back to the kitchen to wait for Lotus and Nancy to finish with their work. Sarah was in the office working at her desk, Jane beside her with a book so that they might share the same candle. Nell was in the drawing room alone playing the piano, with only the fireplace giving her a little light. She did not play well, but it was company for her when others were busy, as she did not care for reading or sewing. Suddenly out of the night came a thunder of horses' hooves as a party of men rode around and around the plantation house shouting and cursing. Those inside came together quickly and after their first alarm stood at windows and waited for the men to approach and make known their purpose. They did not, and after continuing the exercise a few minutes longer, they rode away. Sarah and Floyd exchanged speculations but could make nothing of it.

Nell was certain they meant to return later and burn the house down over their heads as they slept. They did not, but they came again the next night at an hour when the house was dark. The performance was repeated, and again they rode away without making the purpose of their actions any clearer than before. They then skipped a night, but on the night following, they came three times, at nine o'clock, at twelve-thirty, and at just past two in the morning. Sarah and Floyd decided they were merely nuisance raids meant to wake them and worry them. Then they came no more, and Floyd resumed his trips to the Shelter, which he had abandoned because of uncertainty about the night raiders. They never found any damage in the mornings other than the expected trampling of the grounds by the horses.

They had begun to speak to each other cautiously if not hopefully about Christmas, and Sarah was thinking of asking Bruce and Doreen and James and Benjamin to come for Christmas dinner when on Monday night of the third week of December another kind of visitor came, as unexpected as the night riders had been. Again Sarah and Jane were in the office. Immediately before supper Floyd had been there with Sarah, and they had agreed on his starting for the Shelter later that evening when the roads were quiet. He would ride the mule Bartholomew, who almost knew the way himself by now and who was, for a mule, a tractable animal not objecting to night labor. On impulse Sarah had given Floyd a copy of Melville's *Typee* as a surprise for Daniel. Slipping it into a pocket, Floyd smiled and said, "You've adopted him, have you?" When he left her, she realized that his little joke had annoyed her. Why shouldn't she be thoughtful of Daniel? He earned his keep. After all, Floyd had Lotus and a baby coming. —Then she was vexed with herself at having made a comparison in her mind.

Nell had said good night and gone up to bed a few minutes before the knock came. It was not at the front door or the back but on a windowpane of the office where they sat. Jumping up, Sarah and Jane went to peer out. They saw no one. Throwing open the window, Sarah called, "Who's there?"

A voice replied, "Roscoe Elk."

The name of her old enemy still had the power to stop her heart, until she remembered that this could not be a voice from the dead and answered, "Let me see you."

From the shadows the boy came to the window, which was at ground level. Shielding the candle from the draft of the open window, they could see the blue of his eyes and the freckles on his light-colored face.

"Who is with you?" Sarah demanded to know.

"I'm by myself."

What do you want?"

"Speak to you," he gulped.

"About what?"

"If I come in a minute, only a minute—"

"Who sent you here?" Sarah asked.

"I just came!"

"Wait." She closed the window. Jane followed her into the hall and to the front door. When Sarah opened it, the boy stood there on the porch. She looked beyond him to be sure he was alone; then without a word she let him in. Jane showed the way with the candle back into the office, Sarah closing the doors behind them. "Now," she said. The boy looked around the room he had never seen before. Watching him, Sarah was reminded of his grandfather's standing in that room when he was overseer at Beulah Land, usually for an interview that turned into a confrontation with her or Leon, or both. Studying the boy's face, she saw a resemblance to the dead man, but she also saw agitation, and her voice was kinder when she said, "Now tell me why you are here. And how did you come?"

"Tied the horse to a tree in your orchard." She nodded and waited for him to go on. "I had to tell you they'll be coming. I heard them."

"We've had many raiding and foraging parties."

He shook his head. "Something else. I don't know. I heard them talking."

"Who, boy?" she asked.

He seemed to be sorting his thoughts. "Captain Ponder comes to see us. Him and Papa have business together, but he comes just to see us too, and eat supper with us. He even comes in the daytime when Papa's not there, and him and Mama talk. They don't notice me. He promised her a ring for her finger. Tonight was different. He's still there, Captain Ponder is, with Papa. At supper they held up their glasses and did a toast before they drank." He paused as if to gather courage as well as breath. "Captain Ponder spoke the toast. He said, 'To no more Beulah Land—tomorrow!'"

The three stood still, Jane holding the candle. Sarah said, "Well, they do seem to be eating us away little by little."

"They don't mean that!"

Sarah saw tears on his cheeks. "Why have you come to tell me this?" she asked faintly.

"I don't know!" he declared miserably. His tears came then in earnest. Turning, he ran from the room. Sarah reached the hall after him only to see him fling open the front door and go racing down the carriageway. "Roscoe!" she called, but he did not stop or turn; and while she hesitated, Jane came to stand beside her, and they heard the sound of the horse being ridden away.

Soon after, Sarah sent Jane upstairs to bed. She sat alone in the office, not working, a glass of brandy in her hand which she sipped from time to time. She did not believe the boy had been sent by Junior Elk or anyone else, but why had he come? And was he being fanciful—he was certainly overexcited—or had he actually heard something that meant more harm to Beulah Land? She blew out the candle and continued to sit. She needed no light to see in this room, or indeed in any room of the house. Her other senses knew every board and shadow of it. After a while she drained her glass and left it on the desk. Through the window at which the boy had tapped she saw that a half-moon had risen and glowed in the dark sky. She went into the hallway, and then into the drawing room and stood before the fireplace, still showing a few rose-gray embers. Above the mantel was the large full-figure portrait of her husband, which Casey Troy had painted many years ago. He stood handsome and solid-looking against the background of Beulah Land, as if he would always stand so, and it could never change. But he was dead by his own hand, and tonight a stranger had proposed a toast to "no more Beulah Land."

The little porcelain clock Leon had bought for her soon after they were married sounded ten dry, delicate chimes from the low table beside Nell's rocking chair. She picked it up and held its cold face against her cheek. Going through the hallway again, and the breezeway, she went into the back yard, as Floyd walked Bartholomew out of the nearest barn. He did not see her until she stepped out of the shadow of the trees and the moonlight revealed her.

"Are you all right?" he said, leaning down toward her from the mule's back to speak quietly. In that instant she decided not to tell him of the warning.

"Yes," she said. "Only restless. Do you have a pocket left to carry this?" She held the clock up, and he took it.

"I'll be home tomorrow before midnight."

The lights were all out at Oaks, and not even the faintest smell of woodsmoke came to Floyd on the road when he passed the plantation. The moonlight whitened the clay road which in daylight showed red. It had not been a very cold day, but the ground was hard, and as he went along, Floyd could almost hear the frost stiffening the twigs of roadside bushes. When he was half a mile beyond Oaks, he knew he was no longer alone. Deciding to challenge instead of waiting to be challenged, he pulled the mule to an abrupt halt and shouted, "I see you there! Come forward!"

The figure that had been following a parallel path in the fields by the roadside immediately clambered down the bank on foot. "Floyd? It's me, Benjamin."

"My God!" Floyd laughed with relief. "Where do you think you're going this cold night?"

"With you," Benjamin said, encouraged by the laughter.

"No, you're not. How did you know I'd come by? —Never mind. You and your sister have ways of telling each other. She knew she mustn't try to come, so you decided to. Is that it?"

"Well," Benjamin almost agreed, "we thought one of us ought to see Daniel without waiting too long after he left us." He put blandness into his tone when he added, "He's our cousin, you know."

"Mm," Floyd said. "You better go back home before somebody wakes up and finds out you're not in your room."

"I'm not a youngun any more, Floyd. Nobody looks into my room at night. I left a note in the dining room. They'll find it at breakfast."

"And be worried to death. Uh-uh, no."

"Floyd! Let me come—they won't care if they know I'm with you!"

"Now go on back, you hear?"

"Floyd!"

"What do you think your grandpa would say to me?"

"Aw, Floyd."

"I'll tell Daniel you wanted to come see him."

"Will you?"

"Straight home now, and slip in so you don't wake them."

Floyd watched the boy running back along the white road; then he jerked the halter, and Bartholomew continued on his way.

21.

When the morning passed without untoward event, Sarah decided that the youth Roscoe had got his elders wrong, or had taken seriously what had only been meant as a party jest. A portion of her mind listened a little harder perhaps than usual, but she went about her daily jobs as ordinary routine prescribed. Because of the cold Nell walked only a few minutes in the yards to take her exercise, and after dinner went directly to her rocker in the drawing room, adding a single piece of wood to the fireplace. Picking over her jewelry recently to send the best pieces to the island Shelter, she had found a cache of old letters and had now spent a couple of days happily deciphering them, particularly entertained by those that had not been written to her but to her sister Deborah and to Sarah's Aunt Penelope, both of whom were in their graves.

Jane was in her room sewing. Sarah checked the poultry yard again for eggs that might have been laid since morning. Two of her most productive hens were unaccountably trying to "set" and were disposed to lay their eggs where they could not be easily found. When she came in from the yard, she stopped in the kitchen to talk to Lotus about what they would have for supper. Nancy was finishing the dinner dishes. Then making her way back into the main part of the house, she glanced through the open doors of the drawing room, where Nell had dropped the letters to the floor beside her chair and sat with her hands folded in her plump lap and her eyes closed. She snored lightly and regularly.

Smiling as she entered the office, her eye caught movement through the front windows. Although she had heard no sound of

their approach, she counted nine men walking their horses along
the carriageway. She recognized none of them, and as they came
around the house, she followed them window by window, and
through the hall and breezeway, and stood ready to meet them
at the back door when they began to dismount. One of the nine
left the others and approached. He was a short, fat man whose
precise movements seemed to contradict his grossness. Coming
directly to Sarah, he announced himself as Sergeant Billy Smede
and said that he was there on orders from Captain Abel Ponder.

"Why has he sent you?" she asked.

"He has heard that you are hiding a deserter from the Union
Army."

"That is not so."

"I will make a search."

"General Sherman has given orders that you are not to enter
our houses."

"Captain Ponder has ordered me to find the man. We will
search the cabins and barns first." He turned to the men behind
him and called, "Simon." One man left the others. "Stay here
with her. Don't let her go back in the house or talk to anybody."
The soldier nodded and took a position a few feet away from
Sarah. The sergeant and the remaining seven men fanned out;
four, including the sergeant, heading toward the barns and the
others trotting away to the slave cabins, rifles in hand.

Sarah folded her arms, not looking at the soldier. Presently
Jane came running along the breezeway, and when she saw the
soldier, stopped beside Sarah. Shifting her eyes, Sarah noted that
Lotus and Nancy had seen what was going on and remained
quiet, as they had been told to do.

A quarter of an hour later Sergeant Smede returned with his
men, three of whom now carried axes they had found in the
barns.

"I told you I was hiding no one," Sarah said to the sergeant
when he came up to her.

"You swore there was no white man living here, but one was
seen before we came."

"No one has been here today," she said, pretending to misun-
derstand him. "However, many of your men have been here before today. We gave up our guns as directed, and they have
taken all they wanted of our horses and food supplies."

"I'm not talking about today. I'm talking about before the

Army came through this part of Georgia. There was a white man working here. People have sworn to it. Some of your own slaves say so. Now don't try to lie any more."

Sarah appeared to consider. "Perhaps they mean our cousin. That must be it. I assure you he was no Yankee deserter, but a Southerner. He was here a few days, and he did help some with the work because we were short-handed. But he was not living here, and you can see for yourself no one is living here now except us."

"Where did he go?"

"Down to the southern part of the state where another branch of his family lives."

"Where down there exactly?"

"A farm near Brunswick in Glynn County." She spoke calmly, having prepared herself and Jane for these questions after her first denial of Daniel's existence to the three scouts.

"What's the man's name?"

"Todd."

"Not Kendrick?"

"He was not related to my husband, but to my father. He is a cousin, one we hadn't seen for a while."

"Just appeared from nowhere, did he?"

"No, he had been wounded in the fighting above Atlanta and was sick a long time. That's why he was discharged from the Army and allowed to go home. He stopped on the way and let us fatten him up a little before he made the rest of his trip."

The sergeant smiled. "Just like you're helping to fatten us up too!" He touched his stomach in a gesture of mock appreciation and then looked quickly at Jane. "Is she telling the truth or telling me lies?"

"The truth," Jane said promptly.

Sergeant Smede continued to look at the child. "Pretty little thing," he said. "How'd you like to give me a big hug around the neck, girl?"

Jane did not move or answer. Sarah allowed herself only to take her hand.

Sergeant Smede looked back at Sarah. "I guess we'll have to go into your house, woman, and see for ourselves how much of the truth you're telling."

"I forbid you to enter," Sarah said.

"I don't see that you're in a position to forbid me much of anything," the sergeant said. "If you hid any of your guns, we'll find them, and it will go hard for you." He turned his head sharply. "Ready to start, men! Go in and cover everything like we said."

The eight soldiers let out a whoop, and Sarah realized they had been waiting for the words to release them. "Stop, for God's sake," she begged the sergeant. "There's an old lady, my aunt; they'll frighten her!"

"She'll get over it," Sergeant Smede said. "And if she don't; well, you say she's old."

Nancy screamed when two of the men went into the kitchen, but they joined the others again after a quick search of the storerooms beyond the kitchen. For a moment Sarah could not believe it was happening, but the sound of the men tramping through the breezeway drew her after them to the wide hallway. When two of them went into the drawing room, Sarah followed. Nell woke, speechless with astonishment.

"Lord!" she cried when she found her voice. Slipping to the floor, she began to pray. "Blessed Savior and Redeemer, be with us this hour and shield us from our enemies!" The soldier nearest grabbed her by the hair and dragged her. Sarah ran to them.

"Stop! Leave her alone!"

"You tell her to cease praying!"

Nell lay where the man had dragged her, and Sarah knelt to comfort her. The sergeant came to the door. "You're wasting time," he told them. "Go to work. There's a piano. I want the wire." With four heavy blows of his ax, one soldier made splinters of the piano, and the sergeant took out a hunting knife and began to strip the wire away. The other soldier tore the curtains from the windows and left them on the floor where they fell.

"Where is Jane?" Nell said, sitting up.

"I forgot the child!"

"Go and find her," Nell said.

Sarah ran from the room calling, "Jane! Where are you, Jane?"

Sounds from her office across the hallway drew her into it, but Jane was not there. A soldier was knocking ledgers and books from the shelves. He had already pulled drawers out and turned them upside down on the floor. Sarah heard the tramp of feet above and hurried up the stairs.

She found Jane in her room holding tightly the doll's trunk Leon had given her years before, the repository now of the treasures she had not been able to part with, even to let Floyd carry them to the island Shelter. There were two soldiers in the room, one with an ax, the other using a heavy knife to prize open locked drawers and rip pillows apart. Turning to Jane at the moment Sarah entered, the soldier with the knife tried to wrench the trunk out of her arms.

"No! No! No! No!" Jane howled. "Leave it alone! It's mine! It's all I have!"

The soldier let go the trunk and slapped her hard. The trunk flew from her arms, and he carried it to the fireplace and smashed the locked lid with an andiron. Jane's body writhed with outrage as Sarah held her. The soldier first discovered the miniature painting of Leon and bit into it to test its composition before throwing it aside as worthless. Next he found the hand mirror cased in tortoise shell which her father James had given her when she was a baby. In it she had been shown an image of herself for the first time. The soldier looked into the mirror briefly before smashing glass and shell and dropping the pieces into the fireplace. He frowned hopefully at the piece his fingers now brought up from the floor of the trunk. It was a cameo of George Washington which Nell had given Jane on her seventh birthday. Nell herself had worn it, and Deborah had worn it before Nell. The soldier turned it over and, deciding the clasp was gold, slipped it into his pocket.

The last thing he found was the lock of Leon's hair which Floyd had taken from the coffin to give Jane. When the ribbon split, he shredded the hair with his fingers. The other soldier dragged the feather mattress from the bed and ripped it apart. The air was suddenly thick with floating feathers. "Like snow," Sarah thought as she held Jane against her. Jane sobbed angrily. Presently Sarah realized that the men had gone on to another room.

She waited, but no one came back. Jane freed herself and found the broken doll's trunk where the soldier had dropped it in front of the fireplace. Crawling, she found the discarded miniature and searched the floor for strands of Leon's hair, as the feathers from the mattress and pillows still floated and billowed about her. Sarah took her by the hand again and led her into the upper hall and down the stairs. The office was empty now. Nell was alone in the drawing room, where she had left her when she went looking for Jane. She was sitting on the floor beside a piece of the piano keyboard, and as she touched one key after another, she seemed puzzled that they gave no sound.

"Aunt Nell," Sarah said.

Nell jerked her head up as if she had been sleeping.

"Aunt Nell," Sarah said, "I want you and Jane to go back to the kitchen with Lotus and Nancy. Stay there. It's better if you are all together and I know where you are."

"Yes," Nell said docilely, "all right."

"Come with us, Grandma," Jane said.

"I'll be along soon."

The old woman and the young girl took each other's hand and went out, not looking around at the wrecked room.

But Sarah looked at it. No piece of furniture was left whole and standing. The portraits had been pulled down from the walls. She found Leon's, slashed twice across. She tried to pull the parts of canvas together but saw that it was useless. She went again into the office. It was like the drawing room, everything chopped or pulled or stomped apart, pages torn from books, carpet ruined with thrown inkpots, curtains down, wallpaper slashed, windows broken. She looked into the dining room but did not enter it. The floor was covered with splintered glass and china. All the silver had been taken.

There was nothing to do, she decided, but to wait for them to finish and leave. She might as well go to the kitchen and be with the others. But as she reached the breezeway, she stopped a moment to listen to the racket from upstairs. They were running about. Doors slammed. Laughter, high and out of control, mixed with the sound of wood being broken. She could not go away, and so she went back. Shock had carried her beyond fear. Fear was something she might feel for others but could not now feel for herself; and the others were together in the kitchen.

She went from room to room upstairs, not trying to stop their plundering, and knowing that begging would save nothing at all. They had found Leon's clothes, some of them worn lately by Daniel, and one man was making a bundle of them which he proceeded to secure with a silken curtain cord.

As she walked among them, they did not even notice that she was there, such was their concentration. As if she were visiting the ruin of a house she had known whole and long ago, she said to herself: "This is the room where Uncle Felix died. This was Leon's and mine, where we slept side by side on separate beds for thirty-three years. And this is the room where Rachel was born. Here Selma stood one day and let herself be dressed in her bridal gown, and here she returned twenty-four hours later. Here, and here—"

When she roused herself finally, she thought she must have been alone for a long time and in a kind of stupor. She had found her way back into her own bedroom, a shambles like the others, and she was sitting on a footstool that had somehow survived. Looking about, she saw that her wardrobe had been upended and everything turned out. A pillow from her bed, its linen casing looking absurdly white, had been used by one of the men for evacuation, and he had taken a nightgown to clean himself, leaving it smeared brown beside the pillow on the floor.

She turned her head to listen and heard nothing. Had they gone? She had noticed no sound of horses, but that had no significance. She would go and find the others. She did not want to go. She did not want to ask or answer a single question. She would like to go down the stairs and out the front door and never look back.

She left her room and went downstairs and discovered that the sight of wreckage had lost the power to shock. She could look about her and say, "Yes, this has happened; now we must clear it up." She thought that she was beyond shock, or any feeling at all, until she approached the kitchen and heard sounds she could not name, and then knew to be the voice of weeping exhaustion.

Lotus was trying to raise herself from the floor where she lay sprawled on her back. Although a few rags remained, she was all but naked. Sarah helped her up, and Lotus said with difficulty, because her mouth was swelling and bleeding, "Go see to Nancy. I'm all right or will be. I heard her in there—"

Sarah found Nancy stripped and unconscious in the first storeroom off the kitchen. The air was heavy with the smell of blood and spilled semen. As she stared at the girl, Sarah was joined by Lotus. "She looks dead," Sarah said.

Trying to kneel by the girl, Lotus fell, and Sarah helped her up again. Shaking her head, Lotus knelt again beside the girl.

"Where are Jane and Aunt Nell?" Sarah asked. "Where's Lovey?"

"Lord, I don't know." Lotus shook her head. "They tried to help us. Then Miss Nell pulled the child out the back door. Lovey, I don't know. She was here. You better go look and see. I heard her squawling while ago. Sounded like it do killing hogs. You go; I'll take care of me and Nancy."

When she went into the yard, the fig tree fixed her attention for a moment and she had to force herself to concentrate to see beyond it. There was no sign of men or horses. So they had gone. They had done what they came to do, and now they had gone. As she thought it, Nell came around the corner of the smokehouse.

"Oh," she sighed in relief, seeing Sarah.

Sarah went to her quickly. "Where's Jane?"

"I took her to Floyd's cabin. I stayed there with her till I heard them in the yard getting ready to leave, and then I came back out. They sounded right proud of themselves."

"Is she safe?"

"What a question!" Nell exclaimed softly.

"Did they touch her?"

"Not a hair," Nell said. "Do you think I'd have let them? When they threw Lotus and Nancy down and started doing things, I took her out. I couldn't help, and they wouldn't listen to me, though I begged and begged. I asked them to just go and leave us alone. I said 'for pity's sake.' Lord, Sarah, I don't understand what's happened to us, do you?"

"Have you seen Lovey?"

"Lovey's dead."

"Where is she?"

"They dug up Ezra's grave. They said we must have gold and silver hidden under the tombstone, because they knew we were rich! She tried to fight them, and they hit her with an ax. She must be over there somewhere."

22.

Sergeant Billy Smede was acting on orders from Captain Abel Ponder, as he had said. Although not overnice in his feelings, Captain Ponder left ways and means to the sergeant, knowing from the past that these could be as severe as they were usually effective. Having also decided that it would be polite for Sergeant Smede to leave the scene when his mission was completed, Captain Ponder had waited for the right moment to give his orders. He knew that his subordinate had a wife in New Jersey who was dying of cancer, and he found his moment when Smede received an urgent family summons and presented his case for what was called "compassionate leave of absence." Captain Ponder had granted that leave yesterday, and it was to begin tomorrow. Whatever sequel today's performance might engender, the principal actor would have left the stage, carrying with him a share of the spoils of the day as a death dowry.

Having finished the first part of his job, Sergeant Smede rode with his eight men and their booty to a grove of pine trees halfway between Beulah Land and Oaks, which he had chosen as a place of rendezvous. A dozen fresh men had ridden out from town and waited there. The eight who had conducted the raid on Beulah Land related something of their recent experiences and displayed samples of their gains, after which they rested before returning to Highboro. Sergeant Smede, whose endurance was famous among his fellows, led the twelve new men to Oaks. On the way he issued orders and outlined a simple plan.

When they arrived, nine men of the party continued around the house to search and ransack the barns and slave cabins of whatever was worth taking. Sergeant Smede and the remaining three men dismounted in the front yard and marched up the steps to the porch. Bruce Davis, who was as alert as Sarah Kendrick to anticipate raiding parties, opened the door a moment after the sergeant knocked.

"Are you Bruce Davis?"

"I am."

"Owner of the plantation called Oaks?"

"This is Oaks."

"You are the owner."

"Yes."

"You are charged with treasonous acts against the armed forces of the United States."

"Who are you?"

"Sergeant Billy Smede, acting on orders from Captain Abel Ponder."

"I do not admit the authority of Captain Ponder to decide on matters as grave as treason."

"You admit to such acts."

"No such thing. Whatever I've done, I've done as a believer in the justness of the cause of the Confederate States."

"You have given supplies to the Rebels?"

Bruce nodded firmly. "We call our country the Confederacy."

"You have given, so we are told, beyond any demanded subscription."

"No demand was necessary. I gave what I could and gladly."

"You do not deny that you helped in every way you knew how to further the cause of what you call the Confederacy?"

"I certainly do not deny that. However—"

"Have you arms?"

"We were ordered to give up all arms, and I have done so."

"You've kept none back for a time such as today?"

"I have not."

Sergeant Smede turned to the soldiers. "You, Prince, and Johnson. Go over the house for weapons." The two designated men drew their pistols and held them ready. Going past Bruce into the hallway, they trotted up the stairs together.

"Information has been given that you are planning to organize and lead a counter-rebellion against our Union forces."

"That is a lie. I have followed all orders put out by your Captain Ponder and his deputies."

"Do you wish to repudiate your connection with the Rebels?"

Bruce hesitated. "We want to survive, with honor if we can."

"Are you ready to sign a paper condemning your part in the rebellion?"

Bruce shifted his weight, and the sergeant gave him time to think about it. "What is all this?" Bruce asked. "Something new? Are you going around to everyone?"

"We are here."

"I understand that, but when and how did it start?"

"All you have to do is answer my questions," Smede said in a reasonable tone of voice.

"I think you had better escort me to your Captain Ponder," Bruce said after staring hard at the man for another moment.

"He has authorized me to deal with these matters here."

"And how do you propose to do that?" Bruce said slowly.

"That will be seen," Sergeant Smede said.

As if in answer to the hinted speculation, however, there came then two screams, one from a horse and the other from a woman.

Bruce turned and ran through the hallway to the back of the house. The sergeant and the remaining soldier followed on his heels, and the three leaped from the back porch into the yard together.

Two of the group that had been sent to the barns had found Pharaoh and led him into the yard to study him the better. They had managed to saddle him, but Pharaoh would not allow either to mount him. When Smede's two men, Prince and Johnson, were sent looking for weapons, they encountered Doreen, whose first thought was for the safety of Pharaoh, and of taking him if she could to the hiding place in the woods she had prepared. She'd gone directly into the yard, and when the frightened horse and the apprehensive woman had seen each other, each had screamed, bringing Bruce and Sergeant Smede on the run.

Doreen went to calm the beast, but she was unable to do so because the men holding him would not give him to her, and he continued to dance nervously trying to get from them to her.

"Hockinson!" Smede called to a soldier just emerging from the barns.

The man trotted over. "Sergeant?"

"You call yourself a rider, don't you?"

"I can ride anything," Hockinson said.

"Let's see you ride that. If you don't, you lose your share today!"

"You mustn't!" Doreen begged. "He isn't to be ridden by anyone but me. He is not used to any other hands or voice. You can see what a state he is in now."

Rubbing his palms together at the challenge, Hockinson crowed, "Woman, I can ride anything with four legs and most things with two!"

"He won't let you! —Please listen to me, and let me calm him!"

The Negroes of the plantation who were not at work when the raiders arrived had been turned out of their cabins by the soldiers. They did not come close but stood watching from a distance, seldom speaking more than a few words of wonder.

With the help of the men who had discovered the horse, Hockinson managed to get into the saddle, but when the two let go the bridle, Pharaoh reared and danced on his hind legs. Other soldiers came from the barns and cabins, drawn by the commotion, and they laughed when Doreen ran to the horse; but the soldiers who had held him now caught and held her. She could only call Pharaoh's name as the terrified animal reared and plunged, emitting shrieks of rage. Hockinson was cursing him, jerking the short rein hard and digging spurred heels into his sides. Pharaoh's eyes rolled, his quivering mouth flung foamed spittle as he strained ever backward and higher to get away. Finally he and the man, concerting their contrary efforts, produced a fall that dislodged the man, who rolled free, and broke the horse's rear left leg. The crack of bone was followed by an agonized wail from the creature before Sergeant Smede stepped forward with his gun and silenced him forever.

The hot quiet moment that followed was ended when Smede said, "He'd have been no use to us anyway; too wild." He laughed as if unconcerned by the incident. "Too wild even for you, Hockinson? Don't be so quick to brag next time."

Freeing herself, Doreen ran to the horse and lifted his head, heedless of the blood pouring upon her.

"Will you look at that?" Hockinson said in disgust. "Never seen a woman take on so. Did you, Meecham?"

"Well—" The soldier Meecham assumed a comical expression. "It's sure funny, but rest your eyes on that big thing he's got down there. I hear there's crazy old maids get a big excitement playing with such! No wonder he wouldn't let nobody else ride him! —I don't know!"

His joke was received with slaps on back and shoulders by those nearest and laughter from the rest of his fellows.

Prince and Johnson, the soldiers who had been sent to search for weapons, came out of the house marching James and Benjamin before them. Benjamin held his father's arm and tried to guide him so that he did not stumble and fall, for they were being pushed along roughly. Prince still held his pistol ready at the back of their heads. Johnson carried a sword and a rifle he had found in James's room, after he found James and Benjamin in Benjamin's room. The boy had been reading to his father from Homer's *Odyssey* and the soldiers had surprised them. Although Benjamin attended no regular school or tutor at present, James had, with Rector Throckmorton's advice, assigned him certain studies at home.

"Where are we now?" James whispered.

"Back yard," Benjamin answered.

"If there's a chance, get away. Wait at Beulah Land till we come for you."

"No, Papa!"

"Do it!"

"Shut up!" Prince pushed them forward, and Johnson called to Sergeant Smede, "Look-a-here what we found for you! Big warrior and his cub reading poetry together."

"I see what else you found," Smede said, and took hold of the rifle.

"This here's an officer's sword. He says he should be allowed to keep it, 'courtesy of war'!" Johnson giggled.

Smede said, "I guess we've flushed a real mess of mean Rebels here. What do you say to this rifle, old man?"

"It's a hunting gun," Bruce answered. "Where did you find it?"

"*His* room," Johnson replied when Smede looked at him.

"I didn't know where it was. I had forgot it. You can tell it hasn't been fired recently. It was never used except to kill a squirrel or rabbit."

"It could kill a man if you hit him in the right spot. I don't have to tell you this bears out everything we've heard about you, waiting your chance to pick off some of us one day."

Bruce stared at Sergeant Smede. "Take me to Captain Ponder," he said. "I insist on your doing so. I'll tell him whatever he needs to know, but I can't seem to make you understand."

James said, "You must take us both. If your Captain Ponder is an officer, he may be a little more of a gentleman than you. Take us now, and leave my sister and my son alone, as they deserve."

Meecham guffawed. "Robert E. Lee is now laying down the conditions of surrender! Just listen!"

Prince gave James a hard shove that sent him stumbling further into the yard. When Benjamin tried to help him, Johnson grabbed the boy. Benjamin struggled with such force that he freed himself until Sergeant Smede hit him with the butt of the rifle he still held. Stunned, Benjamin tasted blood and realized that some teeth were loose.

In the middle of the yard James held out his hands, groping to find something to touch. Meecham rushed at him playfully from behind, kicking the back of his knees so that they buckled and chanting, "Blind man's buff! Blind man's buff!"

Another soldier darted in, and another, until there was a ragged circle around James, who swung his arms desperately, trying to find something or someone to hold. Whichever way he turned, there was always a man behind him to push or kick him. Smede watched the game with a half smile on his face, letting the soldiers have a minute of fun before he announced, "All right, enough. We've work to do."

Everything stopped at the words, everyone listened. James was left to grope air alone as the soldiers closed around their leader.

"Mendel and Clark."

"Here."

"Tie the old man to a tree so he faces the house and can see, but not too close." They took hold of Bruce and forced him to walk with them.

"Lipscomb and Meecham."

"Here, Sergeant."

"Take the woman to one of the cabins and tie her up."

Doreen was still on the ground with the corpse of Pharaoh. She made no resistance when Lipscomb took her arms from behind and pulled her to her feet. Meecham slipped his hunting knife from its sheath and quickly cut off the horse's genitals. Holding the bloody parts in front of Doreen's face, he said, "Want these for a souvenir, ma'am?" Doreen collapsed and had to be dragged by the two men.

"Scarborough."

"Here."

"Tie up the blind man, so he don't get into mischief. Don't matter where. Don't have to worry about him watching us, do we? Greene, take the boy somewhere out of the way, maybe one of the cabins. Tie him good and leave him. Mendel, when you and Clark get through with Grandpa, hitch the best they got to the biggest wagon they got. The rest of you, go through the house. I don't have to tell you what to look for, do I? Everything worth taking."

The soldiers set to work. In less than an hour the wagon was loaded. In the distance the Negroes stood watching silently. Sergeant Smede made a tour of the house when he was told the job was finished. So thorough had his men been, he found nothing to add to their plunder. Returning to the yard, he studied the loaded wagon with satisfaction, after which he whispered a few words to Clark and Mendel. They trotted back into the house, and Sergeant Smede went to the tree where Bruce Davis was tied. Bruce did not look at him, did not, in fact, look at anything. His eyes were open but lowered and empty of expression.

Sergeant Smede gripped Bruce by the hair to raise his head so that he was obliged to see. "What do you think of that?" he said. "I knew I was going to kill you when you opened the door today." Taking his pistol from its holster, he put the muzzle to Bruce's head and fired.

23.

Sergeant Smede saw the treasure wagon on its way to Highboro and then gave orders as to which of the remaining livestock was to be left and which driven along with a second wagon the men had loaded with food stores and such useful items as harness and well chains. That done, he told Clark and Mendel he had another job for them and that they were to come with him.

It was dark as the three trotted their horses off the main road and through the orchard. They found Sarah and Jane standing together in the front yard gazing off at the glow in the sky over Oaks. Sarah did not appear surprised to see the sergeant, but she took Jane by the hand.

"Thought I'd find you fine ladies working to get everything tidy again," Sergeant Smede said as a greeting.

"Have you come from Oaks?" she said.

Smede followed her eyes.

"Why have you come back?" Sarah asked.

"Well, you see," he said solemnly, "we didn't finish the job; and that's what we've come to do now."

"You mean to burn us too?"

His face relaxed, his eyes seeming to congratulate her on her quick understanding. "If we'd done it before, they would have seen it; and we didn't want them to expect us."

Clark and Mendel came up to stand behind the sergeant and stare at Sarah and Jane, and they shifted their feet as if impatient. "Maybe there's some little thing," Smede suggested, "you'd like to look at or take out before we do it."

He had surprised Sarah with the offer. "I can't think," she said. "I'll give you a minute. Clark, Mendel. Go in with the ladies."

Sarah appeared reluctant, but Jane said, "We can get our clothes."

Smede beamed at the child. "You go bring out what's most important to you."

"There's no light—" Sarah stopped, seeing the sergeant grin at her.

They found candles and lit them in the hallway. Then each of them, accompanied by a soldier, went into her room and gathered together her best articles of clothing. Sarah went into Nell's room and added some of hers to the collection she carried over one arm. When they came downstairs, Jane wanted to go into the drawing room. Clark accompanied her, Mendel following Sarah into the office, where she found two ledgers on the floor and a box containing documents. Going to find Jane in the drawing room, she saw that the child had retrieved the portrait of Leon that had been slashed. "I don't think it can be mended," she told her.

"I want it," Jane said.

Sarah's eyes caught Nell's rocking chair in the dim candlelight. One of the rockers had been broken and both arms were torn, but she decided the chair could be made good and that it might prove a comfort to Nell. Using its seat to carry clothes and office documents, she picked the chair up and followed Jane, who was dragging Leon's portrait with one hand as she held her own clothes on her other arm. The soldiers carefully blew out the candles when they reached the porch and stuck the stubs into the earth of a flower box.

Sergeant Smede, who sat on a garden bench a dozen yards beyond the porch, rose to meet them. He looked over the things they had set down on the ground in order to rest their arms. Picking up one of Jane's dresses, he ran a hand inside it. "Pretty," he said to her, and then to both of them, "These are the things you want most?"

The woman nodded, and so did the girl.

"You'd better move back a little way. It looks to me like the place will go up fast. How does it look to you men?"

Mendel said, "Oh, it will make a fine smoke."

"And a great fire," Clark added.

"I depend on you," Smede said. "Go to your work." But when

they started again to the house, his voice stopped them at the steps. "Come here a minute." They returned. "Take these things inside. They don't look like much to me."

Clark and Mendel looked at each other and then at Smede, but he had his eyes on Sarah and Jane.

"You mean their stuff here?" Clark said.

"Take it," Smede said.

The soldiers picked up the chair and the painting and the office records and the clothes and disappeared into the house again. Without a word Sarah found Jane's hand and led her into the dark and around the house. Smede did not stop them. Five minutes later the house began to burn. As Mendel had predicted, it made a fine smoke; and as Clark had added, it made a great fire.

24.

Daniel and Floyd never found much to say to one another, and their exchanges were spare as they returned to Beulah Land from the Shelter. Otis stayed on as guard and keeper. When Daniel announced his intention of leaving the island, Floyd told him that Sarah Kendrick would not approve his doing so. Daniel did not argue; he merely repeated that he was going and added, "If Miss Sarah does not want me at Beulah Land, I'll move on." He insisted upon walking all the way, although Floyd offered him turns on Bartholomew and even got off the mule now and then to walk for an hour as encouragement to the other to ride.

Thoughtful of Nell, Daniel had snared four rabbits before leaving the island that morning. Gutted but not skinned, they were tied together, two dangling from either side of the mule where Floyd had slung them in front of the saddle. The mule's motion brushed cold fur and stiffened claw against the hand he rested on the saddle horn. They kept a steady pace over the firm ground of the woodland trail, not stopping but eating as they went, sausages and baked sweet potatoes whose skins they peeled and dropped. It was dark when they passed through the site where the sawmill had been. Minutes later they entered the main road at the place Floyd had discovered Benjamin the night before and turned him around to go home.

"Something's burning," Daniel said.

Floyd pressed his knees into the mule's sides, and Bartholomew quickened his walk.

The road turned. Through the trees they could see that the Davis house stood no more. There were no people about.

"Do we go in?" Daniel asked.

"We go home!" Floyd replied hoarsely, his knees now clenched into Bartholomew's belly so hard the big mule began to trot, and so did Daniel, to keep up with them. A long curve of the road brought them in sight of the orchard, but when they took the carriageway through it, they saw desolation at its end. Nothing of the house was left except the two principal chimneys. One had served the drawing room and two bedrooms directly above it; the other had served the office and dining room on the ground floor, as well as rooms above them. The air was still warm from the fire. Bits of ash blew into their faces as they raced around the remains of the house to look for the living. The fig tree that had shaded the back steps before Floyd was born was burnt to a snaggle of stump, and the oaks that had gentled the suns of a hundred summers were blackened with soot.

The nearest barns were gone too. Beyond the water wells and the farther barns they came to the Negro living quarters and there finally saw people. The children were not playing but hurrying on errands in a hysteria of self-importance. Old men and old women stood together mumbling speculation and waiting for someone to pay attention to them. Sliding from the mule, Floyd went directly into his house. Lotus held a rolled mattress in her arms which she was about to carry next door. Seeing Floyd, she dropped the bundle and lurched toward him with her arms stiffly open.

He took her and held her hard. "They came."

"Two times. After dinner and again tonight."

They said no more until their hands had groped over each other, wanting evidence of wholeness after assurance of survival. There Lovey lay on the bed, eyes closed, hands folded over her Then he said, "Where's the mistress?"

"Next door in your mama's house. I was taking this mattress to her. Her and the child and Miss Nell. She says that's where they'll stay. Their house is gone now."

"I saw."

"*Gone!*" she repeated, incredulous.

"Is Mama here?"

"Lovey?" He knew she was dead by the way Lotus said her name.

"What happened to her?"

"Well, she tried to stop them from digging up your papa's grave. They knocked her in the head same as you'd kill a hog."

"Where is she?"

"I just finished washing and dressing her." She motioned her head toward the bedroom beyond them. Floyd went to the door. There Lovey lay on the bed, eyes closed, hands folded over her bosom as no one had ever seen them. She looked nothing like Lovey alive. Lotus had come to stand beside him, but neither moved into the bedroom.

Floyd turned then and looked sharply at Lotus. "Did they— did they *do* you?"

She would not look at him, but stood with head bowed as if in apology. He put a hand to her face and felt tears. "My poor baby," he said, meaning her as well as the child she carried.

Encouraged, she said, "They like to have killed Nancy. I went to help her and then's when—"

"Sh. Sh." He patted her face with both hands. "I better go see about things."

She was as eager for him to leave her as she had earlier been for him to come to her. "They need telling what to do. Some run off to the woods to hide. Some run off, it looked like forever. You go tell *everybody* what to do and they'll feel better!"

Daniel had gone to the door of Lovey's house as Floyd entered his. Stepping from the yard directly into the kitchen, he found Sarah and Jane. They were at a worktable, Jane peeling turnips and Sarah peeling onions. Seeing him in the doorway, Jane dropped her work and ran to him. When she threw her arms around his waist, he bent to hug her clumsily, looking over her head at Sarah, who was motionless, staring at him.

"They burned Oaks too," Daniel said. "We passed it on our way but met nobody."

Sarah said, "We saw the fire before they came back to burn us."

"They killed Grandpa!" Jane keened against him. She had not wept since the soldier smashed the doll's trunk that afternoon.

"Did they?" he said in soft astonishment, and patted her shoulder.

"Doreen and James are all right," Sarah said.

Jane let Daniel go and turned to hide her face. Her tears stopped as if she willed them to, ashamed of them. "Yes," she said. "That is surely a good thing, isn't it? Benjamin is all right. They only beat him a little and tied him down for a while."

"Floyd told me he tried to come with him to the Shelter last night."

"I wish Floyd had let him!" Sarah declared.

Daniel said, "Miss Sarah, why did they come? They've been here so many times taking and stealing. Why did they want to do all this to you?"

Jane looked at her grandmother as if to silence her, but Sarah was already answering. "Who can say? Maybe they had new orders."

"How many were there?"

"Eight at first, led by a Sergeant Billy Smede. Then the sergeant came back with just two—new ones I'd never seen before; and they put the fire to us. That was after they'd done it to Oaks."

"Benjamin was here and told us," Jane said. "He came when he saw us burning, but then he went back. He wouldn't stay."

"Thank God Floyd is home," Sarah said briskly. "He'll look after the people."

"I'll go help him however I can," Daniel said. At the door he stopped. "Miss Sarah, what are you going to do?"

She looked at him interestedly as if he had asked a question she had not yet considered. "Well," she said when she had thought a moment. "One thing we've all forgot, even Aunt Nell, is to eat. I know it's late, but late's not going to mean a thing this night. Lotus brought some onions and turnips, and one of the other women gave Nancy a piece of fatback, and she gave it to me. I told Lotus I'd cook for all of us tonight; she's got so much else to do."

Nell came from the other room. "So there you are!" she said in triumphant accusation when she saw Daniel. "Now see what your fine soldiers have done to us!"

"Aunt Nell!" Jane screamed at her.

"Don't holler at me, child!"

Daniel looked about to cry, and Sarah thought he had never seemed such a boy to her.

"Miss Nell? I was thinking about you this morning before we left the island, and I've brought you something. Wait a minute." He ran out the door and returned before a minute was up, holding the four rabbits high in one hand.

"Well now!" Nell exclaimed, as they all stared at his gift. To Daniel she said, "Thought of me, did you? You're not such a bad old boy. Take them out, and skin the things, and bring them back. Be sure you wash them good if they've been dead all day! They took the chains off the wells, but somebody has rigged a rope on one of them. We'll have us a big stew, won't we!" Daniel left with the rabbits, and she turned again to Sarah. "I'll just build up the fire in this stove while you peel onions." Wadding a handful of her skirt, she opened the hot iron door of the fire compartment and threw in a piece of wood. "Old stove wasn't used much, was it? Wasted on Lovey; never cooked at home, let her family eat in our kitchen. That's why they grew up fat and strong. Only used when Ezra steamed his cures and remedies." Satisfied that the fire was going well, she slammed the door on it. "They'll smell our cooking, and everybody will come."

She was right. Smelling the food, they did come. No one bothered to sit down; but at one time or another more than a dozen came and filled a plate from the big pot on the stove, to which Sarah and Jane continued to add ingredients as they were offered. One brought potatoes, another a string of onions and a hunk of ham hock, another a sealed jar of tomatoes, and another a handful of rice. Nell presided over the stew pot and served the plates held up for her. When someone asked timidly if there was enough, she said merely, "A gracious plenty. It's like the loaves and fishes in the Bible; it multiplies to fill the need. Have another spoonful. I didn't mean to be stingy with you." In years to come they would talk of Nell and her stewpot that night. It was something they all remembered.

Sarah was in and out. Sometimes alone, often with Floyd, she went the round of the cabins and the barns left standing, to reassure and comfort where she could, to assess what had been lost and what had been spared to them. Most of the poultry had been taken; only a few guinea fowls and geese remained. There were three old cows and five hogs that had turned wild and vi-

cious, as swine will, and resisted capture by the raiders. No horse
was left to them, but two oxen remained, and two of the older
mules. And there was Bartholomew. There was no flour and little
cornmeal. Four hams, two tubs of lard, six gallons of syrup, and
a couple of dozen feet of link sausage had been hidden successfully in a corncrib where nobody, curiously, had bothered to
search. The dried corn still on the cob had not been touched by
the raiders, who did not want the trouble of milling it when
cornmeal was already in good supply.

No head count of people had been made, but there appeared
to be still between twenty-five and thirty, mainly the young and
the old, but a few in the middle years who would earn their
keep. Together Sarah and Lotus went into each cabin to make
certain everyone had a quilt to cover him for the night and to
give a promise of sharing things out evenly tomorrow. The
Negroes had been robbed of money and their belongings as had
the Kendricks, and some had been beaten when they resisted.

But people will yawn though the gallows wait, and sometime
after midnight Nell and Jane went to bed in what had been
Lovey's room. Daniel took as his the little room off the kitchen
which Floyd had shared when he was a boy with his father's sick
animals. Sarah did not want to sleep. Wearing her old brown
shawl, she went about counting and sorting, touching and holding. At four o'clock in the morning she found Floyd in the blacksmith shed, where Zebra was finishing work on Lovey's coffin.
They watched him hammer in the last nails as he took them from
his pink mouth, and they decided to bury Lovey at first light.

When it was finished, they took the coffin to Floyd's house,
where Lotus had slept a few hours beside the corpse. They ate
milk and bread together, and then Sarah and Lotus put Lovey
into the coffin, and Floyd and Zebra closed it and nailed it
securely. The two men carried the long box to the grave where
Ezra's bones waited to be reburied. They attempted no service
or ceremony, but settled the two coffins snugly together at the
bottom of the dark cavity. Floyd and Zebra filled in the loose
earth and then, grunting and swearing, shifted the heavy slab
onto the double grave. The two women stood watching, hugging
themselves against the morning cold. If any said a prayer, he
said it to himself.

25.

When she had seen Lovey buried, Sarah went back to the cabin that had been Lovey's and now was hers. She did not disturb Nell and Jane, but unrolled the corn-shuck mattress Lotus had brought the night before and stretched it on the kitchen floor. Lying down upon it still dressed, she slept for an hour, waking and sitting bolt-upright when she heard whispers. She had been dreaming. Of what? The images vanished the instant she woke. Nell and Jane were gazing at her. "Go to the well and get fresh water," she said to Jane. Jane hesitated a moment before reaching for a bucket on the floor by the cook stove and going out.

"Funny way to sleep," Nell said. She peered into the woodbox behind the stove and found two sticks of pine kindling. "There was plenty of room on the bed with me and Jane. She's skinny and I'm short."

"We'll have things orderly tonight," Sarah said.

There was the sound of a rooster crowing. "Listen to him," Nell said. "There's a bundle of feathers that hasn't been plucked to stuff a Yankee's gut." She shook down the ashes in the stove and started a fire, adding pieces of stove wood when the kindling caught properly.

Sarah dragged the mattress into the bedroom out of the way, then tied a kerchief around her head, seeing that her hair was askew and not wanting to take time to make it neat. When she returned to the kitchen, Daniel was coming through the door with a pail half full of milk. "All the old cow would give," he said, setting the pail on the table.

"I'll strain it," Sarah said, and looked around for a clean cloth.

"Bet it tastes funny," Nell said. "The least thing can change the taste of milk. The worst is after they've eaten chinaberry leaves. We had to throw away four gallons one time when the cows wandered and nobody saw them till too late. Remember?"

Jane came from the yard with a bucket of water. "Zebra's got another well working," she said. "See what he gave me?" Setting the water down, she presented them with four eggs she had carried in the lifted hem of her skirt.

"Breakfast," Nell said with satisfaction.

After breakfast Floyd and Daniel settled to the day's work. Daniel, it was decided, would lead a party of men to clean out and reorganize the barns. The ashes of the old house were still smoking in some places, but in others it was possible to begin salvaging bricks and carting away melted glass and charred timbers and other such debris. Several days would be required to clear the ground, but Sarah had told Floyd, and he had agreed, that it should be done as soon as possible. She would not look on that waste longer than necessary; nor did she want their people to do so. When he opened the question of where she and Nell were to live, she said, "Where we live now."

"You could move into town and be comfortable while we build you something better."

"Lovey lived in it most of her life. We'll manage."

Sarah and Lotus, accompanied by Jane, went in and out of the cabins doing more thoroughly what they had done hastily the night before: providing assurance that Beulah Land would go on and finding out what was required most urgently by the families, with particular attention to the old and the ailing.

Nell attended to the visitors, who began to arrive before nine o'clock. During the course of the day half the town and county came, compelled to see with their own eyes that the great house was indeed no longer there.

Beulah Land had a special meaning for those who knew it. Their feeling was not love, but it sometimes included it. Rather, it was a kind of dependence. It had been there all their lives. They had seen four generations of Kendricks live and die in scandal and decorum. Though the land remained, the house had been the symbol of Beulah Land, and so the shock of its destruction was great.

It was certainly greater than Captain Abel Ponder had anticipated, and as word came to him of the heavy flow of people and gifts to the Kendricks, he began to worry. Determined to get what he could from his position, he nevertheless understood that if his administration stirred up unrest, he would pay for it.

On the evening before, when Sergeant Billy Smede had given a report of his day's work, Ponder had been pleased. Going to supper at Junior Elk's, he found only Dorothy and her son to give him company. Junior would return soon, Dorothy promised. He had wanted to watch the fire and had ridden out to his own farm, still called the Anderson Place from the name of the family that had lost it to Junior's father. The Anderson Place bordered short sections of Oaks and Beulah Land, and the old man had hoped to increase its acreage at the expense of Beulah Land's. Captain Ponder was not sorry to be alone with Dorothy Elk and took advantage of their near privacy to give her a ring of oriental topaz that had belonged to Nell Kendrick, and which was a minor item in his share of the spoils. If the boy Roscoe would leave them, he thought, he might suggest a really private meeting with Dorothy, who sat simpering with pleasure over the ring and turning it under the oil lamp to examine it. But Roscoe sat glowering at both of them, hardly looking at his plate as he ate, although not neglecting it either. Junior returned before they finished their meal, and then the evening became one of mutual congratulation and planning. Dorothy sat twisting the new ring on her finger, and yawning, but the boy listened to all they said until his father sent both him and Dorothy to bed.

"Fine son," Captain Ponder observed mechanically, his eyes on Dorothy Elk's behind as she followed the boy out of the parlor.

Junior frowned thoughtfully. "I'm thinking of sending him up North to school, to get him away from down here a while. Be a good idea, you think?" Captain Ponder grunted politely. The evening ended with expressions of trust and confidence and with unexpressed doubts. When Junior closed the door on his guest, he went to the dining room for a glass of brandy and returned to sit in the parlor alone for an hour with no light but that from the fireplace. Once he laughed aloud, thinking how his father would have enjoyed the sight of the burning plantation house. He had got Captain Ponder to do what he wanted, and the next moves would be his. However, if he needed more favors from the commander, he knew the way to get them. He had not missed the ring on Dorothy's finger, and he had understood the implication of nobody's speaking of it.

Geraldine, the woman who kept his house and sometimes shared her bed with him, came into the room. She collected the glasses and coffee cups from Captain Ponder's visit and, starting out of the room, paused to say, "You want me tonight?"

"When I want you, I'll come."

She left him, and he slowly finished his brandy. Looking into the fireplace, he thought again of the larger fire, seeing in this little one before him a miniature reenactment of the day's main event. With surprise he felt himself getting an erection. He waited a little while, expecting it to subside, and when it did not he got up and walked through the dining room and the kitchen to Geraldine's room just beyond. She was undressing and stood in the middle of the room, her dress over her head. When she saw him, she said, "Oh."

Captain Ponder was relieved when the next afternoon Sergeant Smede took his written orders, his horse, and a mule to carry his belongings and rode out of Highboro. The trains had stopped running, and he would have to make his way to Savannah to find a boat to take him home to his wife. Floyd was another witness to his departure. He had taken Bartholomew into town to see what he could buy to replace broken farm tools and to inquire cautiously about the man who had led the raids yesterday. A sentry, who did not know or care who Floyd was, seemed proud to point and say, "That is Sergeant Billy Smede. There he goes now. See him? Fat, short fellow and mean as a snapping turtle. On his way home, done with this war. Whatever you want with him, you're too late. You wouldn't have no chewing tobacco on you, would you, nigger?"

At Beulah Land the callers came and went, and Nell received them, explaining that Sarah was busy sorting out the plantation's business. Only the most determined found her to pay their respects and to offer their sympathy. Some were honest in their concern; others merely wanted to tell acquaintances they had seen the mistress of Beulah Land and that she was a defeated woman. It was like the instinct that makes long lines file past the coffins of the great, furnishing as it does a comforting sense of superiority to the living herd of commoner men and women. One of the more persistent who found Sarah was Stewart Throckmorton. She was inspecting a box of cheese she had hidden in her outdoor earthen icehouse, which the soldiers had not discovered. After a few words of sympathy the rector expressed it as his earnest hope that she did not hate her enemy.

"Oh, but I do," she admitted.

"You mustn't, my child. The Lord commands us to love and forgive."

Sarah stared at him briefly. "Perhaps you should go to my

friend Bruce Davis and do what you can for him—and for his son and daughter."

"Do not trouble your heart there. Rest assured: all has been done. I have just come from them, having gone out with the elder daughter, Mrs. Saxon, who arranged for the coffin and took charge of other practical matters. It is a great tragedy."

"Surely you mean a great crime."

He smiled admonishingly. "And one we may never altogether understand. There is talk in town that the Union commander had received information that Mr. Davis was preparing to lead a counter-rebellion, and they did, in fact, discover on the premises a supply of hidden weapons."

"Lies!" Sarah said.

"Which of us knows his neighbor?" He smiled patiently. "I repeat only what is common currency. I do not say I put full faith in it; I am certain there must have been a great misunderstanding. I daresay Captain Ponder acted with sincerity and conviction, however mistaken he may have been in his overall suspicions." Sarah looked at him, astonished. "There has also been considerable speculation about the unknown white man who has been seen working with your people. Some have suggested—"

"He is a cousin," Sarah interrupted brusquely.

"Ah. And is he then—?"

"I must ask you to excuse me, for I am very busy today."

Most of the callers, however, were content with being received by Nell Kendrick, who was attended by Nancy. With the resilience of youth Nancy had recovered some of her verve and had even begun to find events interesting. She also enjoyed setting the visitors' gifts in orderly rows, and when the kitchen became crowded with the offerings of foodstuffs and clothes and quilts and dishes, she moved the more ordinary items into the bedroom. Her favorite among the presentations, and undoubtedly one of the most exotic, was a gilded birdcage that was the contribution of a choir singer named Eloise Kilmer, who also enjoyed local renown as a poetess and read to Nell and Nancy a poem she had composed for the occasion. Nancy was much moved by it and responded with a graphic account of her own misadventures during the attack.

"I reckon I have been through as much as anybody," she declared. "They raped me; so many of them, we all lost count."

"You poor creature!" Miss Kilmer exclaimed. "Surely you are not fit to be up and around but should be resting in bed!"

"Well'm," Nancy said agreeably, "that may be so, but if you had been through what I have, you'd think twice before you flopped on your back and closed your eyes, not knowing who might come along and take advantage."

Of the many who attended them that day, Selma, with Lauretta and Pauline, were among the first. They urged Nell to persuade Sarah to move immediately to town. Selma insisted that she could easily accommodate them in her house. Nell, who had been born in the town and lived there most of her married life, had no desire to leave the country; she had long ago learned to appreciate its isolation and abundance. So she said, "Sarah wouldn't hear of it, try to persuade her though I might." She accorded them a sigh. "She will stay on here, I am perfectly certain."

"Then *I* shall persuade her, see if I don't!" Lauretta declared, and marched out of the cabin to look for her sister. She found her in the chicken run, face to face with an enormous goose, each looking alarmed and threatening, both hesitating to give an inch lest she be attacked. Lauretta picked up a stick and threw it at the goose, hitting Sarah on the knee but surprising the goose into turning away as she approached. Studying her sister disapprovingly, Lauretta said, "I wouldn't be seen in that dress if they asked me to play Juliet's nurse."

Rubbing her knee, Sarah said, "What do you want?"

"*You* appear to be on the wanting end of the stick this time, dear Sarah. How you survived the night I cannot imagine. Tell me what I can do for you and I shall do it."

Sarah said, "Find me five horses, a dozen mules, and a hundred workers to make Beulah Land what it was again."

"Beulah Land is gone. It no longer exists."

"Look around you."

"I've come to tell you we have all decided you are to move to Highboro and live with us."

"It wouldn't suit me, thank you."

"Beulah Land is in ashes. You are no longer mistress of a great plantation."

Sarah took a breath, held it as long as she could, and let it out. "Nevertheless, I intend to stay."

"You mustn't expect us to encourage your pride."

Sarah turned and went into a corncrib, Lauretta following her. Three old women were settled on the floor shucking corn. Without greeting them, Sarah began to work with them, throwing the clean ears into a center pile. "Thank God there's corn left to us," she said. "If you want to help, Lauretta, start shelling the kernels into one of those pans. We're getting it ready to send to the mill. They took all our meal."

"I did not come out here to shell corn."

"Then you may watch us." The Negro women continued working after brief glances at Lauretta, whom they knew as well as they knew each other.

"Poor Sarah," Lauretta presently observed, as if to herself. "To care so much about anything."

Sarah held her breath again, letting it out only when she had to. "You've heard about Bruce Davis, I trust."

"Yes!" Lauretta relaxed visibly as if she felt herself on safer ground where they might finally exchange sympathy. "Poor old Bruce, how I pity him and grieve over what has occurred. And when I think of what might have been! If not for Annabel Saxon, I could be his widow!"

"Did he ask you to marry him?"

"I have every reason to believe he was on the point of doing so. You will agree that I have experience in these matters."

"When did Annabel perform such a disservice to you?" Sarah said quietly.

"I don't like to remind you at a time like this, but it was on the very night Rachel died."

"Ah," Sarah said. "He asked me to marry him a month before."

"Asked you? Asked *you*? Can you be serious?"

"Yes, certainly; it was not the first time; he was forever asking me."

Lauretta slapped Sarah so hard the ear of corn she was shucking flew from her hands, almost hitting one of the Negro women, all of whom stared at Lauretta as if she had gone mad. Sarah began to laugh.

"You fool!" Lauretta screamed. "What do you have to laugh about?"

"It simply occurred to me that something finally has happened I can understand."

Lauretta turned and swept out of the corncrib.

"Lauretta!" Sarah's voice was urgent. Lauretta paused, but she did not look back at her sister, who continued earnestly, "If you'd like to do something helpful, send me some salt. Nobody has thought of it, and I can't eat without salt."

26.

At Oaks there were visitors too, many of them the same as had gone first to Beulah Land. Oaks, although nearly as large as Beulah Land, always came second to mind, almost as if it were a part of its neighbor, such were the long and often intimate connections between the Kendrick and Davis families. Annabel Saxon did not arrive until midmorning, although she had been sent news the night before of the raid's toll. She came with the rector and a coffin for her father. If she did not bring much comfort to the survivors, she was at any rate ready with criticism and commands and slipped easily into the role of hostess to visitors who followed her with condolences and more practical aid. James was fit to see no one. Doreen and Benjamin were busy. Bruce, funereally garbed and coffined, provided grim illustration to Annabel's recital of woe and hate.

The night before had been a long and busy one at Oaks. When the raiding party left death and destruction behind them, the Negroes came in from the safe distance where they had stood watching. Unused to commanding themselves, they drifted about exclaiming at what they found until one among them named Zadok assumed command. He sent Flossie to look for Doreen and tell her what had happened. He found James and released him, giving him into the care of his wife Rosalie when he saw that James was incapable of helping them or himself. By this time Benjamin had been discovered and freed. Together Zadok and Benjamin untied the ropes that still held Bruce's bleeding body to the tree and laid him on the ground. Passing his hand gently and curiously over the still face, the boy closed the man's eyes and continued to squat beside him a minute or two longer. Then he and Zadok, with no spoken agreement between them,

went about giving practical directions, the presence of each en-
forcing the new authority of the other. By the time Doreen had
collected herself enough to join them, she saw what they were
doing and was glad to acknowledge them by referring others to
them for decisions.

There was no question of attempting to put out the fire. The
house and all in it were beyond saving. But a party of four men
was told to collect all the livestock they could find and put the
animals safely into the barn farthest from the blaze. Two women
were assigned to take Bruce Davis's body to one of the cabins, to
bathe him, dress him, watch over him. Another several women
offered to bring together all the food supplies and to cook
enough to feed those who remained. After consulting with
Doreen, Zadok arranged that a hole be dug beside Pharaoh's
carcass and that he be buried in it immediately. This was done
while the big fire still lighted the night. At some time Benjamin
ran over to Beulah Land, gave Oaks' news, heard theirs, and refusing to linger, ran all the way home again. He went with Flossie to take food to his father. James listened silently to what Benjamin had to tell him, and the boy spoke plainly and
unemotionally. It was not that he had no feelings but that he instinctively put them aside for the time so that he could act.
James began to accept bits of food from Flossie, and Benjamin
left them together, going back to stand with Doreen as the men,
using ropes and two oxen, pulled and finally tumbled Pharoah's
body into his grave. When they covered him over, they began to
stamp and press the earth in firmly. Doreen and Benjamin
walked over the wide grave with the men, round and round,
pressing their feet in deep and hard, as if performing some ancient ceremony.

Zadok said he would stay awake and keep watch over the fire.
For a long time a little crowd watched with him, but one by one
they talked themselves out of words, and shook their heads out
of wonder, and drifted away to sleep what was left of the night.
Finally none was awake but Zadok. Benjamin slept on the
ground beside him, his body curled in a fetal circle on a couple
of cotton sacks somebody had put down for him. He had refused
to go with Doreen to Flossie's cabin for the night. Now and then
Zadok looked from the slowly dying fire to the sleeping boy, and
for a minute he would close his eyes, but he did not sleep. As
day broke, Rosalie brought fried meat and flour hoecake in two

tin pans. Zadok woke Benjamin, and they ate together. All his life Benjamin remembered that as the night he and Zadok came to know each other. Zadok had seen the boy every day since Benjamin was born, but neither had been much aware of the other. It had taken the eruption of violence to make them know they shared a commitment. That is how it sometimes happens. After eating they walked about looking at things and talking as if they had done just that every morning of their lives. Only once did their words show the newness of their present relationship. Benjamin asked Zadok how old he was.

"Thirty-one," Zadok answered.

"I wonder if I will live to be that old," Benjamin said.

Zadok did not laugh or try to reassure the boy, but said seriously, "I don't know, Mister Ben." It was the first time Benjamin had been called "Mister" and it made him feel grown.

27.

Sarah had lived through crises enough to know that every hour she could put between herself and a bad event helped preserve her sanity. She never stopped that day. Even when she appeared to, her hands and her voice were busy. She was sustained by a fever of energy such as great pain or great happiness engenders for a time. As she went here, there, and yonder, she was both inside and outside herself. "That is me," she would think, "talking calmly to this woman as if I had good sense, when what I feel like doing is screaming my head off, or cursing God, or shooting down the whole world if I had a cannon big enough."

When late in the afternoon Nancy came running to find her to say that Captain Abel Ponder was waiting at Lovey's cabin to see her, she believed for an instant that her brain had cracked; but she breathed, she blinked, and Nancy was still there before her waiting to hear what she would say. What she said was "Well," adding a moment later, "I'll come."

Word of the district commander's presence had spread among the Negroes, and since he had ridden up alone and it was the end of the day, they left their work and gathered about Lovey's cabin, maintaining a polite distance but making a strong presence as they waited to observe whatever was about to occur. Inside the kitchen Nell sat on a hide-bottomed straight chair that had been Lovey's, Jane standing beside her. They were as motionless as if posing for a portrait photographer. Abel Ponder stood uncomfortably outside the doorway. He had not expected his meeting with Sarah Kendrick to be so largely attended. As he saw her approaching, he stepped forward to meet her.

"Mrs. Sarah Kendrick?"

"I am."

"I have come to see you." When her eyes refused to acknowledge that she knew who he was, he added stiffly, "Captain Abel Ponder, commander of this military district."

She nodded once and waited.

"Can we step inside?"

Sarah glanced around, becoming aware for the first time of the groups of silent, watching Negroes. "I cannot think anything you have come for would be improperly spoken in front of our people. However—" She gestured for him to enter the cabin, and when he had done so, she followed him, and the groups of Negroes edged closer.

Another silence ensued. The commander had no gift for words, and he had not thought before he came of just what he would say. Soldierlike, he trusted circumstances to point the way. "I came to ask you some things and to tell you some things. —Do you want the child here?"

"She was present during the—visitation of Sergeant Smede and his men. It is her home as well as mine."

"First I ought to tell you: Sergeant Smede is no longer active in my service forces. He has been given leave to go to his wife, who is, I believe, ah—deathly ill." Sarah's face was impassive. "I have thought perhaps that fact, the fact that he knew her to be so sick, may have influenced his actions yesterday." He paused, frowning, as if inviting her to share his speculation, but she did not. "He is a very efficient, I grant, a most conscientious soldier. However, he may have gone a little further than his orders strictly intended. Now, my understanding, the report he gave me before he left the company today, was that you and this lady here and the little girl were uncooperative in the extreme." Sarah could not help it; her eyebrows lifted, but she managed to stop the words that came into her head.

What she would not say to oblige him, Nell did. "Un-co-opera-tive!" she exclaimed. "Did he expect us to kiss the ax he raised to our heads, sir?"

"Aunt Nell!" Sarah's tone commanded her to be quiet.

"Your savages—yes, *savages*—have done their worst!" Nell continued. "Have you come to tell us now that it was a mistake?"

"Aunt *Nell!*" Sarah pleaded.

"Since you cannot unburn a house, unmurder an old woman who tried to protect her husband's grave from desecration, and cannot unrape our younger women, may we assume that after your apologies, you intend to return all that was stolen?"

"Madam!" the Captain thundered, strengthened by her out-burst. "I make you no apologies! I offer to return nothing! You are Rebels! Will you try to understand that? Rebels! Not fine la-dies any more, ordering your slaves around and trying to break up the Union! My men came to you on a serious mission—to look for a man said on authority to be hiding here and said also to be a deserter from the Union Army and a traitor to the United States of America!"

"I told the sergeant there was no such man and never had been," Sarah declared.

"Do you tell *me* that?"

"I do," she said as quietly as she could. "There is no such man. Our cousin was here for a time, but no one we should have re-ported to you—"

The door to the room off the kitchen swung open, and Daniel came in. His face was pale, his manner agitated.

Captain Ponder drew his pistol and held it in the air without pointing it. "Who are you?" he demanded.

"My cousin," Sarah supplied quickly.

"Confound you, madam! You have been silent enough till now, God knows. Let the man speak for himself if he can!"

"Daniel Todd by name," Daniel said.

"You do not have the Rebel sound in your voice."

"I grew up in Missouri, far from these good people," Daniel said.

"She says you are a cousin."

"Yes, sir."

"You are no Southerner."

"My people took the side of the Confederacy."

"You fought with the Rebels?"

"Yes, sir. C.S.A."

"You claim to come from Missouri—"

"I do, sir."

"Born there?"

"I was."

"Raised there too?"

"Yes, sir."

"What relation are you to this woman?"

Daniel looked at Sarah. "Her cousin."

The commander turned to Sarah. "Will you say again that he is your cousin?"

"Yes. Of course he is."

"And from Missouri?"

Sarah remembered then, a second before he reminded her, and remembered too that there had been no time to tell Daniel. "Yet you told Sergeant Smede the cousin staying with you was on his way *home*. Headed *south* when he left here." He faced Daniel quickly. "Where were you going when you left, *if* you left?"

Sarah said, "A farm in Glynn County, near Brunswick, Georgia."

The commander blinked angrily and said to Daniel, "Where is Glynn County?"

"South of here," Daniel said.

"On the coast," Sarah said.

"Will you keep silent until I ask you to speak!" He addressed himself again to Daniel. "What do you grow on this farm in Glynn County?"

"Rice. It's low—coastland. Like my cousin has said. I was telling her about it."

To Sarah he said, "You assured Sergeant Smede he wasn't here."

"And so he wasn't when your men came."

"Where were you?" he asked Daniel.

"I'd started on my way, but I've been sick, and I was weaker than I knew. I was sure I couldn't get back to Missouri, but I figured I'd be better off if I could get to this other part of the family down in Glynn County near Brunswick, Georgia."

Nell said, "He's had the dysentery. That's why they let him out from the Army."

"After Atlanta was taken," Jane added.

"What was your outfit?" the Captain asked Daniel.

Daniel had planned that answer. "Second platoon, Company C, First Battalion, Missouri Rifle Volunteers."

"Missouri is not part of what you call the Confederacy."

"No, sir. We were all volunteers."

"You feel strong about the Rebel cause?"

"My pa did. He was responsible, you could say, for my going into the Army."

Captain Ponder looked from one to another in the room, and then his eyes repeated their inspection of the faces. When he came to Sarah's for the third time, he said, "Tell me again: who is he?"

"He is our cousin," Sarah said.

"How is he your cousin?"

"My father's name was Pennington, and so was his mother's. They—we were Savannah people. I was born and grew up there on Broughton Street. His mother went with a party out to Missouri, where she married a Todd. Daniel passed through once or twice before when he went to stay with his other folks down in Glynn County. We did not keep in close touch, the various branches of the family; but we always knew generally where each other lived. Names and news get repeated sometimes by strangers traveling, not just in letters. Southerners are great travelers and talkers."

"So I understand," he said grimly, and looked at Daniel. "Now you tell me again."

Daniel said, "It's just the way she says."

When he glanced at her, Jane said without being asked, "Yes, sir, he's our cousin, from Missouri and Glynn County."

Captain Ponder's eyes came to rest on Nell. "You are an old woman and can't have many years left to speak truth or lies. Do you swear on your soul this man's a relative and not a Union soldier?"

"Old woman indeed! Just the kind of thing I'd expect a Yankee to say; no manners—"

"Answer me, old woman!"

"He is one of us," Nell said. "I swear it on my soul—and yours, if you've got one."

Abel Ponder opened the door, then lunged back suddenly to grab Daniel by the shoulder and thrust him into the open yard.

The two women and the girl followed. The commander still held his pistol in one hand, not threateningly but as a reminder of his position and power. The Negroes stopped their talk and stood still. "Who is this man?" the Captain asked at large. "Who will tell me who he is?"

Nancy came forward. "Mister Daniel!" she cried. "I declare, I thought you was long gone from here, on your way down to them other folks of yours in Glynn County! Did you get to feeling sick again?"

"Yes, Nancy," Daniel said weakly.

"Ain't that a shame! Same trouble you been had?"

"Just the same."

"Enough," Ponder said. Lotus stepped forward and took Nancy by the arm. "You, woman. Will you tell me who he is?"

Lotus said, "Everybody knows that, sir. Miss Sarah's cousin."

Captain Ponder slipped his pistol into its holster. Without looking again at Sarah or Nell or Jane or Daniel, he called, "Where has my horse got to, you lying black bastards? Bring him to me!" Through the quiet crowd of men and women, Zebra came walking the commander's horse.

28.

At noon Annabel Saxon had decided that it was not fit that her father's coffin be any longer on display in a slave cabin, although an hour before she had found satisfaction in the incongruity of it. She announced to Doreen and James that she was taking the body to Highboro, where their large acquaintance might see their parent decently mourned and properly buried from her own house. Doreen sought a private moment to ask that her sister take James to stay with her until she sorted out matters at Oaks and decided how they were to live. Annabel was glad to accede, for the arrangement seemed to defer to her superior position. James making no objection, indeed looking on it as his duty to accompany his father's body until its final disposal, they soon set off for town. Annabel promised to return late in the afternoon with whatever necessaries and home comforts she could spare to those remaining on the plantation.

So many things begged to be done there was no wasted effort that day by Zadok and Benjamin and the Negro workers. If the central blackened gap left by the burnt house was hard to look around or beyond, still they did what they could, all possessed of an energy and inclination to make things orderly again. Although Benjamin had considered his going about the barns and fields with his grandfather a form of play, their tours now proved their value. He knew where everything was or should be, and he understood pretty clearly how everything ought to be done. So, of course, did Zadok, who might have spent his life at Oaks preparing for this moment to become its overseer. Bruce Davis had been his own plantation manager. Zadok would be Benjamin and Doreen's. There was no question of treating James as the master of Oaks, except in the ways of courtesy and family feeling. He had not accommodated himself to his blindness when he suffered the news of his wife's death, and his state of distraction at that had been compounded by the murder of his father. He would discover his place perhaps when life returned to simpler patterns. Until then, it was natural for Benjamin and Zadok to take charge. The men accepted them easily. Benjamin's lack of age and experience were less important than the fact that he was male and white and a true Davis who had been observed being trained to his position by the old master of Oaks.

With Rosalie's help, Doreen organized the women's work. Flossie and the cook Marie did well enough if they were given orders and watched, but they had no initiative. Nor, Rosalie decided, had they much gumption when it came to meeting new circumstances. With people coming and going, Doreen was often required to drop her ordinary tasks after Annabel left, and to assume the role of hostess, or at least receiver of guests.

Two of these, who came together in their buggy at four o'clock, were the sisters Ann-Elizabeth Dupree and Margaret-Ella Singletary. They had been Annabel's friends since they were girls and rivals as to whose sitting to the painter Casey Troy would produce the most elegant portrait. Mrs. Dupree and Mrs. Singletary had been loyal lieutenants to Annabel's bullying captain through the war until for practical reasons they admitted Union officers to board at their houses, whereupon Annabel heaped her curses upon their heads and declared there could never be reconciliation. Annabel had always patronized them for having only daughters whereas she had produced sons. They had, over the years, rubbed one another raw in a hundred daily ways. Now natural enemies had found reason and excuse enough for mutual disfavor and estrangement.

In the past Margaret-Ella and Ann-Elizabeth had had no time for Doreen, she being younger by a couple of years when they were all young, and a spinster since the sisters were married and mothers. With the burning of Oaks, however, they were moved to magnanimity and arrived in their buggy carrying a pan of gingerbread and several old frocks they told her might be useful for the slaves, although they were "good enough for anyone to wear," they felt satisfied. Doreen thanked them for their gifts and found seating for them in the cabin.

Having looked about them before they entered, they were ready with words of despairing comfort. "Horrible, horrible!" Ann-Elizabeth cried. "The very worst thing that could have happened to anyone!"

"Mr. Davis such a *good* man!" Margaret-Ella observed.

"A generous master, a kind neighbor," Ann-Elizabeth intoned.

"All that has happened to us and ours pales into insignificance compared to your misfortunes—"

"How can the Lord allow the wicked so to prosper?"

On they went, gratifyingly deferential to one they had hitherto snubbed or ignored, until Doreen began to wonder when they would finish and leave her to get back to her work.

"Of course, we used to be such friends with your sister, but Miss Annabel simply would not understand that we were looking out for the good of our own families when we allowed Union officers to take their board at our tables. I hope you do not censure us for treading what we consider the prudent path."

"Oh? Certainly not," Doreen said. She had been only half listening. "I'm certain you've done whatever was best."

"Exactly," Margaret-Ella agreed. "It meant we didn't have to beg our very bread. Pride is all very well, and we wish we could afford it, but it would have been better perhaps for some others if Miss Annabel had tried to cultivate the spirit of resignation and compliance."

"Better for *you* if your sister had not marched all over town with her harmful talk."

They paused to allow Doreen a moment to absorb the implication.

"What do you mean?" she said.

"For one thing, that fine horse of yours—"

"They killed Pharaoh," Doreen said.

"We heard about it. Shocking."

"A good horse *these* days, to simply—"

"Miss Annabel told everyone you'd no right to hold on to such an animal when he might have been useful to our army. But since the Yankees have come, she's missed no chance to say you kept him for a purpose: because your father intended to organize and lead secret forces against our conquerors!"

"Annabel said that?"

Ann-Elizabeth turned to Margaret-Ella. "Have you not heard her say so, Sister?"

"A dozen times at least."

Ann-Elizabeth nodded. "So has everyone with ears to hear, including those who *above all* should not have heard!"

Doreen looked bewildered. "Do you mean she said such things where the Yankees might overhear her?"

Margaret-Ella and Ann-Elizabeth exchanged glances. "Perhaps we shouldn't bother you with such matters now."

"When it's too late to actually warn you," Margaret-Ella suggested.

"Are you saying that Annabel was so unwise as to—"

"Foolhardy!" Ann-Elizabeth stated unflinchingly.

"As if she dared them to do their worst," Margaret-Ella confirmed.

"And now they have done it."

Doreen shook her head. "I can hardly believe that Annabel—"

"My dear Doreen," Ann-Elizabeth commiserated, "everyone has been talking of her dangerous boasting, done deliberately, I assure you, to provoke the wrath of the Yankees. I have heard them speak of it among themselves at my very table."

"And I at mine. When we sought to make light of her boasting, they simply thought we were being loyal to our own and trying to cover up a genuine conspiracy."

"That isn't all, of course. She bragged about the help your papa had given the Cause."

"Far in excess of anything required, she claimed."

"She involved your brother too."

"James? How could she do that?"

"Well, *we* had been told that he lost his sight in a camp accident, but Miss Annabel put it about that he was blinded leading a charge."

"What!"

"Furthermore," Margaret-Ella took up the report, "all of us know that your brother was, if anything, reluctant to go to war because of his strong family attachments, whereas most of the others, at least at the beginning of the thing, were champing at the bit in their eagerness to enlist."

"James was a farmer," Doreen said. "He thought his place was here."

"Precisely," Margaret-Ella agreed with a toss of her head.

"But that isn't the way Miss C.S.A. told it—"

"No, ma'am, it was not!"

"She described him as the fiercest of fighters, one who would never accept defeat—"

"To hear her tell it, he was as bloodthirsty as Attila the Hun!"

"James!"

"Oh, indeed yes, and your father too."

"My poor father?" Doreen's voice shook. "I've seen him step over an ant!"

"Well, Doreen, you know how she can talk," Ann-Elizabeth reasoned. "Not that we doubt, or have ever doubted, her sincerity in supporting the Cause right up to the very end."

"But there are times to hate and times to hold your foolish tongue."

"As the Bible tells us."

"I don't understand why Annabel—" Doreen shook her head. "That pride of hers!"

"More than pride—"

"Arrogance!"

"Surely you knew what she was saying?" Margaret-Ella pleaded.

Doreen shook her head as if she would shake it off. "Nothing. Not a thing. Not one word."

"I'm afraid we've upset you," Margaret-Ella said slowly.

Ann-Elizabeth said, "We'd better go."

Getting up, the two sisters gathered shawls and gloves and reticules, looking around the poor cabin compassionately. "Anyway," Margaret-Ella said. "I certainly hope you-all enjoy the gingerbread."

"Thank you," Doreen said.

Lifting one of the dresses they had brought, Ann-Elizabeth said, "I always liked this one. I wish I could still wear it, but I've got too stout. Why don't you try it on and see if it'll fit. You're taller than I am, but the hem can be let out. Shame to waste it on a darky, and it's perfectly good, *too* good for one of them."

They left, but she could not put what they had told her out of her mind. Rosalie came in from the barnyard, where she and two other women had been cropping the wings of poultry. The hens especially had turned flighty, with an inclination to perch on tree limbs and roof ledges, after so many of their number had been chased and caught by the raiders. Seeing the pan of gingerbread on the table, Rosalie took a piece and began to eat it. It was already cut into squares. Copying her without thinking, Doreen did the same.

"Heavy," Doreen said.

Rosalie nodded. Picking up the dress Ann-Elizabeth had seemed to regret giving up, she sniffed the armpit where the stitching had come loose. "Sour as vinegar," she commented.

Benjamin entered carrying a huge pumpkin. "Look what I found."

Rosalie had taken over the cooking from Marie. "Put it over here," she said. "I'll do something with it later." She frowned. "Cut it up and stew it maybe with a little syrup and nutmeg."

"Have some of this." Doreen held out the pan, and Benjamin helped himself. "The Sefton sisters brought it." Sefton had been the maiden name of Mrs. Dupree and Mrs. Singletary.

"I saw them. I waited till they left. It's as lumpy as they are, but I'm hungry."

"They told me something peculiar about Annabel."

"I'd believe it, whatever it was," Benjamin said, and opened the door to go out again. "Will you look who's coming now?" he said softly.

The surprise in his voice drew the two women after him into the yard. Eating gingerbread, the three stared frankly at the man getting down from his horse. Although he smiled at them confidently, he did not dispose of his horse, for to do so would have appeared to expect a welcome they were unlikely to give.

Holding reins in one hand, the man removed his hat and bent his head courteously. "Good evening, Miss Davis. Mr. Davis."

"You're Junior Elk," Doreen said.

"Yes, ma'am," Junior said firmly. "I've seen you in town off and on; not lately though."

She nodded and waited.

"We heard about your misfortune. I came to say how sorry I am it had to happen." She bobbed her head to acknowledge his sympathy. "Your father, Mr. Bruce Davis, was a man I always respected. He and my father had occasional business dealings, as I expect you know." It was his turn to pause.

Benjamin looked questioningly at Doreen, who said after a moment, "I do remember there was—something."

"Slaves. My father bought a few from Mr. Davis."

"So he did. I recollect being told about it. It was after the warehouse burned down and we lost the cotton."

"The way the war goes, it looks like not having been such a beneficial transaction!" He made his tone jocular so that they would know he was speaking ironically.

"We are all losers by the war," she said stiffly.

"None more than you," he said with sober respect.

Benjamin stared at their visitor, wondering why he had come. Although the Davis family had no reason to think of the Elk family's founder as villainous, their difference in color and the loyalty of long friendship with the Kendricks would have prevented any close acquaintance. And Benjamin considered himself as much a Kendrick as a Davis.

"You will not be having an easy time," Junior said.

"We'll manage," Benjamin said.

"I hope so, I'm sure." Junior was surprised at his speaking up so boldly. He would have liked his own son to show more spirit, but resented the tone of the Davis boy. Sensing his mistake, Junior realized that he had made this trip to Oaks too soon; yet he had been unable to keep away altogether from the two ravaged plantations, and for him to have approached Beulah Land was unthinkable. "I come to offer, in addition to my profound sympathy, any help that may be in my power to provide."

"We've nothing to ask of you," Benjamin said.

"I own the little farm between your plantation and Beulah Land," Junior said, addressing himself to Doreen. "It amounts to nothing, although I keep a family on it to work the fields and keep it up. Should you ever think of selling a few acres, please remember that I would not mind adding to my own paltry holding." Although he was looking at Doreen, he did not miss the boy's resentful start. "You have so many things to think about. I beg you to understand that my visit is well-intentioned, meant only to your possible benefit. Good evening, Miss Davis. Evening, Mr. Davis." Mounting his horse without waiting for them to speak, he trotted quickly around the burnt-out house and down the carriageway.

"The scoundrel!" Benjamin said when he was out of earshot.

"Do you think so?" Doreen hedged mildly. "Oh, I know what Aunt Sarah feels about all the Elks. But we've lost so many of our people I can't help wondering how we're going to put in a new crop next spring."

"It's only now happened, Aunt Doreen!" Benjamin's voice both pleaded and accused. "I'm going to find Zadok." He walked away on his dignity, and Rosalie drew Doreen back into the cabin by suggesting that if she was going to stay outdoors, she'd better have a shawl, for it was getting colder with night coming on.

Zadok was in the biggest barn, where they had moved all the remaining livestock. Benjamin told him about Junior Elk's visit, and Zadok said nothing, but listened with frowning intensity as he held a dried ear of corn carefully through the bars of the pen until one of the hogs grabbed it. They then went around the barn observing the last feeding of the animals, one minute discouraged that there were so few, the next marveling that any had been left to them. Benjamin put off going to the cabin. He had been busy and it had been a long day. It would have been natural to leave the rest for Zadok and the hands, but Doreen wasn't anyone he wanted to talk to just now. He missed Jane. He ached for his grandfather.

He was relieved to see Annabel arrive in her buggy with her younger son Bonard, just when he had decided to go in. That gave him reason enough to stay where he was. He and Zadok made another round of the animal stalls and pens, deciding that, although the cow was old and dry, it was possible she would freshen. The hogs would grow tame again after a few days of quiet and regular slops. They would feed them in addition some of the dried corn they needed to make cornmeal for themselves, because they would be starved of fresh meat long before the winter was done, and it was no good killing skinny hogs. There would be no lard, and the guts would have to be used for chitterlings because there wouldn't be enough meat to make them into sausages.

They paused a long time with the oxen. These had been used at Oaks for slow, heavy hauling, but not for plowing. However, with all but two of their oldest mules taken from them, they would have to be used. Zadok said he would try them out, training them to the plow as he trained himself and another hand or two to the oxen. They were having a comfortable and comforting talk when startled to silence by a woman's scream.

Benjamin expressed their first fear. "The Yankees are back!" But as they ran together toward the cabin from which it seemed to come, they saw no soldiers or horses, and Benjamin identified the continuing protest as his Aunt Annabel's.

Benjamin opened the door, but it was Zadok back of him who said, "God-a-mighty!" before they went inside.

Annabel had arrived with Bonard a quarter hour earlier, bringing some old household linens and a few kitchen utensils her cook assured her had seen their best wear and were practically good for nothing. She might have left the things in the buggy and told Doreen to have one of the women fetch them in, but enjoyed bearing the gifts herself, with Bonard's help. Bonard had been more excited than shocked by his first glimpse of the ruined plantation house, although his mother's partiality chose to read his liveliness as outrage. ("Mama, *look* at it! Just look, I say—ye gods above us!")

They entered the cabin without knocking to find Doreen and Rosalie sorting food supplies brought by callers during the day.

"Here you are," Annabel said in what Ann-Elizabeth Dupree had once referred to as her "God and I are one" voice. She and Bonard plunked down their burdens on the floor, he then stepping into the biggest pot and denting it further than it had been. It had a hole in the side, but as the cook had pointed out, it was fairly high up, so that if they cooked something low in the pot, they would have no difficulty. "These things ought to be a big help to you," Annabel told Doreen. "I can't think you'll want anything for stove or bed very desperately after you look through what we've brought you."

"Ann-Elizabeth and Margaret-Ella have been here," Doreen announced. If Annabel had been sensitive to her sister's disposition, she would have known that the tone was ominous.

"Brought by curiosity, I've no doubt. I do not speak to them, you know, now that they have opened their houses to Yankee soldiers and made their dining rooms places for common board."

"They brought some old dresses and gingerbread," Doreen said.

"Can I have a piece, Aunt Doreen?" Bonard asked.

"No, you may not," Annabel told him. "*You* have plenty to eat at home, I thank the Lord, and you mustn't take from those in need."

Rosalie offered the pan to the young man, who accepted a piece and began to gobble it. "Good!" he pronounced it, blowing sticky crumbs.

"As for the dresses they brought," Annabel said, "I take that as an insult to me. As if I wouldn't take care of my own sister. I don't know that either of them has a stitch of clothes I'd be caught dead wearing if I'd been stripped naked. However, you're not that particular, I realize."

"They had things to tell me," Doreen said.

"I wish you could see Papa. Of course, you will tomorrow morning when you come in for the funeral. I'll send the buggy out. He looks very dignified in my middle hallway, where people can come in and view him without damage to my Aubusson."

"We put him on sawhorses," Bonard said, swallowing the last of the gingerbread.

"They told me you'd been talking a lot about us."

Annabel said, "Of course, there are big pots of fern on the floor around him to hide the sawhorses. I'm really terribly put out with Throckmorton. He insists that the funeral be what he calls quiet and take place at eleven tomorrow. A morning funeral is common, and I said so, but when you make critical observation to him, he just turns it off by talking about God."

"They said you told whopping stories about Papa and James for everybody to hear—"

"The best time is three o'clock. That is proper, but at eleven everybody's thinking about dinner."

"Did you let on that James and Papa were fire-eaters?"

"What are you talking about, Doreen?"

"Mama put a Confederate flag over the lower part of the coffin, Auntie D."

"Did you make out James went blind leading a *charge* in *battle?*"

"What if I did?"

"Did you tell people Papa was going to lead us against the Yankees?"

"I think you're going crazy—"

"Did you tell them I was keeping Pharaoh from our army and saving him for Papa to ride when we rose up to fight the Yankees?"

"I make allowances for what you've been through, and I know you were devoted to that stupid beast and therefore cannot be rational where he is concerned. However—"

"Did you deliberately make the Yankees think we were going to make trouble?"

"I think we'll go now, Bonard. Your aunt cannot control herself, apparently."

"It's true—what they said is true! You did it to make yourself feel Big. —You did it for spite on the Yankees! —It's you as much as put the Yankees up to coming out here and doing what they did!"

"Bonard, go out," Annabel said. He did not move.

"You're going to answer me!" Doreen said.

Annabel faced her squarely. "Very well. I told them we were true, proud Southerners. Anyone who does less is a traitor to our noble Cause!"

Doreen sprang at her, snatched off her bonnet and grabbed her hair with both hands. It was only then that Annabel, who had always despised her younger sister, considering her plain and of no consequence, realized the seriousness of the occasion. It was her first scream on that realization that had interrupted the barn conversation between Benjamin and Zadok and brought them running. Doreen let go hair with one hand and used it to slap Annabel repeatedly, her own angry cries now all but drowning her sister's screams of outrage. It was at this point Benjamin had opened the door and Zadok had called upon the Almighty to witness such unsisterly behavior.

Bonard was gazing at his mother and aunt with simple astonishment. Rosalie stood, arms akimbo, studying the two with detached interest, as if she might be asked to give a considered opinion on the seasoning of a stew. The only shock evidenced was that of Benjamin and Zadok, whose reaction had the effect of bringing that of the others into more conventional if not a truer focus. Suddenly Bonard cried out, "Mother!" and moved ineffectually to help her. Rosalie wrung her hands and said, "Miss Doreen!" Doreen saw Benjamin, ceased abusing her sister, and commenced crying. Annabel drew aside, recovering self-possession with her bonnet and gloves. As she moved to the door, she raised her voice to be heard. "I'll send one of the boys for you at nine. Be ready, you and Benjamin. You'll want to look at our papa a while before the funeral. I don't excuse your intemperate attack upon me, but I shall try to forgive you in time, as the Lord commands us to do."

No one held Doreen, for there had seemed no need. But still weeping, she flew at Annabel again, smacking her smartly on the jaw with her fist. Annabel made haste to exit; and in the days that followed had reason to be glad of her long black veil.

Doreen was now hysterical. The man and the boy looked on helplessly as she babbled vilifying phrases into the air, stopping often, and finally altogether, to merely sob. Rosalie had her arms around her shoulders and was murmuring words that would no doubt have comforted on a more common occasion. Tonight they did not, so Rosalie found a fruit jar of corn liquor among the gifts of food that had been brought that day and made Doreen drink a glass of it. Within minutes she grew calmer. Rosalie renewed her murmuring, which now appeared to be having greater effect. Ten minutes after the first glass of liquor, Rosalie offered another, which Doreen did not refuse. She wept and talked, and Rosalie after another little while led her off to the bedroom next to the kitchen. There she wept and talked more, wept again and slept. She did not once wake screaming as she had done the night before, with pictures in her mind of bloody testicles slashed from flesh still hot with life, with the sound in her ears of Pharaoh's last cries of confusion and terror.

When the sounds from the bedroom were quieter, Benjamin said to Zadok, "I'm going over to Beulah Land tonight."

"Don't you want to wait for Rosalie to fix supper?"

"They'll give me something," Benjamin said.

29.

Lotus offered to cook supper for everybody, but Sarah told her
to attend to her own family after she'd seen that all the old
Negroes left without family were taken care of for the night.
With Nancy helping, Sarah prepared a pot of dried black-eyed
peas with a piece of cured hog's head and a pot of rice. It was,
as Nell said filling a plate, "fare despised by the Yankees as too
coarse for their pampered palates." Nell and Sarah and Jane and
Daniel sat around the table in the center of the kitchen, and
Nancy took her meal a few feet away from them standing by the
cook stove, though she joined in the general conversation when it
suited her. Talk abounded in such phrases as "this time yesterday" and bemused speculations running to: "Who'd have
guessed they'd want that?" —"Why do you reckon they smashed
everything if they were going to burn it anyway?"

Their feelings were as tired as their bodies, and they were still
too close to awful events to have found the cold comforts of hate
and regret. They spoke matter-of-factly, with no self-pity, and
they might have eaten at the kitchen table all their lives, so easily did they accept the circumstance. They fed eagerly, as survivors will, Nell extracting the occasional pig bristle from her teeth
without comment, and Jane evidencing only mild surprise on discovering a white hog's tooth in her own mouth as she chewed a
salty piece of jowl. Nell had thought to liven the plain victuals
by opening a quart jar of cucumber pickles which Miss Ophelia
Pepper had brought as a gift, together with a pair of good down-
stuffed pillows. They had supped to satisfaction and a pensive
quietness when a knock came at the door and Benjamin entered
without waiting for invitation. "Lotus told me you-all were here,"
he said. They welcomed him, making room at the table, and
Nancy heaping a plate of food for him when he allowed that he
was hungry.

He told them some of the day's adventures at Oaks as he ate,
and they told him some of theirs; and when he came to relate the

attack of Doreen upon Annabel, everyone at the table was delighted. Jane asked him to tell it again, and he did, seeing it himself this time as a funny event, and they all laughed as heart- ily as they had done on first hearing it. Nell then decided that she was tired and would go to bed. Catching a look from Sarah, Jane offered to attend her. First she accompanied the old lady to the nearest of the outdoor privies. It was cold and the wind was rising, and they were soon indoors again. Passing through the kitchen, they bade everyone good night, including Floyd, who had joined the group at the table, and went into the bedroom. They would share the double bed, Sarah having set up a single one for herself.

Jane helped Nell to undress and then undressed herself. Yawn- ing and heavy with tiredness, they did not talk much as they plaited each other's hair. Nell had one knee on the bed to get into it when she said, "No, I must say my prayers."

"Say them in bed," Jane urged. "I do sometimes when it's cold."

Nell set both feet on the floor again. "No, I won't. Tonight I must thank the Lord properly for sparing us."

She slipped to her knees, and Jane knelt beside her, their hands folded and held erect in prayer. Finishing, Jane opened her eyes. Presently, Nell opened hers, said, "There," with satis- faction, and attempted to rise, but found she could not. "I got down, but I can't get up. Help me, child." Jane did, and both climbed into the bed and went through the motions of settling comfortably for the night. Nell said wonderingly, "I can't think when it was I last slept with anybody but myself." They had blown out their candle, but Jane could imagine her great-aunt pursing her lips in the dark. "It must be sixty years," she decided. "You kicked me in your sleep last night. If you do it again to- night, I'm going to shove you right out of bed onto the floor." Jane giggled, and a minute later Nell began to snore lightly. For a while Jane watched the flickering candlelight that showed under the door to the kitchen and listened to the mutter of the men's voices and the murmur of her brother's and her grand- mother's, and then she slept too.

In the kitchen they sat on, Sarah and Floyd doing most of the talking. Nancy had finished her work and gone to the cabin nearby which she shared with three old sisters named Verbena, Daisy, and Honeysuckle, two widowed and the other a spinster whose face had been burnt and left scarred when she fell into an open fireplace as a child. Benjamin was asleep in his chair, head resting on folded arms on the table. Daniel was silent, listening to the other two. At a pause Sarah's eyes settled on her grandson. "He thinks a lot of their Zadok."

"He's a good man," Floyd said. "I've seen him work."

Benjamin's eyes opened. "Did you call me, Grandma?"

"You've been asleep," Sarah said.

The boy woke fully. "I thought somebody said 'Zadok.' I better go home."

"Spend the night," she said. "It's late and cold. I'll put down a pallet."

"You can sleep with me," Daniel offered. "I don't mind if you don't."

"I don't mind," Benjamin said.

"Well then," Sarah said. "Show him, Daniel, before he goes to sleep again sitting there."

"Used to be my room when I was a boy," Floyd said. "Papa just about always had something brewing on that stove for his ailing animals. I'd hear him moving around late at night. He didn't sleep as much as Mama did."

"It was just this morning," Sarah said, as if she was ready to dispute her own statement, "we buried them together."

There was silence, thoughtful but not embarrassed. Floyd said, "This room always had a few animals he was tending. I remember when a hen got tired of brooding and left the nest with only half her eggs hatched, he'd bring the others in here. Put them in a box with a sprinkle of meal to make a soft bottom, and set the whole thing in the oven with the door open, keeping a slow fire going. Pretty soon, they'd hatch themselves. Many a night I'd wake up and hear Papa in here talking to his biddies, and them cheeping away."

Benjamin looked as if he might cry, and Sarah guessed he was remembering Bruce Davis. "Grandpa's funeral is tomorrow at eleven o'clock," he said.

Sarah nodded. He had told them before. "Now go to bed," she said.

"Got to go outside first." Daniel rose and followed him out the door. They did not bother with a privy, but went around the cabin to a dark place under a tree and peed. It was cold, and when they were done, they turned and ran back into the cabin.

They bobbed their heads at Sarah and Floyd, who were talking again and did not notice them. The slope-roofed room they went into had been added to the kitchen when Floyd was a boy. Nancy had made the bed. Keeping on underclothes for warmth, they hopped into it shaking with the cold, for little of the kitchen's heat penetrated the room, although sounds from the kitchen did. It wasn't a large bed, and the shuck mattress was cold, but each kept politely to his side as he trembled warmth into himself under the heavy, worn quilts.

When he woke, he thought at first he hadn't been to sleep. Sarah and Floyd's voices still came through the thin wall from the kitchen, but he realized that they were talking about something other than practical next steps in getting order back into the plantation and its people. With something like shock Benjamin realized they were talking about themselves and how they felt. People that old didn't do that, he thought with resentment before he understood in one of those flashes of illumination that make learning possible that he was being a child in his thinking, and that of course they had their own worlds just as he did. Before that moment he had always assumed that his world was the only real one and that they, and by some unspoken agreement, *everyone* acknowledged this to be so. He listened. They were arguing, or at any rate in disagreement.

Floyd was speaking. "He's heading for Savannah, and he's traveling alone."

"Let him go."

"I can't."

"What would you do if you found him?"

"Tell him who I am. Then tell him what he did."

Sarah said, "He knows well what he did."

"I want to tell him. Say: I'm Floyd Kendrick. You raped my wife. You dug up my papa's grave hoping to find money hidden in it. You killed my mama when she tried to stop you and left her dead on the ground."

There was silence before Sarah asked, "Then?"

"I'll tell him I'm going to kill him."

"He'll have a gun and a knife. What will you have? You can't run the risk of carrying any weapon."

"My hands will have to be enough."

"He might kill you first," Sarah said.

"He won't think I'm dangerous to him."

"He will when you tell him what you said."

"By then it won't do him any good. I'll have his gun and his knife."

They were silent again until Sarah said, "I won't try to stop you. It's you I worry about. God knows, not him."

"I'll be home in a day or two."

"What if they catch you?"

"They won't," Floyd promised.

"Do you know it's almost Christmas?"

"What do you want Santa Claus to bring you?" he teased.

"When is it? Three days?"

"Four. —I've lost track; I don't know. Zebra will carry things on. I'll talk to him before I go, but nobody else will know except you and Lotus. Send Zebra to the Shelter for anything you need there."

"I can manage."

"I know it."

"I've hated just one man my whole life," she mused. "He's dead, but I don't stop hating him. He wanted to steal Beulah Land from us. I don't mean just the land and house, everything. He wanted to own *us*."

"He's a long time dead," Floyd said.

"I know. But when I remember him, I can't breathe for a minute. Now it's the same with Smede. In a few hours he did what Roscoe Elk wasn't able to do his whole life. He spoiled what he and his men didn't want. If I hadn't seen, I couldn't believe men would take pleasure in spoiling, ruining, destroying."

"When I come back, we can both forget him."

"Oh, no. I'll never forget him. —Floyd, you've got to come back, you know. I can't do it without you."

"I'll be back. You get some sleep. I'll talk to Lotus, then go early, before day. I won't see you."

"I'll be walking beside you every step of the way. Take Bartholomew."

There was silence. A door opened and closed. Presently Benjamin heard Sarah moving around. Then the light under the door went out.

Much had happened in the last day and a half, not only at Oaks and Beulah Land, but to Benjamin. It had begun to happen before, but thinking about it now, it seemed to Benjamin to have begun the night before last when he tried to follow Floyd to the

secret place. Wide awake now, the boy felt that he alone was
awake in the whole world. And what a world it had become: one
without Bruce Davis and without the house he'd been born in,
the ugly, roomy old house that had seemed ageless and indestructible. He had heard the shot that killed his grandfather. He
had felt the heat of the fire that burned the house. He had
known what it was to be by himself but not what it was to be
alone until now. *Where did everybody go?* The terror of the
question was so strong in him he thought he had spoken it aloud
when he heard Daniel say, "How long you been awake, Benjamin?" Relief welled in him, and presently manifested itself in
great sobs that shook the bed more violently than ever their combined chills had done when they went to bed. Daniel lay still for
a few moments, then turned and hugged himself around the boy.
He did not speak, but his warm, bony feet were eloquent in their
rubbing against Benjamin's. Both were comforted, and soon
slept.

30.

The next time he woke, Daniel was gone. It was dark outside,
but in December that didn't mean early, and Daniel might have
got up and started some piece of work that was on his mind to
do. Benjamin lay on his back to warm his rump. The quilts had
slid and bunched during the night, and he had waked with his
backside cold. As he gathered his wits, a rooster crowed. He
remembered what Floyd had said about his father's hatching
eggs in the oven. The next sound he heard was from the kitchen:
someone was starting a fire in the cook stove. He dressed quickly
and went to find out who it was. Nancy had got the fire going by
then and turned with a smile of surprise. "Morning, Mister Ben.
You still here?"

"Morning, Nancy. I slept with Daniel."

"Come warm your hands. There's heavy frost this morning."

He joined her at the stove. "What time is it?"

"Law, I don't know, but folks is stirring. You staying for breakfast?"

"Nobody's awake yet. I might as well go."

"Don't know what there is, but I could fix you something. Got to fix myself something. Likely be a mix and a mingle."

"Much obliged, but just tell Grandma I went."

She nodded. "Mister Dan was walking past to the barn when I come out my door little while ago."

With a last rub of his hands together over the stove, he went out the door. It was light enough to make out shapes of cabins and barns, and he passed no one as he headed for the main barn. There he found Floyd and Daniel, who stopped talking as soon as they saw him. It was the first time he had ever felt in the way with either of them. Nobody spoke a morning greeting. Floyd's face was set sternly. He had just put a saddle on the mule Bartholomew and was securing a bundle behind the saddle.

"I'm on my way home now," Benjamin said.

Floyd nodded, and turned his back to tighten a line around the bundle.

"Thank you for the share of your bed," Benjamin said to Daniel.

"All right," Daniel said. "Take care of yourself, Benjamin."

"I will." It wasn't until he was halfway home, going at a trot to keep warm over the shorter back way between the two plantations, that he came to think of Daniel's words as a kind of goodbye.

In the barn Daniel said to Floyd, "No. I'll take what you say anytime it's about work, because I promised Miss Sarah when I came. But this is not work we're talking about."

"Finding the man and dealing with him is my business," Floyd said.

"No more than mine."

"It's my people he wronged," Floyd reminded him.

"It's me that caused it."

"That's not so."

"Didn't I hear with my own ears what Captain Ponder said?"

"What you heard was their excuse. If there'd been no you, they'd have come just the same and done it just the same."

"That may be so," Daniel admitted, "but I don't feel right about it, letting you go and not going myself. Look at it this way. Who's more important to Beulah Land, you or me? You are more important to it and to Miss Sarah than I am, or anybody."

"I won't be gone more than a day or two," Floyd said. "No longer than going to the Shelter and back."

"Maybe so. But it's a whole lot different than going to the Shelter and back, you'll admit."

"You mean dangerous?"

"I sure do. What do you reckon they'd do to you if they caught you?"

"What do you reckon they'd do to *you* if they caught you?"

"I'll take my chances."

"And I'll take mine," Floyd said. "You wouldn't get through town without their seeing you and stopping you."

Daniel thought for a moment. "Then let's do it together. They'd find it less odd than you traveling by yourself, or me either."

Floyd got on Bartholomew's back and began to walk him out of the barn, but Daniel ran after them and grabbed the bridle. Even as he did, his look apologized and his voice pleaded. "Floyd, I owe it!"

Floyd looked at him long and hard. He didn't like him, but he could no longer deny him. "We'll take turns on the mule."

Daniel breathed out heavily. "You ride him. I'll walk. I'm a good hard walker. I can walk anywhere."

"We'll take turns like I say," Floyd repeated irritably. "There'll be times it will look funny if they see a white man walking and a Negro man riding."

"Do we have to go through Highboro?"

Daniel had let go the mule's bridle and was following mule and rider around the ruins of the house to the carriageway. "It's the only way that makes any sense if you want to hit the road to Savannah. Any other is too long, and I want to make up time."

"We'll make it up," Daniel said. "He won't be in a hurry now."

They passed no one. The road was theirs. Before it turned and brought them into sight of the first houses of the town, Floyd got down from the mule. "You ride through town."

"No, we'll both walk," Daniel said.

"If you're going, you have to do it the way I say! I know everything about this country, and you know nothing."

Daniel mounted the mule slowly, and they went on. They saw a few people, even a few soldiers, but nobody stopped them, or spoke to them, or paid them the least attention. It was that way all day long. People had their own affairs to think about, and the sight of the two men and the mule was not such an unusual one. They paused once to eat cold victuals Lotus had put up for Floyd, and to feed and water Bartholomew. Daniel insisted on walking all the time except when they were passing close to a big farm or through a town. They did not talk except to say what was necessary. They continued for a couple of hours after sundown, stopping finally at a deserted farm cabin just off the road because it had a well. The cabin was filthy, and they decided after a look to only sleep in it, building a fire in the yard and roasting a rabbit on a spit Floyd whittled with his pocketknife. Daniel had run the rabbit down and knocked him on the head with a stick during the afternoon. Soon after eating they rolled themselves into the two worn quilts Floyd had brought and went to sleep. They had both walked a considerable distance and were tired enough to sleep even in that rough way.

When they woke at dawn, Floyd went into the yard ahead of Daniel. Following, Daniel heard him say, "Well, I will just be damned."

"Morning, Floyd."

It was Benjamin. He and Daniel stared at each other but did not speak.

"How'd you get here?" Floyd said.

"Walked some. Got a ride or two on wagons."

"What do you want? Somebody send you?"

"I figured it was my job more than yours," Benjamin said.

"Your job to do what?" Floyd said.

"What you're doing."

"What is that?" Floyd said carefully.

"Finding Sergeant Smede."

"What do you plan to do if you find him?"

"Kill him," Benjamin said. For the first time that morning Floyd and Daniel looked directly at each other. "It's my place to," Benjamin went on. "He killed my grandpa. He burnt Oaks and Beulah Land. I'm close-connected to both, because both will be mine to take care of one day."

"You're thinking a long way ahead," Floyd said.

"Yes, I am."

"Well," Floyd said. "I see how your thinking runs, and I don't quarrel with it. But you're not needed. *He* says it's his job, and I say it's mine."

After a pause Benjamin said, "Maybe it's for all three of us."

"Three against one?" Floyd said.

"The odds favored them more than that when they came after us, and they had guns. We didn't have anything."

"Did you let anybody know what you were up to?" Floyd said.

"Zadok won't be surprised. I slipped off after Grandpa's funeral. They were all talking to each other and not noticing. I figured when they all got home, they'd each think I'd gone with the other. When they get worried, Zadok will tell them."

"How did you know we were here, inside?"

Benjamin nodded toward the mule. "You didn't hide Bartholomew."

All three looked at the mule. Floyd said, "It's a long way for you to walk back, having just got here, but we're going toward Savannah, and you'll be headed in the opposite direction, to Highboro."

"No, I won't. You made me go home once before, but you won't this time. If you don't let me go with you, I'll go by myself; but I won't go home till Sergeant Smede is dead. Confound it, Floyd, I've got to go. You know as well as I do my daddy is blind. I'm the new man at Oaks with Grandpa gone."

Floyd looked hard at the boy, as he had looked hard at Daniel the day before, and he saw a determination in him that was more than a boy's, and he saw too and respected a need to prove himself to himself. "Well," Floyd said slowly, "Daniel here is a good rabbit catcher and I'm a good mule tender. What are you good for?"

31.

Near sundown, they overtook Sergeant Smede.

Benjamin and Floyd and Daniel were footsore, each having determined not to ride the mule while the other two walked. Bartholomew had had an easy day, as unburdened as they ex-

cept for the half hours Daniel or Benjamin had straddled his
back when they were passing through a town, or met with soldiers or other strangers.

Knowing they were on the right and only track, they had not
indulged in inquiries lest they be remembered later. They went,
if not blindly, uncertainly; for the man they sought might have
stopped off the road to rest an hour or a day (unlikely, they
agreed), or might have joined a pack of Union soldiers for
slower but safer passage. They calculated, however, that he
would prefer to travel alone without explaining the mule that
carried his personal spoils of war.

They stopped at only one farm, needing fresh water for themselves and the mule. That was at noon, and they interrupted the
midday meal of the old couple whose home it was.

When she saw Daniel at the kitchen door, the woman dropped
the iron spoon with which she had been feeding herself and exclaimed, "Yankees again!"

Startled, Daniel then realized he had not been recognized as a
Yankee but merely assumed to be one, as strangers would be,
since few of the soldiers wore enough of a uniform to identify
them.

The man pushed his chair back from the kitchen table and
came to the door to stand beside his wife. "No use you stopping
here," he said. "They been four times and cleaned out everything. Taken the corn, leaving only shuck and cob."

Peering into the yard, the woman cried, "A nigger Yankee too?
Lord preserve us! —And a boy. How come you take to soldiering
at your age, youngun?"

Daniel explained quickly that they were not soldiers, only
travelers wanting water.

"If that's all, help yourself from the well," the man offered.
"Only thing I got that ain't give out on me."

"Much obliged," Floyd said, leading Bartholomew to the well.

"Have you seen a man today," Benjamin asked, "not very tall
but fat, riding a horse and leading a mule?" Floyd had described
Sergeant Smede as he saw him leaving Highboro.

"You sure you ain't Yankees?" the woman said.

"Do I sound like a Yankee, ma'am?" Benjamin said, smiling.

"No, you don't," she admitted, "but he does." She nodded toward Daniel.

"I'm not one of them neither," Daniel said.

"Well then, we did," the man said. "Like you say: he was fat and riding a horse and leading a mule. Standing at the road I was, to see what I could see, and there he came. Peculiar thing, a cloud of winter flies round his head like his flesh was sugar candy. He didn't look hungry, so I told him we was and asked could he give us something; but he cussed me and trotted off, flies and all."

"How long ago would that have been?" Daniel asked.

"Hour or two," the woman said.

"Less'n two," the man corrected her.

"Don't keep from your dinner," Benjamin said.

"It's nothing but soup from a cabbage stalk and an old potato," the woman said before looking at him speculatively. "Are you hungry, boy? It tastes all right if you're hungry, and you're welcome to some."

"We stopped back a ways to eat, but I'm much obliged to you, ma'am, for offering to share."

Daniel and Benjamin joined Floyd at the well. They and the mule drank deeply. Benjamin, after a word with the others, returned to the house to thank the old couple.

The man said, "See your nigger didn't drink from the side of the bucket but used his own cup. Shows he's no Yankee nigger, don't it?"

The woman said in an anxious tone, "Try to go home, boy. I bet there's somebody worrying after you."

"Yes'm," Benjamin said.

They went along confidently now. The encounter made Daniel thoughtful, and presently he broached an idea to Floyd and Benjamin. It wasn't a plan but a suggestion of how to begin when they caught up with Smede, and it had come to Daniel because of things the old couple had said. There were people enough on the road coming and going to make the threesome appear to be nothing extraordinary, especially so since they went on their way in the most unconcerned manner. They might have been going a mile only and the people of passage were all strangers to each other.

As they followed a sharp angle in the road, they were all but upon him. Benjamin leaned down from the saddle to say to Daniel, "There he is; that one is Smede."

"You sure?" Daniel whispered.

"I'm sure," Floyd said quietly.

Daniel nodded. "Let's do like we said."

Floyd put his hand on the bridle and halted the mule. Benjamin slid down the mule's side to be less visible, and together they watched Sergeant Smede draw ahead. Daniel continued walking, but slackened his pace, so that presently there were a couple of Negroes between him and the sergeant. Then a family party came from the opposite direction in a wagon and stayed between them long enough for Daniel to drop farther back.

He did not want to approach the sergeant yet. Smede paused once to look off the road into a clump of trees; then evidently decided against making camp there and went on. Half an hour later Daniel was alone on the road with the sergeant, the other travelers having made their choice of a resting place. He kept a good distance between them without seeming to mark it. He was certain that Smede, being a soldier, would know there was someone behind him even though he never turned to look, but he would have no reason to be apprehensive of whoever it might be; nor was there any need for him to exercise caution unless he felt himself followed too closely.

Daniel had begun to wonder if Smede intended to go on for half the night when he saw him stop at a bridge that crossed a narrow creek. Trees came down to the road, and after a pause Sergeant Smede dismounted and led horse and pack mule into the woods. Daniel continued walking a quarter of a mile before he allowed himself to look around and another quarter mile before he turned back.

He found the creek and followed it into the woods, knowing that Smede was likely to make his night camp alongside it. After a few minutes he saw a glow and crept on toward a sandbar where he could now see a fire was laid. The nearer he came, the more caution he used. Smelling the horse, he inched his way until he made out silhouettes of horse and mule beyond the fire where the trees loomed. The man was not in sight, and Daniel was wondering where he had got to when he felt a poke in his back. He knew it was a gun muzzle when the man spoke.

"Walk ahead to the fire."

Daniel did as he was told.

"Now face me."

Daniel turned and saw the sergeant close for the first time.

"You've been following me," Smede said.

"Yes, sir," Daniel admitted.

"State your purpose."

"I've come to give myself up to you," Daniel said.

Sergeant Smede's eyes popped wide open, then narrowed. "You don't sound like a Rebel."

"No, sir, I'm not."

"Who are you?"

"The one you were looking for."

"The one *I* was looking for?" he said carefully.

"Asking for anyway."

"Where was that?"

"The plantation they call Beulah Land."

Smede's eyes opened wide again. "You mean to say you were hiding there? You couldn't have been. The men looked everywhere."

"They didn't look in the woods."

The sergeant studied him briefly. "Deserter?"

"Not meaning to be. I got scared and then got lost from my platoon after some fighting. Went on, not knowing where. Found myself there and they let me stay."

"Deserter," Smede decided.

Daniel shrugged. "I didn't mean to. It was just that every day it got harder to go back. They said nobody'd believe me if I told the truth about getting lost and being scared. They worked me."

"Why didn't they give you up when we came?"

"Afraid they'd get into trouble."

"Why didn't you give yourself up?"

"Likewise afraid."

"What changed your mind?" Daniel tried a shrug as answer. "Why didn't you turn yourself in at Highboro headquarters?"

"Too many. Figured I might get one man to believe me better than a whole company and commander."

"How did you know me?"

"I was in the town when you left. Heard soldiers talking like they wished they was you, saying you were out of it, going home."

"You figured to tail along home after me?"

"Yes, sir, that's right."

Smede lowered his gun and let out a bellow of laughter. "If you ain't a simple bastard! —Where you from?"

"Vermont."

"What part?"

"Farm north of Rutland."

"That's back of nowhere, so they say. How'd you get in the Army?"

"Pa took me to Rutland and good as sold me."

Smede chewed the inside of his cheeks before he nodded again. "A simple country bastard. What do you reckon I'm to do with you?"

"Well—" Daniel's voice took on strength and what sounded like joking hope. "I don't reckon you're going to turn around and march me all the way back to Highboro!"

"You don't, do you?"

"No. I was told you've got a wife."

"You being a deserter, I could kill you. Just what you deserve, and leave you right here. Nobody'd ever find you, or know who they'd found if they did."

"Please, sir, don't do that. I'll work for you, make your traveling easy."

"You appear mighty anxious to get home yourself. Wonder why, if your pa sold you to the Army. Ma crying her sweet old heart out for you?" Daniel shook his head. "Got a gal, then."

"Might say."

Smede spat. "Big-tittied country heifer?"

Daniel let his voice turn a little sullen. "Just a gal."

The sergeant blinked and studied Daniel. "You are truly a simple country bastard. —You come here by yourself?"

"Who'd be with me?"

"You tell me."

"Nobody."

"Pull out the pockets." Daniel did so. "Take off that jacket, turn it inside out, then upside down and shake it." Daniel followed the instructions. Nothing fell, for he carried nothing with him. The sergeant frowned but looked easier. "You can put it back on. Clean your hands in the creek. I'm going to turn you into my cook, among other things."

Daniel squatted, scooped up sand and scrubbed his palms. After rinsing them in the creek, he wrung his hands, which were near numb with cold, and held them to the fire to warm and dry.

Smede found a fruit jar of whiskey in a saddlebag and unscrewed the lid to take a swallow. "Better," he said to himself, and shivered as the hard whiskey hit his stomach. Rummaging in the saddlebag, he brought forth a frying pan and a coffeepot.

"Here." He handed the utensils to Daniel. Going to the mule, he removed two packs from his back. From one he took a bag of coffee and a linen pillowcase that held slices of raw ham. Selecting a thick piece, he slapped it into the frying pan. "That's for me. If I leave any, you can have it. If I don't, there's plenty bread in the bag there."

Daniel was hungry and would have felt it if his mind hadn't been on other things; but he hardly noticed the rich smell of the meat as it sizzled in the pan over the flames, except once to wonder if it had ever hung in the smokehouse at Beulah Land. Sergeant Smede rolled a short log nearer the fire and sat on it, pulling an army blanket tight around his back and shoulders. He held the whiskey jar between his knees and now and then unscrewed the lid and took a swallow. If it warmed him, it did not appear to cheer him, for he stared glumly into the fire as he waited for his food to be cooked. Only occasionally did his gaze shift to Daniel, and then his eyes took on a mocking, superior glint.

The sergeant ate with his knife directly from the frying pan, sopping up the grease with bread, leaving no shred of meat. Daniel dipped water from the creek and boiled coffee. "Proper wife, ain't you?" the sergeant observed. When he finished his rough meal, he told Daniel he could have what was left of the bread and coffee. Daniel crouched by the fire, tearing the bread and feeding pieces of it into his mouth. Smede had settled back to the whiskey. Presently he grinned. "You look like a dog." Making no reply, Daniel continued to chew and swallow the bread. "You hear what I said?" the sergeant asked a minute later. "I said you look like a dog. A goddam dog." The sergeant was silent again, drinking from the jar, looking into the dying fire as gloomily as if its images showed the death of dreams. "Going home to a rich wife," he said. "War over, going home. —Say something."

"War's not over yet, Sergeant."

"'Tis for me." Smede snorted. "'Tisn't for you!"

"You're lucky to be going home to a rich wife," Daniel said.

"Didn't say I had a rich wife," Smede said sourly. "Said I'm going home to a *sick* wife. My wife has been sick ever since the day I married her. She's had everything the doctors got a name for. Start from the top of her head: headache. Go right on down to earache, toothache, sore throat, stomachache. Down through every organ. Down to the corns on her little toes. She's not rich, she's sick. I'm rich, she's sick. If I told you half of what I've got in those bags over there—" He shook his head. "But I won't or you'll get ideas." The sergeant seemed to grow sober with the thought. "Don't you get ideas, because if you do, you're a dead man. —Most of it from that place. What do they call it?"

"Beulah Land."

"Fool name."

"Comes from the Bible," Daniel said.

"It don't come from anywhere now. I stopped it good. Sergeant Billy Smede and his merry men burnt Beulah Land down to the ground! Then I took what I wanted and left. Before I left I had me a piece of pussy. Fact: I had two pieces of pussy. One, a little nigger gal and the other a big nigger woman. Kept saying, 'Don't do it to me, Massa; I got a baby in me!' Know what I told her? I told her, 'He better make room for me, woman.' That's what I told her. I said to her, 'You got a baby in your belly, I'll just give him a sip of my buttermilk.' All the men watching laughed when I said that. Why don't you laugh?" The sergeant drank again from the jar and locked it between his knees without screwing the lid on. "Little white gal there, pretty as could be. Reminded me— She didn't take to me though. Could see she didn't, way she looked at me and looked at her grandma. Her grandma was no bad-looking woman for her age either. I had a mind to give her a taste of my dick too, but I didn't. That little gal now, I told her to hug my neck, but she wouldn't. I might just not have burnt that house down if she'd hugged me good. Prettiest thing you ever saw; pretty and clean. I'd have eat a yard of her shit just to kiss her ass, and so would any man. —Hey! Why you looking like that, dog-boy? You been in nigger country so long you don't know what a white man looks like?"

Daniel hugged himself hard with both arms. "Cold," he said to excuse and explain whatever his face had betrayed.

"Go to bed." Smede laughed. "Bet you got a hard-on from what I been telling you. I'm going to sleep right here by this fire, my head on this log. You got no bed, have you, not even a blanket? Well." The sergeant yawned loud and long, then coughed and spat into the fire. Fixing his eyes on Daniel, he appeared quite sober. "How far can I trust you?"

"As far as forever," Daniel said.

"You make a wrong move, and I kill you, boy. Some have said

I got eyes in the back of my head. That don't half put it. I got eyes in the soles of my feet and sewed onto the very buttons of my clothes. You be careful. If you're going to pee, go now. I don't want to hear a twig snap once I lay my head down. If I do, you'll be dead before you can pull your peter out. Here's something else for you to chew on. When my eyes are closed and I'm snoring like a cataract, I'm still nine-tenths awake. I never been more than one-tenth asleep, and when I'm one-tenth asleep, I'm still more awake than God was when he decided to call the dark 'night.' You hear me?"

Daniel nodded. "Yes, sir."

He continued to crouch by the fire when Sergeant Smede turned and urinated into the creek. Smede then farted and stretched and shivered. Turning back, he carefully selected and added two small pieces of hard dry wood to the fire. He set his rifle flat on a scatter of leaves behind the log. Removing his holster, he took the pistol out, then wrapped the blanket around him and laid himself down.

Daniel had moved to the other side of the fire and sat with arms clenching knees and legs, face down on knees. It was quiet. It remained quiet. Daniel became aware of the cold again. He counted up to a hundred slowly. He tried to count backwards, forgot his place and started again, lost his place again. He counted forward, one to a hundred, slowly once more. He was about to raise his head when the sergeant said, "You're not asleep."

"No," Daniel said, raising his head briefly, then rested one cheek against his knees, so that he faced the sergeant.

"If you'd pretended you were, I'd have killed you." Daniel saw that the sergeant's hand covered the pistol beside him. But in another minute the sergeant began to snore. Daniel could only guess and hope, since he had no way of knowing whether the man was asleep or testing him. Holding his breath, he righted and raised his head. The sergeant's eyes were closed; he continued to snore. His heart thumping, Daniel slowly lifted his hands and arms above his head, the signal they had agreed he was to make when the sergeant slept. They had chosen it because, should the man be awake, the gesture could be read as a stretch, unthreatening. He wondered if they were there in the dark and if they had seen him. He had not heard a sound when he saw Floyd's face rise suddenly from behind the log on which Sergeant Smede rested his head. Smede's eyes opened and he shifted his weight to one elbow, raising the pistol to aim at Daniel. "What are you up to, country boy?"

Floyd was upon the man as the pistol fired. Daniel dived for the pistol when it fell. Benjamin secured the rifle and stood with it aimed at Smede's head. Daniel said, "Sergeant Billy Smede, you are caught."

Floyd ran his hands over the short fat man, finding three knives and taking them. Then he let him go. The sergeant stood and shook himself, cursing savagely for a full minute before making an accusation without conscious irony, "You son-a-bitching thieves!" and a threat without realizing its impotence, "I'll find you and kill you wherever you run to hide!"

For a moment no one moved. Then Floyd said, "You won't find us because we've found you."

"Who's that boy? Step up to the fire so I can see you!"

Lowering the rifle, Benjamin came to the fire where he could be clearly seen.

"You're one of them Davis people."

"My name's Benjamin Davis. I'm the man at Oaks since you killed my grandpa."

"You're nothing but a shit-tail youngun!" Smede jeered, raising his hand as if he meant to swing a slap.

Daniel thrust the pistol closer. "Touch him and *you're* dead, *boy!*"

Smede looked with respect at the pistol, since it was his and he knew what it could do. "You change sides so fast I reckon nobody knows which way you'll jump next."

"I'm done jumping," Daniel said.

Smede's head jerked to bring Floyd into his sight. "Who's the nigger?" he asked.

Floyd said, "Floyd Kendrick. Son of the man whose grave you dug into and of the woman you killed when she tried to stop you."

"That was a misunderstanding," Smede said.

"It was my wife you raped," Floyd added.

"I didn't know you niggers got married." Smede's voice was husky but he spoke rapidly now to Daniel. "You're not such a simple bastard you'll let them use you, are you? They'll turn you in and keep your share. Whatever they promised, I double it. You point that pistol toward the nigger, away from me, and you've made your fortune. I'll see you get home to that gal. I'll see you get no punishment for deserting. I'll share half of all I got on that mule's back, and it's more'n you'll ever see in your life, boy, if you live to be a hundred years old. —What do you think of that? Me and you riding free, here to Savannah, me on the horse, you on the mule, singing and drinking all the way to Savannah. Get us a boat, and home by New Year. Eighteen sixty-five will see you a rich man! Turn that fucking pistol, boy, or give it to me!"

Smede held out an open hand. Floyd and Benjamin stood still where they were. Daniel held the pistol as he had pointed it at Smede, but it was lower than it had been. A hand will not hold a pistol steady and true for more than a few moments without the weight of it making it waver. Taking advantage of the silence of the others, Smede pressed on. "You may have a grudge against your pa for putting you in the Army, but you can't deny the Union, and that's what the fighting is for, to preserve the Union. You said you're from Vermont?"

Daniel nodded.

"Was that the truth?"

Daniel nodded again.

"Well then! We're on the same side, you and me. It's our job to keep the Union together, to stop the niggers and Rebels from dividing us, turning brother against brother. Don't you understand you go against the law of the Union and the will of God if you throw in with them?" Smede paused for his words to make their effect.

"Think what you did," Daniel said.

"What did I do? I fucked a nigger or two. I burned a house or two, but they're *Rebels!* They're not like us, they're the *enemy!* Can't you understand that?"

"No."

"Well, can't you understand money either, you ignorant country bastard? When I say you'll be rich, I don't mean fifty dollars and a tin pocket watch. I mean *rich.* You can buy yourself a farm if that's what you want. You can buy your pa's farm and kick his ass off the place, if that'll give you pleasure. You can forget farming, settle in town, open a store, marry yourself a town girl, drive your own buggy, have people take off their hats and call you 'Mister' —Are you hearing what I'm saying to you?"

"Every word," Daniel said.

Smede came to attention. "Give me that pistol, Private!" he commanded.

Daniel raised the pistol to the level of Smede's heart and held it steady.

"Wait," Floyd said.

Smede turned to face Floyd.

"Take off your clothes," Floyd said.

"Why?"

"Nobody's going to rape you."

Benjamin raised his rifle. "If you don't, I'll blow your brains out."

"Listen to the—"

"Take off everything you're wearing," Daniel said.

"Let me tell you something: you shoot a gun and you'll have the Union army on top of you. They're all around here, waiting for you son-a-bitches to make a wrong move!"

Floyd advanced toward the sergeant.

"Get away from me, nigger, don't come no closer! —Private! —You, boy! I'm a white man. You going to, both of you, let a nigger threaten a white man? Are you going to do that? You do and he'll be after you next!"

Floyd swung the knife Smede had earlier used for eating. It caught the man in the neck, and blood poured. Smede staggered backward, his eyes stony with disbelief. Benjamin dropped the rifle and took up one of the knives Floyd had found on the sergeant. Daniel took the third. Smede fell. Floyd dropped astride him, turned him on his back and ripped his upper clothes away, exposing his fat chest and belly to the firelight. On their knees Daniel and Benjamin scrambled to the man and stabbed him until there was no life left beneath their hands, and the sand was black with blood. All this they did without voicing any sound. They paused finally, breathing fast and hard.

Daniel looked from one to the other and then at the dead man. "He's dead."

The men leaned back on their haunches, heaving air into their lungs, and the boy, observing them, did the same. Their breathlessness was occasioned partly by the brute exhilaration of the killing, but more by the strain of the last hours they had lived through.

Finally Floyd said, "We've work. Wash first."

Daniel said, "Did you pass any camp when you followed him and me?"

"No," Floyd said. "There's nobody but us. We've got the night if we need it. Build the fire up, Benjamin, when you wash yourself."

Benjamin squatted at the side of the creek and splashed water over his hands and face, not minding that his clothes got wet too. When he turned to work on the fire, Smede's body had been stripped of its remaining clothes and dragged into the shadows.

There had been no way of planning it, but the three now worked together as if they had. A few yards into the woods Daniel found a natural trench, and Floyd helped him carry Smede's body to it. They placed him face down and covered him with lengths of moss they tore from the low limbs of trees. They then added heavy underbrush and left him. Benjamin had glanced in their direction as they worked, but he did not join them. He didn't want to see Smede again, and nobody wanted a hint of ceremony in his disposal, although it had been Benjamin who suggested the stabbing, telling the two men that morning about Julius Caesar.

When Floyd and Daniel returned, Benjamin had a strong fire going. They examined Smede's gear, burning all letters and papers. They removed identification from clothing, since they could not bring themselves to destroy it. They made a bundle of it, deciding to leave it on the steps of the first country church they came to, where it would be found and do somebody some good.

Benjamin discovered that the horse which Smede had ridden was, as he had suspected from seeing him on the road, one from Oaks called Bob. The mule was declared by all of them likely to be one of Beulah Land's, by the way Bartholomew, when he was brought into the camp by Floyd, went straight to him and made friendly sounds. They would know in daylight.

Daniel took bread and whiskey from the saddlebag, and they ate and drank. Benjamin did not like the taste of whiskey, but he accepted a swallow at Floyd's direction to help him sleep. As the fire died, they wound blankets and Floyd's old quilts about them, stretched out on the sand, and slept.

At first light Daniel built the fire up and boiled coffee, which they had with the last of the bread. By the increasing light they assured themselves that the horse was indeed Bob and that the mule was one of Beulah Land's called Do-all. In the packs Do-all had carried they discovered jewelry belonging to Nell and Sarah and Doreen, and silver pieces that had been taken from both plantations. After a rough sorting of the items, they redistributed them in various bags and pouches and loaded the horse and mules again. Kicking the fire into the creek, they mounted: Benjamin on Bob, Floyd on Bartholomew, and Daniel on Do-all.

Sometimes they rode together abreast, sometimes in a line; but they did not talk of what they had done. Benjamin asked if either remembered the day of the week, and Floyd said he thought it was Saturday. Benjamin said, "Tomorrow is Christmas." They spent the night at the abandoned farm where Daniel and Floyd had stopped and Daniel had cooked his rabbit on a spit. They finished Smede's store of ham, which they fried over the fire Benjamin made. Although they could not agree as to whether it had come from Oaks or Beulah Land, they declared that it had surely come from one or the other, because the hogs of the two plantations fed on corn that tasted like none other they knew.

32.

Having gone and come a long way, Floyd and Daniel were content to maintain the same pace for the last mile of their return; but Benjamin, feeling an explosion of energy, was suddenly eager for the sight of home faces and coaxed Bob into a gallop. Recognizing his neighborhood, Bob was willing. Not quite by chance, Nancy was the first to see Benjamin and give him welcome when, late on Christmas Day, he turned into the carriageway of Beulah Land. She had found herself worrying about him, and when she was not wanted for work, had taken to wandering along to the old stone bench that had been the goal of Nell's occasional walks. Standing on it. Nancy found that she could use it as a lookout to the main road. When she saw Benjamin, she jumped down and went running to meet him before he turned in.

"Mister Ben!" she called. "You back! Where you been to?"

"Hey there, Nancy!"

"You scoundrel! Slipping off like you did and everybody wondering—"

"How is everybody?"

"We all fine. Did you follow Floyd?"

"Why would I do that?"

"To get that Yankee that stole and burnt us! —Merry Christmas! Christmas gift, Mister Ben!" So did the servants traditionally demand presents on the anniversary of the Savior's birth.

"Merry Christmas, Nancy. I'm sorry I don't have a present for you."

"That don't matter none; you're welcome anyhow!" As he continued along the carriageway, but slowed politely to a walk, she sidestepped in a quick, dancing way to keep up with him. "Are you hungry?"

"I am, surely."

"Where the other ones?"

"Who do you mean?"

"Ah, you teasing me! —Floyd and Mister Dan is who!"

"They're back of me!" His saying it that way seemed to please both of them, for they laughed.

"Did you *get* him?"

"Get *who?*"

"You know who. The one they went to get!"

"You want to know a lot, don't you?"

"Did you?"

"Yes," he surprised himself by saying, for he had meant to save the news.

"*Did* you?"

"I *said* yes!"

"Oh, Mister Ben, you have revenged my honor!"

Benjamin looked startled and blushed.

"I hear them talking about revenging the honor of us all. Miss Sarah tried to keep it from Miss Nell about Floyd's going, but you know how long she could do that, I reckon! And Lotus, she tried not to tell me; but Lotus too good to hold a secret; she have to share everything she got. So we all of us knew before long. Why else would Floyd go off and leave us? You answer me that."

"Well, I guess you're right. We went for Oaks and Beulah Land."

"Lord God Almighty—I'm one proud girl! Y'all did it for me as much as Lotus and your grandpa and old Lovey! Didn't you? Now didn't you?"

"I reckon we did, Nancy."

They had come to Lovey's old cabin, now used by Sarah; and Nancy turned Benjamin over to Sarah and Jane when they raced out of the house together. Nell waited at the door, no less part of the occasion for merely looking on. Slipping down from the saddle, Benjamin gladly allowed himself to be embraced and scolded, all of them laughing, and Jane crying as well. When Nancy offered to take the horse to the barn, the others went indoors.

Benjamin soon learned that Doreen had spent the day at Beulah Land and had left them to walk home less than an hour ago, wanting, she said, to be there with their own people, and most especially in case Benjamin should come back. He must go home presently, Sarah said, but not until he'd had a share of their Christmas dinner. They had not done badly. The day before, Miss Eloise Kilmer had brought them a good-sized piece of corned beef. (It was she whose less practical gift of the gilded birdcage had so pleased Nancy the day after the raids.) Lotus had supplied sweet potatoes and rice and a cabbage. Doreen had brought with her a spice cake which Annabel had graciously sent her when Doreen refused her sister's invitation to take Christmas fare in town with her family and James.

Soon after Benjamin's arrival, Floyd and Daniel came. The greetings and embraces, the laughter and tears, the questions and answers were repeated, and many times again before the company broke up nearly two hours later. Benjamin, after Sarah had urged him the third time, said he would fetch Bob from the barn and go home. Floyd went to his cabin with Lotus. Sarah and Nell and Jane and Daniel sat on, tired and comfortable, around the kitchen table, smiling at each other and agreeing that it had turned out to be one of the happiest Christmases they could remember, as they went over the same incidents and made very nearly the same comments on them they had already made so many times during the past two hours.

Benjamin departed reluctantly, for he knew that Oaks would offer no company so pleasant as that he left at Beulah Land. He found Bob readily enough, having carried a candle with him from the kitchen. The horse had been unsaddled, brushed, and given hay, but was presently unattended, or so Benjamin thought until, having resaddled the horse, he remembered that his saddlebag was missing. Lifting the candle above his head, he surveyed the immediate vicinity of the barn, as if the saddlebag must surely be within sight if he could light his way to it. As he looked, he heard a giggle, at first smothered, then boldly repeated.

"Nancy!" he said, recognizing it as hers.

"Surprise!" She slid down from a hayloft over his head to land almost beside him outside the horse's stall. "Bet you looking for this!" She held up the missing bag.

Taking it, he said, "I wondered where it had got to."

"Thought there might be something in it special, so I stayed to take care of it for you."

"You're right. I thank you, Nancy, and I'm sorry you had to wait."

"Oh, I didn't have much else to do." He stood smiling at her, and she smiled at him. Finally she said, "How old are you, Mister Ben?"

He frowned. "Not so young, you know. Nearly twelve, or twelve, you might say." He was lying by a year, but then he felt so very much older than he was anyway.

"Well," she said in a tone that seemed to hedge and reserve what she might have said, had he been older. "Twelve is not very old. I was twelve all last year."

"But I'm a boy," Benjamin said. "I've done a lot of things girls don't do."

"Bet you haven't done much I haven't!" she boasted.

"Well, I—" He was unsure of himself suddenly, not knowing whether he wanted to go ahead or not; or rather, knowing that he did, but afraid.

"Did you hear what the Yankee men did to me when they were here?"

"Yes, I did, Nancy; and I was sorry."

"It was pretty bad," she said.

"It must have been," he agreed. "Anybody'd do such a thing is a low-down boll weevil."

She nodded thoughtfully, although her frown seemed to deny total agreement. "Did you ever think about doing things like that? —You know what I'm talking about, don't you?"

"No, Nancy; I declare I never did."

"I don't mean to me," she said hastily. "I mean anybody."

"No indeed, Nancy!"

"Well," she said meekly, until she looked at him below his waist. What she saw made her giggle triumphantly. "If you never thought about it how come your thing sticking up like that?" He pushed at himself desperately. "Don't do that," she cautioned. "You might just hurt yourself. Mustn't go poking, I been told, lest you do a damage. I don't know much about it, but I been told menfolk is weak down there." Her hand had gone to him as if to protect him from his own hand, then to idle and press and stroke when his flesh responded. She blew out the candle he held. They were quiet, almost not breathing.

Then she said, "You right, I expect. Twelve is not so very young, for a boy. I'm going to climb up into that loft again. You want to come with me?"

"I better get on home," he said, ashamed of his fear.

She shrugged and climbed the ladder quick as a cat. He hesitated, until hesitation became lingering. His eyes were used to the dark now. There was brilliant moonlight, and it shone through cracks in the walls of the barn. He looked toward the horse. The horse turned his head and looked at him. The horse looked away, and this Benjamin interpreted as showing he was in no very terrible hurry. Still, he waited. Then burning head to foot, he put hands and feet on ladder rungs and began to climb. He smelled her before he saw her, and then he saw her only dimly, which made it easier for him, as she began to make it easier for him too. She loosened his trousers until they fell about his ankles. She touched his knees, encouraging him to kneel over her when she lay back, and he came down upon her gingerly until she guided his penis between her open legs and set it to enter her.

A minute later she said, "You don't have to be in such a hurry. That pussy ain't going to run away." That was all either of them said until it was over for him. She stroked his back intuitively to soothe him after his final spasm, and they both lay still. Presently he rolled off her but not away, pulling at his trousers because he was beginning to feel the cold.

"Did I hurt you, Nancy?" he asked shyly.

"No!" she said cheerfully. "You wasn't nothing at all like them big old dirty mens."

"Well, I—"

"Don't mean to hint you wasn't big enough for the job," she said quickly. "You a right good size for a boy not yet grown."

"Have you seen a lot of boys, Nancy?"

"Oh, a few. Seen 'em, that is. They like to show off theirselfs trying to make your eyes pop."

"Who does?" he wanted to know.

"Oh, this one and that one. I reckon you not specially close to either one of your cousins, Miss Annabel's boys?"

"I hate them," Benjamin said. "You mean to tell me you've seen *them?*"

"I sure have."

"When?" he demanded to know.

"One time 'bout a year ago they was out here visiting with your grandma. Their mama was. Both of them slipped away from the porch and coaxed me to the barn. Said they had something to show me and cornered me in one of the cow stalls. Pulled their things right out, just like they was play-pretties everybody was dying to see."

"What did you do?"

"Laughed." She laughed now.

"You did?" He laughed with her.

"I sure did. They was no bigger than a thimble and just as easy to lose, I told 'em."

"You *did?*"

"I sure did. Now you're a proper right size, but not them boys."

"Huh," he said, trying to keep the pride out of his voice. "I never did think much of them, and now I think even less."

She smiled. "Did you have a good time?" He nodded. She had pulled her dress well down and sat with her arms hugging her knees. "Everybody made different, and you can't tell looking at them with their clothes on. Some big boys got little things, and some little ones got big ones. You know that boy they call Pike, son of Delia?"

"I think so. Short and skinny?"

"A runt. He could walk under a toadstool without ducking his head, and him fifteen years old. Well, they say his growth all went to his peter. Me and three, four other girls one time coaxed him to follow us into the field when the corn was high last summer, and we told him we'd heard about him and we'd give him our next piece of company cake if he'd show it to us. He was ready to oblige, and it was just like they'd said. It's so long he have to tie two knots in it so it won't trip him up when he walks."

Benjamin laughed until he was weak and felt blessedly helpless and friendly, and all he could say was "Oh, Nancy!" now and then before going off into more laughter.

"It's a fact," she declared solemnly, which only set him to laughing the harder. "Time for you to get on home now and stop Miss Doreen from worrying about you. Zadok, he been over here twice. He worrying 'bout you too."

"You right, I better go," he said, and felt his way to the ladder. "You coming?"

"In a little while. You go on."

"All right." He paused on the ladder just before his head disappeared. "Nancy?" He wanted to thank her, to make a statement of his friendly feelings and his gratitude, but she saved him from it.

"You have revenged my honor," she said, "and now I don't have to think about them bad mens no more."

"Good night, Nancy."

"Yes," she said, and yawned.

In the dark below he found Bob, secured the saddlebag, and led the horse out of the barn. Walking him and making as little noise as he could, he took his way around the black patch of earth that was the only sign left of the big house. He did not mount until he reached the main road. Then the tired boy on the tired horse went home finally to Oaks, now shivering in the cold moonlight, now and then laughing aloud as he remembered the girl he had left in the hayloft and the things she had said.

33.

They were drinking a glass of scuppernong wine. "Youth and age lie down together." Sarah smiled at Daniel as she said it, and he smiled at her broadly, the width of his mouth cracking his face in two. Nell and Jane had gone to bed an hour before. When the two awake were silent, as they had been for a few moments, the sound from the next room of the old woman's snoring alternated with the sigh of the young girl's even night breathing. Sarah rose from her chair at the kitchen table and closed the door, which had swung open. "You are tired too," she said. "Go to bed when you feel like it, I generally stay up a while after everyone else has gone off."

"I'm tired, but I'm not sleepy," Daniel said, as if it were a conundrum.

"That's the way it is sometimes." She lifted her head and looked about the kitchen slowly, deliberately. "I never expected to live in one of these cabins; yet how well I know them. I used to hold a little school in one for the servants' children. It was the beginning of the school my sister-in-law keeps in town now."

"Miss Selma?"

Sarah nodded. "It started because I began to teach a boy named Roman. A very special boy."

"I've heard some about him," Daniel said.

She looked at him keenly to gauge how much he had heard, and her words hinted a warning, if warning was needed. "He was my first friend here. I'll tell you about him—some other time."

"It was his clothes I wore just after I came."

"You soon grew out of them."

"You said he was the son of the master of Beulah Land."

Her face closed, then opened again with a softer look in her eyes. "Yes. My husband fathered him before we were married, when he was himself no more than a boy. Roman's mother was a Negro girl named Clovis, who married Roscoe Elk."

"It's complicated."

"Yes," she said, this time with irony. "But simple too. Or maybe I mean: given what everybody was like, it was bound to happen." She shrugged. "Things that seemed important once don't any more."

"It was before you married." His voice sounded almost angry in its offer of comfort.

She smiled but said, "I would not have missed Roman for a thousand infidelities."

"What happened to him?" Daniel asked.

"He killed a man, and they made him go away. The man was

his half brother, Junior Elk's brother." Hearing the coldness in her own voice, she added quickly, "As you said, it is complicated. —How very strange for you! To be here now, a Yankee boy with a Southern family, knowing so little of its history."

"I don't think of myself as a boy, Miss Sarah."

"If you were as old as I am, you would not take offense at my using the word."

"I don't think of me as young or you as old."

"You are learning to flatter like a Southern gentleman."

"I will never be a Southern gentleman, Miss Sarah."

"Are you thinking of leaving us?"

"Not if you let me stay."

"It isn't for me to give you permission. That's between you and Beulah Land."

"Then I'll stay."

"And become a Southern gentleman." Her tone teased him a little.

"No, ma'am." He smiled. "When you say 'Beulah Land,' you make it sound like something with its own heart and soul."

"It is!" she said as if surprised that he had just discovered it. She studied him silently for a few moments. "I wish I'd had a son like you."

"I couldn't think of you being anybody's mother."

"Well—" She laughed, not quite with humor. "Nor am I."

Sarah was perfectly well aware of the undercurrent of their conversation. She had tried, although not very determinedly, to discourage it. Now she looked frankly at the young man who sat across the table from her. Since he insisted that he was not a boy, she would consider him as a man. His face was lean but no longer skeletal as it had been the night he arrived with Lauretta. His forehead was high with a bony ridge just above his eyes. His eyebrows and hair were thick, light brown. His stare was as serious and intent as a bird's. She noted the big, well-shaped nose—nothing boyish there, nor in the full mouth below it. The chin—yes, it trembled slightly, as a boy's might, under her scrutiny. Seeing him this way and thinking precisely of how he appeared, she knew it did not in the least signify whether she considered him as man or boy. He was Daniel, and he was looking at her with love and fear. In that moment she knew that she would have to resist to her utmost loving him too, and in the same way. It didn't matter that she was in her fifties, and he not yet twenty. She wanted to lean across the table and touch him. She would like to feel his hands on her face. Sarah and Daniel were not the first or the last to love someone the "wrong" age. It is a common enough accident of timing that is one of the many accidents in life people deal with one way or another, and it has nothing to do with wanting to be younger or older. As she looked at him, not knowing that she appeared beautiful to him, she realized that she had allowed the pause between them to become too long and too full, and she sought words to break it.

Before she found them, Daniel said, his voice raw with feeling, "Miss Sarah, I—I want—I want you to know—I'd do anything in the world for you!" It was the best he could do, although not what he wanted to say.

However, it served to give her voice. She thrust out her hand, open and palm up, and when he reached to her, she took his hand and shook it warmly, to his disappointment and relief. "Daniel," she said, "you are our good friend. You are *my* good friend. I bless the night you came here. This is your home."

It was not what she wanted to say either, but it would have to do for both of them. They looked at each other with apology and forgiveness, and Sarah hurried to put words after the moment, lest it go wrong, as she knew it might. "Dan! Tomorrow after you've rested some and maybe feel more like it, I wonder if you'd be willing to go to the Shelter and stay a few days, so that Otis can come home and have time with his people?"

"Surely, Miss Sarah."

"Zebra has been back and forth, but nobody else; and he must want badly to come home. He hasn't been here since our trouble. Also, I'll tell you some things we need I'd like him to bring. Not so many because the Yankees may come again on one of their visits. I promise not to wait too long before somebody comes to relieve you."

"I'll go, Miss Sarah." Daniel's voice sounded sad, for he had offered everything, and was merely being sent on an errand.

Seeing his disappointment, she continued, "Floyd will think he ought to go, but Lotus has been worried and needs him with her a day or two. And it will be good for him to talk to the hands we have left; get them settled down and put a little resolve into them."

"I'll be glad to go, Miss Sarah," he said a little more brightly.

"Now you'd better get some sleep. We have to be up early to-morrow."

He rose from his chair awkwardly, as if he were being dismissed. Feeling guilty, she frowned and would not look at him until he got to his door and stood there, making her look at him before he would leave. When her eyes met his, he said, "Good night, Miss Sarah."

His not daring to ask more brought her from her chair and to him at the door. She lifted a hand to his face, as if to test his cheek for fever. "What you went with Floyd to do—I'm obliged to you. They say vengeance must be left to the Lord. I can't help it, I feel better for what you've done, you and Floyd and Benjamin. But if you hadn't been any part of it, you'd still be welcome here to make it home. You'd still be my friend. You are a good—man." She did not draw her hand back when he caught the mound of it lightly with his teeth, but took his shoulder with her other hand and shook him with affection that denied anything stronger between them. "Merry Christmas, Daniel."

Turning, he stumbled into the lean-to room that had been added to the cabin when Floyd was a boy. She closed the door and went back to the table. Without sitting down she finished her glass of wine, and then his, which he had left half full. Blowing out the candle, she went to the door and, opening it, looked out. The moon was bright, the place was still. All appeared dead, or sleeping. For a few moments the cold air felt good, and then it chilled her, and she shut the door. She had always been able to see in the dark, even when she did not know a place any better than a few days' residence had taught her this cabin; but she found her way easily into the bedroom, slipping out of her shoes and dress and getting quickly into bed in her petticoat.

For a time she listened to Nell's snoring and Jane's easy breathing. She was thankful that Daniel was no nearer, for had he been, he would have heard her thoughts and come to her. Did he lie awake? Or did he, because young, sleep deeply without troubled dreams or wakeful, hateful desires? For the first time Sarah felt herself old. She was tired, she was old, and she loved a boy. Tears came until her face was wet and her throat thick. Fighting to draw breath, she opened her mouth, and her inhalation was a cry that frightened her and woke Jane. She commanded herself to be still and was unable to obey. She wept, making as little sound as she could, but it was enough to bring

Jane to her. Without a word the child slipped under the covers and held her. Sarah gave herself up, and Jane held her in her warm, small arms, cooing love and reassurance until Sarah exhausted herself and slept.

34.

Having gone to sleep with her own tears, Sarah woke to those of another woman. Recent months had so alerted her to deal with crises that she was out of bed and at the back door in bare feet before she quite realized what had brought her there. The door was being pounded from outside and penetrated by angry wails. Opening it, she was confronted by a woman named Josephine who had washed all the clothes and house linens of Beulah Land as long as they had them to wash. Flinging herself upon her mistress, so that Sarah had to catch her in her arms whether or no, Josephine poured out her troubles.

"Miss Sarah, I have killed him! You better send-see, but if he ain't dead, he got more blood than a ox!"

"Who, Josephine? *Who*'ve you killed?"

"Who, you say?" Josephine appeared astonished that such a question could be put. "*Napoleon* is *who!*" She wept.

At that moment they were joined by two others, roused by the racket. Daniel had his trousers on and was pulling a shirt over his head. Jane arrived in her nightgown, carrying shoes and dress for Sarah. Over the shoulder of the woman she held, Sarah said to Daniel, "Tell Floyd to see about Napoleon *directly!*" He nodded and was gone. Sarah slipped her feet into the shoes Jane set ready and guided the big black woman to a kitchen chair, where she collapsed with her head in her hands, moaning.

"Now don't cry, Josephine. It'll be all right. I've sent Floyd to Napoleon, and he'll take care of him!"

"No'm, he won't. I killed him, I tell you—"

"Now don't—"

"Stabbed him with the very knife he use to cut the corn!"

"What did you do that for?" Jane asked.

"Shoulda stabbed that bitch Corinne too!"

That told Sarah what had happened.

Corinne was what Lovey used to call a twitchy-tail, unable since she was ten to keep from flirting with everything male that came her way. When she was fifteen, she was married to a man named Alf, who had made her behave, but Alf was one of the hands taken to Savannah six months ago to work at dredging the harbor. In his absence Corinne had reverted to her early flirty ways. Josephine's Napoleon (she had asked to change her name from Betsy when she married him) had been susceptible. It was one of the recurring plantation problems Sarah found most difficult to deal with, for she was able to see every point of view, and general sympathy is not helpful in settling such matters.

"Tell me what happened," Sarah urged.

"Oh, I can't ma'am!" Josephine wailed, and then after blowing her nose on her skirt, proceeded to do so. "Well'm. I see he been sniffing round that heifer. She draw a bucket of water and start to tote it to her cabin; she say, 'This sho is feel heavy today!' —like water change his weight one day to the next. —Napoleon hear her—she wouldn't say it if a man warn't handy. First thing you know, he toting for her. Well, I put a stop to that. But then she use other tricks she got. Happen along when Napoleon knock off his work, scratching her ass more like rubbing or patting, you know the way I mean, purely inviting a man to do the same or leastways fasten his eyes where her hand is. Then we was dancing last night, it Christmas and all, but not like it use to be; not so many things, but us making our own good time. And Napoleon dance too much with Corinne. I had to hit him side the head to get him home, and everybody laugh at me. Well, we went to bed. Then middle the night he must have sneaked out on me. I woke up, he gone. First I think the privy, but I remember it cold weather, and Napoleon won't go when it cold. I lie awake, I toss, I turn. After while I get up and wait. So there I'm waiting when he come sneaky-tail home before daybreak. We have us a fuss. First he deny, make innocent. But when I tell him I smell her on him, he say proud as you please he done it! Yes'm, say he done it! That when I grab up the knife. —Oh, God, Miss Sarah, what I gone do without Napoleon?"

Sarah had managed to get her dress on during the recital, and Jane had started a fire in the cook stove. Fully clothed, Nell opened the door from the bedroom and asked to be told what all the clamor was for. While Josephine repeated her story with embellishments, Sarah boiled some of the parched peanuts they used instead of coffee. By the time Daniel returned to say Napoleon had stopped bleeding and started crying, the three women and the girl were drinking the bitter but comforting hot brew.

"You see, Josephine?" Sarah said. "It'll be all right again. You go on back and have a talk with Napoleon."

Josephine ruminated. "If I send him to you, will you tell him not to mess around no more with that woman, Miss Sarah?"

"Well, I'll say something to him," Sarah promised.

Nell said, "You so worried about him, I'm surprised you can sit there drinking coffee knowing he's alive and not dead after all."

"I'll go presently," Josephine said, and sipped from her cup. "Do him good to dread my coming." Her face took on a brooding look and after a moment she gave voice to her thoughts. "Lord God. Lord God-a-mercy." The dark mood passed with a few more sips from her cup, and she looked brightly at the man who was helping himself to a cold biscuit from the stove. "You say he crying, Mister Dan?"

"That's right," Daniel affirmed, nodding and chewing.

"Well!" Josephine said.

And so another day began at Beulah Land, different from every other and like every other.

Morning fires were lighted, food was cooked and eaten. There was no formal call to work, but as the men emerged from their cabins, Floyd set them jobs. All the stock were fed and watered. The women fed and counted and scolded the chickens and other barnyard fowls, and counted again until they came near agreeing on their tallies. They searched for eggs and sometimes found small caches of food that had been hidden from the Yankees, reporting them to Sarah or Lotus after taking a share they did not report. No one considered it stealing when they took from the general provender more than was their proper portion.

Standing and studying the black bare earth where the big house had stood, Sarah and Floyd agreed suddenly that it should be plowed. In Floyd's absence the debris had been cleared away, salvaged or buried or thrown into deeper parts of the creek that meandered through the woods. Zebra hitched Do-all to a plow and broke up the ground at Floyd's direction. It was not that they intended to plant it now or ever, but Sarah had suggested that breaking it up would break the curse of the destruction, and her reasoning pleased everybody. They would stop walking around the scorched place as if on hot coals; they would stop respecting the old definitions of walls and doors. They would cease reminding one another that *there* was where the drawing room had been, while the central hall had stretched from here to here, and the breezeway— As soon as the plowing was begun, they all smiled and moved about more freely and easily than they had done.

Midmorning Nell directed Josephine to build a fire under the largest of her black washpots in the laundry yard. Together they boiled up a great mess of lye hominy, stirring it with the wooden paddle Josephine had used to stir boiling linen. The soapy, unpalatable smell of it filled the air and was somehow a comfort to those it reached, for it assured them they would not go hungry, however much they might grumble at the dullness of such lowly fare.

Jane went with Nancy to dig potatoes from the hill of earth where they were stored, accompanied by a group of little girls. Mom Patience, the oldest of the remaining old women, went to the woods to look for certain leaves and bark and winter berries she said would provide elixirs to repel the illnesses of early spring. Bartholomew appeared willing enough when Daniel set a saddle on his back and, taking instructions from Sarah as to what things Otis must bring with him when he rode back on the mule, made his departure.

In these ways they lived the day, not forgetting their private hates and hopes, but working around them, everything finding its place and moment in the texture of the life they shared. Daniel was gone. Sarah was aware of it and missed him. But here was a pretty freckled egg one of the women brought her. And soon Jane and Nancy came back trailed by the children, all trying to share the handle and the burden of the bushel basket of new-dug potatoes, all giggling.

Alone, Daniel sorrowed for the love he had not been able to speak, but a turn of the road brought a muddy creek smell that put his mind on catfish, and he thought that tonight, or tomorrow when he was alone at the island Shelter, he would catch a fish and fry it, and count the bones when he had eaten it, making a wish for every bone; and stir the ashes of his fire when he sat quiet before sleeping, free to think whatever came into his mind, free to feel whatever was in his heart.

35.

It was a time of tears. Men as well as women shed them without embarrassment, even with pride. Children who suffered the loss of a parent—and many died aside from those who fell to gun and sword—were too warmly pitied, and encouraged to grieve too passionately. As for the old, some of them stopped crying only to eat, and some not even then, for, being old, they claimed a larger acquaintance than their juniors, and the day seldom passed that the dark angel did not give the kiss of death to at least one who had been known to them. It was a time then of sorrow, most of it genuine but some of it not. Weeping might almost be said to have been in fashion.

Annabel Saxon had altered truth until it became romantic fantasy; but whereas those who listened to her might be persuaded to see her and themselves in the self-flattering light she shed over the past, Annabel herself still knew an apple from an onion. The only time she was surprised to real tears was on a morning she entered her drawing room with something else entirely on her mind and happened to find herself looking straight at her portrait over the mantel. It had been painted by Casey Troy during his months of residence in the neighborhood when he painted most of the local gentry. Seeing that early likeness without forethought, face to face as it were with her youth, Annabel could not but be struck by the realization of how beautiful she had been and—turning from portrait to mirror nearby—how the years since had hardened her eyes and chin, softened the flesh of her neck, and begun to gray her hair. She was not yet thirty-five, but she fully looked her age.

It was the fault of early marriage. A child she had been, gay and triumphant at marrying young. But of course it meant that now she had two sons nearly grown, and people would soon begin to think of her as old. She had endured enough, she reckoned irritably, to make her look twice instead of just her age. The war had not gone to her satisfaction; and now although all knew defeat to be unavoidable, none could say when or how the end would come. People only agreed that the old ways were lost forever. With the war's end Colonel Blair Saxon would return to Highboro and work again with his father in the bank, for no matter who wins or loses a war, there is always money to be changed for those who survive it.

There were, to be sure, her sons, but she was not willing to live entirely through them; and doting though she seemed to friends and family when she spoke of Blair Junior and Bonard, she admitted to herself that there was something of character lacking in both of them. A year of direct involvement in the war would have done them good, she felt. She had encouraged them to think too highly of their prospects and abilities.

Annabel had made the most of family misfortunes, of her brother's being blinded (in battle, she had claimed), of the Yankee raids on Oaks, and of her father's murder; but the novelty of these tragedies had passed, and they were in danger of being lumped together in people's minds with the general woe, leaving Annabel with no particular distinction.

To top it all, her old rival, Margaret-Ella Singletary, had recently had the luck of being made a widow. Her husband had actually been killed in the fighting in Tennessee. As if that were not enough, Annabel suspected a budding of tenderness between her brother James and the new widow. The similarity of their situations had waked a sympathy in the heart of each for the other. Margaret-Ella's widowhood had provided the occasion for reconciliation with Annabel. Annabel could not chance looking mean by continuing to snub one who had made "the great sacrifice for our Cause," albeit somewhat late in the game. Social intimacy was resumed. Annabel had to content herself with the crumb that it was the younger, plainer sister who put on crepe. Had it been Ann-Elizabeth, who was Annabel's exact contemporary and principal rival of the two, life would have been insupportable.

Since his residence in town began, James had become something of a pet of the circle of women dominated by Annabel. He was handsome in a country-man way. He was still young. (Men were accounted young much longer than women—oh, unfair, unfair!) He was of good family. He owned property, for whatever it was worth. He had served honorably in the war. He combined in his person the authority of masculinity with the vulnerability of blindness. More than one of Annabel's acquaintance had felt the attraction of being useful to one so eligible. James, who had loved only Rachel, who indeed had thought of none other— James, who had spent most of his days on the land and in the elements, had taken with surprising ease to life indoors and to the company of women.

There was little choice for him, so many men having been claimed by the war. Although one or the other of his nephews steered him through the town every morning for his exercise and he was stopped on their excursions for a remark or a discussion by sundry townspeople, he felt easier at home, where the sounds were not so many as to confuse him. He required the reassurance of the known. The silence of his mind was fearfully jarred by the unexpected. Like them or not, he knew what to expect of Annabel and her sons and of the two house servants, Millie and Old Fox.

Nothing had been quite real to him from the day he lost his sight, and the fact that so much had happened and that of so violent a nature since then merely compounded the sense of unreality. He knew that Rachel and his father were dead; he had attended the funeral of one and touched the tombstone of the other, tracing her name. He knew that Oaks had been burned to the ground; he had felt the heat and smelled the fire. So he understood that the life he had lived as a working farmer was no longer possible to him. That Oaks had been destroyed so soon after his ability to function there even made its destruction seem peculiarly and awfully appropriate. In feeling so he did not consider the feelings of his son and daughter, it is true, nor of Doreen, who had been the one of his original family closest to him in love and understanding, but self-concern is not an accusation often brought against those afflicted as James had been.

Hence, he had learned to sit patiently in a room with nothing but his thoughts and the ticking of a clock for company. Homely sounds and silences were more agreeably broken by female voices than by male, he discovered. At first he merely endured the visits and attentions of Annabel's female acquaintance; then he learned to be grateful to them and to look forward to the visits. He liked the murmur of their voices asking and answering questions that hardly needed to be asked and answered, so known and worn were all areas of daily concern. He liked the fact that many of them carried sewing about with them, because he could fancy they were not staring at him, and he discovered that he could be useful if only in such little ways as holding up his hands as frames from which they wound their knitting yarn. He did not know how much he charmed them as he sat, a listening frown on his face. He was, as one said privately to another on leaving, "such a *man*, yet so unforbidding." To use him as a winding post was like plaiting the mane of a wild horse.

One afternoon as he sat contentedly so, it happened to be Margaret-Ella who wound yarn into a ball from the posts of his lifted hands, and Margaret-Ella's voice that sweetened the air with trivia. Annabel suddenly remembered something she had meant to tell Millie and plunged from the room without excusing herself. She did not return immediately.

The realization that they were alone together was instant for Margaret-Ella. It came only gradually to James.

"Miss Annabel appears to have deserted us," Margaret-Ella presently observed.

"Has she?" James did not care that she had gone.

"I mean to say she left us several minutes ago without—"

"Yes?"

"—without saying what she was about to do or how long she would be."

"Annabel comes and goes. They all do," James furnished, only for something to say.

"I suppose it must be distracting for you?"

"No, I'm used to it."

Margaret-Ella took advantage of their privacy to enjoy a close, unhurried examination of the man on the settee before her. He sat with his back stiff, head cocked alertly. So still was he the very muscles of his thighs seemed to bulge his trouser legs. Indeed, he sat more like a soldier than a farmer; he had, of course, been both. Yet his big, well-proportioned body seemed perfectly at home in this parlor with its feminine furnishings, and that indicated to Margaret-Ella that he had the temperament of a true gentleman. He was a handsome man, she decided, and wondered why she had not before been aware of it. Well, she answered herself, they had both been married; and when they were younger, *he* was the younger by one or two years. That would still be so, she admitted, but it signified less now than it had in their extreme youth. His hair was clean and neatly trimmed, as were his fingernails, she noted, leaning toward him as she wound the thread.

He seemed to sit more attentively, feeling perhaps the warmth of her sudden closeness, or catching the moist fragrance of her scent. Her voice was little above a whisper when she said, "You must feel very alone without a wife."

His answer was not immediate, but when it was given, it was thoughtfully spoken. "And you without a husband."

"Yes." She caught her breath. "Oh yes," she added in a rush, "I have been without him for most of the war, you know."

"Longer than Rachel and I were separated," he said deliberately.

"He was one of the first to volunteer."

"Yes."

Her voice was seductive in its shyness. "I believe such as we suffer more than those who have lived entire lives alone."

"It may be so, ma'am."

"The single bed can surely be no colder than the double bed that once was shared." She laughed shakily. "I am not a brave woman. You will despise me for this self-pity."

"No," he protested.

She sighed. "It is hard."

He blushed so violently she became alarmed. Staring at him full again, she soon perceived the reason for his confusion in the bulge of his trouser front. His hands, still upright as they dutifully held the loops of yarn, rendered him helpless. Without a word Margaret-Ella quickly spun the remaining thread into the full ball, releasing his hands so that they might drop to his lap to cover what had been revealed to her. As she glanced at him again, she felt her eyes fill with tears of sympathy. Not thinking what she did, she reached a hand to his cheek. "Thank you, my friend," she whispered.

"Well, whatever are you doing!" Annabel exclaimed, returning. "Both of you quiet as mice stealing cheese. Nothing at all to say to one another? My! —The most surprising thing: I had just finished speaking to Millie in the kitchen about the dried peaches and was returning to you here when I saw through one of the windows coming along to the side door—not the front nor yet the back, but the *side* door, mind, which you will agree shows a nicety of intention and exactness of judgment, now won't you?"

"What are you gabbling about, Annabel?" James asked severely.

"Well, heigh-ho! And don't you growl at me, my good fellow,

when I have news for you. *Good* news. —No less than an offer for Oaks!"

"What kind of offer can you mean?"

"An offer to *buy* the place, dunderhead! What else would I mean?"

"Go back to the beginning, Annabel. Someone was coming to the side porch entrance."

"Just as I said."

"Who?"

"Junior Elk. Exactly. And Negro or not, one of the richest men in the county."

"What do you say he wanted?"

"To make an offer for Oaks, I tell you!"

"Now that is very odd!"

"True!"

"If he had been serious, he would have asked to speak to me."

"I told him you were engaged and urged him to say what his business was to me, promising to—"

"I really must get along home," Margaret-Ella interrupted them to announce.

James faced the direction of her voice. "Miss Margaret-Ella, I beg you not to trouble yourself so much as to—"

"Well, if you must," Annabel acquiesced, leading the way into the hall so promptly that Margaret-Ella found herself fumbling to gather her knitting into its carrying bag and follow her with no more than a nod to James, which he, of course, could not see. Her leaving was without dignity, attended by the barest courtesy. James felt it all and was angry. Hearing the front door close and Annabel's returning footsteps, he slapped the arm of the settee and exclaimed, "Annabel, you really have no manners at all!"

"Oh, don't make such a fuss—"

"That poor woman, bereaved as she is—" Annabel sniffed. "And one of your oldest, dearest friends!"

"Lord, yes. I've known her and Ann-Elizabeth cat's ages, haven't I? Since we were little girls and you were crawling around in rompers. We don't stand on ceremony with each other, you see. They treat me the same, never fear."

"I have never known Miss Margaret-Ella to be anything but gentle."

Annabel looked at him narrowly. "You don't know anything about women, James. Mama and Doreen spoiled you, and

Rachel was the first and last woman you ever noticed—" She sat down opposite him, taking the chair the visitor had lately occupied. "See how you have distracted me when we have such an important family matter to consider!"

"You go about everything the wrong way. Junior Elk, you mean?"

"Of course!" she said satirically. "It is just what everyone wants, you will agree: to be rid of those big old places. We do not pass a friend on the street or talk to one at church of a Sunday who doesn't say the same. Everyone longs to sell, and why not? The war is all but over, and we the losers. That gorilla Lincoln and his black Republicans have taken our slaves, and there is no other way to work so many acres. I've heard you say as much yourself."

"Yes," he agreed tentatively.

She clapped her hands. "What luck for us then that he chooses to fancy Oaks!"

"As I remember," James said, "his father always wanted to own Beulah Land."

"Then we are double lucky the son wants Oaks, are we not? I say let us talk with him and hear what he has to say. If he makes a reasonable offer, and I have no doubt from what he has said that he is prepared to do just that, needing the merest encouragement to understand that we are not entirely cold to such a proposal—"

"There are many matters to consider."

"Oh, yes. We must ask for more than we expect him to pay, and leave a little room for gee-ing and haw-ing. How often have I seen Blair and Papa Woodrow carry on so at the bank with some poor soul."

"We must consider other people."

"None but ourselves surely."

"The Kendricks."

"D'you mean Auntie Sarah?"

"*She* would never sell, you may be sure."

"Perhaps he knows that, and so he comes to us."

"Nor would she welcome my selling Oaks to Junior Elk."

"It is certainly none of her affair what we do with our property."

"We are old neighbors. If I should sell, she would have a new neighbor."

"You are surely being oversolicitous of one who is no blood relation."

"Davises and Kendricks have always been close, not just neighbors, but related by marriage for the last two generations."

"Well," said Annabel, "surely *that* is over now, for Beulah Land no longer has Kendricks to marry Davises! Beulah Land itself, if it survives the war, will certainly go to your son Benjamin, for who else is there? You are needlessly cautious in your concern. Auntie Sarah worships her grandchildren, and they are your children!"

"I should keep Oaks to pass on to Benjamin, as it was passed on to me."

"And let him have both Oaks and Beulah Land? What on earth would he do with three thousand acres and not a single slave to work them? Indeed, why should you assume that Oaks is yours to pass on to *your* son? I too have sons."

"They have a father, and *he* has a father, and *he* has a bank."

"That has nothing to do with it. I am talking about property."

"I shall naturally consult with you—if indeed there is anything in the man's offer."

"Oh, there assuredly is! Would you like me to send for him?"

"No."

She hesitated, considering the matter. "Perhaps you are right. We must not appear too eager. On the other hand, there should be no trifling with such a golden chance."

"How was it left between you?"

"Why, I said I would tell you what he said. He thanked me and asked if he might call again to know your views. I agreed."

"I shall go to him. I do not like the idea of conducting business talks in your home."

"Lord, if that's all that worries you, you must forget it. When Blair was home, the only thing he ever found to say for himself was something or other to do with the bank."

"Nevertheless, I shall go to him."

She appeared to yield. "As you please." She sighed, but then she added, "This afternoon."

"Tomorrow perhaps. No sooner."

"First thing in the morning. You mustn't leave it too long."

"I shall be the judge of when to see Junior Elk."

She decided to leave it there.

36.

One of the lesser properties Roscoe Elk had accumulated was a two-room structure on a lane just off the main thoroughfare of Highboro. It had been a shop that failed to earn a living for two successive owners before Roscoe began to use it as an office. It was still so used by his son, who kept it deliberately shabby to reassure and disarm those who found themselves doing business with a Negro. From the old desk facing the front window Junior Elk could see all who passed or approached. When, late in the morning after his call at the Saxon house, he saw James Davis escorted by the Saxon house servant, he knew he was going to have his way about buying Oaks plantation.

Opening the door, Junior raised his voice in surprise. "Mr. Davis! —Junior Elk speaking to you. I say so because there is no way you should recognize me by voice. I was hoping that you would send for me, for I never wanted to put you to the trouble of finding my poor place of business."

"Good morning to you," James said formally. "My sister Mrs. Saxon has told me—"

"Oh, yes? Mrs. Saxon!"

"If you will be so good as to direct my servant where to seat me?"

"Indeed!" Junior made a bustle of clearing papers from a worn leather chair beside the desk.

When he was sitting, James said, "Thank you, Fox. Now why don't you go along and attend to those errands Miss Annabel wanted you to do for her, and then come back for me?"

As Fox left them, Junior said, "I have seldom said more than 'Good day, ma'am,' to Mrs. Saxon before yesterday, but of course I am well known to her husband, Colonel *Blair* Saxon, and to his father, Mr. *Woodrow* Saxon, from my dealings—and those of *my* father before me—at the bank!"

James nodded.

"It was a terrible thing that happened at Oaks," Junior continued. "I don't wonder that you now choose to make your home in town with Mrs. Saxon."

"I have another sister and a son who remain on the old place," James observed.

"Yes, sir. I paid them a short visit soon after the calamity, to let my sympathy be known and to offer any help it might be in my power to give at such a time."

"Did you?" No one had told James.

"Your sister, Miss Doreen Davis, was most polite although—poor lady—she seemed to be still in the grip of the cruel thing that had happened. However, on that occasion she saw fit to remember that your father and mine once arranged a little business between them."

"I see." Again James nodded, weighing the tone as well as the words and unable to detect anything other than respect and deference in the man's voice.

"The recollection of that transaction is, in part, what gave me the idea, what even leads me to *hope*, if I may so put it, that you may be prepared to consider selling off some of your abundant acreage."

Taking the last words as a point of comment, James said, "So many acres it is not easy to put them to practical use these days. There are no longer the men necessary to work it all properly."

"Exactly, sir. Now let us look to the future. I would not be ambitious to keep such a large place myself, knowing how impractical it will henceforth be to operate profitably."

"Then I don't understand your interest in the possibility of my being willing to sell; yet that is what Mrs. Saxon led me to believe."

"Oh, another use, sir," Junior said confidently. "I would not envision keeping such a place whole, nor would you, I imagine, care to see it kept so by a new owner, for it would be too painful a reminder of the past. However, this war which we have all suffered long, but which, if the good Lord so decree, will end one day, has uprooted many people. Some will not find their way home but will endeavor to settle wherever fate has scattered them." In talking to whites Junior sometimes assumed the rhetorical manner of his father before him, a way of speaking that had once made him laugh but which he now employed with a kind of self-irony to screen some of his shrewdness. "Do you begin to divine my drift and meaning, sir?"

"Say on, if you will."

"People will live and they will build a new life. I have wondered if there may not be a market in the future for many small farms where the great plantation of Oaks has flourished all our living days until now."

James was thoughtful. "You mean: cut it up, sell it by parcels?"

"Yes, sir."

"That would surely be a long and tedious business with an uncertain outcome."

"For *me*, sir, not for you. I am prepared to make an offer for the entire acreage *now* and make it my own concern to have new wells dug and fences posted, and to dispose of it as separate farms if and when such a market opens up. I may be wrong. It is a great gamble, but one I am prepared to take."

James held the inside of his cheek between his teeth and pressed slowly until he tasted blood. He had suddenly remembered one day when he was a boy and his father Bruce had given him a plot of the land to farm as his own. How proud and determined he had been then. It was always he, not his elder brother Adam, who had cared about the land. "All this is—I mean to say, we are only talking, you know."

"Yes, sir. But to a purpose, I hope. I realize that you must consider various aspects of the question, think it through most carefully, that is. You may even—" Junior's voice seemed to hesitate with honest doubt. "I do not know how ownership is arranged, but it will perhaps be necessary for you to obtain the consent and agreement of others. I do not know."

"I am the sole owner," James said shortly. "What I decide will settle the matter."

"Ah, then that will make it simpler, sir, will it not?"

James paused to check his resentment at the other's suggestion that the disposal of Oaks might not be entirely in his power. He wondered if Annabel had indicated any such thing in her exchange with Junior Elk the day before, or if even her father-in-law, with an eye to her interest and that of his grandsons, had rubbed his nose in the meaningful way James had seen him do, and coughed, and implied vague doubts. "What I decide will settle the matter, you may be sure. Still, I must think about it carefully before I make any decision."

"Just so, sir," Junior said with respect. James could not see the amused contempt that showed in his eyes. "Just so, indeed," he repeated. "No sensible man makes quick decisions on matters so momentous as those we have been turning over. I myself will think about it further also. Yet I am fairly certain in my own mind that some such speculative venture as I have put before you might turn out well for all concerned, might eventually and with a great deal of work, and of course investment, prove itself a good thing in the long run for whoever is prepared to be patient. I will even go so far as to tell you, sir—although I would speak of it to no other saving perhaps Mr. Woodrow Saxon, who has some confidential knowledge of my various small affairs—I will tell you, sir, that word has come to me that a number of farmers in our part of the state who have large holdings are entertaining the idea of getting rid of them, in part if not altogether, being of the opinion that farming as we have known it on a large scale is done for in our section. So, while we must not move forward too quickly on the one hand, we must not on the other move too slowly—if we intend, that is, to move at all."

Understanding the bluff behind the earnest tone, James began to redden, and Junior watched his expression come to the point of anger before he offered mollifying words. "There is no question that I would consider buying anywhere but from you, if you choose to sell, sir. There is no land so desirable for the purpose I propose as your own. The soil is rich—it has been said that you could grow anything you put your hand to. The land is well situated in terms of town and railroad to all markets. A man would be a fool to buy elsewhere if he could buy from you, sir. Believe me truly; I understand that."

"How many acres would you think of?" James asked presently.

Junior's answer was prompt. "All of Oaks if you are prepared to sell. How many acres is that?"

"Fourteen hundred, and something more than. I would have it newly surveyed, it has been so long since that was done." He paused, and Junior chose to remain silent to see if silence would loosen the blind man's tongue a little. He would like to enjoy the interview a bit more. "It is true that I— Well, I am blind now, as you know. It is true that I would find it no easy matter to manage Oaks again even if other things were as they used to be."

"I understand, sir," Junior said with dignity that did not presume sympathy.

"However, it is to be all thought over carefully." Junior allowed himself a smile. It was his experience that men who protested so much that they must further consider and reconsider had already made up their minds. "Yes. I should probably —if I make up my mind to dispose of any of it, in fact—want to keep a piece of it for my son."

Junior shifted his chair. "Ah, I see your servant returning."

The door opened without permission asked. "I'm back, Mr. Davis," Fox said.

"Wait for me outside, Fox."

"Yes, sir." The door opened and closed again. James rose from his chair.

Junior said, "I must thank you for doing me the honor of coming here, Mr. Davis. I had not intended to put you to the trouble."

"I take my exercise every morning. This morning I walked this way instead of another, you see, so there was no trouble about it."

"Even so, I thank you for coming and hope that it may not turn out to have been an unrewarding exercise."

Another silence followed, James standing still, Junior rising from his chair behind the desk. Junior watched James's face, reading it easily, knowing the question behind it, letting embarrassment become evident before exclaiming, "Forgive me, sir! I must not have my wits about me this morning. In all our confidential exchange, I have not asked you to set a price at which you might consider my offer to buy. May I know what you have in mind?"

James swallowed and relaxed his shoulders. "I have nothing in mind. The property has not been bought or sold for nearly a hundred years."

"Ah, that is so."

"Since the matter has been on your mind longer than mine, perhaps you would care to name a price you would be ready to pay."

Junior's voice was importantly businesslike. "That would depend on so many things, sir. How much land you are willing to dispose of. How soon you might decide. Whether you wish to keep back a little bit for your son or a large amount. You understand?"

"Still, some figure must have occurred to you," James insisted.

"I confess it has. I would be willing to pay in gold, seeing there is so much fluctuation in the value of our paper money these days. Gold keeps its value. That might take a little arranging, but my wife's family have banking connections in Savannah, and those connections extend as far as New York and Boston. If, let me say, you wanted to sell the main part of your plantation, I am prepared to pay the equivalent of twenty dollars an acre."

37.

"That is how we left it," James was saying to Annabel an hour later.

"Twenty dollars an acre." She wet her lips with her tongue in the ancient gesture of avarice. "In gold. I have heard of fifteen offered *not* in gold but in Confederate paper, a sack of which will hardly buy a bushel of potatoes."

"It is a consideration," James agreed.

"You must do it," Annabel announced. "You will then be independent and not have to worry about being blind the rest of your life. Why, it will be a cushion for all of us in these uncertain days."

"I have told you: I shall think about it." James was not displeased at the morning's interview with Junior Elk. He had returned home determined to give Annabel only the bones of that interview, but she would not, of course, be satisfied until she had made him dress the bones in every ounce of their original flesh and gristle, decked finally with the skin stretched smooth over all.

"You will be a fool not to jump at it."

"Thank you, Annabel. Now let us talk no more of it."

"I say what I think."

"No one will deny that." He sighed.

"And why should I not give my opinion, pray, on an important family matter, to the only brother I have left?"

"If it were just your opinion, there could be no objection. But you have a way of giving opinions as if they were new commandments thrown like thunderbolts from the mountaintop."

"I say you must take it before he changes his mind! *He's* no fool, nor is he the novice in business affairs I fear you are. Why, I have heard Papa Woodrow say that had Junior Elk and his father been white men, they could have owned this state."

"Then we must thank God for his merciful wisdom in making them black."

"Your affliction has given you a waspish tongue."

"Had I a thousand eyes, you would still try my patience."

"Nearly thirty thousand dollars—in gold!" she squealed like a girl.

"You must calm yourself before you go mad with joy at my good fortune in having Oaks burned down over my head."

"Listen to you!" Annabel laughed in something near admiration. "Do you think up these hateful things to say to me when you are left alone? —Now, since you insist on the courtesy, and that is all it is, an *indulgence*, we had better get it done. I'll order Fox to hitch up the buggy after dinner, and I'll drive you out myself to tell Doreen what we are about to do."

"You will do no such thing. I can speak to Doreen better alone. And I must talk to Benjamin about it too."

"He doesn't count; he's a child."

"It is only your sons then who matter?"

"They are years older than he, practically grown men; and they have had the advantage of a town rearing, with school *and* a tutor. They are therefore more capable of understanding great affairs than your son."

"I hope Doreen and Benjamin will not hate the idea of leaving Oaks."

Annabel snorted impatiently. "You must not ask them what they think but merely tell them what you have decided. When people are asked what they think, they are invariably disagreeable, I have noticed."

"You must make a little book of your observations and give it to your friends on their birthdays."

It ended in his going to Oaks alone, or rather with his being driven there in the buggy by Fox; but his session with Annabel made his noon dinner sit lumpily with him, and he arrived belching nervously and in a temper, unprepared to reason calmly, fit only to command, and that harshly. When he told them of Junior Elk's proposition, Doreen was at first silent and then began to weep. His offer of comfort was so rough that she wailed louder. "What is to become of me?"

"I will get a house in town," James said, "and you will live with me."

"I don't want to live in town," she declared. "I have never got along with town people. I never have anything to say to them!"

"You will learn," he said coldly, "as I have."

"Oh, James! Things are not the same any more!"

"No," he agreed testily, "they certainly are not."

"I know that yours has been the heavier tragedy, but we have all suffered!" She wept again, and he made no move to touch her. James was tired of tears and had begun to distrust them, noting that they seldom kept the weeper from speaking whatever was on his mind, but served to decorate or vary such statements, as fern is used to make an effect in a vase of flowers.

"It has been especially hard for you, Doreen," he said automatically.

The mildness of such sympathy served only to anger her. "So now I am to be wrenched from what is left of my home, this poor place once lived in by Negroes and still smelling of them—"

"Exactly," he snapped. "Wrenched from this cold cabin and set down in a decent, comfortable house in town. You will make friends. You will find it easier to talk to people. It is likely that, given time, you will decide to marry, you know."

"I? I, marry? —By that you must mean that you are thinking that *you* will marry again. Well, who is she to be, have you decided? I can tell you she will not want your unhappy sister dumped on her doorstep!"

"I do not intend to marry again!" James cried.

"But it is you who spoke of marriage, James," Doreen said logically. "I don't know why you will treat me so unkindly when we have always been particularly close. You have changed since going to live with Annabel. She has infected you!"

James shook his head in exasperation. "Benjamin, are you here?"

Benjamin grunted.

"Where are you?"

"Here, Father."

"You were so still I thought you had slipped away."

"No, sir."

"Then what have you to say?"

"About what?" Benjamin answered sullenly.

"About what!" James roared. "Am I raising a stupid son?"

Doreen's tears stopped. "You haven't done much about raising him at all, have you? —Off at the war. And when you were home, no time for anyone but Rachel. You and Rachel! The love story of the county! So wrapped up in each other, neither of you cared about anyone else. And when you were away, Rachel was just as bad. Did nothing but cry for you like a child, leaving her own children to be brought up anyhow by anybody with a minute to spare and the pity to notice them. The way you behaved, you *and* Rachel, no one would think they were your children!"

"Doreen!"

Her hands flew to her mouth as if they would keep her from speaking ever again. Staring at him, she whimpered once. Her hands then reached out to him, but she did not dare touch him. "James! —Oh, James, I am sorry for that. I didn't mean it, you know I didn't. You know I couldn't have said it if I'd thought. I swore to myself I would never speak of it to another living soul, that I would never think of it, never ever again! Forgive me. It is my poor, lonely jealousy that said it, not I. I have always loved you so. Forgive me! —I wish I were dead! —*Please* say you forgive me?"

James sat pale, unmoving. When he spoke, his voice was faint, but there was in it a note that tried to caution her. "Yes. Very well. Very well, Doreen."

"No, you will not forgive me!" she cried, and ran out of the room and the house, slamming the door behind her. The man and the boy sat together in silence until James said, his voice still low, but determined, "Now you must tell me what you think of Junior Elk's proposition. You know how we are situated. You understand that the loss of sight makes it impossible for me to work again as a farmer the way I did." He paused, waiting.

Benjamin had felt embarrassment at Doreen's behavior, but it had passed and been replaced by curiosity. He tried, however, to answer his father. "Well, sir, I know it is a good offer. I've heard about others wanting to sell, or saying they do. It's true we've lost a good many of our hands. But I believe with time that Zadok—he and I have worked together since it all happened. Zadok is a good man."

James shook his head. "Zadok can't run the place by himself. You know that."

"I don't mean we could run it the way you used to with Grandpa, or even the way Grandpa managed after you went to war and the men started to leave. But we could keep it going. We *have* kept it going, sir. I'm learning more every day, and Zadok—"

"Zadok! —Benjamin, I'm proud of you for thinking that way but—how old are you exactly?"

"Eleven."

"You're doing well for somebody far beyond that age. I was like that too when I was a boy. Thought: if they'd only let me, I could run this place by myself. But it wasn't true for me, and it isn't true for you. It won't be good enough, however fast you learn, nor however much help Zadok is."

"I wish you'd let us try before you—"

James was shaking his head too decisively for Benjamin to continue the argument, and Benjamin's mind and will were not concentrated on it, but still with what Doreen had said, or almost said. There was a secret. It involved him. There was something he did not know that they had long known, and he was at the center of it. It all had to do with him. "What did Aunt Doreen mean?" he said abruptly.

James jerked his head upward and toward the sound of the boy's voice. "She is upset."

"Yes, sir, I know that."

"She is more attached to the old place than I realized—as you are too, it seems."

"There was something else."

"Nothing to concern yourself about."

"She said—about Jane and me not being your children. What did she mean, sir?"

"You are certainly my children." His voice was stronger.

"She surprised herself, and you. It slipped out, and she was so ashamed she couldn't let it be."

"I've told you it's nothing, Benjamin."

"I can't believe it was nothing. It was about me."

"Yes, but it's nothing you need to know."

"Sir, if it's about me, I want to know. It's important, or she wouldn't have been so upset. Aunt Doreen has taken to crying a lot more than she used to, but not about nothing."

"It's nothing that concerns you," James repeated.

"How can it be about me and not concern me, sir?"

"Because it happened before you were born!"

Benjamin pressed his mind to remember everything he had ever heard, or heard hinted, about that time. "Mama was sick with the fever before you married. She caught it, they all thought, from your brother Adam, who had been to Savannah and come home, and who died of it. He would have been my Uncle Adam if he had lived, but he died. All that is so, isn't it? Then—" His breathing was quicker. "I've heard it said he and Mama were expecting to marry?" He said it as if he expected to be laughed at and contradicted. He said it without believing it, as the young never believe that anything real happened before they were born. "Were they supposed to marry each other?"

James closed his blind eyes. "Yes," he said dully.

Benjamin flinched with shock. "They were engaged to each other to be married," he said carefully, still tentative in his acceptance of it as truth.

"They were." The words were like a sigh.

"He died," Benjamin said slowly. "And she was sick. Then you and she got married." He hesitated. "I was born." He paused again, studying the face of the man before him. "You were not my father."

"I loved your mother all her life, and she loved me."

"Yes, sir. Everybody knows that, like Aunt Doreen says, but you were not my father, were you?"

"We are the same flesh and blood."

"I think I know how you mean that, sir." The boy choked and coughed and wanted to spit, but swallowed instead. "Like livestock. But I am not your son." Knowing now that what he said was true, he could not yet accept it. His mind had raced too fast. He must stop and try to see how he fit into everything. "I am not your son, am I?" Again, the manner of the question begged for contradiction. It did not come. "Grandpa—he was my real grandfather, wasn't he?"

"Of course he was. He was Adam's father as well as mine."

Benjamin smiled with relief. "Then that was all right." His eyes clouded. "Did everybody know about me when I was born?"

"The close family."

"Grandma Sarah."

"Yes."

"Great-grandma Edna."

"Yes, yes."

"Grandpa."

James nodded quickly.

"Aunt Annabel. Aunt Doreen." James made no acknowledgment of these. "The people on the plantation, they must know. And those at Beulah Land, they must know. They know that Uncle Adam was my real father, don't they?"

James shrugged helplessly, impatiently.

The tears would not be stopped; Benjamin could only try to keep them quiet.

"Jane is my half sister. She feels like my sister though. She doesn't know, does she?"

"No."

"Don't ever tell her!"

"I have always thought of you as my son as much as I've thought of Jane as my daughter."

"Excuse me, sir. It is important to me to know who I am. I feel downright simple not having known when everybody else did!"

"Not anyone but family."

"What was Uncle Adam like?" He suddenly had to know. Benjamin had heard little about Adam other than the hushed words that had told of the "great tragedy" that had taken him so young. Benjamin had never been interested in him, never known he had reason to be. Adam had seemed no more than a family name surrounded by a mist of romantic sadness; one of theirs, of the family, not real to Benjamin because he had never seen him. He was a name on a stone in the cemetery. But that young man who would always be unknown to him had felt passion, and that passion had gone to make him.

"I ask you to forget it," James was saying. "I want you to put it out of your mind. Think of it when you are alone, if you must; get it clear for yourself. That will be best, I suppose. But I don't want to hear you talk about it any more. You are my son—in all ways. You are my son to me and to the world. I came out here today to tell you and Doreen that I am going to sell Oaks. I want you to come to town and live with me when I get a house. You haven't been to school properly. You must get some real learning, not just what you pick up from—Zadok! And others."

"I want to stay here, sir."

"You can't."

"Oaks is home. I was born here. I may not have known who my father properly was, but I've always known Oaks is home."

"Well." They were silent again, each thinking, and their thinking taking them further apart. "I may not sell all the land. If you feel so strongly, we'll keep a hundred or so acres for you to have when you're grown."

"I don't want to sell any of Oaks."

"You have nothing to say about it," James said coldly. "It belongs to me."

"If my real father had lived, it would not be yours to sell; it would be his!" Benjamin declared.

James got to his feet and found the door. Opening it, he shouted, "Fox! Where are you? Bring up the buggy! We are leaving!"

Having worked for Annabel Saxon for nearly eighteen years, Fox knew how to accommodate himself to the moods of the master race. He and Millie had been given to Annabel and Blair by Blair's father Woodrow Saxon as a wedding present in 1847. By developing a blend of arrogance and servility, which are closer than is generally assumed, being nurtured by the same principles; and by cultivating his natural skills as liar, thief, philosopher, and buffoon, he had survived. He was, therefore, unsurprised when James, half an hour after demanding that he be driven home "as fast as the horse can go," said, "Instead of home, I want you to take me to Mrs. Singletary's house."

When they arrived, Fox stopped the horse in front and said, "Here we are. Mrs. Singletary's house like you said."

"Give me the reins to hold. You go to the door and ask if Mrs. Singletary is at home."

"Yes, sir."

The half hour since his provoking interview with Doreen and Benjamin had done nothing to cool James's temper, and now as he sat alone in the buggy holding the cold leather, he felt useless and ridiculous as well as angry and hard done by. He did not know what he would say if asked why he had come. It happened that his appearance was not put to question. After being subjected to Doreen's tears, Benjamin's passionate inquiries, and finally to Fox's sly patience, he was now roused from unhappy self-contemplation by a warm, womanly voice charged with concern and invitation. "Captain Davis!" it said. "Do take my hand and let me show you into my house."

"Mrs. Singletary?"

She claimed his hand as soon as he dropped the reins, and the soft touch of her seemed to give him eyes, for he put his foot securely onto the little step-down from the buggy and was instantly beside her.

Fox said he'd wait, and James found himself walking in the most natural and pleasant way along a short brick path that led to a door that had been left flatteringly open by his hostess, an indication of her eagerness to welcome him.

"There are three roses on that bush by the door. Think! Roses in January— I wish you could see them." Her words were brisk and cheerful; they made him feel considered but not pitied. Without the sensation of being led, he found himself indoors. The room he was in must, he thought, be small, for it was quite warm, and he felt a glow of his face reflecting the heat of a fire. There was a clean, fruity scent on the air. Perhaps he sniffed, because she said, "It is an orange. My daughter Prudence won it at a church drawing. She remembered oranges when they were common, because she is not thirteen. Prudence was so pleased. She came running laughing home and said, 'Guess what, Mama, I have won an orange, but I am not going to eat it. I am going to stick cloves into it and put it on this table near the fireplace in your sitting room, where the warmth will draw out the scent and we can enjoy it privately.' She did, and we have." Margaret-Ella laughed quietly. "Even the cat. Sit here, sir." She put his hand to the arm of a chair. Its movement told him it was a rocking chair, and that fact somehow made it easier for him to seat himself without awkwardness.

"What a cozy room this is," he said, turning his head as if he were looking around it.

"It is my own little sitting room. It is for me and my daughter, and particular friends. I allow the Union officers the use of the parlor. It gives them a feeling of home, and I do feel sorry for them. They have been a help to me in many ways since I took them at my board. If you will be content to sit, I'll get us some sassafras tea. Do you like it?"

"Yes," he said.

"So do I. Almost better than the other, although I suppose I should like the other better if it were common and sassafras were rare. I shan't be long. And if you feel a claw, why slap or stroke as pleases you, for it will only be my old puss Susie. She will not leave this room because of the orange and cloves, but she loves a lap to sit on and will try yours if you let her."

"I really can't tell you, Mrs. Singletary, why I came—" Before he finished saying it, he heard the door close softly, and was left to suppose that she had not heard him. He held his hands out to take warmth from the fire. He was glad he had been warned, because the next minute he felt something land on his lap; and when a tentative claw explored his trouser leg, he knew he was being used as a cushion by Susie. He touched her back with the back of his hand, and she purred. He pushed the floor with his feet, pressing back, and rocked himself lightly.

He stayed for more than an hour. Long before he roused himself to go, they were calling each other by first names. She told him she had always hated her full name and asked him to call her Maggie, which, she said, her father had used to call her, although her friends insisted on Margaret-Ella, double names being considered more elegant among them when she was growing up.

As they walked together to the buggy, where Fox waited asleep in the seat, she said, "I hope you will come again, soon and often."

He smiled. "I feel that I can see your face, I know so well how you must look. Though we have known each other all our lives, I have not known you at all until recently—indeed, not before today, I vow. Things are so often awkward at Annabel's when visitors are there."

"To tell you the truth," she said, "Annabel has always brought out the worst in me. She and my sister Ann-Elizabeth were particular friends, I suppose, or 'friendly rivals' is to say it better, and they tolerated me because I was close enough to their own age, though younger, of course. I was part of their schemes and feuds without feeling much about them. I am myself only in my own house."

He found her hand—it was not far from his—and held it after shaking it. "Thank you, and I shall come again, if you are sure I shan't be a nuisance."

"No one else will be as welcome," she said.

Again he managed the buggy step without fumbling, possessed of new assurance she had given him.

"Home now, Cap'm, or somewhere else?" Fox asked with a chuckle.

"Home," James said grimly.

38.

Junior Elk also had a busy day, the difference between his and James's being that one responded to events while the other ordained them. Junior would not have claimed that he knew just how things would happen, since no man can, but he was prepared to manipulate situations that were largely his creation.

Five minutes after James left his office, Junior locked the door and strolled along to the main throughfare and into the headquarters of the Union forces. There he called upon Abel Ponder, whom he knew to be a troubled man, for Captain Ponder had told him so and told him why. He had, it seemed, received two sharply worded dispatches from his commanding officer in Savannah asking him to make a full statement forthwith upon his activities in administering the military area under his control for the past two months. His wisdom and discretion were questioned, and there were hints that complaints from a "person of substance and probity intimately acquainted with the locality" had found the ears of Authority in Savannah. Captain Ponder did not specify to his friend the charges, which included looting and fornication with Negroes, thereby, the dispatches intimated, creating an abomination and gratuitously insulting the principles of the defeated peoples.

There was no need for him to specify, for it was Junior Elk who had supplied the charges, not directly but through those "banking connections" he sometimes referred to, in reality simply his wife Dorothy's father in Savannah. Junior had written to her Negro mother advising her to deliver the complaint to her white father—each had married color to match subsequent to their liaison—and suggesting further that the Union commander at

Highboro constituted a threat to Dorothy's virtue and good name. Bankers and conquerors know how to perform little services for one another, both being realistically aware that all human existence must be based on order and cooperation, the latter sometimes between seemingly unlikely allies.

Junior had decided that he no longer wanted Abel Ponder in Highboro. The Captain had served his purpose, and his continued presence would only remind people of the killings and burnings of the recent past and invite their speculation upon the Elk-Ponder friendship. Junior had also decided to rid himself of Dorothy, and he thought he knew how to do it with Captain Ponder's unwitting aid.

A man in trouble with his superiors will not ask much in the way of sympathy and understanding. A shaking of the head, a murmured "tsk-tsk" will be magnified in the heart of the pariah into the most tender compassion. Seated privately with the Captain now, Junior supplied the head-shakings, and Ponder supplied the rest.

"You know it is all false," the Captain said, having given Junior an indication that "personal appropriation of goods belonging to others" was one of the accusations against him.

"Certainly," Junior agreed solemnly. "Everyone understands that your appropriation of food supplies was for the common good. It is acknowledged that you have been entirely honest and evenhanded, taking from rich and poor alike no more than was available."

So earnestly was it spoken that Ponder heard only the sound of it and not the sense. He struck the palm of one hand with the fist he made of the other. Then taking a paper from the desk to read again, he said, "A new dispatch this morning. However blameless we both know me to be, I have been summoned to Savannah to make a direct accounting. My written explanations are not deemed sufficient."

"What, sir! Are we to lose you?" Junior appeared much cast down by the thought and was forced to support his head for a moment with a hand that hid his eyes.

"I hope not permanently," Ponder said, "but I am to go. I shall arrange affairs here as well as I can and leave in a day or two."

Junior shook his head sadly. "It is a mistake, some misunderstanding surely."

Captain Ponder nodded but took no comfort from the suggestion. "I wonder who can have—well, damn it, *somebody* told *lies* that made for this result!"

Junior considered. "One thinks first of the Davis and Kendrick families, I suppose, as who might consider themselves aggrieved, however unjustly. Then there is Sergeant—what was his name?"

"Smede, do you mean?"

"He has recently passed through Savannah, has he not?"

Ponder snorted. "It's unlikely that *he* would have dared to put up lies about anything that happened here."

"Ah." Junior shrugged. "Does one ever know who to trust? He may not have thought he received a fair share of— Naturally, I do not know how these things were managed." Junior coughed. "And so on and so forth."

"He had no reason to be dissatisfied," Ponder said, but his eyes narrowed.

"A man will sometimes brood on another's gain instead of being satisfied with his own." Junior was thoughtful again and presently remarked, "What can I say? Except that I am distressed for you, and for the town, sir, which you have administered so well—to *my* satisfaction, at any rate. I wish there were something I could do to help you, but of course I have no power, no influence in high places."

"No," the Captain agreed, with due sense of the compliment the other paid in his desire to be of service.

"Mrs. Elk will be inconsolable. I despair at the idea of her knowing."

Captain Ponder's eyes took on a soft expression, as near as they could. "She has been good to me. I shall not soon again meet a kinder friend than she—and you have been."

Junior held up his hands deprecatingly. "We have done little, sir. What was ours was yours, but I cannot say it was very much."

"A great deal to one far from home and hungry for the society of ladies, I promise you."

Junior put on a warm smile. "She would be gratified to hear it from you, sir. This is lamentable! I dread to make her unhappy with such sad news. No, no, I cannot tell her myself." He paused and then seemed to discover a way out of the problem. "I have it, Captain! *You* will tell her for me. She will take it better from you. Now, it happens that an urgent matter has arisen this very morning that requires my riding immediately into the country.

The place they still call Anderson's, you know, next to Beulah
Land. My father acquired it many years ago in payment of a
debt by the last of the Anderson men, and I keep a family there
to see to the land although in truth it hardly pays me—but I
shan't trouble you with details. What it means is that I shall miss
my dinner at home in order to attend to this nuisance. I fear it
will take the entire afternoon, trivial though it be. Ah, me. One is
ever at the mercy of obligations. You, sir, I beg: you, sir, must go
home in my place and tell my wife the news *now*. You can console her by asking her to console you. You will do her a great
favor if you stay with her a little while. —Indeed, you must eat
the dinner that I shall miss."

Captain Ponder did not grasp new situations quickly, which is
the reason Junior continued to talk, saying the same things in
only slightly different ways in order to give the military mind
time to see a possibility of advantage for itself. "Well, now, I—"
was the first hint that it had. Abel Ponder thought of the beautiful Dorothy Elk. He remembered her dining table that had so
often given him pleasure, visualizing the succulent dishes he had
enjoyed from it and would shortly enjoy no more. (Geraldine
had been trained to the kitchen by Junior's mother, as she had
been trained to the bedroom by Junior's father.)

"Come, sir," Junior urged him. "You will do me the greatest
kindness. More than you know. I beg you to agree."

The Captain sighed, then smiled generously. "Well, friend Elk.
How can I refuse you if you put it so? Although the need for
consolation will, I'm certain, be greater for me than Mrs. Elk."

"You will fortify one another," Junior assured him. "If I may
just write a note for you to take to her?"

"Pen and paper over there," Ponder said briskly. A nod of the
head indicated the orderly's table.

Going to it, Junior said, "How good you are to do this for me."
He scratched quickly with the pen, waved the paper in the air
until it was dry and then folded without sealing it. Handing it to
the Captain, he said, "I will see you again?"

Ponder nodded. "Oh, I am not to leave for another day or so."

"I wish it were never! Now I must make haste. I paused for a
mere greeting and would not have stayed except for your dire
tidings."

When the door closed after him, the Captain remained a moment at his desk before going to the window and looking out. He

found Junior Elk's back, and sure enough he was walking away like a man with no time to lose. Returning to the desk, Ponder opened the unsealed note and read it. "Business takes me from town the rest of the day. You must show our friend *every* hospitality."

Junior's haste did not keep him from returning to his office and writing a note to Geraldine. "Watch and encourage. Sweeten the trap with wine. They will not expect me." Geraldine was in his confidence and would take his drift. Then going to the livery stable where he kept a saddle horse, Junior instructed an underling to deliver the note to his housekeeper at his back door. Mounting the horse made ready, he trotted him past the Union headquarters before taking the road out of town to the Anderson Place.

Dorothy Elk was idling in the room only she called her boudoir when her son came in. "Haven't I told you to knock on that door, Roscoe?" Her scolding was automatic, as much from boredom as disrelish for the boy.

"Yes'm," he admitted. "Captain Ponder's here and wants to see you."

"To see me?"

"That's what he said."

"Not your papa? He didn't ask for your papa?" She did not move her elbows from the dresser top where she leaned toward the mirror, almost into it so that her breath clouded it; nor did her eyes leave the reflection of her face after they had caught his image behind her. "You ought not to stand on one leg that way. I don't know, it makes you look biggety to your mama. Where is your papa?"

"How do I know?"

She flung a box at him so carelessly he did not bother to step aside. It fell open as it hit the floor, spilling face powder.

"Is he with the Captain?"

Roscoe shook his head.

"Pick up that box from the floor," she said. When he made no move, but continued to seek her eyes in the mirror, she added, "Answer me when I say something."

"No'm."

"Can't you say anything but yes'm and no'm?"

"Captain's by himself."

She touched a silver comb to her hair, frowning with concentration. "Your papa's right about sending you off somewhere to go to school. Get your blue eyes out of my sight and tell the Captain I'm coming along directly."

When the boy left her, Dorothy changed the brown dress she was wearing for one of pink silk, leaving the red ribbon at the throat loose enough to bare the upper oval of her breasts. Applying rouge, she examined herself in the mirror glass again and was satisfied.

The sight of the man alone in the parlor when she opened the door, sitting with forlorn face before the fire, made her hope briefly that he brought news of some accident to her husband. "Captain Ponder! Is anything the matter? My clumsy boy said you'd come to see me, but I did not credit it."

"Is it strange that I should come to see you?" He rose to take the hand she extended. Having held it and pressed it, he appeared to be undecided what next to do with it until she withdrew it gently, placing it over her heart to suggest that it was the more valued by her for its recent contact with him.

"You are always welcome." She smiled and slowly turned the topaz ring which he had given her.

"Even when I come alone?"

"Especially."

"And find you alone?" he ventured boldly.

"Especially!"

Captain Ponder was aware of a sensation in his penis. Whether it stirred or merely grew a trifle warmer he did not speculate, but the atmosphere between him and the woman had brought it to a degree of alertness.

"Sit down," she said, and dropped into a small wooden chair. It was painted gray and gold and cushioned in gray; she knew that it made a complementary background to her warm, dark beauty. "Mr. Elk is away from home."

"I know." He drew a chair matching hers close to the one she sat in. "In fact, I am his messenger."

"And I thought you were your own!" Abel Ponder presented the note Junior had written in his office. She opened and read it. "He says that I am to entertain you. Will you stay and have dinner with me? I hate eating alone, and the boy is no company."

"Gladly, I thank you."

In truth, Dorothy did not at all mind eating alone. Her thoughts seldom acknowledged the company of anyone and never the need. "That is good!" She smiled prettily. Rising, she went to the door and called to Geraldine, who came quickly, having received her own note and seen the Captain arrive. Dorothy told her to bring a glass of wine for the guest. When she returned to her chair, the Captain was looking at her so admiringly and longingly he would perhaps have appeared absurd to anyone other than the object of that admiration and longing. She enjoyed his look and said nothing to distract the thoughts that sustained it until Geraldine came in with a tray. She had not, as was usual in such a situation, brought a single glass of wine. The tray held two glasses and a bottle of Junior Elk's Madeira.

Geraldine did none of the common cooking, but had hastily made a chocolate pie when she knew the Captain would be staying for noon dinner. After baking it she had set it to cool, but it was still warm under its high-piled, delicately browned egg-white meringue when she put it on the table for her mistress to serve at the end of the meal.

Roscoe had eaten with his mother and Captain Ponder, but he did not speak beyond a mumbled request for a dish to be passed to him; nor was he spoken to as they made their way through dishes of fried chicken, hot biscuits, rice and gravy, sweet potatoes, and pickled cucumbers, the man and woman all the while declaring to each other their acute disappointment in not being able to continue their present, precious friendship. Finishing his pie, Roscoe asked to be excused from the table, and his mother obliged him.

Captain Ponder went about the consumption of his dessert with the unflagging relish of the gourmand. The pie had not quite set, so he used a spoon for it, licking it shiny clean of the creamy chocolate with every spoonful he took. Bits of the sticky meringue clung to his mustache. Geraldine had brought a second bottle of wine to the table, and it had been entirely drunk by the time Dorothy led the way again into the parlor and urged the Captain to smoke her husband's cigars. These were supplied to him regularly throughout the war by an acquaintance in Cuba, in spite of the blockade. Ponder thanked her and accepted one, but instead of lighting it immediately, he stood in front of the fire warming his behind and preparing the cigar for smoking. They spoke seldom, wanting few words, each occupied by agreeable thoughts that needed no voicing. The food and wine had made them easy with one another. Dorothy hummed tunelessly and showed off her several rings again, explaining who had given each one to her and on what occasion. She examined her hands and held them up delicately when he praised their shape. She pulled her bodice about this way and that, seeming dissatisfied with its fit, and he told her that her bosom was the finest thing he had ever seen on a woman. She took no offense at the compliment but indeed began to press and mold the flesh, not enticingly but as if it were her duty to present the admired feature at greatest advantage. During this process Abel Ponder slowly licked the cigar all over with a look of concentration not unlike that of a dog washing his genitals.

The cigar was never lighted.

By the time the Captain was ready to apply an ember to it, Dorothy was saying that she had suddenly taken it into her head to try an old gold necklace her father had given her when she was still a child against the pink silk dress. He asked to be shown it, and Dorothy rose to fetch it. Warm from the fire, the food, the wine, and his own desire, the Captain dropped the cigar to the hearth and followed her. Dorothy herself had drunk enough wine to make no objection to his presence in her boudoir, and she hardly noticed when he closed the door behind them. She was a woman who loved compliments on her appearance but who had lived largely without them during the years of her marriage. If she had been able to enjoy the admiration of others, to which she felt herself abundantly entitled, she would not perhaps have been forced to provide it for herself. She was not of a passionate nature, but as they lingered in her boudoir and he exclaimed insistently over her beauty, she was encouraged to reveal more of it, chiefly with the wish to thank him and to deserve his praise.

However, when the door from the hallway opened and Junior Elk entered, he found his wife and his military friend very nearly naked upon her bed. The Captain's drawers were bunched about his knees. His plump, pale, hairy rump was the most prominent object presenting itself to Junior's gaze, and although the Captain had not yet been able to effect entry of his hostess, he was making a manful effort to do so, and his tool for the task stood at its greatest distension. Neither saw the intruder in the doorway, the Captain's backside effectively blocking Dorothy's view. Neither was aware of being discovered until they heard the exclamation, "Oh, for shame! I am betrayed!"

The cry caught the Captain with his body arched at an angle close to ninety degrees, and for a long moment he held his exposed buttocks suspended at their peak. But then they began to tremble, and he slumped to the bed and off it onto the floor as though he had been shot. His hands clutched and pulled garments about him. He did not dare look at his host, although he might safely have done so, for Junior had covered his face and turned away as if the sight before him held the power to blind and blight.

After quickly drawing the counterpane over her more vulnerably exposed parts, Dorothy Elk remained as she was. Junior Elk moaned lightly and kept it up as Captain Ponder, crouching and crawling, managed to get himself out of the room and, when he had somewhat arranged his clothes in a manner that was passably seemly, out of the house. He repaired directly to his office at the Union Army headquarters, where after a while he reread, and not for the second or third time, all the dispatches he had received from superiors in Savannah, concluding that the future appeared gloomy. From hoping to clear his name so that he might resume his administrative duties in Highboro, he inclined to a soldierly request for reassignment to the field, wherever it might be as long as it was not in Georgia. Sherman's main forces, he had heard, were now in Carolina.

Hearing the front door close after the military guest, Junior stepped back into the hallway, where Geraldine presently found him. "He's gone," she said, looking at him steadily. Junior nodded his head twice as if to be doubly sure it was so.

"Do you have it?" he asked.

She held out a buggy whip he had told her to fetch him as soon as he arrived at his own back door. He took it from her. Going into Dorothy's room, he found her as he had left her and closed the door. Geraldine put her head against it to listen. She heard the woman inside begin to cry before she received a blow. After the first cut of the whip Dorothy screamed, "Don't mark my face!" After that the sound of the whip and the angry wails of the woman filled the house. In his room Roscoe held a pillow over his head and wept too, but he did not dare intercede on his mother's behalf. He knew she did not love him, but he had always thought her the most beautiful thing in the world.

39.

During January and February most farmers talked uncertainly of what they would do, but at Beulah Land they plowed as they could and planted the seed they had in hope of an eventual harvest. So did they at Oaks. Sarah and Floyd told each other it was too soon to plan when each day brought word of further depredations and humiliations to those they knew, but they were people who could not see a leaf fall without wanting to put a seed into the ground; and so they plowed and sowed and talked of the future.

There would be another house at Beulah Land, not grand as the old one for all its homeliness had been, but a comfortable sort of farmhouse, Sarah said, commodious enough for the visiting of relatives and friends but with nothing merely for show. Floyd, she declared, would live in no cabin but have a house suiting the worth and needs of the man who was the work boss of Beulah Land and her best friend. They laughed together and at each other as they planned arrogantly and generously.

They knew they must wait, not only for the end of the war but for a time they might build without threat of destruction. They argued and puzzled about how they could work the land again with the small number of hands left to them. Like all defeated peoples, they studied the conqueror to learn how to deal with him. The present need was to keep as much as they could while taking care of their own. The next need was money, or what would pass as money and do its work, for they must pay the hands who tilled the fields as well as providing their families with food and shelter. It would be many months before the land returned a yield. Meantime, they had a sawmill.

They decided to reassemble it on the afternoon they heard that Captain Ponder was to go to Savannah. Rumors cling like vermin to armies, and people who speak the same language will exchange truth as well as lies, however much they appear divided in sympathy. Therefore, the town of Highboro knew that the Captain had been summoned to Savannah almost as soon as he knew it. Benjamin brought the report to Sarah.

The afternoon after James's visit to Oaks, Benjamin rode into town with Zadok, thinking that together they might persuade James to let them continue to manage the plantation. Their joint plea made James jealous and angry.

"No!" he declared at the first pause, having kept still as long as he had in courtesy to Zadok. "It is settled. I will sell. I talked again with Junior Elk this morning and we are agreed."

"We've started plowing and planting—"

"I told him I would keep a hundred acres for you to have as your own since you feel so strongly. He has come up with a different proposal."

"But, sir—" Benjamin protested.

"Be silent and listen!" If the boy had said "Father," he might have held the man's ear, but "sir" stung like briars after their exchanges the day before. James proceeded to outline Junior Elk's idea. Benjamin was so surprised by it that he left off trying to beg James to let them keep Oaks, and he took his leave eventually with few words. When he and Zadok paused at the drygoods store to see if any nails were to be had, they were given the rumor about Abel Ponder's departure. Benjamin told Zadok to take his mule on home while he stopped at Beulah Land; he wanted to talk to his grandmother.

It was a warm day for the time of year, and he found her coming out of the tool shed, where she and Daniel had been examining hoes. Sergeant Smede's men had broken the handles of all their hoes during the raid, and Daniel had replaced them as best he could. The new wood he'd had to use in most of them was unsatisfactory because it lacked the rigidity of seasoned wood, and all the field hands were complaining.

Benjamin's telling her was the first she had heard of James's intention of selling Oaks, and she quickly led the boy away from the buildings into the fields where they might walk without interruption and talk in privacy. She shared his horror at the decision to cede Oaks to Junior Elk, and when he presented her with James's offer of land of his own, she was as surprised as he had been.

"Wait!" she exclaimed. "Tell me again—"

"Junior Elk is to have all of Oaks. He has offered twenty dollars an acre—"

"So much?"

"Yes, ma'am."

"Money goes; land stays."

"My father—" With Sarah he could still use the word he shied from in direct address. "My father is willing to give me the two parcels of land that used to belong to the Andersons and the Cokers."

"They belong to Junior Elk. *His* father bought them—or bought one and got the other in a debt settlement."

"Yes'm, that's what I'm saying. If my father will sell him all of Oaks in one piece, Junior Elk will hand over the two farms as part of the business. Elk doesn't intend to keep the place whole for himself but cut it up into little farms and sell them off."

"I must say I'd welcome that more than having Junior Elk lording over the big estate next door!"

"Weren't the Cokers—?"

"Of course they were. Your other grandmother's people. Gertrude Coker married Bruce Davis. They all called him Rooster then."

"Rooster!"

"Yes. She was so pretty when I first knew her. Her brother Orin had a grudge against Bruce, and after she died there was a big falling-out. Then the Cokers got bad off and Orin sold the farm to Roscoe Elk instead of Bruce. He went off with his two clabber-faced sisters to Alabama, I believe, to live with their other brother Lester. God knows what Lester must have thought when he looked up and saw them coming! Of those five sisters and brothers your granny was the only one to marry. Peculiar family. I don't think Bruce ever heard of them again."

"It was before I was born," Benjamin said as if that explained his vagueness, although every Southern child heard family history from cradle days.

"Ben!" Her mind had been working ahead as she remembered the Cokers for him. "That's not so bad, if you think about it. You'd be getting a good little farm that used to belong to your grandmother's family. You could almost say you have a kin claim on it anyway. And there's the Anderson Place besides? That's a tidy piece of land altogether, nearly a hundred and fifty acres and right next to Beulah Land." She was thinking that one day he might simply add it to Beulah Land.

"That's what Zadok says. We could manage it, him and me, with some little help."

"You could. And won't you feel better on a place new to you than you would huddled onto a tacky bitty piece of leftover Oaks? Every time you looked around at what you'd lost, your heart would hurt you."

"Where would we live?"

"There are two houses. Used to be the Andersons' and the Cokers'. The Anderson house is better, and plenty big enough for you and Doreen."

"Junior Elk has Negroes living there."

"Who do you think lived where we're living now?"

They laughed for the first time.

"You don't think it's such a bad idea?"

She shook her head. "If it has to be sold. —Your father is firm, I imagine; there's no changing his mind?"

"No, ma'am. I tried hard."

"The Davises can be stubborn. They get it from Edna. Thank God she's not here to see what's happening to Oaks!"

Benjamin wasn't interested in what his great-grandmother might have thought; to him she seemed dead a long time. "Well," he said speculatively. "Well now!"

They walked and talked for an hour more, saying eagerly the same things over. Events of the last months had taught them to accept what would have been unthinkable a year before. So full of the one topic were they Benjamin had started home and had to turn back to tell Sarah the news about Captain Abel Ponder; and to her exclamations at that account and her questions he only replied, "I don't know! They say it's a fact, but they don't say why."

Away he rode again, taking the shorter way to Oaks on his horse Bob, through the fields, into the woods, and finally into the Glade, that high, sheltered place of rocks and trees, with a narrow brook running through it from an artesian spring. It had been the "secret" place of more than one Kendrick and Davis. Lovers had met there for privacy, and an act of violence had been done there that triggered more violence. It was the place too where Adam Davis and Rachel Kendrick used to meet and where, in fact, Benjamin had been conceived. He had been there many times but never felt a mystic kinship to it, nor anything in

particular except that it was a pretty place. Today he paused
and after looking about him for a few moments slid down from
the saddle, not bothering to tie Bob to a tree, both of them
meandering free.

Benjamin found violets, mainly blue, but with a single cluster
of white ones among them, and he picked a few to carry to his
aunt. When he mounted to leave, it was twilight. Without his
being directed to do so Bob walked around in a full circle, and
Benjamin found himself thinking, "When I get older and times
get better, I'll build me a house here." It was part of Oaks but
joined to the Anderson Place. He would ask his father to make it
over to him as part of the transaction with Junior Elk.

Sarah was waiting for Floyd when he returned from the fields
with the plowing gang at the end of the day's work. She told him
the news about Abel Ponder, and they speculated on its meaning. Floyd was sensibly matter-of-fact. "He may be coming back,
or they may send somebody worse to crack the whip over us."

Sarah nodded to acknowledge the truth of what he said, and
they were silent as they walked toward the cabins. At her door,
however, she turned and said, "I don't care, Floyd—we're going
to bring the sawmill back now, and we're going to put it together
here. We've got to start again sometime."

"They could take it away from us."

"I won't let them."

"Going to stand guard all day? Every night? What with, a pile
of rocks beside you to throw?"

"We won't put it back where it was, we'll have it *here*. When
we've got our crops in the ground, we can cut the timber and
drag it here to saw into planks. We can start building our houses.
We know just where we want them. Yours with the grave just at
the side the way you said you'd like it; mine not facing the road
the way it used to but half turned toward the fields and woods.
All *right here*, Floyd. They won't dare interfere with us after the
things they've already done. And others will see what we're
doing and come wanting to buy timber. We'll cut it and sell it to
them, and that way we'll have the money to keep Beulah Land.
They aren't going to take anything else from us, Floyd, because
I won't let them; do you hear me?"

Floyd had begun to laugh, moved by her exhilaration but
thinking he should try to scorn her to caution with his laughter
too.

"I mean what I say, Floyd!"

"I know you do; oh, I know you do!" Laughing again and shaking his head, he turned in the direction of his own cabin, where Lotus stood waiting in the doorway.

"Don't you want your baby to live in your own house instead of a slave cabin?" Sarah called. He stopped, turned, and looked at her. "Well?" she challenged him.

40.

Sarah was sitting alone at the table that had become her desk, in the kitchen that was office and living room and dining room, as well as cooking room. Daniel and Nell and Jane had gone to bed, and so had the Negro workers. It was quiet outdoors and in, the only sound other than an occasional arpeggio of snores from Nell being the rasping of Sarah's pen as she worked at numbers. She added and subtracted and then crossed out everything she had written down. She was trying to come to an estimate of the output they could expect daily from the sawmill, when two knocks came. Getting up, she opened the door a crack and stared in surprise at Roscoe Elk.

"Please let me in."

"Have you come to see me?"

"Yes, ma'am, I have."

"You by yourself?" She peered behind him into the yard. "It's beginning to rain."

He nodded his head. "I slipped away when they—that don't matter."

"Well, come in." He did so and she closed the door. "How did you know which cabin was mine?"

"It was the only one with a light."

She hesitated before sitting down and motioning him to another of the straight chairs at the table. "Sit down if you want to. We'll have to be quiet not to wake the others." When he looked at her apologetically, she added, "Aunt Nell Kendrick and my granddaughter. Our cousin Daniel—you'll have heard about him." He had begun to glance about the room, and she studied his face. It showed a combination of embarrassment and determination. She looked for reflections of his grandmother and grandfather without finding them. "You came before to warn me. Although as things turned out, it didn't do much good."

"I'm sorry."

"I didn't mean it the way it sounded," she said. "I'm grateful to you for letting me know. It would have been worse if I hadn't expected them."

"It was beautiful out here," he said softly, "but they burned you down."

"Well." She laughed abruptly without humor. "Before they did that, they took everything they could carry and broke the rest. You might say that not everything was entirely wasted, since some of it may be giving use or pleasure to someone else at this moment. They left us ashes and memories, and we've tried to bury both. Have you come to warn us again?"

"No, ma'am."

The boy seemed hardly to listen. She continued speaking because she saw that he was agitated by some struggle within himself. "A few came after them. I didn't care then, just stood in the yard and laughed at them. Told them they were too late, we'd been eaten out. Not even the bummers stop here any more."

"I've come to say goodbye," he declared suddenly.

She thought but did not say that there was no need for him to take farewell of her wherever he was going or for however long a time. Smiling slightly, politely, she waited for him to continue.

"They're sending me to school. —Not 'they.' Papa is. We had trouble at our house. Nobody wants me there. He's sending Mama away too—to Savannah! Captain Ponder is to see we have 'safe conduct' it's called. I'm going with her and then I'm going to be sent by myself on up to Baltimore, or maybe somewhere else, I don't know." He paused, and she watched him, although he had turned a little away from her. Some part of her thrilled at knowing there was trouble in the Elk household, her old hatred of the boy's grandfather stirring again, but as she looked at him, she began to feel a little pity. He was not merely a plain boy, he was ugly. His head appeared too big for his body. His ears and nose were large, yet they lacked definition, as if they were still wet clay the sculptor had applied to his work without deciding yet on the final form they were to take. His front teeth were crooked, and the upper ones did not make a neat closure with the lower ones. Only his eyes were good, but they redeemed all. They were large, deep, and intelligent, his present distress showing in them the depths of feeling of which he was capable.

She reached impulsively and took one of his hands. "Is there anything I can do?"

He stared at his hand in hers and pulled it away. "No, ma'am. I came to say goodbye, that's all. I'm not saying goodbye to anybody or anything else, but I came to let you know."

She could not answer that, so she said, "You will come back one day? The time will pass. You won't be homesick for very long, there will be so much new and interesting for you to see and do."

"I won't be homesick, Mrs. Kendrick. —I hate all of them, 'deed I do! They don't care!" After the outburst his embarrassment returned. He scrambled hastily from his chair and went to the door. Following him into the yard, she said, "Wait!" and when he stopped, continued, "Will you come see me when you come back?" By the glow of light from the window she saw his face gather reserve and distrust. "I want you to."

His eyes did not change expression, but he bobbed his head once.

"I hope you have a safe journey." She expected him to go then, but he stayed. "I'll say goodbye." She held out her hand. He did not touch it.

Instead, he edged away but then turned and blurted, "Let nothing bad happen to Miss Jane!" With that he fled. Alone, she held out her hand again palm up. The mist of rain was so light she could barely feel it.

It was true that Captain Ponder was to give Dorothy Elk and her son "safe conduct" to Savannah. On the morning after he had been surprised at his lovemaking, he had received a call from Junior Elk at army headquarters. The orderly, having been given no instructions to the contrary and knowing the caller welcome in the past, ushered him into the commanding officer's presence. Abel Ponder had been standing at a side table examining papers.

Seeing Junior, he blushed deeply. Taking the papers to his desk, he put that object between him and his caller by sitting down.

Junior made no reference to the day before, but said that it had become an urgent necessity for his wife to go to Savannah to attend her mother. His son too required passage to that city. "His benefactor," Junior said patiently, as a teacher will drill a slow class in spelling or grammar, "my banking connection in Savannah, is to make arrangements for him to go to school in some Northern place. Baltimore, or if that is too Southern, perhaps Philadelphia. That will be settled later."

Ponder listened, frowned, and cleared his throat. Junior, knowing the other's mind lacked quickness, said more or less the same thing twice again in a quiet voice that was neither friendly nor unfriendly but aimed to soothe as it penetrated. Captain Ponder was glad enough to see the affair ended in this manner. "I believe," he said finally, "I can oblige you." He coughed and spat on the floor. "The boy too, you say?"

"If you will be so good," Junior said evenly.

Ponder blinked rapidly, and Junior knew that he was weighing his chances of sleeping with Dorothy on the journey. "So be it. I propose starting tomorrow early. What transport have you for them?"

"I imagined that one of your rank and importance, Captain, would provide himself with a carriage—a military carriage, of course, one of those from Oaks or Beulah Land, taken for use by the Army."

"Perhaps that. —Yes. I see. If you will have them and their trunks here by eight o'clock in the morning."

Junior bowed. "I am indebted to you."

Junior Elk and two of his servants arrived promptly in a wagon at the army headquarters with Dorothy Elk and her son and their trunks. The family members exchanged no kiss or other gesture of leave-taking. Those to go merely took their place inside the closed carriage while the servants loaded the trunks. Junior Elk walked away without looking around. Shortly after, he found Geraldine with a second breakfast ready and waiting: fried rabbit, fried ham, batter cakes and cane syrup, real coffee and a pitcher of cool sweet milk. She was wearing the topaz ring Junior had taken from Dorothy's finger the day before yesterday.

41.

To those who insisted that even at that late hour military aid
would arrive from abroad and turn defeat into victory for the
Confederacy, others observed that it would be as useful as applying leeches to a man whose throat has been cut. On April 3,
Richmond, was occupied. On April 9, Lee surrendered. On April
14, Lincoln was assassinated.

Sarah and Jane and Nell were in the yard watching squirrels.
They had returned from a walk to the sawmill, reassembled and
for the first time inspected by Nell, who had complained of the
noise it made, it being but a quarter mile from the cabin at the
edge of the woods.

"When you hear it," Sarah told her, "think of gold and silver,
think of a new house and a new dress. It's close because we have
to watch it. When we don't have to, we'll put it somewhere else."

"Look!" Jane said.

Two squirrels were using the oak trees in the old laundering
area for a lightning game of hide-and-seek.

Her voice cautious as a hunter's, Nell said, "Jane, you reckon if
you picked up that stick and got close you could hit one? Not
enough for a stew but'd make a nice gruel."

We are seldom caught in appropriate attitudes by history. The
ladies of Beulah Land were distracted from the squirrels' play by
the arrival of Annabel and Lauretta, who came clattering along
the carriageway in Annabel's buggy, which she herself drove.
Annabel and Lauretta were not friends; they were not even
friendly; but they were nonetheless willing to share an hour on a
fateful occasion.

With the alacrity of a girl Lauretta leapt from the buggy before Annabel had quite halted it. "Guess, guess, *guess what!*" she
exclaimed, and not waiting to be obeyed or begged, announced,
"That monster Lincoln has been shot! —Yes, it is true, he is
dead. I was teaching the multiplication table, and the children

were being so stupid I was of a mind to slap a few faces when she came in with the news!"

"I knew she'd have to tell it first," Annabel sneered, having stopped the buggy without getting down.

"I've given you credit for bringing the news," Lauretta pointed out.

"I was on my way out here," Annabel said, "to look over Doreen's new domain. Brought some things for her, not that she'll be grateful. Four perfectly good bowls and a churn that only needs careful handling. There's a crack line so thin you can hardly see it because of the bue border, and the milk doesn't seep if you make the butter come fast. Or so Millie tells me. I'm glad to say I've never had to churn in my life. How exhausting it must be."

"I told the children to drill one another in the sixes and sevens—they're pretty good through the fives—and begged Miss Annabel to bring me. I knew you'd want to hear—"

"I had best drive on," Annabel interrupted, "and see if anybody's beat me to telling Doreen."

"How long will you be?" Lauretta asked.

"No more than an hour."

"Don't forget to stop for me the way you did last time. I would verily expire if I had to walk three miles into town."

"Be ready." Annabel slapped the mule's rump with her reins.

Nell said, "Annabel, you look older."

Deciding she could not ignore the old woman, Annabel attempted drollery. "I'm young enough to be able to afford it!"

"You'll be gray as a coon in a year's time," Nell said, shaking her head. "I can remember when people said you were a pretty girl, though I never saw it myself."

Annabel yanked the reins, turning the buggy in a circle.

"Don't hit my flower bed!" Jane implored.

If she heard, Annabel ignored the plea, for a front and a back wheel cut double ruts across a corner of the nasturtiums Jane had planted and tended.

"Well, what do you think?" Lauretta said. "It happened in a theater, so I feel a connection. I suppose *that* ended the performance."

Sarah realized she was trembling. "Why in God's name would anyone—?"

"Aren't you thrilled?"

"No!"

"Well, I for one am," Lauretta said. "It's a sip of nectar between all the cups of gall. We need no longer imagine the old ape's laugh of triumph."

"I cannot share your satisfaction," Sarah said sharply. "Floyd thinks he will—would have been—our friend."

"Oh, well, the Nigras—"

"The friend of all of us."

Lauretta shrugged and pouted, having expected to be praised for her news. "I don't suppose you have tea or coffee, but I could drink a glass of buttermilk if there's nothing better."

"Come into the house," Sarah said, and the others followed her.

Not one to nurse resentment, Lauretta offered another item for their interest. "Blair Saxon is coming home next week."

"So soon? My gracious!"

"Yes." Lauretta laughed, better pleased with her reception. "He sent word."

"Why didn't Annabel tell us?" Sarah said.

Lauretta untied her bonnet. "If you ask me, it explains her bad temper. Not that she's ever a sunbeam at the best of times. Everything I said on the way out here, she bit my head off. If I hadn't wanted the ride, I'd have blessed her out; but beggars can't be choosers." She sat down, and Sarah poured a glass of buttermilk. "Poor man. Imagine. Four years at the war and then to come home to Annabel."

Jane giggled, and Lauretta beamed at her.

"How well I remember my last appearance on a stage up North. It was at the Walnut Street Theatre in Philadelphia, and the play was *Fashion* by Anna Cora Mowatt. When I appeared, there was whispering and finally someone in the gallery called out to accuse me of being a spy for the Confederacy! We tried to go on, but I was hooted from the stage, and the play was stopped." She sipped from the glass of buttermilk, which gave her a thin white mustache. "You see how strangely these things happen? Now, in another theater four years later, the wheel turns a full circle."

That night a son was born to Lotus. She bled a great deal but was happy when they showed her the perfect boy. She had feared every day that some flaw would be the consequence of the attack upon her by the raiding party.

They had talked of names, but nothing had been decided. Floyd had rejected the suggestion of using his own if the child was a boy, and Sarah had vetoed the use of Leon's when Floyd asked her about it. Nancy helped the midwife and was attending Lotus when Floyd brought Sarah to his cabin an hour after the birth.

Drawing a chair to the bedside, Sarah said, "Can I hold him a minute? I'll give him back if he cries."

Floyd lifted the boy from his mother's side and set him down on Sarah's lap.

Nancy had been uncharacteristically quiet. "I been studying about him," she said finally. "Let's call him Abraham."

Each looked from one to another tentatively.

"I favored Ezra for his grandpapa," Lotus said.

"He can have both," Floyd said.

"Abraham Ezra Kendrick." When Sarah pronounced the full name, it was as if she had christened him.

Wanting Lotus to rest well that night, Floyd made a pallet in the kitchen to sleep on. For a long time he lay on his back with the thought "I am a father," after which he slept deeply. He was wakened, however, at daybreak by the frantic crying of the newborn. Listening, he got up from the pallet to investigate, for there was something unnatural in the sound that warned him. Lotus had bled to death in the night, and the baby's jaws, between squalls, clung to her cold breast seeking life that was not there.

42.

The death of Lotus saddened everyone, for she had been a woman who gave without making a virtue of it, one who sweetened the lives of those around her by her good humor and good sense. None mourned her more truly than Nell.

"She does very well," Nell conceded of Josephine, who had left her washtubs for the new Kendrick kitchen, "but her biscuits taste of—*soap*." It was an accusation she made at every meal, and she always whispered the last word of it, as one whispered the scandals of kings.

Having observed that Nell's enjoyment of her victuals was in no way impaired by Josephine's perversity with biscuits, Sarah smiled at Daniel, seated on her right at the round dining table Otis had made.

Passing along the humor, Daniel winked at Jane, diagonally across from him. "Miss Nell," he said, "I think me and Benjamin had better go fishing this afternoon and catch something to whet your appetite. What would you say to that, ma'am?"

"You certainly cannot go fishing on a Sunday," Doreen pronounced.

"I do enjoy a good fish," Nell answered thoughtfully. She stared briefly at the clean bone between her fingers before dropping it to her plate and considering the choice remaining on the platter that had been piled high with fried chicken and set in the middle of the table by Nancy at the beginning of the meal.

"Pass me the rice, please, Grandma?" Benjamin said.

"Look at him!" Doreen ordered them. "He won't touch it at home when Rosalie puts it before him." Everyone was used to the fact that almost everything Doreen said nowadays was a judgment. No one minded; if that was her way, then that was her way.

"I have to have something to put under this good chicken gravy," Benjamin said. Having helped himself to the by now congealed rice, he spooned gravy over it. The gravy was thick with bits of crusted chicken and browned flour, the top of it layered with clear grease. He stirred the mixture with his fork, tasted it, and smiled appreciation. "Let's do go fishing, Daniel. I don't think I've been just for the fun of it since I used to go with Grandpa." There was a blank moment before he continued. Such silences were common social punctuation following the war and the March, as Sherman's campaign was called, when someone was mentioned who had been a particular victim. "If we catch only one or two, they're for Aunt Nell, but if we catch a lot, you all have to promise to come to *my* house to eat supper! Is that all right, Aunt Doreen?" Sometimes Benjamin would go in one breath from assurance to uncertainty, knowing himself to be no longer a boy and not yet a man.

"The family never needs an invitation to take a meal with us," Doreen said, but she looked mollified at having been consulted.

"Jane, honey," Nell said, "you just pass me that dish of butterbeans, and I'll dance at your wedding."

"I don't know if Aunt Nell will want to walk that far," Jane said.

Taking the bowl from her, Nell slapped her hand. "Mind your business, Miss Puss. I'd walk from here to Savannah for a good mess of fish."

Benjamin reached to the platter for another drumstick, and as he began to eat it, he moved a foot, touching his young hound Delilah. She had slipped into the dining room when their heads were bowed and Doreen, who more than ever fancied praying aloud, asked the Lord's blessing. It was considered a compliment for the hostess to call upon a guest to perform this service, and Sarah called on Doreen for it when she was present, knowing that it pleased her. Looking around the circle of faces, Benjamin decided that he loved everyone present, even Amos Twiggs, who sat silently eating prodigious amounts, interrupting himself only to say some such as "Thank you for some of that okra, ma'am," or "Much obliged for the stewed tomatoes, sir."

It was the middle of June and the first Sunday dinner which Sarah had made an occasion for the family. It was, in fact, a double occasion, to celebrate the new house and to mark Jane's birthday, which had occurred two days before but which with everyone busy had waited for Sunday to be observed. At the table were Sarah and Jane, Nell and Doreen, Daniel, Benjamin, and Amos Twiggs.

Amos Twiggs, or Mr. Twiggs as he was called by all, was one of those mysterious strangers who appear from nowhere in the aftermath of wars and natural disasters. He had simply been sitting on a log in the yard one morning in late April when they came out to begin the day's work. He asked to see Mrs. Kendrick.

He was a small man, ordinary but neat in dress, his hair and beard streaky brown and gray. His eyes were brown, but they had a yellowish cast like a goat's, and they looked at Sarah mildly and seriously as he explained that he had heard she was building a house. "Happens I know something about it, ma'am."

As it turned out, he knew everything about it. He looked at

the several plans Sarah and Floyd had drawn, and he pulled his ears gently, first one and then the other, and he presently began to murmur suggestions that improved the plans and omitted all of their more impractical vagaries. They had not begun blindly; they had hired four men from Highboro who were known to be best in the local building trades. Mr. Twiggs deferred to these until they saw that he knew more about their own work, which included bricks and chimneys and windows and doors, than they themselves knew. He never commanded, but before his first day was out, he was in charge, and nothing of importance was being decided without someone's saying, "We must ask Mr. Twiggs."

At supper that night Sarah expressed her confidence in him and asked him to name a price for his services. He would not, he told her, want anything but his keep. He was given a cabin to himself, and he ate every meal with the family. There were times Sarah thought he must be younger than he looked, and there were times she was certain he was older, but aside from wondering about that, neither she nor anyone else at Beulah Land found themselves speculating about Mr. Twiggs. He was never known to make a personal observation about himself or anyone else. His accent was neither Southern nor Northern. He volunteered nothing of his background and asked nothing about theirs. The nearest he ever came to explanation of his presence was his early statement of "having heard that Mrs. Kendrick was building a house."

It was done now, except that it lacked paint, and the paint was on the way from Savannah. Blair Saxon had arranged for it. The house was all on one floor with a living room, a dining room, an office, four bedrooms, a kitchen, and a storeroom-larder. Mr. Twiggs had shown Sarah how more rooms could be added in future if they were required. It might ramble almost as she pleased. The one adornment—and that was practical, considering the climate—was a porch that ran across the front and wrapped around both sides, thus affording cool shade at all times of day in any but the hottest weather.

Floyd's house had also been built, but the original plan had been modified after the death of Lotus. It was square and consisted of four rooms: an office–sitting room, a kitchen, a bedroom, and another room the size of the bedroom but standing empty except for a few special farm implements Floyd would not leave in the barns lest they be stolen. The vacant room would be Abraham's when he was older, but the baby was now being cared for by Nancy, who had taken the job upon herself without being asked. She lived with Abraham in the cabin where he was born. There was mention of another woman's sharing it with them, but there were more cabins than people, and no sharing except for convenience and company was necessary.

Since the war's end more workers had left the land, most of them finding their way to bigger towns and cities to explore the meaning of freedom, and some of them falling again into slavery of one kind or another. The South was invaded by all manner of vicious and virtuous men from the North, eager to profit from catastrophe. One of the darker maneuvers was to hire a gang of workers, paying them something in advance and transporting them to seaports where their work was supposed to be done. They were then shipped to Cuba to be sold as slaves. Junior Elk had been involved in such transactions, but not as a principal. He played his part at the beginning, with a little money and the promise of work in Savannah, where he was known to "have connections." A score of men who had once slaved in the fields of Oaks and Beulah Land now slaved on plantations of sugarcane and tobacco with the Cuban sun on their backs. The cigar Junior enjoyed next winter might be made from leaves they had picked.

Benjamin had only two men to help Zadok on the new farm. Called the Anderson Place for as long as anyone could remember, even when it was owned by the Elk family, it was soon referred to in the county as Ben's Farm, perhaps because of the novelty of its being in the charge of a boy. James had been true to his word; the farm, including the Glade, was the property of Benjamin Davis.

At Beulah Land, aside from the very young and the very old, there were eleven workers where there once had been a hundred, and they were paid fourteen dollars a month in addition to their keep: clothes, food, and medicine included. Each of them also was given two acres to use as he would. When a branch of the Freedmen's Bureau was set up in Highboro, work contracts were duly signed by Sarah, who had taken the Oath, and given the mark by those who could not write their names. From superstition some would not make the mark but only touch the pen that had written their names. The touch was supposed to bind them legally but, in fact, contracts were frequently broken by both the farmers and the men and women who worked for them.

Floyd and Sarah had little trouble with their workers, for they were known to be fair, and they were not mean with food and clothes, although no more was allowed than they thought just and necessary. Somehow, Floyd managed. Daniel supervised the work on the land, mainly planted in corn this year. Floyd concentrated on the sawmill, which was more important to them because it provided cash. But everyone worked where he was needed. One day would find Floyd with a hoe in his hand and the next see Daniel balancing a plank on his shoulder as he stacked a pyramid of lumber.

When even Nell had stopped eating, Mr. Twiggs decided that he would like one more boiled potato, which he ate with the solemn relish he had accorded his first taste of the table's bounty. They watched him, not rudely but with the kind of satisfaction they had learned to know at the rare sight of abundant food being abundantly enjoyed. When he was done, Sarah called to Nancy in the kitchen to bring the birthday cake. Josephine began to clear away used plates, for Nancy had made the cake herself and claimed the privilege of bringing it into the dining room. She now did so as slowly and deliberately as a bridal attendant marching down a church aisle. There were no candles, but there was pink icing. Nancy had used beet juice to achieve the color, and no one except Sarah had seen the cake after it was made until now.

There were exclamations and a general shifting of chair legs, during which Delilah's tail was caught under someone's foot. She let out a modest yelp, more of warning than pain, but it was enough for Doreen to discover her presence. Everyone else had known she was there, Doreen being the only one Delilah practiced to avoid.

"Benjamin, I've told you!" Doreen cried. "You've let that confounded hound in again!"

"Never mind," Nell said. "A man wants his dog with him. Jane, cut the cake while I make a wish for you. I wonder which slice will have the button." To Mr. Twiggs, who was staring at her gently, she explained, "Whoever gets the button will be an old bachelor."

43.

Captain Abel Ponder's successor had been sent from Savannah to Highboro the day after Ponder had added his verbal account and explanation to what he had already written of his administration. The Captain's bluster of outrage that his honor should be in question was met with rude laughter. It was pointed out to him that if further proof had been needed, it was furnished by his arrival in a stolen carriage with a Negro woman he had been accused of corrupting. His request for reassignment was granted before he had stamped the travel dust from his boots, and Colonel Ward Varnedoe set off with a single orderly to replace him in Highboro.

Colonel Varnedoe's rank was, even in those easy-ranking times, too exalted for the post he was going to assume. He was sixty years old and in the ordinary course of events would have been on his way home, but he had taken his new assignment with the understanding that he should be relieved of it within six months. So much was known of him within hours of his arrival in Highboro, which happened on a Saturday. When he attended church services the next day, the fact was favorably remarked. And when on the Monday following he respectfully begged to be excused from receiving Junior Elk until he had had time to study his position and the general situation, that too was noted. Junior had come to call on the new commander to discover whether he was as big a fool as his predecessor; but finding himself rebuffed, he was content to remember that Colonel Varnedoe was in residence temporarily.

The requisition of foodstuffs continued, but the raids stopped; so, therefore, did the looting. Colonel Varnedoe was prompt and firm in the application of new regulations that arrived every day concerning the governing of the conquered, but he was reasonable and he was responsible, and it was being said presently that were he not a Yankee, he might be considered a gentleman.

If age be the great Subtractor, as is generally averred, still some of the things it eliminates are well lost. Ward Varnedoe was no longer ambitious to do more than his duty, knowing that to be difficult enough. While retaining reasonable pride, he had shed most of the vanities that make old men tyrannical. The more familiar he became with his own faults, the less inclined was he to look for faults in others. A wart was a wart, but not sufficient reason to cut off a hand.

In acquainting himself with the town, he accumulated a fair knowledge of the people and their activities. He was surprised to learn of Selma's school for Negro children, for it was the very kind of thing the Freedmen's Bureau was set up to encourage. He would pay a visit to the school, he decided. But as matters more urgent required his time, it was not until a morning in May that he found a free hour to call upon the schoolmistresses. Lilac answered the door and ushered him to the office, where Selma was working. Selma received him courteously and suggested that he might like to observe a class in session. Agreeing, he was led to a room in which Lauretta drilled a dozen young ones in the spelling of simple words. Lauretta's back was to the open doorway. A child named Jenny was having trouble with the word "because," and when her large eyes caught sight of the Colonel's blue uniform, she plunged gratefully into a terror that was almost entirely assumed. "Yankees!" she cried.

Lauretta wheeled full about, arms stretched wide as if to save her charges from harm. "What! Do you now invade the very schoolroom?"

The situation was quickly set right with explanations by Selma, who then withdrew to her office. A chair was found for the Colonel, and teaching was resumed. The session was turned into a spelling match. Lauretta and her pupils instinctively collaborated in showing off, Lauretta calling out words they knew best and the boys and girls working their faces and voices into tortures of indecision before triumphantly producing the right spelling, immediately followed by the correct pronunciation of the word, the way they had been taught.

For five minutes they made a studied pretense of ignoring the Colonel, as he had asked them to do; but they could not keep it up; their eyes *would* dart to his mild, interested face. Soon every one of them was flirting openly with the good man, whose lips now and then bent with humor, try though he did to remain serious. When at the end of half an hour a boy named Monroe was proclaimed the champion speller, they applauded him as if he had slain dragons, although he always won the spelling matches and so was loathed by every one of his classmates. The Colonel produced a five-cent piece and asked Lauretta if he might give it to the boy. She smiled permission. The prize was given. The children were allowed a recess and dashed into the yard to spend in games the hysteria they had accumulated during their performance.

Colonel Varnedoe complimented Lauretta on the good conduct of her class and asked if he might visit the school again. She assured him that he would be welcome. So began their friendship.

Another friendship grew beyond its bounds and sought new dimensions. James Davis proposed marriage to Margaret-Ella Singletary and was accepted.

Watching her carefully remove curling tongs from her hair, Ann-Elizabeth observed, "I don't know why you bother to make yourself pretty for a blind man." Dropping the tongs to the dresser, Maggie slapped Ann-Elizabeth as hard as she could. It was the first time Ann-Elizabeth had been afraid of her younger sister, and the first time she believed there might be something of true regard in her feeling for the man she was about to marry. Almost everyone professed himself against the match except the two principals.

The wedding took place at three o'clock on the afternoon of Saturday, June 24, 1865, in the living room of Annabel and Blair Saxon. It was remarkable for the fact that faces remained as solemn at the end of the ceremony as they had been during it. Only the families were asked to attend. Annabel and Ann-Elizabeth were united as never before in their disapproval. The difference in ages, although amounting to just over thirteen months, the lady being that much longer upon God's earth than the gentleman, might have been thirty years by the way they harped on it. Remarks like "indecent haste" and "want of proper feeling" were exchanged by the two matrons even as James and Maggie exchanged their vows, and Nell was moved to declare when her disappointed eye assessed the meager refreshments that she could quite believe "the funeral bak'd meats" had been called upon to "coldly furnish forth the marriage feast."

The real reasons for dissatisfaction were as several as those who suffered them. Annabel did not like to see James and his new money leave the family. Ann-Elizabeth resented the double consequence accruing to her sister of a second husband and a fortune—and these too directly on the heels of her distinguishing widowhood! To Benjamin the marriage seemed to further separate him from the man he had until recently considered his father. Jane was simply jealous of the fact that Maggie's daughter would now have the right to call James "Papa," and at the wedding when Prudence made friendly approaches to the younger girl in light of their future sisterhood, Jane snubbed her with blazing, tearful eyes. Doreen had never liked Margaret-Ella and Ann-Elizabeth and saw the alliance as a betrayal of the devotion she had given James all his life. To Sarah it was evidence that James's love for her lamented Rachel was dead.

The day was hot, and even the older men of the party availed themselves of the splintery palmetto fans Annabel had scattered about the room for her guests. When they had all gone their gloomy ways, she tried to quarrel with Blair, who would not take her seriously; she rebuked Blair Junior and Bonard for flirting with Prudence Singletary, which only inspired them to nudge and wink at each other; and she criticized Millie and Fox for both the arrangements and their performance, which set them to talking in the kitchen in bold, wounded tones about "de 'Mancipation Proclamation." Then with a headache she did not have to invent, she announced that she was going to her room and to bed. She could not, however, sleep, as she complained the instant Blair joined her a couple of hours later. She was, she confessed falsely, resigned to James's marriage, but the awful thought that now possessed her mind was that soon—ah, all too soon!—her sons Bonard and Blair Junior would get themselves married and thereafter be lost to her.

Sitting on the side of the bed, Blair removed his stockings, first shaking them out and then sniffing delicately at the toes. "You must think of it this way," he said as solemnly as if he were reading a Psalm, "you will not be losing sons but gaining daughters."

"Poppycock. The advantage is all on the other side. —However, I shall, I hope, know my duty when I see it. And I shall watch Benjamin too, and make every endeavor to assure that he does not marry unsuitably when the time comes."

"He's still a boy!" Blair protested, draping his stockings over the tops of his shoes and setting them beside the chamber pot.

"Poor mite," she continued. "Within a year to lose his mother

—not that she was much good to him or to anyone else, as James's rash remarrying surely indicates—and then his grandfather, and now his father!"

At that moment Annabel's "poor mite" was in the Glade, where he and Nancy met, never by prearrangement, for neither of them knew when he and she might be free; but their convenience and inclination contrived to bring them there at the same time moderately often. After they had "done it," as both then referred to the act of sexual conjunction, Benjamin worried about his size, as boys will.

"Everything that don't wither, grows," Nancy teased him. "Stop your grumbling. 'Tain't always the biggest bird that sings the sweetest song."

Prudence had gone to Ann-Elizabeth's house to spend a few days so that, her aunt explained to her stiffly, her mother and Mr. Davis might have the opportunity of adjusting to their new living arrangement, an explanation Prudence received with grave face and merry heart.

James and Maggie had her house to themselves, the army boarders having been turned away when it was decided that James would make it his home after the wedding. His trunk had been brought over that morning by the slyly chuckling Fox, who had declared for the hundredth time to Maggie's cook Tenah that he had had a large part in the development of the romance that now so displeased them all, for he had "taken Mister James in the buggy to see the lady when he was powerful low in his spirits."

However that may have been, James was not low in his spirits tonight. He and Maggie were as glad to be rid of their families as the families had been to finish with them. Closing the front door, they made themselves at home, reveling in the knowledge that they were alone. They walked about arm in arm from one room to another. Already James found the house easy and familiar, from his frequent visits. They sat for an hour, she on his lap in his favorite rocking chair, as the cat Susie stared at them, but could not stare them out of their friendly behavior. Tenah had left a cold supper on the table, thankful at being allowed to go early to her own house at the foot of the vegetable garden in the back yard.

They drank a little punch, they ate of the roast chicken, they talked almost without stopping. And when they entered the bedroom at last, it was without the nervousness of the uninitiated, but with the readiness of two who are eager to become lovers. In a few moves James shed his outer garments. Finding her as she was beginning to follow his example, he said, "Let me undress you."

She smiled and nodded, which he almost might have seen from the way he began to undo her clothes. She let him manage it without help or coy hinder, only now and then pressing her lips to his when they happened to be near and when he paused in his work to marvel at her. Settled finally in bed, he said, "You forgot to blow out the candle."

"I wanted to see you," she said.

"Blow it out, so we'll both be in the dark."

In the warm summer night they made the sweet sweat of love.

44.

The baby Abraham on her hip, Nancy stood watching Sarah as she sorted plums one morning in the storeroom behind the kitchen. Both Nancy and the baby were getting over colds, or the same cold, according to Nancy, who referred to it as "our cold." She occasionally wiped the baby's nose with her skirt, but only snuffled her own. Very early that morning she had taken a bucket and Abraham, and a kitten to occupy Abraham's attention, to the orchard, where she had picked the ripening plums. Quiet as she watched Sarah pick over the plums, she finally said as if she had been saving it, "He's gone."

"Who? Who's gone?" Sarah exclaimed fearfully. Her mind had suddenly leapt back over the years to another morning when Floyd had left Beulah Land to be a world wanderer for a time.

"Mr. Twiggs," Nancy said, swinging the baby up into both arms and jouncing him.

Sarah was instantly relieved. "Oh!" She had known Amos Twiggs would go without saying goodbye, that his sudden absence would serve notice of his departure, even as his sudden presence had announced his arrival.

"Well'm, he done all he could, didn't he?"

"Yes, he did," Sarah agreed.

"Even to waiting till you was painted."

"He's a good man," Sarah said.

Nancy pursed her lips consideringly and glared at the baby to try to scare him into smiling at her. "Spooky, you ask me. However, he left you a sign."

"He did?" Sarah was surprised. "Where?"

"Ask me no questions, I'll tell you no lies."

"In his cabin?"

"You'll find it."

"Why can't you tell me?"

"Just remember: I didn't move a thing!"

Laughing and swinging the baby to left and to right, Nancy left the storeroom and went directly into the yard as if she had important business there.

After a few words with Josephine in the kitchen about how much sugar to use with the plums, Sarah, who was curious as well as amused by Nancy's mystery, let herself drift in the direction of the cabin that had been Amos Twiggs's. The door stood open, but that was as it always had done in warm weather. Mr. Twiggs had nothing to close a door upon. She walked into the cabin's one room. The bed was neatly made. The one chair was drawn up beside the one table. On the table was a cold candle in its chipped saucer. The nails on the wall behind it held no hat, no coat. Mr. Twiggs was surely gone, as Nancy had said; but what had she meant in telling her that he had left a sign? There was nothing of him at all.

Then she saw it, neatly placed, not fallen or forgotten, beside the candle holder. It was the button Mr. Twiggs had found in his piece of Jane's birthday cake, that had made them all laugh so, even Doreen. Mr. Twiggs, on leaving, had made a little joke.

Touching the button and smiling, she was roused by the sound of Lauretta's calling her name. Going to the door, she saw her sister crossing the yard under the big oak trees looking as if she would go in four directions at once. "Here I am!"

Seeing her, Lauretta ceased her frenzy and came on to the cabin as dreamily as a sleepwalker in a play. Still smiling, but quizzically, Sarah drew aside to allow her to enter. Lauretta walked straight to the chair beside the table and sat down, shaking her head.

"Whatever is the matter?" Sarah said, knowing Lauretta well enough to suppose it might be little, or nothing at all.

Lauretta turned on her a look of awful intensity. "Would you hate me if I married and left you?"

"Great God in heaven!" Sarah cried.

Lauretta shook her head again. "I ask myself if I am worthy, and I know I am not."

"What are you talking about?"

"I ask myself: can I learn to be worthy? And I don't know—I declare I just don't know!" She took a handkerchief from her dress pocket and blotted her palms. "It's so hot already and not yet ten o'clock." Sarah waited, supposing from her past performances that Lauretta merely wanted to be begged for her secret. Lauretta was looking down at herself, as incredulous as an infant discovering it has a foot. "I came just as I was, for there seemed no necessity to change, as he said I looked perfectly lovely. I can never quite decide whether lavender suits me. I had told him we must see you first before I gave him an answer."

"I am wiser than to try to be your guardian," Sarah said drily.

"Don't tease. I left him sitting on the porch and came to look for you when Nancy said you were out here somewhere."

She would humor her; it was a morning of mysteries. "Left who?" she said firmly.

"Colonel Varnedoe, of course. Who else could it be?"

"I was not aware that he was your beau," Sarah said.

"You surely don't suspect me of trifling with a man like Colonel Varnedoe?"

"You have been known to trifle with the devil himself," Sarah said.

Lauretta giggled. "I never dreamed—" She paused to remember. "Of course, he *has* taken to stopping at the school fairly often, but I thought it was no more than his interest in the teaching of the pickaninnies. He always asked Lilac to direct him to my little group, however. I thought nothing of that. —No, really, Sarah dear. No cause for you to look at me so skeptically. I assure you the Colonel is not the sort of man one flirts with." Sarah lifted herself to sit upon the table. Lauretta leaned toward her confidingly. "Isn't he fine-looking? So very distinguished, like an ambassador or a really great poet perhaps. No, not at all like a poet. They're either mad and twenty or terribly old and drip egg in their beards. I have no use for them. Colonel Varnedoe is not so terribly old, do you think?"

"I've seen him but once or twice, and never speculated on his age."

"Not too old for me? —I mean, we shouldn't look ridiculous together?"

Sarah bit down a smile. "If you find yourselves suited in other ways, I don't see that that need trouble you. Now, back to beginnings. Am I to understand that Colonel Varnedoe has made a proposal of marriage to you?"

"Why else would we be here?"

Sarah shrugged helplessly. "I am still in the dark."

"Oh, it isn't true about my not flirting with him, I have. But I never dreamed— He is such a shy, such an innocent man where women are concerned."

"Do you think an innocent man is quite the kind to make you happy?"

Lauretta clapped her hands. "Wait until I tell you!" She looked Sarah straight in the eyes. "I have told him everything."

"That must have taken a very long time."

"It all came tumbling out. I told him about running away when I was a girl, leaving you with Aunt Penelope in Savannah, marrying Douglas Savage. Becoming an actress. Finally discovering that we were *not* married."

"What did he say to that?" Sarah asked.

"He was angry with Mr. Savage. If Mr. Savage had been present, he would have suffered at the Colonel's hands."

"I'm glad to hear it."

Lauretta laughed. "Oh, Douglas wasn't such a bad man, you know. Rapturously handsome—do you remember? And so much in love with me he couldn't keep himself from telling me lies and marrying me when he already had a wife."

"And a child," Sarah reminded her.

"I told him about Bonard Davis," Lauretta continued eagerly.

"How much?"

"About his being married to Selma but her not living with him. About our running away together and traveling as man and wife in the West, and about Bonard's being a gambler—"

"How did Colonel Varnedoe feel about that?"

"He was most angry with Bonard too. He said that with me to inspire him, what could a man not have done?"

"From your reports Bonard did quite a number of things."

"I believe," Lauretta said, shading her voice modestly, "Colonel Varnedoe meant things of a noble nature."

"Did you tell him how Bonard died?"

Lauretta nodded as matter-of-factly as if the cause had been pneumonia. "I thought he would weep. I assured him, of course, that Bonard was not cheating, that I was later told by a most reliable witness that he had drawn his cards honestly and held a winning hand. That only appeared to make the Colonel sadder."

"He is tenderhearted for a soldier."

"Oh, he is, Sarah. How he feared for me, knowing that I was friendless and alone in that barbarous California town where everyone was aflame with gold lust!"

"To save his sensibilities, you told him quickly, I trust, about your rescue by Mr. Robb Quale Tilly."

"I told him everything about the wretch—and about his ogre of a wife, who arrived on the scene by clipper ship to the consternation and confusion of us all!"

Sarah nodded. "Colonel Varnedoe spoke of horsewhipping, I imagine."

"Well, no. In fact, he laughed. And once he began, he laughed so hard the tears actually did come. We laughed together."

"I begin to hope for Colonel Varnedoe, even perhaps for you."

Lauretta appeared to hesitate. "One thing I did not tell him."

"I think you may keep one secret from a suitor."

"I did not tell him about Leon and me. Nor about Rachel." As Sarah stared at her, Lauretta's voice and eyes faltered. "I was too ashamed to tell him that."

"You did right not to," Sarah said evenly.

"But I did tell him everything else; I did, truly. About the acting—he's not the least straitlaced about my having been in the theatrical profession. As a matter of fact, he's *interested*. I shall have so many funny stories to tell him that will make him laugh! —if, I mean to say, we decide to go on together." She sighed.

"Since you have come to me, I suppose I should ask the proper questions. Has he told you anything of his background?"

Lauretta nodded. "His wife died ten years ago. He has two sons, grown and married. No daughters or other dependent female relatives. Isn't that lucky? He is not rich, but he has what he calls 'substantial holdings' in Maryland. His house is at Oxford. That's the Tidewater part. Maryland is *almost* Southern."

"Are you certain that you want to marry, Lauretta? You've been your own woman for a long time."

"Yes, and I am sick of it. I should like to know that someone— not just someone, but Colonel Varnedoe—cares what happens to me."

Sarah studied her sister's face.

"Oh, Sarah, do you think I dare? I meant what I said. I am not worthy of him and I know it. He is a good man. Why is it I never cared for a good man before?" She then said as if it answered her question, "No good man ever cared for me."

"I think if he had lived, Bruce Davis would have—"

"No, you were right. I have thought about it. He would never have been happy with me. Sarah, *can* I make a man happy?"

"I don't know."

"The town will be scandalized at my marrying a Yankee, won't they? How Annabel will thunder and roar! I would almost do it for that alone."

The two sisters sat quietly for a few moments, each occupied with her own thoughts until Lauretta said, "I don't suppose it will be a very passionate marriage. But who can say as to that? A gentleman has the right to expect, at the very least, an amiable compliance from the woman he marries. I shall manage it easily enough, although truth to tell, passion died for me with Bonard. He was a scoundrel, but he was *my* scoundrel. Do you know he never looked at another woman when we were together? I had his undivided attention in those ways. A man who gives that cannot be faulted altogether."

"You were lucky," Sarah conceded, "in your excursions and alarms."

"Yes, I was. I had so much, so many, whereas you, my poor Sarah, have had only that—traveling portrait painter, if I am to believe you."

"I should never have told you about him," Sarah said.

"Forgive me for saying it, but I pity you."

"He was worth a hundred."

"Easy to boast so if you have no comparison."

"Meow," Sarah said.

"I'll sheathe my claws forever if you will come and curtsey to my Colonel. I thought—or rather he thought that I—"

"Never mind," Sarah said. "Let us go and beguile the conqueror."

Rising from her chair, Lauretta looked about the room, her eyes settling on the button on the table. "What is that for?" she said.

"Nothing to you," Sarah said, picking up the button and making a fist to hold it tightly. They went out of the cabin.

"See him? Looking toward us so anxiously."

"I can see him," Sarah said, "but I cannot see that he is looking anxious. What eyesight you still have."

Lauretta linked arms with Sarah and kissed her on the cheek. "Smile," she commanded. "As we grow older, we must try harder to please."

"I am smiling," Sarah said.

45.

When word got about, as it very soon did, of the proposal of marriage and its acceptance, there was indeed a certain amount of verbal commotion. Annabel Saxon, by general acknowledgment the town scold, announced that the entire structure of Southern society had crumbled and said that woe would certainly betide those who had so recklessly effected its erosion. However, clocks will continue to tick if they are wound, and dogs continue to bark at cats and cows, and after the first mild sensation the news became simply another topic of conversation and interest, of no great account. This is not to say that people approved. There were cluckings and pursed mouths over the fact that Colonel Varnedoe was a Yankee, although his Maryland origin was held by some to be an amelioration. Dissatisfaction was expressed mainly on account of Lauretta's being rewarded for a lifetime of indiscreet, often as not scandalous, behavior. The Lord may rejoice in the salvation of a single sinner, but his followers are slow to take his example.

The wedding would take place on the new big porch at Beulah Land in the last week of July, it was decided, and it would coincide with Colonel Varnedoe's relinquishing his post as commander of the military forces governing the district. Although Lauretta had leaned toward a church ceremony with a little avenue of crossed swords at the exit, Sarah insisted that it be performed at Beulah Land, knowing as she did the impropriety, indeed the impossibility, of Lauretta's being married in church. A general invitation was circulated for eleven o'clock, the Saturday morning of July 29. The couple would go immediately by the restored train service to Savannah, thence to Baltimore by coastal packet. As her oldest relative, albeit no blood kin, Nell, to her huge delight, was to give the bride in marriage.

One of those most interested in the setting of the wedding date was Junior Elk, for it would signal the assumption of power of Captain John Struther, whose acquaintance he had already made. Captain Struther had been a lieutenant to Captain Abel Ponder, and Junior thought he could be counted an ally. To that end he had made certain overtures that had not been discouraged.

Junior was in no hurry to divide Oaks plantation into small farms and to sell them. Although he spoke warmly, he spoke vaguely of the plan when he met James Davis and his wife on their morning walks and once so answered Annabel Saxon, who pursued him out of the bank to ask him graciously how he was getting on with his "little project." He was accountable to no one, and none knew it better than Junior Elk. He owned the land.

He had, in fact, started to build a house for himself on the exact foundations of the old Davis house, buying lumber for it from the Kendrick sawmill, which he still coveted. He could buy it nowhere else, but he would have bought it from Sarah and Floyd had there been a dozen mills, for the opportunity it gave him of spying on them and of weighing their circumstances and expectations. These latter did not comfort him. With his father before him, he now had come too far to be content with anything less than ascendancy. It was not a question of proving anything to anyone; he must know it himself. So the old foundations were cleared and reinforced and, where necessary, enlarged. His house would be grander than the Davis house had been, and its grandeur would mock the past.

He would do this, and he would still cut up the old plantation, keeping a choice four hundred acres to surround his house, and selling the other parcels as farms that would have the appearance of mere serf holdings to the great lord. —If only he had a son as worthy of him as he was of old Roscoe Elk. He reminded himself that he was young enough to beget other sons if he lost all hope of the one he had sent away to be educated. Or perhaps it would all, being finally accomplished, end with him. His ambition was not to establish a dynasty but to be first in his own lifetime and know it.

For that, he must not only build but destroy. It was not enough to complete the Elk fortune if he did not obliterate that of the Kendricks. In actuality there were no Kendricks. Leon Kendrick had been the last to carry both the name and the power the name conjured. Sarah Kendrick was not a blood Kendrick, nor did she have a child who was. When she died, the name would die, among whites anyway. The child she had claimed, Rachel, had been her sister's and, it was commonly assumed, her husband's, for why else would they have raised her as their own and married her to the neighboring Davises?

However, Rachel had had children, and they grew and flourished, did *Miss* Jane and *Master* Benjamin, although they bore the name of Davis. There was another he could not forget: his own mother's son by Leon Kendrick and hence his half brother, Roman. Roman "Elk." Roman *Kendrick*. But he was banished for having killed Junior's real brother, who had wanted and finally raped Sarah Kendrick.

Aside from these there were some others who loved the Kendricks and who made the Kendrick destiny, good and bad, their own; and the chief of these was Floyd Kendrick. The women Selma and Pauline didn't count, for they were unnatural as well as women. They could be, would be forgotten. But Floyd must be dealt with, for he had long made the Kendricks strong.

46.

On a late afternoon in early July, Benjamin waited at the Glade, having left Zadok and their two helpers arguing amiably in a cornfield below. They had pulled a few ears for eating before today, but today they had given themselves the satisfaction of walking between the rows and speculating on the eventual yield. The stalks were strong and green from the right combination of sun and rain; their leaves would provide good fodder. The ears, although not mature enough to show brown in the silk tassels, were growing thick and heavy, the promise fulfilled of the verse they quoted when they dropped the seed kernels into the ground: *One for the blackbird, one for the crow; one to rot, and one to grow.*

It had been a hot day, and Benjamin was barefoot. After cupping his hands and drinking water from the brook until he belched, he waded to get his feet clean, using his toes to pick up pebbles from the bottom. Benjamin didn't mind waiting for Nancy if she finally came, although he liked it better if she was there waiting for him when he arrived. It was—he searched his mind—more seemly. But he was never to forget the loneliness that overcame him when he waited and she did not come, and after putting off leaving a little longer and a little longer, he went home without seeing her. She was his playmate, the only one with whom he did not try to be older than he was.

The farm was coming on pretty well, according to Zadok, who encouraged the boy more than anyone else. For Sarah, the affairs of Beulah Land always came first. James's silence, compounded of envy and uneasiness at having sold Oaks plantation, had the appearance of fidgeting impatience when Benjamin went to see him and made dutiful reports of progress. Any cheerful statement of their prospects only saddened Doreen, who would shake her head and remind him of what they had lost. Daniel was a frequent visitor, but it was not in Daniel's nature to offer encouragement. The New England part of him distrusted hope.

When Benjamin and Zadok took over the farm, the preparation of the fields for planting had hardly begun. The little that Junior Elk's men had accomplished had an air of excuse as if to say, "We'd have done better if we'd been serious about a crop." Zadok and Benjamin were serious. Although the new hands they were forced to hire balked initially at taking orders from one as young as Benjamin, white or not, they worked well enough when they saw the way he worked beside them. He was a strong boy and could guide a heavy plow as steadily as they, although he did not have their strength and endurance. The fields began to look more promising than they had in anyone's memory. Neither the slaves who had kept the farm for Junior nor Junior's brother

Alonzo when he was its tenant had any interest in it; and the Andersons and Cokers, who had owned the acres before they fell to old Roscoe, had by general opinion been a sorry lot.

What Benjamin and Zadok were doing to the fields, Zadok's wife Rosalie was doing to the house. After paint had been applied to the new buildings at Beulah Land, there was enough left to give Ben's house a coat of gray with white trim, and the hangdog look of uncaring neglect it had worn for years was suddenly gone. With Rosalie's example of energy before her, Doreen began to lose some of her apathy and to find skill as well as interest in making flower beds and a kitchen garden. Annabel was good enough to bring her slips from her own gardens, as she frequently confided to acquaintances in town. It had, she affirmed, been her husband Blair who succeeded in obtaining Sarah's paint from Savannah; and so she might claim a little credit, she thought, for the better appearance of the place. She allowed that it was beginning to look quite respectable, but added that Doreen could never be happy there and would go to her grave grieving for their old home.

After scrubbing one foot with the other in the brook until they were both clean, Benjamin sat on a rock dreaming and sulking. Seeing him so a moment before he discovered her, Nancy almost put off to another time the decision she had made, but his first words, gruff with pride, made it easier for her to keep to her resolve.

"I was about to leave. Thought you weren't coming."

"I told you never to expect me, for I never know when I'll be here."

She had indeed told him that, but it was a Thursday, and he knew that she was more likely to come on Tuesdays and Thursdays than other days. Lovers of whatever degree of casual fidelity quickly learn the times they may expect to find one another. "Have they been after you, keeping you busy?"

She tossed her head. "I do what needs. Nobody bosses me."

"You do what Grandma tells you to do."

"She don't have to tell me. I see it and I do it." She put her thumbs in her ears and waggled her fingers at him.

Knowing that any reference to her special charge was likely to mollify her, he asked, "How's your—how's that baby you take care of?"

"Abraham," she reprimanded him.

"Abraham," he apologized.

She had time to turn his question to her own purpose. "He's one of the reasons I got to stop coming here—"

He knew that was too dangerous to acknowledge. He would divert her. "Rosalie says he's the smartest baby she ever saw."

"She do?" Nancy smiled. "Well, I reckon he is!" Pleasure turned to suspicion. "When she say that?"

"This morning at breakfast," he lied.

"She haven't dropped over to see us since last Sunday. Funny, her to say that about him this morning for no reason."

"I guess she was just thinking about him," Benjamin answered slowly. He had gone far enough in making himself agreeable. Frowning as he stared at her, he felt a mixture of irritation and need. "Well," he said after a moment, "are you ready to do it?"

"Am I ready to do what?" Her words arched and fluted with vagueness.

"You know what!"

She mocked him. "Just like that he say, 'You ready to do it?' Like I s'pose to drop my drawers the minute he tell me to!"

Childlike, he seized on one part of her statement to salvage his pride. "You don't *wear* drawers. You go around with your bottom bare."

"That's all you know about what I'm wearing *today!*" she assured him haughtily.

"Let me see!"

"No such a-thing!"

He reached for her skirt. She slapped his hand and ducked away. He grabbed. She ran. He chased after her. Suddenly they were their calendar age, racing through the Glade, screaming and laughing like children let out of school. When he grabbed her again, they fell together and rolled struggling on the ground, no longer laughing, their combat almost becoming lovemaking. Nancy pushed him away fiercely, and he knew she meant it. They sat up, separate and offended.

"You *are* wearing drawers," he accused her.

"Didn't I tell you?" she said savagely.

He apologized even though he did not know what he apologized for. "I'm sorry." Then he said accusingly, "What did I do?"

"You hurt me."

"Well, I didn't mean to."

"Well, you did!"

"Show me where."

"I don't have to show you where!"

"I didn't," he declared again.

"You did so!"

"I thought we were playing."

"Always want to play—like a little boy, not the grown man you want everybody to think you are."

"What did you mean while ago?"

"While ago when?" she hedged.

"That thing you said. You said—you said like you weren't—"

"He can't say what I said. Shows he don't listen to nobody but his own self!"

"What's the matter with you, Nancy?" he begged in innocence that was largely real.

"Huh. I reckon if you don't know, I can't help you."

He shook his head desperately. "I think you've gone crazy. I think you got bugs in your head and they've affected your brain."

"Well if I got 'em, you got 'em too!"

For a little while he sat and stared at her. She sat and glared at him. Then each of them made an elaborate play of not letting their eyes come to rest on the other. Still sitting, she swung suddenly so that her back was squarely to him. "I am not," she said carefully, "gone to come up here with you any more." He said nothing, but now he could look at her back and hate her for turning it to him. He could pretend to himself that he despised the spiky pigtails of her hair and the two rings of sweated dirt that showed around her neck. "I am not gone to do it any more with just anybody, and you in particular."

He had known for the last few minutes that was what she had come to say to him, but to hear the words was another thing. "Well, if that's how you feel, you better go."

She did not move. "You can't make me do nothin'. Like everybody else now, I'm *free*."

"If you're free, that means *I'm* free *of* you!"

"Talk mighty big for a little old boy."

"This is my land!" he declared angrily. "And if you don't like me any more, you can just get off it, you hear?" Without another word she was on her feet running, and he was left with his land, hating her, wanting her to come back, knowing she wouldn't, feeling ugly and young.

Still he lingered. Getting up from the ground, he sat again on the big rock where Nancy had found him. Arms folded on drawn-up knees, he looked down at his clean feet and then he looked through a break in the trees to the green fields below catching the late sun.

"Adam!"

Benjamin had never known such a moment. His spine felt like ice as he turned to watch the figure approaching through the shadowy trees. Scrambling from the rock, he saw that the man was a Negro, although not dark. He was middle-aged and well dressed, and he walked with a limp, but he came on as if he had every right and reason to be where he was. "Who are you?" Benjamin challenged him.

"I knew you couldn't be," the man said, "but the look, I'd nearly have sworn at a distance—" He was looking about the Glade, as one might review the objects in a room once familiar but not seen for a long time.

"You're Roman!" Benjamin discovered. "Aren't you? You're Grandma's Roman!"

The man laughed joyously. "If your grandmother is Sarah Kendrick, then I am indeed her Roman!" He had gone to the big rock and was touching it gingerly, as if touching a sleeper he was afraid to wake.

"Are you Elk or Kendrick?" Benjamin had never been clear about that.

"I'm known now as Roman Kendrick, though I was called Elk when I was born." He looked at Benjamin again as he left the rock. "Adam died, and Rachel married James."

"They were my mother and father."

Roman studied the boy's face. "Yes," he said softly. "I see."

Benjamin blushed. "You knew Adam Davis, did you?"

"He was almost an idol to me."

"Tell me about him."

"Another time I will." Roman moved to the brook and squatted to touch a shelf of slate under the water. Benjamin followed and squatted beside him. "Adam's tutor was a man named Driscoll Proctor, who became a friend of mine. When he went away to the North, I went with him, and we taught in a school in Philadelphia."

"Like Aunt Selma and Pauline," Benjamin said.

"Do they still keep the school?" Roman asked.

"It's in town now, part of the house they live in."

Roman smiled. "That school was started by Sarah Kendrick because of me. —How much do you know about all this?"

"All," Benjamin fudged. "Well, some. Not everything. Will you tell me what you know? The Davises and Kendricks keep a lot of secrets."

"All families do."

"Some of them I've just been finding out."

"I know how that feels." He dried his fingers on his trouser legs. "Whenever there's more than one, you have secrets—and lies."

"What are you doing here?" Benjamin then thought to ask. "I don't mean why you came home. Everybody comes home, but why did you come *here?*"

"That's a thing I don't think I'll tell you." Roman rose from the side of the brook with a mild groan. "How can so much have happened to me, and this place be the same! How old are you?"

"I own my own farm," Benjamin said.

Roman began to stroll, touching a log with the toe of his shoe, pulling a leaf from a tall weed.

Following, Benjamin said, "Did you use to come here?"

Roman nodded.

"It's mine now," Benjamin said. "Part of my farm."

"It was always part of Oaks," Roman observed.

"There isn't any Oaks," Benjamin said. Roman stopped walking and stared at him. "The Yankees burned the house, and later on Junior Elk bought the land. Zadok tells me that some are even starting to call it *Elks* instead of Oaks. I don't care. If it's not ours, I'd rather they stop calling it Oaks. Don't you know what's happened to us?"

"My last letter from your grandmother was a year ago." Roman looked a question too huge to ask.

"I could tell you all of it," Benjamin said, "but she'll want to. Haven't you seen her yet?"

Roman breathed in a spasm, as if he had stopped breathing and started again. He shook his head and swallowed. "I've been wanting to see her ever since I went away, but when the train got in today, I left my trunk and started walking. I came here first, and I can't tell you why." He hesitated. "I know the way, but I'd be glad of your company."

Benjamin turned and chose the path that would take them down through the woods and fields. "Grandma talks about you a lot," he said.

Roman laughed. When Benjamin next turned his head, he saw tears in the man's eyes. Roman shrugged. "To hear Sarah called 'Grandma.'"

A dog raced around them and stopped in the middle of the path, looking back and hassling as if she had run a long way.

"Belong to you?" Roman said.

"Come here, Delilah," Benjamin ordered. She ran to him, wagging her tail and twisting her body in greeting. Benjamin bent, grabbing her head with both hands and kissing the top of it.

"I'm glad you're not too old to kiss a dog," Roman said.

Benjamin looked surprised as Delilah ran ahead, leading the way to Beulah Land.

47.

Jane was shocked as well as puzzled, seeing her grandmother greet the dark stranger, with Benjamin standing by as if he understood everything. Sarah did not merely shake his hand; she embraced him, she kissed him on the cheeks. She wept and laughed, pushed him away to look at him and then embraced and kissed him again. Jane knew that her grandmother could do nothing wrong, but the man was a Negro, however light-skinned. When she learned from their exclamations that he was Roman, she accepted their behavior, but only with an effort; for, having heard Sarah talk about him, she had always thought of him as a boy; yet here he was, not only a grown man, but middle-aged. However, when it came her turn to make his acquaintance, she gave him her hand, and as he spoke to her freely and gently, she almost accepted him as one of them. He had known her mother, he told her. They had picked pomegranates together when she was so small she could hardly run without falling, and he was forever having to pick her up.

"I remember that day," Sarah claimed, unwilling to be left out of any memory of Roman's in the first hour of his return.

And then Nell, whose judgments of people Jane knew to be mainly severe, came out on the porch where they were and clapped her hands together with: "Lord, help my time; it's Roman come home!"

Nothing would do but that a watermelon be fetched and cut then and there when Nell discovered he had not tasted one for several summers, and never mind that supper would soon be ready, for when did a piece of watermelon hurt anyone's appetite. When Daniel came in from the barns and was introduced, Jane noticed that he watched the newcomer with even more reserve than she had felt, and something like jealousy; so she stood beside him for the rest of the time they were all together to assure him that his place with her, at any rate, was not affected. Floyd came from the mill smelling of resin and with sawdust clinging to his hair, and there was further happy shouting, and a few tears too. By then a diminution had occurred in the readiness of those less intimately concerned to continue as bystanders, and before long the party broke in two. Jane and Daniel, Nell and Benjamin and Delilah went into the dining room to have their supper, while Roman and Floyd enjoyed theirs with Sarah in her office, where, she said, they might exchange news and reminiscence to their hearts' content without boring anyone but themselves.

After first gladness came realization that the years of Roman's absence had made him in some ways a stranger to Sarah and Floyd. This encouraged boasts that none of them and nothing had changed, which all knew to be untrue; but gradually a feeling of familiarity and ease returned, as the new look of each merged with old images and it was seen that an added wrinkle in the face or mind did not affect essential selves.

Roman was told what had happened, not only at Beulah Land and Oaks but in their surrounding part of Georgia since he last had direct correspondence with them. Floyd and Sarah listened with eagerness and sometimes consternation to what had happened to Roman. He had spent most of the war years in Washington working in hospitals with the wounded. They sat in silence as he told of gangrene and amputations, of the awful tales he had heard from deathbeds of the savagery of Confederate soldiers, of battleground murders and mutilations that had to do with stealing shoes more than winning or losing a battle, and of how he had at times found himself hating and cursing the very people he had come from.

Driscoll Proctor was dead. He had contracted a consumption of the lungs and died last December, leaving his life savings, which were not on a great scale, to Roman. It was on that occasion Roman gave up his work in Washington and returned to Philadelphia. He decided to teach again, but he had no heart to return to the school he and Proctor had conceived and nurtured under the patronage of Miss Eliza Truman, whose zeal it was to have Negro children taught to read and write as first steps toward becoming responsible for themselves. Discerning in Roman's voice a recurring thread of yearning after the past and origins, Miss Truman had engendered a plan.

Why not return to his homeland and do what he could, preferably in schooling, where his experience lay, to advance the progress of black children? It required little to persuade him to it, and she was not a woman to admit "practical" obstacles. Money? She would find it. Her work had made friends as well as enemies, although some of the former declared themselves sick to death of the cause of Negroes after the long war. Others listened to Miss Truman and pledged support.

Roman reminded her of a thing she had been told and had forgotten, that his leaving the South had not been quite voluntary. He had, in effect, been banished for killing his half brother Alonzo. Miss Truman traveled with Roman to Washington, where the rap of her umbrella handle opened doors that might not have been opened readily to him alone. The end of it was that, in consideration of his record of public services, he was given a paper pardon for the old crime and encouraged to return to Georgia to work in educating the children of former slaves. He was free to follow his own course with tacit sponsorship by the Federal government.

During the rehearsal of these encounters and decisions Sarah and Floyd exchanged looks of many meanings, some of them proud and approving, some uncertain and disturbed as they considered the possible local attitudes toward Roman's return and new ambitions. But they did not speak of these doubts.

They discovered that it was late only when they agreed to walk the nearer reaches of Beulah Land together, these three who had shared so much of its history, and found that others of the household had retired to their rooms for the night. As they strolled the grounds, Roman began to feel at home again. The new Beulah Land was not so very different from the old, as every night scent and murmur reminded him. Floyd offered to share his house with him, and Roman accepted gladly. Breaking a short silence, he clapped Floyd on the back and teased, *"Papa Floyd!* I won't believe it until I see that youngun."

"Tomorrow morning," Sarah said.

"Now," Floyd said, for they found themselves pausing just at Nancy's cabin.

"If you wake that baby, Nancy will skin you alive," Sarah said, "and I won't plead for you."

When Floyd knocked at the door, Nancy opened it cautiously in the dark; but when she saw who it was, she scolded him so shrilly that the baby woke and began to cry. Floyd went past her and lighted a candle, and after promising to be quiet as ghosts, the others followed. The child stopped his bawling and stared at their faces in wonder. Nancy muttered that no one was to pick him up, on pain of such punishments as she did not specify but would take pleasure in devising. Roman hesitantly put out a finger. When the child reached up to investigate it, Floyd said, "That's my Abraham."

Floyd and Roman walked with Sarah back to her house before going into their own. Sarah's office, although it still seemed new and raw to her, was the place she most often ended her day, and she found herself going to it now, although the hour was late. She must always have a little time by herself to consider the events of the day. With the dining room and Daniel's room the office made a short wing separate from the other family rooms.

Sarah had set her candle on the desk and pulled out a chair when a single tap sounded behind her. Opening the door, she found Daniel. Although she liked feeling his presence next door when she was working at night, he seldom made a move to join her, understanding as he did her need for privacy. "Is anything wrong?" she asked. His face, set and solemn, told her that he had waited to speak to her alone. She remembered the night of his return from the hunt for Sergeant Smede. "You wanted to see me, something about the men? With Roman's coming home we've had no time to talk about the work."

He shook his head and came into the office without asking if he might, leaving the door open behind him. "I've been putting off telling you and tonight decided I must do it. If I waited till morning, I'd probably put it off again, and you ought to know." She waited for his determination to overcome his uneasiness. "After the harvest is in, I'm going."

"Where?" She studied his face, but he had closed it to her. "Back North?"

"Maybe. Yes, ma'am, that's what I'll probably do with myself."

"I thought you'd begun to feel that home was here with us."

"I won't be going home."

The other time when he had tried to speak his mind to her, she had deflected him for both their sakes. Now she would not. "Why do you want to leave, Daniel?"

"You don't need me here any more. And now this new"—he swallowed—"who's come, you need me even less."

"I assure you Roman won't be helping with the farming. He never did. He has his own kind of work to do, now more than ever."

"Well, it's not that, not his coming that made up my mind."

"I don't understand," Sarah said.

"Nothing to understand, Miss Sarah."

"If you want to make a life for yourself without us, I shan't try to dissuade you. But if you go, we'll miss you."

His eyes blazed. "No! You won't miss me," he declared. "Good night, Miss Sarah."

"Wait, Daniel—"

But he had left her and a second later she heard his door close quietly. She wanted to go after him. She knew that she could make it right with him, put an end to his misery, but her own reticence and awareness of consequences forbade her doing any such thing. She blew out the candle and sat down, folding her arms on the desk and resting her head on them. Presently she was overcome by a terrible and shaming wave of self-pity and wept.

48.

"Niggers ride and white folks walk."

The cue for this observation by one Union sentry relieving another was the arrival at army headquarters of the buggy from Beulah Land driven by Floyd with Roman as passenger. The buggy was a put-together affair of half-rotted wood, rusted metal, and threadbare upholstery. Several spokes were missing from its wheels, which were caked with red clay made adhesive by the drizzling rain they had come through to Highboro. Sorry sight though the buggy was—and it was kept shabby to discourage envy and theft—Floyd had bartered a half gallon of seed corn and a pair of guinea hens for it because he insisted that Sarah have a vehicle to take her to town when that journey was necessary. She in her turn had insisted that the two men use it for their errands on the morning after Roman's return.

Roman went into the headquarters and Floyd waited, but he wasn't used to staying still, so after a few minutes he got out of the buggy too. He ran his hand over the mule's flank, loosened a harness strap that needed nothing done to it, and then picked up one of the mule's hind feet to examine its condition. The sentry, who was watching him, sidled over. "What you got there, Mose?" he said.

Floyd turned to him with surprise, for after noticing him when they arrived, he had not looked at him again. "Mule and buggy," he answered easily enough.

"Don't take no farmer to know that's a mule, though I've seen better in a knacker's yard; but call that a buggy?"

Floyd smiled obligingly. "Best we can do."

"Reckon it's typical of this God-forsook part of the country."

To get away from the sentry Floyd moved to the other side of the mule and fiddled with the harness.

Tilting his head, the sentry pursed his lips and let spittle ooze out in a thin stream before expending the rest of it with a great plop on the sidewalk. He then resumed his post.

Roman came back and the two got into the buggy and drove to the depot. The rain had stopped, and people were stirring out of doors, so they were not surprised to find a little crowd of men gathered around the steps at the station, waiting apparently to see the morning train come through. Although he could have put a name to most of them if he set his mind to it, Floyd knew them only in a general way as the town loungers and drifters. They were chorus and witness, the watchers of funeral processions and fires and the coupling of stray dogs.

They were not, however, facing the way the train would come; their eyes were on Roman. Floyd doubted that any remembered him, for Roman had been away twenty years, and town memory of individual Negroes was not long. Perhaps they only wondered who the stranger was. Roman saw them watching, and Floyd walked protectively a little ahead of him as they went up the steps toward the freight office to claim Roman's trunk.

"Morning," Floyd said without picking out a face to say it to, and Roman nodded courteously.

Floyd then saw one among them, Charles Byrne, whom everyone knew, for he had been sheriff of Highboro for twenty-seven years. Sheriff Byrne stepped forward and addressed himself to Roman. "What's your name?"

"Roman Kendrick."

"Once known as Roman Elk?"

"I was given that name when I was born."

"Why'd you change it?"

Roman hesitated. "I decided to take the name of my owner when I got my freedom." There was a snicker from the crowd. Floyd saw a shifting at the side as Junior Elk came out of the freight office.

Sheriff Byrne said to Roman, "You had better come along with me to the jailhouse."

Floyd said, "What for, Sheriff?"

Byrne turned mild eyes on Floyd. "Breaking the law. That's why I usually take a man to the jailhouse."

Roman said, "I don't know what law you mean, sir. I came to town just yesterday and went directly to Beulah Land."

Junior Elk joined the central figures. The crowd of men closed around them, not in a threatening way but wanting to see and hear as much as they could. Since the matter appeared to be entirely among Negroes, it did not concern them other than possibly providing entertainment for an idle hour. The sheriff said to Junior, "You recognize this man?"

Junior and Roman looked at each other. "He's the man that killed my brother, Alonzo Elk."

Byrne nodded. "Due to what they called 'special circumstances,' they didn't hang him but let him go free. Judge Maynard decided the case, as I remember, more or less privately." The sheriff's eyes were on Roman now. "Do you deny you're who we say you are, whatever name you now call yourself?"

"No, sir," Roman answered.

"The rest of Judge Maynard's letting you off was that you were to get out of Highboro, get out of the county, get out of this very state, and stay out and never come back. You broke that condition, and so I'm arresting you."

"I've been pardoned," Roman said quietly.

The sheriff looked puzzled. "I can't understand you. You don't talk like a Southern nigger."

"I was given a pardon."

"Now who by?" The sheriff's tone was slyly coaxing.

From his coat pocket Roman produced the document he had presented earlier to Colonel Varnedoe at army headquarters. The sheriff took it, frowning, and read it slowly and carefully. He read it again before passing it to Junior Elk. "Says so, be damn. Federal pardon from Washington, says."

"The Union commander saw it this morning," Roman said, "and his clerk registered it."

"That so?"

Junior Elk handed the document back to the sheriff, turned, and walked away. The sheriff read the paper a third time before giving it to Roman. "Looks to me like you ought to have showed that to me when you first stepped off the train."

"I'm sorry, sir," Roman said. "I thought today would be soon enough, and I was anxious to get home."

"Well." The crowd relaxed ranks and broke as one, and two, then all turned their attention to the train whistle that sounded in the distance.

"Am I free to go?" Roman asked politely.

"Reckon." Still frowning, the sheriff remained where he was until he stood deserted and alone.

During the incident Roman and Floyd had not looked at each other, knowing as they did that any look they exchanged would be interpreted as collusion or complacency. Without speaking to each other they claimed Roman's trunk and tied it to the back of the buggy. Only when they turned the buggy around and gained the relative privacy of a side road did they relax their caution.

"Junior will try to kill you," Floyd said.

Roman nodded. "I don't think he loves you either."

"He wants our sawmill," Floyd said. "He and a man named Abel Ponder, who was the first Union commander here, were thick as thieves until the Captain was called to Savannah. It was them sent Smede to burn Oaks and Beulah Land. I know it as well as I know today is Friday and there's fish for dinner. The Yankees are just greedy, but Junior is nursing his father's hate." They rode in silence until Floyd said, "You had enough of Highboro for one morning or you still want to stop at the school?"

"The school, if it's all right."

"Sure enough." In a few minutes they were with Selma and Pauline and Lauretta, who gave them a friendlier reception. Lauretta took Roman by both hands, produced a flow of welcoming tears, and reminded them of the way he had come to her rescue that night in Philadelphia when she had been turned off the stage at the Walnut Street Theatre, accused of being a Confederate spy.

"I never asked," Roman teased her. "Were you?"

"No, but I wish I had been!" All of them laughed.

"Fine talk," Roman said, "for one who's soon to become the Colonel's lady."

"You know from Sarah," Lauretta said, gratified.

"It was the first thing she told me," Roman said.

Lauretta nodded, believing him. "What color are they wearing in Washington this summer?"

49.

Her gown was the color of old ivory and of so sheer a muslin Nancy swore that if you dropped it from the roof, it would take an hour to float to the ground. Knowing the store Lauretta would set by her wedding dress and the difficulty and expense of finding anything of good quality, Colonel Varnedoe had begged to be allowed to supply it. Permission was given, traditional niceties not being then strictly honored. Contrary to expectation, the wedding was a happy occasion. God so smiled on the day, Lauretta might have been the most virtuous and deserving of women.

To save trouble and the embarrassment of possible omissions and refusals, the invitation was a general one; and Sarah did not know how many to expect. Nell predicted that the entire county would come, and urged the preparation of great quantities of food. Doreen lent Rosalie. Rosalie, Josephine, and Nancy baked a squadron of angel cakes and prepared a tub of potato salad and a vat of punch into which went ingredients that must never before have flavored a nuptial cup. Otis dug a trench near the sawmill to make a barbecue pit, and after reducing logs to firm smoldering ash, stretched wire across the trench to serve as grill. On it the night before the wedding he spread the dressed carcasses of two goats and a dozen wild turkeys. He tended the grill all night, receiving visits from everyone on the plantation who caught the scent of the meat and was able to walk to its source. He mopped the meat frequently with a peppery, vinegary mixture of his own. Tasting it, Sarah could hardly see for the water that sprang to her eyes, and when she asked what he called it, Otis told her Devil Spit. While initial contact with the sauce was fiery, it's afterglow was magically pleasing.

In the event Nell was proved right. People's early vagueness as to their intentions gave way to an almost universal decision to come. By ten o'clock on the morning of Saturday, July 29, a great crowd was assembling at Beulah Land. The Reverend Stewart

Throckmorton had doubted the importance of the event and found obligations that made it necessary to assign his function to an assistant, but on the day before, sniffing the air as it were, he brushed his best black suit and said he would go himself. Annabel Saxon was stout in declaring that she would ignore the shameful occasion; indeed, she repeatedly invoked visions of wild horses being powerless to alter her determination; but at ten-thirty she arrived with her husband and their two sons. There had never been a doubt of James and Maggie's being present. Miss Eloise Kilmer's offer to sing was accepted, and Roman was pressed to provide further melody with his flute. Nell said to Miss Kilmer: "What are you going to sing? You have to tell me and sing it over a few times so I get used to the words; otherwise, I'll laugh all over my face when I ought to look solemn, and nobody will like that."

Jane's flower beds were in full bloom. Hers was the true gardener's gift, whereas Sarah had no talent for decorative planting, grumbling, "My fields are fair, my plots are not." No matter that it had been the wrong time when Jane set down her seeds and cuttings; they had taken root and grown. Doreen and Benjamin were there as a matter of course. For several nights Benjamin had practiced before the mirror certain gestures and stances he expected would win him a name for adult elegance: one leg straight, the other gracefully bent at the knee, one hand at the small of his back, the other lifted to give expression to whatever he might be saying, which in his sessions before the mirror had only been: "Friends, Romans, countrymen, lend me your ears; I come to bury Caesar, not to praise him." But when he tried it, Daniel asked him with genuine concern if he felt sick. He did manage a look of supreme hauteur when Nancy circulated among the guests with glasses and cups of punch, but the effect of it was spoiled when after passing him she suddenly turned back to find him staring after her with an expression of wounded resentment that made her laugh, however it touched her heart.

Maggie's Prudence flirted with Annabel's Blair Junior and Bonard. James followed the sound of the flute and found Roman. As they remembered Driscoll Proctor together and the days he had been tutor to the young Adam and James Davis, it occurred to the older James to say, "I have worried about Benjamin. Since he has his little farm and is so deeply concerned with it, all thought of other education has been set aside. When his harvest is in—no, before!—I'd like to arrange something. Would you, do you think, have time to tutor him in a few subjects?"

Hearing the last words as she joined them, Sarah said, "What a very good idea! Will you, Roman?"

"Only if he wants it himself," Roman said.

Benjamin was called to them and the matter was settled, although neither Roman nor Benjamin was happy about it, Roman because he expected to be too busy for private tutoring, and Benjamin because he hated Latin and ancient history.

Nancy too heard something of the conversation, and it provoked her into seeking Selma and Pauline in their corner, where they were whispering about the other guests, to ask them if they would let her come now and then when she had the time as a pupil to their school.

One of the town's most persistently cheerful old ladies, a Miss Lutetia Whigham, took pains to compliment Sarah on her new house. "I declare, ma'am, it is the prettiest thing I ever saw!"

"Is it?" Sarah said with surprise, and looked at it good and hard. They were standing in the front yard and she had been about to go up the steps to speak to Ann-Elizabeth Dupree and her husband Charles, who had just found his way home from the war and whom she had not yet welcomed. "Then that must be Mr. Twiggs's doing."

"Who, ma'am?" Miss Whigham asked politely.

Still gazing at the house, Sarah discovered that it *was* pretty. It did not look sudden or accidental but as if it had been there under the trees forever with its broad porch and flower gardens wrapped around it. The realization troubled her, for no one had ever called the old house anything better than "commodious." To allow the new one to be pretty seemed disloyal to the past, even frivolous.

There were no gifts except the few contributed by Colonel Varnedoe's officers, whose presence at the wedding was as discreet as his quiet authority could wish it to be. People walked and stood in the front and back yards to judge the house from all vantage points; they promenaded the porches that followed three sides of the main structure; and the atmosphere very soon became festive. Drawn by curiosity and the prospect of a good feed, they found themselves talking of other occasions at Beulah Land. They could almost believe that it was five years ago until they were reminded of what had happened since by the shabbiness of their clothes and the sight of the blue uniforms of the Union officers.

As to the actual ceremony, which took place on the front section of the porch, it was as though God did truly smile. No chicken cackled, no cow lowed, no mule brayed or broke wind within earshot. The sun was shining and the gentlest of breezes caused flowers to bob their heads in a kind of rhythmic benediction. For a few moments the watching crowd was motionless as Miss Kilmer sang her song. Even the dogs wandering about were daunted by the sudden quiet into listening attitudes. Delilah looked so intelligently attentive that Benjamin and Daniel had trouble holding in their amusement. Then Roman began to play softly on his flute, and the Reverend Throckmorton spoke with stern, unloving authority the old words.

Sarah found herself unexpectedly moved. She was not a lover of weddings as some women were said to be, and for the most part sat through them detached, merely doing her duty by bearing witness as two fellow souls mumbled their way into a union of sorts. As she thought about it, she decided that the special quality of this wedding was the exchange of vows between people as old as her sister and the Colonel, their age making them more rather than less vulnerable to the treacheries of time. She had not anticipated that these two would touch her, and they did.

The ring was given, the kiss taken. Mr. Throckmorton made a prayer of his last words, unwilling to relinquish a performance that he knew had gone well. Then it was over, they were married. Everyone spoke or laughed; everyone moved at once. Sarah reached Lauretta and kissed her. Lauretta said, "No fool like an old one!" For the first time since they were girls Sarah felt affection for her. Stepping away to give others access to the bride, Sarah decided to go and speak to Josephine and Rosalie, although she knew they were ready with the tables of food on the side porch nearest the kitchen, where three small girls standing guard against the flies waved palmetto fronds.

When she returned to the front of the house, she found Lauretta and Colonel Varnedoe sitting in chairs that had been shifted from porch to yard. There was an object set up in front of them she knew to be a camera. Lauretta had told her that Colonel Varnedoe had commissioned a photographer to attend them after the ceremony, some fellow who traveled the military camps recording the faces of officers; for the general populace did not have money for such vanities. The man was at his work when she first saw him, his head hidden in the dark cloak the contraption wore. When he emerged, he continued fussing with the camera, but even seeing him from the back she knew there was something familiar about him. As she moved forward, he turned his face for a moment and looked directly at her before going on with his job. The man was Casey Troy.

The man was Casey Troy, and he had looked at her and not known who she was. She went quickly into the house, finding her room and closing the door behind her. There she sat down abruptly and discovered how weak the incident had left her. A brief palsy enveloped her; she felt wasted and tired. Making herself breathe deeply and regularly, she revived her strength a little. When she felt almost herself again, she raised her head and looked deliberately at her reflection in the mirror across the room from where she sat. Even at that distance, the mirror showed a woman past her prime and growing old.

Twenty years ago she had known Casey Troy for a few weeks. They had loved each other and been intimate for a few nights, and he had gone away. There had been no question of anything more. He was a painter of portraits then, going from plantation to plantation and town to town, earning his keep and taking his diversion where he found it. He had been a frank, confident, good-looking man, and their lovemaking an uncomplicated pleasure to both of them.

That was twenty years ago. She frowned at her reflection; no wonder he did not remember her. A light knock sounded and the door opened before she could speak. Jane entered and came directly to her, touching her back. "Are you all right, Grandma? I saw you leave in such a hurry, I thought you might not be feeling well."

"I simply wanted a minute alone, that is all. Now go back. You and I are together responsible for our guests."

Festivities reached their height as the punch was drunk and the food eaten. Nell had taken the precaution of seeing that a quarter of a goat was set back for the family's later consumption. There were the usual toasts, the familiar jokes, the discoveries that are always made on such occasions by this one that that one is prettier than he had hitherto noticed, more jolly and clever, the vitality lacking on ordinary days lending a glow to the commonest countenance, a lilt to the dullest voice.

Sarah and Lauretta said a firm goodbye as the wedding gown was packed away, the last item to be placed in Lauretta's trunk before it was taken to the depot. Colonel Varnedoe drove the buggy that carried him and his bride, and they were escorted by two of his officers on horseback. Sarah stood on the porch and waved to them, and it was Nell who caught the bouquet Lauretta tossed from the buggy, which amused all except the younger girls, who laughed heartiest to hide their annoyance that such a gesture had been wasted in a joke.

One of the guests produced a fiddle, Roman fluttered a few notes from his flute. The side porch where the refreshment tables now stood empty was cleared, and there was dancing for a couple of hours, Sarah leading the way with Benjamin, Jane partnered by Daniel, and the others pairing themselves as they would. Later Benjamin danced with Prudence and was gratified by seeing Nancy stare at them with stony contempt. Daniel took Sarah through a waltz, and during it she looked about to see if Casey Troy was still there—she had asked Jane to see that the photographer was given refreshment—but he was nowhere.

By late afternoon everyone had gone, even Benjamin and Doreen, for Benjamin wanted to see Zadok about one of their cows he feared was ailing. Saturday and a wedding made no difference to a farmer, he told Sarah earnestly when she suggested that they remain for supper.

It was the four of them, Sarah and Nell and Jane and Daniel, who sat together at their own table that evening to enjoy Nell's hoarding. There had been many parties before the war but few in recent years, and Jane could not stop exclaiming over how happy everyone had appeared to be and what a good time they'd had. Any number, she said, told her it was the best time of their lives, paying her the compliment of treating her as one of their hostesses, seeing that she performed the role. Jane could not remember ever seeing so many people happy and carefree together. And wasn't it, she asked with surprise, odd that Aunt Lauretta's wedding should bring about such a celebration?

"It wasn't anything to do with Lauretta," Nell said. "It was their being at Beulah Land again."

50.

Sarah did not love Sundays. It wasn't that she must always be doing, and for that matter Sunday at Beulah Land was as full of activity as she chose to make it; but she felt there was something bogus about a day set aside for rest and spiritual nourishment. Her spirit fed on life every minute; she did not require hymns and bell ringing to activate it. It made her irritable to see people sitting about with blank looks, or chewing over scraps of old news (for nothing happened on Sundays), or affecting affability and piety in the house of the Lord.

On that Sunday there was no talk except of the wedding. Some of the very people who had stayed too long yesterday came again on their way to or from church to say how very much they had enjoyed themselves. Bored out of patience, she soon left the social chores to Nell and Jane, who seemed not to tire of them, and fled to the barns, where she discovered Nancy and Abraham watching a brood of baby chicks happily racing about on their thin legs under the hot eye of the mother hen. But when even Nancy began to speak of yesterday and asked if she thought Miss Prudence Singletary as pretty as everyone said, Sarah answered her grumpily and went looking for Floyd.

He, thank God, was willing to talk about work. There would not be much cotton this year, at Beulah Land or anywhere else, but what there was was nearly ready to be picked, and then it would have to be ginned. There were markets again in the North and in England. The Kendrick cotton gin had been let alone by the Union troops—Sarah reckoned because they didn't know what it was, but Nell had suggested that they spared it because it was ugly and they only chose to destroy what was beautiful. The sawmill would stand idle for a few weeks; there were not enough men to work the fields and to operate the gin and the mill. Benjamin offered to lend Zadok and his two men when he could, since he had planted late and would not reap much of a harvest this year, although his corn and sugarcane had done well. The women and the children would pick most of the cotton, and even the old people would go through the motions of helping.

When Sarah took a straw hat from a peg in the tool bin and she and Floyd set off to walk the fields—a thing they did every day, hence not a "Sunday occupation"—Daniel joined them. Leaving the Glade, where he had gone hoping without hope to find Nancy, Benjamin spied them and came down to meet them. Sarah was happy with her men, as she called them, until they decided to cool themselves with a swim in the creek, which had the effect of sending her back to the house. As soon as she was alone, she was unhappy, which fretted her with herself until she realized that it was seeing Casey Troy again that had upset her. She had not thought about him very often, but she had not forgotten him either, and she supposed that vanity was stung by his not recognizing her. On the moment she decided that what she needed was a few hours of hard work in the cemetery. She and Jane had not been there since last November. In spite of the pressure of plantation problems, they would go tomorrow.

And so they did, Jane being eager to share that occupation with her because she knew how jealously Sarah kept it a private thing in her life. They found the grass thick and the weeds high and pitched in vigorously with hoes and shears. As she worked herself into a steady sweat, Sarah let her mind wander until, had she been asked, she would have said she thought of nothing at all. After a time, however, she noticed that Jane's eyes were fixed now and then on the nearby church. Looking over at it, she saw only the desultory traffic in and out of the women who came on Mondays to tidy it, and then she paid no further attention to it or to Jane.

"Grandma, there's a man been watching us," Jane said presently.

Sarah grunted. "Maybe he isn't used to seeing women work."

"It's us he's watching, not what we're doing. He goes away and comes back, as if he can't make up his mind."

"Well, he isn't our concern, is he?" Nevertheless, Sarah took off the ragged hat she wore to protect her face from burning. The inside straw was damp. She shaded her eyes with her other hand and peered. A man stood outside the iron gate that led from the churchyard into the graveyard. He was almost hidden by the hydrangea that had for years threatened to block the gate en-

tirely if not cut back or replanted. His frown was intense. Seeing
that he was observed, he opened the gate and came toward
them.

"It's the photographer," Jane said.

Sarah was thinking how little he had changed in twenty years.
His hair was graying, but it was as thick as she remembered it,
and his figure was still lean.

"Mrs. Kendrick," he said when he came to them.

"You are Mr. Casey Troy."

Jane looked at Sarah, astonished.

"I was certain you did not remember me."

Sarah wiped her forehead with the back of her hand, which
was dry but only moderately clean. "This is my granddaughter,
Jane Davis."

Casey bowed. "Miss Davis."

"You took the wedding pictures," Jane said. "I couldn't find
you when I looked for you to give you barbecue."

"Mr. Troy is an artist too," Sarah explained.

"Yes'm, I remember. Mr. Troy, the pictures you made of
Grandpa and of Grandma were burned by the Yankees, and so
were the ones of Aunt Nell and Aunt Penelope, but the ones you
did of Aunt Selma and Aunt Annabel are still somewhere."

Casey smiled before he frowned, thinking aloud: "There was
another young girl like you."

"Her mother," Sarah said.

"Is it that long ago?"

He looked at her as he said it, and his eyes suddenly acknowledged the years her face showed. Seeing that, she felt calmer.
"Since you missed the refreshments yesterday, Mr. Troy, perhaps
you'd like to share our dinner basket today? Leftovers from
then, but you are welcome."

"I would not want to intrude."

"We are about to stop this work. My buggy is in the grove
behind the church. Jane, will you go ahead and see to things?
Mr. Troy and I will be along directly." As Jane dropped her hoe
and set off, Sarah continued, "One of the men came with us to
take the mule back to Beulah Lane, where he's needed today in
the fields. He will return with him later in the day to fetch us—"

Alone with Sarah, Casey let his expression relax. "I remember
being here with you once before. At a funeral."

Sarah made herself smile. "That would seem likely."

"A doctor's wife."

"It must have been Miss Mamie. Yes. She and the doctor are off over there. Their graves are overgrown, I'm afraid. There's nobody to take care of them. They had no children."

"It was the first time I spoke to you alone, although there were many other people."

"There have been funerals for some of them since, Mr. Troy. Look around you. Do you remember Miss Edna Davis?" She stepped to Edna's grave.

"The beautiful old woman." Casey smiled.

"Only you ever called her that, I believe. She is here." She turned to indicate another, fresher grave. "Her son Bruce, who was master of Oaks and who paid you for that portrait of Jane's Aunt Annabel. He was murdered by Yankee raiders. My daughter Rachel was married to his son. Hers is the newest grave. The population here has grown more rapidly in recent months than it has in the town proper. It is what some of us have called 'the night season.'"

He had moved a little beyond. "This," he said, "is your husband's grave, is it not?"

She nodded.

"Jane was much attached to him. Among us, grandfathers and their granddaughters are often very close. She loved the portrait she mentioned. I had a miniature of the face copied three years ago to give her at Christmas. The Union soldiers did not care for it, and so they let her keep it when they burned us down."

"I remember what a kind and handsome man he was." She turned quickly to hide the tears his gentle tone had surprised her into showing. Stooping, she wiped a set of shears on the grass and put them with Jane's hoe on top of the weathered gravestone of Edna's husband, the first Benjamin Davis. Taking a twig broom, she brushed fallen leaves from Leon's grave and turned dry eyes to Casey Troy, who was saying slowly, "I know what has happened to you since I was here. I have asked, but without being indiscreet, I want you to know."

"We are not so nice about discretion these days," she observed. "Not that we at Beulah Land were ever famous for it."

He stared at her, frowning again. "You didn't know me," he suddenly accused her.

Automatically, she denied understanding him.

"You had forgotten me," he said. "You looked straight at me Saturday and showed not a sign of recognition."

She dropped pretense. "It was you who did not remember me, sir."

"*Sir*," he mocked her. "We were once Casey and Sarah to each other."

Her face, already pink from the heat of the morning, reddened. "You are certainly being indiscreet now, to remind me of that."

"Do you deny it?"

Her look faltered. "No, but I have forgotten it."

"I have not."

They were silent until she said, trying to command a lighter tone, "Mr. Troy, what use is this line of talking?"

"I have always remembered you."

"As I was twenty years ago," she observed.

"You are not so very different," he declared.

"Oh, yes I am, and you know I am. I have seen it in your eyes."

"Then you misread what you saw."

"That I did not!"

"Are you to be right and I wrong in everything we say today?"

"Mr. Troy, it is impossible for us to quarrel. We are virtually strangers to each other."

"You were the tenderest, the most beautiful woman I have ever known."

"We Georgians are generous with flattery; we will call any woman pretty. But even when I was half the age I am now, my appearance excited no extravagant comment."

"I have never known a woman less aware of her attraction as a woman."

Panic gave her a new weapon. "Mr. Troy, you are perhaps misled by what you may have been told of my position in the community. I don't understand, of course, what is behind all this, but I assure you that I am not a widow looking to make another match and that Beulah Land is no longer the rich property it was."

"That is beyond indiscreet. It is insulting, and I know you mean it to be. I do not need your Beulah Land."

"Then that is good, for it has nothing more to give you than it has already given. Have you forsaken painting for the camera? I once thought your portraits particularly fine, although of course I am no judge in these matters, except for myself."

"You really do astonish and amaze me!"

"Fortunate woman at my age to astonish and amaze, for whatever reason—"

"You will stop putting me off and pretending I do not exist!"

"I assure you: I am aware of little else at the moment than your existence!"

"Good! Then look at me!" When she turned her face away from him, he took her chin and pulled it back. "I want you to accustom yourself to the fact that I am old."

He had surprised her again. "*You* old? Why you have changed hardly at all."

"Come." He smiled and looked more cheerful. "Admit that you have no time for creaking old boys like me. I saw the eyes of that young man following you everywhere you went after the wedding!"

"What do you mean?"

"Ah, you must tell me, not I you. When any man spoke to you, he looked as if he hated you, thereby revealing that he loves you."

"You are beyond extravagance; you are mad."

"The gangly fellow who waltzed you about?"

"You were not present when we danced."

His voice pounced. "Then you must have looked for me!"

"Daniel Todd is my cousin."

"There seems to be some doubt about that. I also asked who he was."

"You are trifling and familiar. You asked a great many questions for a stranger."

"One led naturally to another after the first answer I was given —that your husband was dead and that you had not remarried."

"You must tell me about the photographs. What is the result? Good or bad or only middling? I believe my sister's husband made arrangements for them to be sent to him in Maryland by a courier package or something of that sort."

"I retract what I said about tenderness. You have grown hard."

"I must go along to the buggy. Jane will wonder what has become of me. I withdraw the offer of sharing our dinner basket."

"You can take your dinner basket and go to the devil!"

As he turned to stride off toward the gate, a heavy clap of

thunder sounded and the rain began to pour. So occupied had
they been with one another they had not been aware of the
darkening day and the heavy stillness that signals thunderstorms
in that season and that locality. Forgetting dignity, Casey Troy
bolted for the church porch. Sarah looked for shelter under the
nearest tree, but there was no shelter, so intense and determined
was the storm. Within a minute she was wet through, and that
on top of the heat she had generated from labor and recent emotion gave her a chill. She cowered miserably until a quake and
flash of thunder and lightning coming together terrified her into
running to the church porch, where she found Casey Troy talking in an easy, amiable way with Miss Eloise Kilmer and Miss
Ophelia Pepper, whose mission it had been that morning to
clean the church after Sunday services.

Struck dumb by her disheveled appearance, Miss Kilmer and
Miss Pepper then proceeded to pity her, and to tell her how wet
she was, and to ask why in Heaven's name she had not sought
shelter when she saw the storm brewing, for there was always
some warning of what was to come, however curt. More practical help they did not offer. Casey Troy also observed that she
was unwise to go about in the rain, but when he suggested that
the most sensible thing she could do was to step inside the
church and take off her wet clothes, the maiden ladies fell to
giggling until they recollected themselves enough to forbid the
action. It would, they agreed, offend the Lord to have a naked
woman in his house, and besides they had just finished waxing
the floor of the vestibule.

There was nothing she could do but hug herself and endure
their prattle until the rain stopped. When it did so only a few
minutes later (but each minute seeming truly an hour), the ladies took their leave, one on either side of Casey Troy, whom
they had remembered from his earlier sojourn in Highboro and
whom they pronounced "not at all like those Yankees but almost
one of us."

Sarah found Jane in the buggy, where she had remained to
keep dry. Jane helped her remove her outer garments, and when
she had drunk a little peach brandy, she began to feel more herself. They ate directly from the basket, and as they talked, Jane
asked only twice if she did not think Mr. Troy an exceptionally
handsome man, at least for one his age.

51.

Selma and Pauline had suspended classes until late October, because children old enough to be taught were old enough to pick cotton, and even the youngest wanted to be where the others were during harvesting. There was, however, activity in the house behind the hedge on the edge of Highboro, the house that once had accommodated a family of whores and now provided classrooms for the children of slaves. The two women welcomed Roman's joining them as they planned for the winter months. With the growing enrollment they needed his gift for organization and his larger experience.

Selma heard that the white school had some old desks they were willing to sell. Roman examined them, and finding them no worse than ink-stained and scuffed, bought them with money from the fund provided by Miss Eliza Truman. He set great store by the formal furniture of education, partly because he loved desks and blackboards as the tools of his trade and partly because he had discovered in the Philadelphia school that children learned more readily with the genuine accouterments of scholars than they did with makeshifts. He also bought, and installed with the help of Lilac, who could climb like a monkey, a bell which he persuaded his doubting colleagues was valuable as a symbol of authority as well as being of practical use. They all smiled with satisfaction when they tried ringing it.

Twice in one week the three teachers visited their pupils in the fields and both times worked alongside them for an hour, to the children's amusement, for none of the teachers had ever before picked cotton, and their clumsiness encouraged the young ones to good-natured derision.

Floyd and Otis readied the cotton gin for the wagons they hoped soon would be waiting their turn to wheel their loads under the great funnels that would suck the raw cotton into the machinery that separated seed and trash from the cotton itself and packed it into bales. Daniel and Zebra headed the force of men working the fields. Sarah was in the house, at the gin, and in the fields from dawn until sometimes dark. Only the sawmill was idle now, its last cutting having been an installment in the continuing order of materials for the building of Junior Elk's new house at Oaks, or Elks as people had grown used to calling it. The change of name had begun as a joke, a play on the sound of words, but when the joke wore out, the word remained and was used by all except the Davises and the Kendricks. Even Annabel Saxon used it as one who graciously sanctions a jest, since she considered the selling of Oaks to have been mainly due to her promoting Junior Elk's interests. She had, in fact, become something of a partisan of his. As Nell observed, there is nothing like money for broadening the sympathies, and she offered it as her opinion that Annabel would embrace Beelzebub if he put a dollar in her pocket. No longer a diehard, she greeted with enthusiasm any project she could call Progress. They must all, she admonished them, move with events and not sorrow over the past.

On the evening of the first day cotton was picked at Beulah Land, Sarah and Floyd sat in the office after supper with no business between them other than that of sharing their satisfaction in having come as far as they had from destruction and the uncertainties that followed it. It was early, but Floyd was yawning when Jane came to tell Sarah she had a visitor. Floyd said good night and left the office by the side door leading onto the porch. Sarah asked Jane what sort of unknowing visitor had come to call after supper during harvesttime. "Come see," Jane said.

Casey Troy rose as they entered the living room.

Nell had drawn her chair to a table and was examining a set of photographs Casey had taken after the wedding. "I declare your sister could be in the very room with us, so like her these are." She frowned as she said it, as if the thought did not altogether delight her.

Sarah and Casey exchanged bows, she looking at him questioningly, he returning her look with one of courteous composure. "You asked about the photographs when we happened to meet at the church that rainy day."

"It is good of you to bring them and show them to us," Sarah acknowledged, curiosity sending her to gaze over Nell's shoulder. Jane crouched beside Nell to share her view, and Casey came and stood so close to Sarah their bodies almost touched, his expression one of anxiety to see if the pictures met her approval.

"They are remarkable," she admitted.

"The spitting image," Nell said. "As if she might step out any second and make one of her silly remarks."

As they examined and reexamined the photographs, Casey managed always to be beside Sarah, so that she was never unconscious of his physical presence. However aloof she kept her face, she found herself remembering his body and the way she had responded to it twenty years ago. He breathed and moved. For a moment when he reached to point to a detail in one of the photographs, she saw the pulse beating firmly in his wrist where the dark hairs curled around it, and she remembered her lips touching him there. She was astonished and dismayed by her quick reaction to him, for nothing could or would come of it.

When Nell tired of the photographs, she said, "I was surprised to see Mr. Troy, thinking he'd be miles away from Highboro, his work here done. Do you remember him, Sarah? Surely you do. He reminded me, though I should not have needed reminding, that he put us all down with oil paint on canvas—how long ago? It doesn't matter. A year is like a day when you come to my age. I hadn't remembered his being so handsome. Isn't he a handsome man? I do like to see a handsome man." She turned to Casey, who was smiling at Sarah in a way that made her want to pummel him. "The older I get, the more I like to see good-looking faces around me. Now I was not like that when I was younger. I was not, you might say, one for the gentlemen. In fact, I never looked at one after I married, and scarcely looked at one before either, except to note whether the body before me bowed or curtseyed. But now I enjoy the pretty faces of girls and the handsome faces of men. I don't know what it all means or will lead to, I declare I don't."

Half an hour later, as Casey Troy left, Nell asked him to return the next evening to take supper with them, if he didn't care what he had, for they never troubled about meals much during harvesttime. Sarah suggested faintly that Mr. Troy's work might engage his attention too fully for him to be free, but he offered himself as happy to come again.

During that supper Daniel had nothing to say to him after saying howdy-do, frowning over his plate and looking up only to see how Sarah responded to Casey Troy's conversation. Sarah herself spoke little at the meal, but Nell and Jane chattered away with as much cheerfulness and animation as any guest might require to know himself welcome. Afterwards, they both told Sarah they found him completely charming, completely the gentleman.

"I wonder," Jane said, "why he has never married."

"Ah," Nell answered, "it was perhaps some early affair of the heart that went wrong."

Sarah said, "I think it more likely to have been his preference for the life of the rover. He does not appear to me to be a man much inclined toward hearth and home."

"And there you are wrong," Nell said. "When you went off to the office with Daniel to talk to Floyd for half and hour, he had much to say to Jane and me on the delights of our new house and of his envy of any man who could call such a place home. Jane then asked him if he had no home himself that he went back to. And what did he say to you, Jane?"

"He said no but that he hoped to one day. He said he was much taken with our part of the country and had begun to think of settling down here if a certain plan he had in mind came to anything."

Nell said to Sarah, "Do you think Highboro might be able to support a man in Mr. Troy's profession?"

On Saturday of the same week, which they at Beulah Land treated as a full working day, Sarah received another caller. She was in one of the cotton fields when Nancy came from the house to say Captain John Struther wanted her. A quarter of an hour later she found him on the porch and escorted him into her office. Captain Struther was a tall man with wide hips, and his uniform fit him loosely, or rather seemed not to fit him at all. He had no beard and he smiled often with his mouth, showing long, crooked teeth with too much space between them. His eyes never changed their expression of watching even when they did not seem to watch, which put Sarah in mind of a cat acting out its game with a crippled dove.

To show that she knew his position, Sarah said, "You have taken over from Colonel Varnedoe as commander of the Union forces."

"That is so and explains why I am here."

Sarah waited, making no effort to match his smile.

"You appear to have recovered your losses very soon," he said, letting his eyes take in the simple furnishings of the room.

"Then appearances are misleading," Sarah said. "We lost everything but the land and our wish to survive."

"Yet you have been able to rebuild more quickly than others."

"We had the advantage of a sawmill."

"And the cleverness to hide it, and many other valuable things as well, I have no doubt. I recollect no mention of a sawmill in the town's inventory when our forces first came here."

"You were with Captain Ponder in his time?" Sarah said.

"That is so, and it is the business of that sawmill that brings me here today." Again she waited, impervious to his steady smile. "It is not currently being operated."

"We do not have men enough to run it during the cotton picking and ginning, even though there isn't much of a crop."

"You speak of 'we.'"

"All of us at Beulah Land."

"You mean no one in particular besides yourself."

"My overseer Floyd Kendrick and I, if you like."

"He is—am I right?—a Negro."

She nodded shortly. "He and his family have long been connected with Beulah Land."

"As slaves, naturally."

"They were freed some years before the war."

"That was generous of the Kendricks when we remember the price of a working man or woman. You did not, however, free all your slaves."

"No."

"These colored Kendricks—it is confusing that you and they wear the same name—"

"Not to us."

"These freed colored Kendricks chose to remain."

"Beulah Land has always been home to them."

"That is so. I see. Ah, that is so. Very true." Although his voice was unemphatic, almost singsong, his eyes were bright with cunning. "This Floyd Kendrick has been valuable to you?"

"Beulah Land could not run without him."

Captain Struther's smile went wider, then returned to its ordinary dimensions. "However, it is the sawmill I am here to inquire about. Its lumber is much needed, as you are doubtless aware, benefiting as you do from that need."

"It was not we who caused the destruction that made so much rebuilding necessary."

"Yet it has not been to your disadvantage, has it? Surely not to your disadvantage?" She waited while he stretched his smile again until the skin of his cheeks was tight. She remembered a day last winter watching Daniel stretch the hide of a rabbit on a barn door to dry before he made a muff for Jane.

Hearing his next words, she told herself she must not let her mind wander. "I understand that people who are eager to build cannot depend on supplies from your sawmill, even when they are willing and able to supply their own stand of trees."

"You are talking about Junior Elk."

He bobbed his head. "That is so. Yes, Mr. Elk and others." He coughed and swallowed to clear his throat. "He has, in fact, come to me with a plan. I consider it excellent and am sure you will agree. He has men in his employ who are idle at this time, since his fields are not as productive as yours. He and I believe it would be an advantage to the community, indeed to the county, if those men could be put to work at the mill producing lumber."

"Under whose supervision?"

"Ah, you are quick. That would be decided. You do not object in principle to the idea?"

"I do, most certainly. To begin, it is not practical. The operation requires skill, and the very man who knows most about it is busy at the gin, and in fact everywhere in our work."

"You mean this Floyd Kendrick?"

She nodded.

His smile gaped to its widest. "Indeed valuable," he murmured in his characteristic soothing tone. "But surely these skills you speak of may be taught. There is no secret, no—magic about it, I trust?"

"The sawmill is mine," she said baldly, "and I will not allow Junior Elk to run it."

"You would not lose by it. He agrees to pay you, the amount of payment to be fairly worked out between ourselves, of course."

"The sawmill is mine. It will run again when the cotton has been picked and ginned."

"He opened his hands in a gesture of genial despair. "A month? Two months?" He shook his head unhappily without giv-

ing up his smile. "Time lost. Lumber lost. Rebuilding to wait."
He sighed. "Mrs. Kendrick—your husband hanged himself, did
he not?"

She stared at him without responding.

"A terrible thing," he continued. "An offense against God. A violent family altogether, I have been told. —However, that is beside the present point. You are the owner of all this because of
his death. So many things you have, and position to do good to
the community. Perhaps you have not considered how much
your management of these possessions can affect the community.
Well, I have done so because it is a part of my job here, and I
am here to tell you that if you persist in being unreasonable, I
am empowered to take over the sawmill and have it run for the
benefit of all."

"Do you not mean for the benefit of Junior Elk, and perhaps
even for your own?"

His smile gentled to sadness but persevered. "I was afraid my
meaning would be misunderstood. Ladies do not always grasp
these matters as they should do. Ladies are inclined, I have discovered, to see everything in a narrow, personal light. —Naturally, I mean the benefit of the population at large. That is so.
Yes, that is so."

"I have much to do, Captain Struther. This is a busy time for
us."

"It is, I must tell you, for me to terminate our interview and
not yourself, madam." She had risen from her chair at the desk.
She remained standing. "Think over what I have said. Ask a
man's advice. I believe you have some family connection with
the Saxons who run the bank."

"I thank you, but I do my own thinking."

"After you have done so," he said soothingly, "I trust that you
will see the positive merit of the plan I put before you."

"Then you trust in vain."

"A soldier, Mrs. Kendrick, is nothing without trust. The interview is now over. Good day to you."

She made no move to accompany him to the door, but turned
her back and leaned against the desk. "Fool, fool!" she called
herself, her face burning. After all that had happened, to lose her
temper in that way, to try to score off the man as if they were

debaters to be judged by an impartial jury—she was a fool. However, it was clear what Struther and Elk intended to do. They would first try to take her sawmill, and then, if that succeeded, they would want the cotton gin; and finally endeavor to realize the dream dreamed by old Roscoe Elk: they would try to take Beulah Land itself. And all this they would do with the trappings of the new "Reconstruction legality."

That evening when she told Floyd what had happened, he listened quietly. Then he sighed. "We ginned just three bales of cotton today."

"Should we set someone to guard the sawmill at night? Junior's father once burned our warehouses and almost ruined us. It could not be proved, but I was sure then and I am sure now it was he who did it. Zebra would not mind sleeping there perhaps. What do you think?"

"Nancy says Abraham's been crying. She believes his gums are sore and he's trying to cut a tooth. I told her he was too young, but she said funny things happen when the daddy is an old man."

"I don't know where she gets it. She makes up a lot of it, I'm certain —You don't think we should worry about them, do you?"

He sighed again, impatiently. "If they would only let us alone for a while. No, I don't think we should worry and wonder what they will do, but wait until they do it. We can't run for shelter every time a cloud passes over the sun."

"James Davis is looking for something substantial to put his money into."

"Mm."

"I don't think they'd try to take a business away from a blind man."

Floyd yawned and laughed and rose from his chair. "I'm so tired I don't think I'll ever sleep again. Do you get like that? When I want to go to sleep, my feet and legs itch. When I do go to sleep, my head spins around like a top and wakes me up. Leon and I used to carve our own tops when we were boys, gouging thin grooves around them to wind the string. I'd forgot all about that. We'd count to ten and let them fly, and the one whose top spun the longest won."

"Won what?"

"Just won."

52.

When a week went by and they were let alone, and when the second and third weeks passed without any further threats, Sarah lost some of her apprehension of what Captain Struther and Junior Elk might next do. The Captain had expected to frighten her into giving way to them, and she had not. At best, it was over; at worst, they were reconsidering their approach. At Beulah Land work went on. Josephine was busy in her kitchen, drying, pickling, and preserving, with Nancy and Jane helping her. Daniel and Zebra saw to the fields and sent the cotton to Floyd and Otis at the gin. Sarah kept track of all and even gave herself a few miser moments of acquisitive satisfaction as she counted the corn and fodder, judged the hogs for what they would yield in meat and lard, and occasionally shocked a hen drowsing in the hot sun by picking her up and feeling through her feathers for the flesh that would eventually nourish them.

Nell had made Casey Troy so welcome that he seemed to come and go as he pleased, although he was careful not to put himself in anyone's way and not to stay very long any one time he came. Sarah almost decided that he had nothing better to do than sit on her porch entertaining Nell and whoever else pulled up a chair and sat for an hour. But when she had settled it so in her mind and begun to feel a not unfriendly contempt for one who allowed himself to be so casually occupied, he would disappear altogether for a few days and when he returned say simply that he had been working. Mr. Twiggs's extensive porching proved its worth during the late summer days. The living room was all but abandoned, and no one felt it improper to drop sweaty and dirty from field or road into a porch chair for five minutes of rest and talk. Chairs were shifted to catch whatever breeze stirred from whatever quarter, grouped and regrouped for privacy, or intimacy, or a more general sociability. They swatted flies and slapped mosquitoes and complained that there was no air anywhere, but they stayed on the porch as much as they could. With Casey so frequently in attendance it became natural to speak before him of matters concerning Beulah Land, and he soon had knowledge of what they thought about everything from the quality of this year's crop of pecans to Sarah's dread of Captain Struther and Junior Elk. If Casey had any ideas of leaving Highboro, he did not make them known, and his friends in the country began to accept that he might indeed stay among them as a town resident.

Roman and Selma and Pauline were happy with their work at the school. The new desks and blackboards were installed, and Roman found and stored supplies of chalk and paper tablets and ink. Miss Truman shipped him several boxes of books, mainly for the teaching of arithmetic and geography, areas hitherto most neglected in the teaching of the Negro children. They waited at the station until the first Sunday Floyd would let Roman borrow a mule and wagon. That happened to be September 3, and without anyone's having suggested or decided it, everyone found himself included in plans for a church party for that morning except Nell, who had announced that she would never leave Beulah Land alive, and so stayed home. Boards were set athwart the wagon to serve as removable benches, and these accommodated Sarah and Jane and Daniel and Doreen and Benjamin, as well as Roman and Floyd. To make an easier load, both Bartholomew and Do-all were hitched to the wagon. They went to the church an hour early in order to visit graves and friends, for no one wanted to linger after services, the men and children being hungry and the women having to hurry home to see to their Sunday dinners.

The young people always arrived early, and Jane and Benjamin were quickly engaged in a crowd that included Annabel's sons, Bonard and Blair Junior, and Prudence Singletary and her cousin Eunice Dupree. Roman and Floyd went along to the depot to collect the books. Roman would stay at the school when the hauling was done, because he was unwilling to leave the pleasure of unpacking the boxes to the next day, and Floyd would return to the church to gather the party for the return to Beulah Land.

It was a clear, hot day. The young ones did not mind the heat but dashed about as easy in their skins as if it had been April or November. Their elders complained and fanned themselves, but their complaints were more social than real and only part of the general way of complaining they had all fallen into about the hard times they'd suffered and were suffering still. Sarah had a few words with James and Maggie Davis. ("How that woman has improved since getting married again! Don't you tell a soul I said so, but I declare it for a fact: I saw the curtains of her bedroom drawn in the middle of the afternoon!" —Everyone gossiped about her cheerfully except her sister and Annabel, who looked sourly on her late blooming.) James asked Sarah if she'd given further thought to their discussion two weeks ago in which he had suggested buying a share of the sawmill, and she said she had and that as soon as the harvest was in, she wanted to have a real talk with him about it that would include Floyd, who knew more about its running than she did.

She then drifted into the graveyard, her excuse the bunch of zinnias she carried for Edna's grave. She seldom brought fresh flowers to anyone else's, for there were rose bushes planted everywhere that never stopped blooming until the weather froze. But she liked to bring flowers to Edna because they had shared so many satisfying hours in the place.

As she progressed from the church to Edna's grave she paused to speak with this and that one, becoming as she did so aware of a similar attitude among old acquaintances. It was summed up by Cora Callahan's remark: "I declare, everything bad seems to happen to you-all out there, but you're better off than anybody else. You're low or you're high, while the rest of us just rust along in between." Lauretta's wedding had been their first real chance of seeing her new house. They resented it, she now discovered, and they resented the fact that she had a harvest to be busy about. There were even sly remarks about the cotton gin and the sawmill—as if, Sarah thought, all these were gifts or luck and had not been sweated for!

She found herself out of temper even before Annabel joined her at Edna's grave. Her first warning was Annabel's laugh behind her, a sound that always put her on her guard. "I swanee!" Annabel exclaimed. "You are the sweetest thing about Granny's grave. I'll vow nobody thinks of her from one month to the next but you, but you are faithful, aren't you?"

"And how is all your family?" Sarah said equably.

"Oh, Blair's somewhere over at the church talking business and crops. You know, married people never see one another at a gathering after they arrive. I hear you're doing pretty well out at Beulah Land this year—"

"Tolerable."

"Better than that, Blair says, now be fair! Everyone says you're well off again. They're also saying you have an almost constant visitor in the person of that Casey Troy. Is it so?"

"He comes to see us," Sarah agreed.

Annabel laughed again, and Sarah reflected that her laugh was generally the preface to her saying something unpleasant. "Everybody's talked about you since they went out there for Miss Lauretta's wedding. The new house was much admired. People say they don't know how you managed it after *supposedly* losing everything you had."

"People say far more than they know anything about."

"Don't forget how they all rallied around after Beulah Land was burned—"

"As if they could not wait to see it with their own eyes." Sarah made herself laugh as if the remark was meant as a joke. "And now it seems that they come and eat my barbecue and bite my back while they're doing it."

"Well, Auntie Sarah, you can't blame people for talking, the way Mr. Troy trots out there every day like he's one of the family. In fact, a lot of people are saying he *hopes* to be, and that he wouldn't unless he'd been encouraged. If you understand what I mean."

"Subtlety was never your way, Annabel."

"I hope not. I say what I think and nobody can accuse me of speaking one thing to them and another behind their backs, now can they?"

"I've never thought about it, to tell you the truth." Sarah moved as if to leave her.

"Needless to say, I've defended you. I've told people when they said things like that to me, hinting, you know, that I might know something, you and I having so many past family connections—I've told them they're crazy thinking anything special will happen between you and Mr. Troy. After all, what is he? A man who travels around making pictures. How can anyone take him seriously, I say to them, especially anyone your age and in your position? A man like that might try to flatter you, of course, because look what he'd have to gain if you were fool enough to marry him!"

"Annabel! If you don't shut up—"

"Don't you fly off at the handle at me. I'm only saying what everybody—"

"You have said enough."

"Here he comes, so I'll leave you to your courting, if that's what you want people to think of you. From now on I shan't try to stop them saying whatever they please. —Howdy-do, Mr. Troy. I am just leaving. Surely they're about to ring the bell to take in church? Are you coming with me, Auntie Sarah?" When Sarah only glared at her, Annabel shrugged and laughed again and went on her way.

"What's wrong?" Casey said.

"I don't know why I let that female make me angry."

"She's too silly to treat seriously."

"If you knew the things she just said. According to her, they're gossiping about us. Did you know that?"

"I've heard a word or two," he said. "I'm sorry if it bothers you. Why don't you marry me and shut their mouths?"

"When are you going away?"

"Do you want me to?"

"It isn't for me to tell you what to do," she said.

"Then I'll stay."

"What do you really want here, Casey?"

"Everything I can get," he said. "I'm always serious, and you always pretend that I'm making a joke."

The church bell rang then and together they left the graveyard and went into church. Casey took a place in a pew at the back, and Sarah joined Jane and Doreen and Benjamin and Daniel in the Davis row in front of that of the Saxons.

Only the old and perhaps those in the throes of adolescent piety followed with real concentration the progress of the service, but all present would have said they were content to be there. Sarah had never been deeply religious, but she had an appreciation of the way the familiar words calmed and comforted her. She enjoyed the singing, and for the time of the service she liked the feeling of rising and making responses as part of a congregation. Gradually she felt her temper cool as she played her part. It was the one daylight hour of the week when all was still outdoors. From eleven to twelve on Sunday no one stirred in the public places of the town. People were either at home or at church. Briefly the birds and bees were lords of the summer air, and theirs were the only sounds that came through the open church windows.

The service was nearly over when everyone heard the shot and thought the same thing: mad dog. Part of the general gossip that day had been of an incident earlier in the week. A Union soldier claimed to have seen a mad dog outside Highboro walking with a kind of stagger and foaming at the mouth. When the soldier approached with his rifle up, the dog slunk into the nearby woods. The soldier, who was alone at the time, did not risk going in to look for the animal. So everyone was alert in some part of his mind for further news and would not rest easy until the dog had been found and killed, or enough time had passed to let them think the soldier mistaken in his supposition. When the shot came, there was a restless stirring, an eagerness to discover whether or not the dog had come into town and been killed.

As soon as the service ended the younger members of the congregation slipped up the aisles and out even more quickly than usual, and the older ones hurried after them with hardly more decorum. Sarah and her family group were among the last to come into the open air, where they found the crowd that had been inside staring silently at an odd thing. A wagon with no visible driver rattled rapidly over the hard clay road toward the church, the mules drawing it clearly in something of a panic.

It was Daniel who cried, "That's our wagon!" and Benjamin who followed him running as he shouted, "Where's Floyd?"

Even then Sarah felt no foreboding. There had been some mishap; the mules had bolted when they heard the shot, or even perhaps had taken intuitive fright at sight of the mad dog. But she hurried too, Jane beside her. Daniel and Benjamin managed to grab the mules, who, recognizing them, became tractable; and when they brought the wagon to a halt, they saw Floyd stretched face down on the floor of the wagon. He had been shot in the back of the head.

What she did next Sarah was not to remember; no one who saw and heard her would ever forget. It was as if she had been struck by lightning. She went rigid and fell without a sound. Jane caught at her, and Casey Troy was there to help her onto the ground, whereupon she came to herself and scrambled to her feet. Throwing herself into the wagon, she turned Floyd on his back and saw that he was dead. Lifting his bloody head and shoulders, she gave a howl of rage and grief such as a savage queen might have uttered on finding her mate slaughtered in battle. She bit and spat and clawed when they tried to wrest her from the dead man, all the time howling like a creature mortally wounded. At last they were able to drag her free and to the church porch. One crowd, mostly women, ready to succor their own as women will when one of them is in trouble, closed around her; a second crowd, mainly men, surrounded the wagon. Boys ran to execute any order given by an elder. Water was brought to Sarah, who would not drink it. She was now so still she might have been struck dumb. Dr. Platt came to her and tried to rouse her. She gave no indication of seeing him. One of the men went off at a run to fetch Sheriff Byrne, and another to find Captain Struther, but the boys were ahead of them; for both Byrne and Struther appeared within minutes of the discovery of the wagon with its dead freight.

Sarah had not been struck dumb; she was thinking with a terrible concentration of her interview with Captain Struther. Seeing the sheriff and the Union commander as they arrived almost together, she wrenched away from the doctor and his helpers and went to them, the women following and the two crowds merging.

To the sheriff she said, "Arrest Captain Struther."

"Mrs. Kendrick, you know I can't do that, and no more is there reason for me to."

"Arrest him. He killed Floyd Kendrick. Floyd is there in the wagon."

"I don't doubt that, ma'am, but why do you have such an idea?"

Captain Struther said, "The woman is crazy. I went to talk to her once, but that's all. She became violent then, I will say."

"Murderer!" Sarah was upon him before anyone could stop her, trying to tear his face. The sheriff and Daniel pulled her away.

Struther said, "Control yourself, woman, or I shall have *you* arrested. There are a hundred witnesses to your attacking a Union officer."

"But no witnesses to your killing my Floyd!"

"*Your* Floyd? I understood he was a *free* nigger that worked for you."

"You or Junior Elk. He wants my sawmill—he wants my cotton gin—he wants Beulah Land. Floyd stood in your way—he and I. Now that you've killed him, will you kill me?"

The whispers ran:

"Where's Dr. Platt; can't he do anything?"

"He's gone to get his bag."

"Can't her folks stop her?"

"I never in all my days heard such a carrying-on."

"It's like they say: he's only a Nigra."

"I've always suspicioned what was going on out there. Him free and staying on. Never marrying either until he was an old man, you see?"

"You *don't* think she would—?"

"It wouldn't be the first time a Kendrick kissed a nigger!"

"Oh, Glory, help us this day!"

"Go get Junior Elk," Sarah insisted. "Bring him. He must face me. If you didn't do this, he did!"

Dr. Platt reappeared with a handkerchief drenched in chloroform and clapped it over Sarah's face, and since people will allow a doctor to do anything, nobody stopped him. Sarah slumped. Daniel caught her in his arms and lifted her to the wagon. Someone had brought a choir robe from the church. Jane covered Floyd with it as well as she could, for flies and a single wasp had come to hover about his head.

The whispers rose and changed in tenor, now that Sarah lay helpless.

"Bring her out of the sun, poor woman."

"Angels, have mercy."

"So much trouble she's had to bear."

"The whole tribe of Kendricks is under a curse—"

"Poor thing, poor thing."

Sarah was carried into the church and put down flat on a pew. Jane and Doreen attended her, and Doreen would not let the doctor use his handkerchief on her again. The doctor found him-

self a busy man, in any case. Now that the first clamor was sub-
siding, others among the women discovered themselves to be in
need of assistance, Annabel Saxon chief among them. Annabel
asked them all to bear witness to the disgrace Sarah Kendrick
had brought upon herself and by reflection on the Davis family
as well, for was she not the grandmother of the youngest Davis
children, and had their families not married once in each of the
two preceding generations? The shame of the connection lay
heavy upon her heart, she assured them.

The men largely ignored the women; they milled and muttered opinions about the killing. No one had seen it happen. All
had heard the shot, if not from the church, then from their
houses. No one, it appeared, had been stirring. The Union sen-
tries on duty were sent for. They knew nothing, had seen nothing. Junior Elk arrived, and Sheriff Byrne advised him not to approach Mrs. Kendrick, although he stated that he wanted to see
her and answer any question she put to him before them all. To
clear his name, he told them where he had been and with whom,
and these were brought to bear witness. (He had been in his
shabby office with two poor white farmers he had lent money to
in the spring so that they could plant a crop.)

It was Sheriff Byrne himself who found what he and everyone
took as final and absolute proof that a white man, and almost
certainly a white *Southerner,* had done the murder. Returning to
the wagon to examine the dead man, the sheriff found a paper
with a message printed on it in ink. The message read: SEND THE
NIGGERS TO AFRICA. KILL THEM THAT WONT GO.

When she was conscious again and appeared to have collected
herself, Sarah was shown the paper and told that even she now
must admit that her lurid accusations were unfounded. She studied the message, and she looked at Junior Elk, who stood at a re-
spectful distance looking back at her with dignity and seeming
candor. Then, as if they were alone, she said to Jane and Doreen,
"Come. Let us go home." Rising, she walked between them to the
wagon. Daniel helped her into it, and the others of the party
climbed in after her. Sarah would not sit on a bench. She knelt
on the floor of the wagon with a hand on the body covered by
the black robe as Daniel took the reins and turned the mules toward Beulah Land.

53.

Pauline and Selma arrived with Roman late in the afternoon. The three had spent most of the afternoon seeing both Sheriff Byrne and Captain Struther, who separately assured them that all would be done that could be done to apprehend the murderer. Roman spoke of friends in Washington and Philadelphia who would be receiving a full report of the event, which only offended the law officer and caused the military officer to vow to himself to suppress any evidence that might come out. He was confident that none would, for he and Junior Elk had planned carefully enough to take advantage of chances that came their way.

Otis made a coffin. It had been decided to bury Floyd the following morning. There was no one to wait for. Pauline was his only blood kin other than his son. His real family had been Beulah Land. When Pauline and Josephine had bathed and dressed him, Roman helped them put Floyd into the coffin, which was closed and nailed shut and set on two sawhorses in the living room of his own house. Zadok and Rosalie came from Ben's Farm to pay their respects. Rosalie was disappointed to find the coffin closed. As she told Zadok on their way home, she never could believe anyone was dead unless she'd seen it with her own eyes.

Daniel was in a fever of anger and indecision. He and Floyd had not been friends, but they had worked together and learned to trust each other, and Daniel discovered that his feelings about the man were more complex than he had supposed. Sarah would not go to the coffin, and she did not welcome any of those who knocked on her door when she had gone into her office. Nell went to Floyd's house and sat a while with Roman, who said he would not leave his friend until he was buried. Jane found Daniel feeding the stock and begged him to change his mind about leaving Beulah Land.

"I'm not going anywhere," he said, making his decision as he spoke the words.

"You're not?" Jane could hardly believe her easy victory.

Daniel shook his head, frowning hard at her. She burst into tears and he had to set down the bucket of slops he'd been about to pour for the pigs in order to comfort her.

There was no sitting to a meal that night, but Josephine and Nancy saw that everyone who wanted it was provided with food, and Nancy knocked on the office door with biscuits and two pieces of chicken on a plate. Sarah opened the door a crack and accepted the plate, setting it on the desk, where Nancy found it untouched next day, except by ants who made a steady line down a leg of the desk, across the bare wooden floor to a window.

Although she ate nothing, Sarah drank a bottle of peach brandy. At dawn she heard the sound of shovels and looked out a window to see Zebra and one of the field hands digging a grave beside that of Ezra and Lovey. She went to her room and bathed her face, then changed her clothes and combed her hair. Calling Nancy, she told her to bring Abraham to her.

Anxious for her charge, Nancy refused.

"Do what I say," Sarah ordered.

Among the things she had remembered during the long night was the time a year ago Floyd had told her he was going to marry Lotus because she was pregnant with his child. It was after she had been to see Edna on hearing that Edna had taken to her bed. It was the night Lauretta came home, bringing Daniel. Floyd laughed at her as they talked and teased her by saying she always took over the children of others. Well then, so be it. There was no formal service at the grave, but Roman recited from memory the Twenty-third Psalm. Sarah held Abraham, and no one thought it strange. The little crowd stayed watching until Zebra and his helper had filled the grave. Jane's placing a bunch of her roses on the mound was the signal for them to turn away.

Sarah held Abraham out for Nancy to take him. "Otis," she said, "I want you and Zebra to operate the gin today as usual. Take what help you need." Otis nodded. "Dan, you go on with the field work, and make them work hard, you hear?"

Mounting steps to the porch, she made her way around it to the outside door of her office, where she found Casey Troy waiting. "I'm going to Savannah on the train. I wanted to see you be-fore I left."

She held the door for him to enter the office ahead of her, and then sat down at the desk, folding her hands and letting him find a chair opposite her.

"I believe you now," he said. "I thought it was old prejudice on your part, but I don't think so any more. I believe that Elk and Struther arranged the killing between them because they wanted to get at you and Beulah Land, and everybody knew he was your strongest support. I don't think you or anyone else will ever be able to prove what they did or how they managed it. What has to be done now is show them you have friends as strong as they. That's why I'm going to Savannah. I know two men high up in the Union command there, and when I tell them what I know, they will make it clear to Struther they are watching him."

"It doesn't really concern you," Sarah said slowly when he waited for her to speak.

"You concern me."

"I've nothing for you, Casey. There have been defeats, but none like this. It isn't what they did to us during the war that matters. It's what they're doing now and mean to go on doing. Junior Elk will be king, and we at Beulah Land the earth for him to walk on. Your friends in Savannah won't stop that. I came late to hating the Yankees, but I hate them now—almost as much as I hate Junior Elk. Don't you understand? Floyd is dead. They've killed *Floyd*."

Casey rose from his chair. "I'll be back by the end of the week."

"Take a boat from there and be rid of us. Don't come back."

"I only seem an easy fellow. I'm as hard and stubborn as you are, and I love you with all my soul."

She looked at him long and shook her head.

He paused at the door but without turning. "I'll be back. Tell Miss Nell and Jane—and tell Daniel."

Part Two

1873-1874

"Passing, I leave thee lilac . . ."
WALT WHITMAN

1.

Naked, Benjamin narrowed his eyes to judge the distance and then ran as fast as he could, leaping from the bank and belly-flopping into the creek at a place Kendrick men had used for swimming for ninety years. Surfacing a moment later, he spouted like a whale and flung back his head to rid it of water. Bonard was on the bank laughing. "Ben, you son of a gun!" Although only April, and the first week of April, it was hot.

"Come on!" Benjamin shouted. "I've been in every day this week!"

Bonard squatted to unfasten his shoes. By the time he undressed and stuck a foot into the creek to judge its temperature, Benjamin had disappeared around a bend. Hearing him splashing and whooping, Bonard waded into the water, wetting himself by degrees before suddenly submerging and rising to swim after his cousin.

The two young men had become companions because each needed a friend and no one more likely offered himself to either. At twenty-three Bonard had lost most of his peers to marriage. His brother Blair had led the way by marrying Prudence Single-tary four years ago and settling to work with his father at the bank. Bonard was supposed to work with James at the sawmill, "to be his eyes," as Annabel put it with conscious eloquence. The mill now had permanent headquarters in the wood at the edge of town where passing armies used once to bivouac. Bonard, however, spent no more than an hour or two a day at the mill, and James complained to Annabel that "Bonard won't take hold, and he doesn't have an idea of how to handle men." Bonard was lazy and restless, and his handsome face had made too easy conquests among the girls of the county whose aim it was to please the boys. As Bonard joked to the loungers on the depot steps, "If they're looking to have their little hearts broken, I reckon old Bonnie is glad to oblige them."

As they thanked him with laughter for passing the time of day with them, one of the men always made the same response: "Hearts ain't all you break, eh, Bonnie boy?"

Benjamin at nineteen found himself isolated, as much by his history as the location of his farm. He looked upon his early adventure with Nancy as a kind of miracle, but it was a miracle that had no resumption. He thought it might, one day when he was fifteen. After the harvest that year, Benjamin decided to build a cabin for himself at the Glade. He had given up his idea of building a new house and living there, but decided that he wanted a place to go and be alone. Zadok helped him clear a space by the brook and together they put up a log cabin, only getting help from a Highboro craftsman to do the chimney and fireplace. The furnishings were few: a bunk bed, a table and chair, a case for what he called his pleasure books, as opposed to those Roman set him to read, although some were the same.

He made it understood at both the farmhouse and Beulah Land that no one was to bother him there. Everyone promptly came, but on finding it rough and ordinary, they were content to leave it to Benjamin. Only one day, goaded by her own unsatisfied curiosity, Nancy went up to the Glade. Benjamin surprised her, and they surprised each other by quickly, wordlessly having sexual relations. Afterward Nancy told him she was never coming back and never again going to do such a thing with him. It was not long after, when Nancy was nearly eighteen years old, that she had a talk with Sarah, and Sarah helped her go to Savannah on the train and find work, giving her the names of family friends to solicit for domestic jobs if she found nothing more to her liking.

Having taken a man's responsibilities at eleven, Benjamin read under Roman's guidance but did not attend a school where he would have known boys his age. When they were still playing marbles and flying kites, Benjamin had been driven by loneliness and longing to every kind of gathering where he might hope to see girls: church every Sunday, funerals, weddings, picnics, violet-pickings in spring, berry-pickings in summer, hayrides and cane-grindings in autumn. His need sharpening instinct and perception, he very soon learned which girls were willing to let him do a little, and which ones more, and the few who were completely obliging.

There remained the need to talk to a fellow male, to exchange stories and do some bragging, for he discovered that whatever a girl might do on a grassy slope in spring or a wagon piled with hay on a dark night, she was not inclined to talk about it later.

It was natural for him to open his mind to Daniel, since they had seen one another daily for half Benjamin's life, but Daniel ignored his hinting until desperation compelled Benjamin to beg, "What do *you* do about it?"

Daniel looked at him blankly.

"About you-know."

Daniel shook his head to deny that he understood and frowned to discourage explanation, which piqued Benjamin into saying, "You know well what I mean. What roosters do with hens and boars with sows. I mean *it*. What do you do about *it?*"

"I don't do anything," Daniel muttered, red in the face.

"Are you telling me you don't even go up in the loft and pump away sometimes?" Benjamin demanded to know.

Daniel turned and walked off, and Benjamin did not broach the subject again, not wanting to embarrass his friend and suspecting that he would get no further.

Benjamin's next approach was to Casey. Although he considered Casey, if not yet old, then getting to be, he guessed that Casey might have had some experience of girls when he was younger. Casey saw what the boy was about and was willing to be his sounding board. His friendliness allowed Benjamin to relax, and they talked for a quarter hour. Casey discovered that Benjamin was not innocent and therefore not asking for instruction, but that he wanted merely to check his experience against that of another. Benjamin plunged along enthusiastically, doing most of the talking, but encouraged by occasional nods and smiles from the older man. Gradually, however, it occurred to Benjamin that Casey's observations were not in the past tense. Although he said what he said with discretion, he was clearly still in the enjoyment of that part of life.

Benjamin had to make sure. "You mean you and *Grandma?*"

Seeing the boy's surprise, Casey blushed for him but answered firmly, "When I gave up the field, I was fortunate in marrying a warm woman."

"Well, I be-dogged!" Benjamin was astounded. "I thought it was all done for people as old as you."

"Do you think," Casey said testily, "it will be for you when you are my age?"

"No, but—"

"But you think you'll never be my age." Casey saw from Benjamin's face that was indeed what he felt, and his good humor saved the moment with laughter, in which Benjamin presently joined, if a little uncertainly, having learned more than he'd set out to discover. But when he was alone and had time to think it over, he found himself as much amused as he had been disconcerted. "Grandma and Casey," he considered, "how funny they must look!"

But of course there was no further discussion with Casey.

Zadok was the one Benjamin spent most of his day with, and he felt as close to Zadok as to anybody he knew, but their closeness did not include casual conversation about personal physical matters. They were, in fact, particularly polite to each other in those areas, never performing a private function together. Even when they were in field or wood and one of them felt the call to pass water, he walked a little away and turned his back, although they often continued to talk as the thing was done. It was equally out of the question for him to confide in Roman. No one had suggested such a thing to him, but Benjamin was perfectly aware that Roman's passions did not include women.

And so one Sunday, meeting before church, Benjamin and Bonard found themselves talking easily and Bonard decided that his cousin was not as slow a horse as he had hitherto assumed him to be. Benjamin saw Bonard as a man of experience who was suddenly approachable and friendly. Grudges of childhood were shed. When two days later Bonard stopped at the farm for no reason other than to talk, it seemed natural enough for them to agree to go to a dance together the following Saturday night. It was a country dance and none attended as couples who were not married. The girls went with their families or in groups, and the men alone or with a male companion.

Soon they were taking each other for granted, and if a week went by without their meeting more than once, both felt the lack. They had little common ground beyond an interest in girls. For Bonard there was the reward of having another marvel over experiences that had become for him commonplace. There was for Benjamin the satisfaction of being with someone he could believe felt as he did, even though in every conversation there were reminders of limits to the mutuality of their feeling and understanding. Benjamin did not like Bonard's careless condescension about farming; nor did he find his cousin's ridicule of "ignorant darkies" witty. Benjamin despised the Negroes who had been set up by carpetbaggers and scalawags after the war to make laws for Southern whites, and he hated the Negro militia who had for a time been used by the Yankees to enforce their rule; but he had known Floyd, and he knew Zadok and Rosalie, and he would never think or talk about "darkies" as though they were all one, any more than he would think of white people in that way. Then too, Bonard talked as if their elders were his enemies to be cajoled or abused as occasion required, whereas Benjamin more often than not trusted older people, perhaps because of his strong early love for his grandfather Bruce Davis.

But Benjamin ignored these flickers of doubt when they were together. How good it was to say "fuck" and "pussy" almost without thinking about it. How it cleared the head to laugh at things that had been throbbing fears at three o'clock that very morning. How fine it was to look another man in the eye as he spoke a name and to say, "Yes, I've been with her too." Young men were as eager to detail dalliance as young women were to pretend that it had never occurred, however much the latter assumed it was not done because it violated the gentlemen's code of honor. And then, the simple fun of it all—as on this hot afternoon of early April when Benjamin had gone to the creek to swim and been joined by Bonard, who came looking for him.

They lay on their bellies after swimming, and the sun dried their backs, and they talked with no awareness, no caring that what they said had been said before, only a little differently, and would surely be said by young men forever when they sought to measure their manhood with the peculiar mixture of truth and falsehood that constitutes masculine intimacy at that age.

"When," Bonard asked, "was the first time you did it? With a girl, I mean."

"I don't remember," Benjamin lied.

Bonard glanced at his companion, recognizing the reply as evasion. "Well, it was old Millie that got me started," he said.

"Fox's old Millie? You don't mean you—"

"No, no!" Bonard turned on his side and threw a pine cone at Benjamin. "She got after me about the sheets. She said if she had to *unstarch* my sheets before she starched them again, she'd up and quit working for Mama. She said it wasn't natural for a boy to mess his bed, and I took what she said to heart."

"I guess it was easy for you," Benjamin said. "Living in town and seeing everybody all the time, you just had to keep your eyes open and decide which ones you wanted to cut out of the flock."

"Oh, I didn't have much to worry about," Bonard agreed. "But the things they make you go through just to get a little piece of pussy! —All the smiling and the bowing and picking flowers. Godalmighty! The violets I've picked. The berry buckets I've had to fill! The sweet-talking I've done when I knew they were wanting to as much as I was!"

Delighted, but still a little shocked by his cousin's free way of talking, Benjamin laughed, his breath stirring the pine needles beneath his mouth.

Bonard said, "When you blush, you blush all over, did you know that? I have to laugh at old maids like Miss Eloise. She ever try to talk to you?" Shaking his head, Benjamin reached to tear leaves from a weed and held them under his nose, enjoying their pungent odor. "When I was about eighteen, she took me aside and said to me, 'Bonard, you may tell me it's none of my business, but I've known you ever since you were a little boy, so I feel free to say what I please.' I smiled and waited. 'Bonard,' she said, 'I've heard that you take a drink. Is it so?' I lowered my eyes and told her yes'm, it was. She said, 'Oh, Bonard, you must try to overcome your thirst for alcohol, for they say it leads men to do terrible things.' I put on the most innocent look you ever did see and asked, 'What kind of things, Miss Eloise?' She bit her lips but looked determined. 'Bonard,' she said, 'I want you to tell me something and tell me true: are you a *good* boy?' I took a long time pretending I didn't know what she meant, and then I let her see I did, and she blushed even more than you just now. I said, 'Miss Eloise, I have to own the truth since you've asked me to. I'm not what you'd call a good boy.' Then, 'Oh, Bonard,' she said, 'you must save yourself for the girl you marry.' That was just what I was waiting for her to say. 'Well, Miss Eloise,' I said to her, 'I haven't run short yet, so I reckon I've got enough to go around.'"

"Now, *hell* you didn't!" Benjamin declared.

"*Hell* I *did!*"

"I don't believe it!"

"Ask her, why don't you?"

The thought of saying such a thing to Miss Eloise Kilmer set Benjamin to laughing again.

"I got a good idea," Bonard said. "Let's go out and see the Crawford girls. It's Friday, and you've knocked off for the day. I drove my buggy to your grandma's. Zadok said you'd be there."

There were five Crawford sisters, the youngest thirteen and the oldest twenty, all unmarried. They lived with their father Alf, who no longer farmed the few acres he owned. After the war he lost most of his land because he couldn't pay the taxes demanded; but he discovered that there was money in making and selling liquor. His wife was dead, and Miss Kilmer sometimes opined that his girls needed guidance. Alf would not have agreed with her; he never seemed to mind if one of them went to the barn with a customer who came to buy his liquor and stayed to talk and dance with his daughters.

"On a Friday there's bound to be others," Bonard said. "We won't be first, I'll vow. What do you say?"

"I told Aunt Doreen I'd be back after while."

"If you're not, she'll know it, won't she?"

"I suppose."

"Come on, then. Dancer will get us there in half an hour, and if you don't want to stay, you don't have to; I'll bring you home."

"That stuff he makes is awful," Benjamin said.

"I know it, but that ain't the main attraction. You can talk to Alvina or Alma or Annie or Abbie or Adeline. Might even get one of them to traipse out to the barn with you—to feed the hogs, I mean to say—but no telling what-all else could happen there! —Look at you! I see you!"

Benjamin rolled over and rose to his feet, hiding his erection. "We'll see, after I swim a little more." Again he ran and belly-flopped into the creek, enjoying the clean sting of the water after the itch of pine needles. When he returned, Bonard had begun to dress. There was no need for Benjamin to say he would go; both knew he would.

Dressed, they made their way out of the woods toward the house at Beulah Land. As they drew near, they could see Jane on the porch in a rocking chair with four young men on the floor making a semicircle in front of her, as if they presented themselves for her inspection.

"Look at that," Benjamin said disgustedly. "They come every

evening. Aunt Nell says she can't use her own front porch any more because of the boys that come to see Jane."

"Which does she fancy?" Bonard said.

"None, far as I know," Benjamin said shortly.

"She's gotten to be a pretty girl," Bonard observed speculatively. "I'm almost sorry I used to fight her. A mighty-mighty-mighty pretty girl."

Benjamin stared at his cousin. "Let's hurry," he said.

Having no sister, Bonard did not understand Benjamin's annoyance, but he slapped him on the shoulder amiably. "Ever hear why all their names begin with 'A'? Old man Crawford told me that when he got married, he figured he'd never get tired of doing it, so he started naming his children with all the 'A' names he could think of, hoping to go straight through the alphabet. After his wife died, he thought about marrying again, but says he didn't have the heart for it. Sometimes he says he didn't have the *hard* for it and gives a wink, which sets all the girls giggling! When I've got nothing better to do, I make a list in my head of what the 'B' names might have been, and so on."

Benjamin knew the story, but he laughed as if he did not, and they got into the buggy, friendly again. As they rolled off down the carriageway, Bonard lifted his hat in the direction of the porch, and Jane waved to them. "Barbara, Becky, Beatrice, Binnie—oh, it goes on forever!"

2.

"What's blue and got the same number legs as a spider?"

"Don't listen to him, Jane. What is it grows a foot a day and wiggles its ears when it rains?"

"Tom Cooper, that's what!"

Jane laughed. "You're all so silly!" She was pert enough to speak the truth and mannerly enough to say it as a joke. They were not town dandies. Thomas Cooper, Frederick Shields, Hobart Kenning, and John Baxter were the sons of neighboring farmers who knew well enough the lean realities of every day, but were still happy to cut the fool when they hoped to entertain a girl they admired. If their banter harked back to early times, it was part of their legacy as Southerners as much as a determination not to allow grace and nonsense to vanish from their world. So they and Jane acted the dandy and the belle none of them had ever been or ever would be. No one was deceived, but everyone was pleased with each other. Thomas Cooper's shirt was so heavily darned it looked embroidered. Frederick Shields had the horny hands of a plowman. Hobart Kenning wore his one pair of shoes only when he left his home farm to visit or go into town on his father's business. And John Baxter knew very well that he couldn't afford to marry Jane Davis or any other girl for another ten years.

"What's blue and wiggles its ears when it *whats?*" Jane said. "I swanee if the whole bunch of you aren't crazy with the heat, and it just April. Lordy knows what you'll be like come August dog days!"

Hearing the stumping of Nell's cane, the boys scrambled to their feet as the old woman came out the door and looked at them sourly.

"Let me get you a chair, Miss Nell!"

"My, you're looking pretty today!"

"Granny said tell you she had more dried verbena than she knew what to do with and wondered if you had any use for it?"

Jane sat quietly, letting the young men fuss around her great-great-aunt, knowing that she required no help from her.

As she settled into the rocking chair that had been brought, Nell said, "Tell your granny I've plenty verbena but I'm obliged to her for offering." She reviewed the four young faces of the boys. "In the sight of the Lord you are equal, but I don't understand why he makes you all look alike."

"Shoot, Miss Nell, you know we don't; you're just saying that. Look at Tom Cooper's ears. Did you ever see such big feet as Hobart's? Fred here is one big freckle! So how can you say we look alike? Miss Jane can tell us apart, can't you, Miss Jane?"

"Well, if she can," Nell said, "it's only because she sees you so often."

Frederick had been studying his right hand. "Miss Nell, I'll bet you remember—what is that old-timey thing you're supposed to say three times to get rid of warts?"

Nell thumped her cane on the porch floor. "I never had occasion to get rid of warts, young man. Make up a charm to suit yourself."

"Aw, but then it wouldn't work!"

John Baxter said, "Miss Nell, you're a big old tease, just like my Aunt Caroline."

Nell peered at him with surprise. "Is Caroline Peabody your aunt?"

"Yes'm, my great-aunt; she sure is."

Nell weighed the matter. "Somebody told me she died."

"No'm, she's still with us, thank the Lord."

"Big goiter, though," Nell observed.

"Well'm, that's so, but she's accustomed, it having come to her before she was thirty, they say."

Nell rocked, pursing her lips thoughtfully. "Big as my two fists, that goiter." She closed her eyes. Within seconds she began to snore.

"Well," Thomas Cooper whispered to Jane, "I for one have got to hit the grit for home."

"Me too," John Baxter said. "I'll walk you till I turn off."

Jane protested politely that they mustn't go, but five minutes later they were all gone.

"I was playing possum," Nell said as Jane rejoined her after seeing the last of the young men go down the carriageway. "So sweet, that wisteria." She had her eyes on a cluster of the lavender blossom, the vine of which shaded the western end of the porch. "You set that out yourself."

"Yes'm," Jane said. "When Grandma first built this house. You remember Mr. Twiggs?"

"Certainly I remember Amos Twiggs."

"I dug in the ground where I knew it had grown when they burned us, and I found one springy root. That provided all this."

Nell rocked slowly, contented. "I wish the fig tree had lived. We'd had it such a long time, we almost thought of it as biblical." She sighed. "What are those on the table?"

Jane went to the porch table and picked up a reed basket, looking at its contents. "Hickory nuts. Hobart always brings something, but these'd be old and probably shriveled inside. You want me to crack one for you and see?"

"No, I'll wait for my supper."

Jane sat down. "I wonder where Ben and Bonard went off to while ago."

"Bonard?" Nell said. "He ran away with Lauretta and got himself killed in California. It was scandalous."

With no surprise Jane answered, "This is his great-nephew, Aunt Annabel's son."

Nell tossed her head. "Only smart thing Annabel ever did was marry the banker's boy, and she treats him like a Nigra, they say. He ought to take a stick to her."

A Negro boy bounded up the front steps and onto the porch, breathing fast and hard. After looking wildly about, he dropped on all fours and crept behind Nell's rocking chair. Nell and Jane ignored him. A moment later Sarah ran up the steps. "Abraham?" she called. "Where are you? What I've got for you won't hurt much!" Finding him, she swooped and grabbed a heel and dragged him, both of them giggling, across the porch and down the steps. "Josephine told me you took an apple tart without asking her. She told me to catch you and wear you out!"

Freeing himself, the boy ran off, laughing triumphantly, with Sarah in pursuit.

"Always was a fool about her Nigras," Nell said to Jane.

"Abraham is Floyd's boy," Jane reminded her.

"Ah, Floyd," Nell murmured. "Floyd was different. Is that Casey coming yonder?"

Casey Troy trotted his horse up the carriageway as they watched him and dismounted just as Abraham appeared again, pursued by Sarah. Seeing his chance, Abraham grabbed the reins of the horse. "I'll take him to the barn, Mister Casey!"

"Thank you, Abraham." Casey caught Sarah around the waist and swung her to him, kissing her smackingly on the mouth.

"That is the kissingest man," Nell complained to the air.

Casey and Sarah came up the steps, their arms about each other's waist. "Yes, and you're about to get one too," Casey warned Nell, going to her and bending to kiss her on the cheek.

Shooing him with her handkerchief, with which she then proceeded to wipe her cheek, Nell said, "Don't come slobbering over me like a fancy man."

"Shouldn't tempt me, sitting there pretty as a bowl of cream." Casey shifted chairs, and they sat four together watching evening fall.

Nell said, "I been meaning to talk to you about Sarah, the way she plays with that youngun. If they were the same color, I couldn't tell them apart."

Casey shook his head. "I can't do anything with her, Miss Nell. She won't behave herself. They broke the mold when they made you."

"That's what Felix used to say," Nell confided mournfully. "You didn't know my husband, did you?"

"Not to say 'know,' ma'am. He was living the life of an invalid at the time I first came to Beulah Land."

"There was a man," Nell informed him.

"I have heard his character extolled by all whose honor it was to claim his acquaintance."

Nell glanced at him sharply in the twilight. "Times, Casey, you sound so Southern I could almost declare you're making fun of us."

"You shock me, ma'am!"

Presently Jane said, "There's the moon."

Daniel came walking from the house that had been Floyd's and Roman's and was now his. He had bathed in the creek after work and put on clean clothes. After they greeted each other, Daniel took his place on the steps near Jane's chair. One of the hounds came around the house wagging his tail, and when nobody ordered him away, he climbed the steps to nuzzle Daniel's knees. "All your beaux left you?" he said mildly to Jane.

"Smarty," Jane said, as if she had been expecting some such comment.

"How many came today?"

"So many I lost count."

"Niminy-piminy," Nell said. "I can't believe that boy's aunt is still alive. If she is, she must be a hundred. Who wants her old dried verbena, I'd like to know?"

"Has Benjamin been?" Sarah suddenly asked.

"That's funny," Nell said.

"What is?"

"Your saying 'Ben been.'"

"He went off somewhere with Bonard," Jane said.

"I wanted to ask him something," Sarah said, disappointed. "Well—"

Josephine rang the supper bell, and they got up from their chairs.

"I miss Nancy," Nell said. "Where did Nancy go? Bless her heart, wherever she is." When Daniel went to help her into the house, she clutched his arm for support and patted his hand with her free one.

3.

Anyone else coming to Beulah Land to see its mistress and being told that she was in the chicken yard would have gone after her, but Annabel Saxon declared herself exhausted and asked Josephine to fetch Mrs. Troy, for she had particular business with her. Sarah came, but in her own time.

"I've been waiting an hour," Annabel said.

"Then you've had a chance to rest. Josephine told me you were tired, and I had some work to finish."

"I wasn't going into any chicken yard wearing these new shoes."

Sarah looked down at Annabel's feet. "Pretty. They look too small."

"If anything, I'll have to pad them at the heel," Annabel claimed.

Sarah laughed shortly. "And if pigs could fly, they'd think they were angels and try to sing, I've no doubt." The mention of shoes reminded Sarah to examine her own. Seeing that they were mucky, she removed them and scraped their soles on the edge of the porch.

"Pee-yew," Annabel protested, fanning the air with both hands.

"You can't expect chicken manure to smell like roses, although I believe Jane uses it to fertilize some of her bushes to good effect."

"Is Jane not about?" Annabel glanced right and left.

"She's probably with Aunt Nell, or working in her flower beds out back. Did you want to see her?" Sarah sat down in her stocking feet beside Annabel.

"You don't mind if Mr. Troy finds you like that?"

"He's found me wearing less without complaining."

Annabel smiled carefully, to show that she understood and did not approve. "And where is he this afternoon?"

Sarah smiled too, but the lines bunched between her eyes. "I believe he's taking some photographs in town. Are we going right through a roster of everybody at Beulah Land, or have you something to say to *me?*"

"I should think you'd hate having your husband pose and photograph pretty young women, seeing that he's a few years younger than you are."

"Perhaps I should, if I were jealous."

"I cannot get used to your being Mrs. Troy, or to your marrying again at all."

Sarah stopped herself from making the reply that came to her. "Ah, well."

"People still talk about it."

"People still talk about Jonah and the whale."

"Your marrying him so soon after your sister married *another* Yankee gave rise to various questions. People have wondered if it has something to do with the seemingly indestructible prosperity of Beulah Land."

"Annabel, you make me tired. Now you surely haven't exhausted yourself driving your buggy out here to tell me what people may be saying about us. If you have, you've wasted your time." Having given her a lead, Sarah paused, but when Annabel did not take advantage of it, continued, "Are you comfortable in your new house?"

"Oh yes. Of course, I've known what I'd do with it for a long time." Two months earlier her father-in-law had died, an event that doubly rejoiced Annabel, for it meant that her husband was now in control of the bank with their elder son working alongside him, and that the old Saxon house she had long coveted was hers at last.

Sarah decided to enjoy herself until Annabel got down to the business that had brought her to Beulah Land. "I suppose Prudence will be making changes in your house too, now that she and Blair have moved into it."

"I hardly think any changes are required."

"I meant that every woman wants a house to be hers, and I believe Blair has actually bought it from you, hasn't he? Maggie said something to that effect when I saw her at church."

"There's some arrangement between him and his father; I'm not clear as to details."

Sarah smiled. "Blair is lucky. Prudence is such a good wife and mother."

Annabel flushed. "I reckon she tries," she conceded tightly, "and well she should after making a match so far above her deserts. I'm sure now that her mother has had it in mind ever since she was born. She's sly, you know. I've even suspected that's why she contrived to marry my brother, to pave the way for Prudence from inside the family."

"It was all so natural," Sarah said, "your having cherished Maggie and Ann-Elizabeth as friends since you were girls together."

"I've come to speak to you about Bonard."

"Have you!" Sarah had never learned that as soon as she let down her guard with Annabel, Annabel would spring a surprise.

"He and Benjamin have become thick."

Sarah shrugged. "They go around together."

"I didn't mind when it started. Benjamin working so hard on his little farm, I thought, might inspire Bonard to apply himself more diligently at the mill; but James says it's made no difference." Sarah waited. "In fact, instead of having a good influence on Bonard, Benjamin is egging him on to be wilder than ever. Did you know they were out all last night?"

"Benjamin is grown; I don't monitor his comings and goings."

"Don't you care that he's getting a bad reputation?"

"He enjoys sparking the girls, if that's what you call a bad reputation."

"They spent the night at Crawford's. I got it out of Bonard after he came home. You know what goes on at Crawford's. If you don't, you're the only woman in the county who doesn't." Sarah made no comment. "Do you mean to speak to him, now that you know?"

"Reprimand him?" Sarah shook her head. "It would be meddling, and it would be a mistake."

"I wish Bonard would marry."

That seemed to Sarah to be safer ground. "You haven't always been so eager in that direction."

"I am now."

Sarah was amused, but she was also watchful. "Of course, good prospects like Prudence are not to be found every day. Do you have anybody in mind for him?"

Annabel looked directly at her. "I think that with a little encouragement he would be in love with Jane."

Sarah did not answer at once. Finally she said, "That is out of the question."

"Why?"

"To begin with, they are first cousins."

"First cousins do marry. There are arrangements about that."

"There will be none involving these two."

Annabel looked away. "Have you ever heard Jane express any —disagreeable feelings about my son?"

"I don't think Jane has thought of marrying," Sarah said, shifting the argument to the less personal.

"She's eighteen. I'd been married a year at her age, and many girls marry younger than I did."

"Boys come visiting and sit on the porch for hours, but there's no special one."

"I think Bonard would beat their time if encouraged."

"Please don't *you* encourage him, Annabel!"

"It would be an excellent thing. You've brought the girl up very well. She is worthy of us, and I approve the family connection that already exists—as much as I disapprove others."

"Has it occurred to you that she might not find Bonard 'worthy'—to use your word? It's ridiculous to talk about it. There is nothing between them, I assure you."

"Would you set yourself against a match?" Annabel asked.

"I would not have Jane make the mistake Selma did in marrying your uncle."

"The two Bonards are entirely different cases."

Sarah said slowly, "Your son appears to me to be growing more like his namesake all the time. I would not say so, for it does not concern me, but you have brought the matter up."

"Would you try to forbid marriage between them?"

"It won't come to that."

"I think you are wrong."

"I don't like to interfere in other people's lives any more than I like their interfering in mine, but if you promote such a thing, I *shall* work against it."

"Everyone knows Jane's devotion to you. Do you think it fair to play on it?"

"Jane thinks for herself; she is not thinking of Bonard."

Annabel rose abruptly, and her chair continued to rock.

"Annabel, don't do this."

Annabel forced a smile. "I'm sorry you feel the way you do. I hope you will change. —Whatever happened to that girl you used to have? The sassy Nigra girl. I've actually seen her sitting down in a chair beside you—"

"Nancy? She went to Savannah to find work."

"They have no loyalty, do they?"

"What brought her to your mind?"

"It's hot, and you haven't offered me anything. She used to make good lemonade. Well, goodbye, Auntie Sarah."

Sarah watched her go down the steps and get into her buggy and drive down the carriageway.

Jane came from the hallway carrying a tray, too late to see the buggy disappear around a curve. "I brought lemonade," she said. She set the tray down and poured two glasses full. "When I came in from my flower beds, Josephine said Aunt Annabel was here."

Accepting a glass, Sarah said, "So she was."

Jane smiled. "You and Aunt Annabel, always at sword points."

"I thought we felt the same about her," Sarah said.

"She's acted nicer to me lately, and sometimes I think she's funny."

"Not I," Sarah said grimly.

They sipped lemonade. "Of course," Jane said, "she'd be awful to have as a mother."

Sarah tensed her feet in her stockings and said nothing.

"I feel sorry for Bonard," Jane said.

"Annabel is worried about him," Sarah said. "She fears he's— he has bad companions."

Jane laughed. "Does she consider Benjamin bad?"

"She means—well, you've heard about the Crawford girls."

"You've told me never to believe gossip. Enjoy it, but don't repeat it, you say." Jane smiled in a teasing way. "I've also heard you say it's better for a man to sow wild oats before he marries than after."

"Some do both. I appear to have said a lot of silly things lately."

"If Bonard finds a proper wife, I'm sure he'll be all right."

"It's none of our affair," Sarah said deliberately.

"Well, he's very handsome." Reading her grandmother's look of alarm as surprise, she continued in a teasing vein. "Maybe some worthwhile girl will take him in hand and make a saint of him. Who knows?"

4.

When free public education was introduced in Highboro, as it was in most of the South in the late sixties, Selma and Roman and Pauline became part of it. Their salaries were small, and aside from the little they spent on clothes, were used for the school. Their school had always been for Negro children, so segregation was not imposed upon it, but merely continued. Miss Eliza Truman had died, and although no money came now from Philadelphia, books and maps were occasionally sent by someone who had known Roman or his friend Proctor, or who had worked with that good bully, Miss Truman, and hoped that their leftovers and hand-me-downs would be of use to the little school in Georgia. When the stationmaster passed word to Roman that another crate had arrived, he usually went to open it and see what was in it before begging cartage on somebody's wagon. Sometimes it was simpler to divide the contents for easier transport.

One morning in late April he was accompanied to the station by three of his younger male pupils. Each carried an old sack that had been used for picking cotton until worn out. The crate waiting for them held a collection of wall charts, most of them useless as well as dull. The duller the chart, the better its physical condition, Roman knew from experience. Two were so soiled and cracked he guessed they were the prizes even before he unrolled them. One showed representations of the land animals of South America and the other simple botanical renderings: a stalk of corn from seed to harvest with illustrations of the plant above and below ground; acorns and pine cones much enlarged; apples in cross section complete with twig and leaf. These, he knew, would delight the children. Looking at them he could almost hear the youngest ones catch their breath in wonder, see their eyes grow larger as if the better to take in the magnifications and their lips part as they studied each item. They were fresh and true and wonderfully literal in the way they saw things; only as they got older did they set up barriers, suspect traps, jeer each other's enthusiasms. Now the little boys gazed at the two opened charts with their hands respectfully clenched behind their backs. Roman rolled them up again and helped the boys pack all of them, good and bad, carefully into the old cotton sacks. They set off importantly for the school while he waited on the station platform for the arrival of the morning train.

He had no reason to meet it; he did so as idly as the loungers on the steps, who from familiarity accepted and ignored him. Although he knew they paid him little attention, Roman found himself playing a part: standing ill at ease, moving awkwardly when he moved at all. It was a defense that had become a device for survival for those Negroes who were without means or patronage. It was not enough for the ordinary Negro to behave in a docile way; he must look docile as well, lest he be thought "uppity." Hence, the side shuffle, the vague hand gestures, the ducked head. Roman recognized these for what they were when he first returned to Highboro and swore he would never adopt them, but he did, at first by unconscious imitation. When he realized what he was doing, he despised himself, but he continued to do it. That he was somewhat lame only gave the game an ironic fillip.

As he waited now, a parody of ineffectuality in the way he stood, he heard his name called and turned to find Jane Davis beside him. The loungers began to watch, having no train yet to divert them.

"Miss Davis."

The loungers glanced at each other. One whispered, "Hear? Calls her Miss Davis stead of Miss Jane the way any other darky would."

"Are you meeting the train too?" Jane asked.

"I came to collect one of my crates," he explained, and told her of sending the boys back to the school with the rolls of charts. "And you? Have you come to meet someone?"

"No. Grandma and I came in the old buggy. She had some business with Uncle Blair at the bank, so I told her I'd wait here. When I was a little girl, Grandpa used to bring me. Grandpa Leon, I mean. He'd hold me up high when we heard the whistle, and I don't know which of us was more thrilled. It was as if we expected the most wonderful things to come on that train, although the train itself was enough." Roman found himself unexpectedly moved, hearing his father spoken of in a way he had never known him. "It was always, every time, the most glorious thing we'd ever seen. So when I'm in town and the time is right, I like to come here."

"Is it still glorious?" He had begun to walk slowly along the platform, encouraging her to walk with him away from the loungers.

"See him?" one said. "Making her go with him."

"Well, they say there's no trouble with him thataway, for he's a morfidike."

"A what?"

"One of them half-man, half-woman critters."

"What you reckon he's got down there?"

"Maybe both. Maybe neither one!"

They all snickered.

In answer to another question Roman had asked, Jane was saying, "We know he should, but he won't. Grandma tries to send him off after breakfast with his books and lunch pail. Then later in the day we'll see him in one of the fields with Daniel or over at Ben's helping them. He just loves the ground, Abraham does."

"He ought to come to school."

"Grandma's already told him he has to next fall every day, rain or shine, sleet or snow or earthquake."

Roman smiled. "I'm only being stern for Floyd."

("See him? See him smile? What you reckon he led her away to say he didn't want us to hear? You have to watch them niggers with learning.")

Jane said, "He'll always be Floyd's boy, don't you worry about that, the way we all talk about Floyd! But you're right to keep after him, and us. We promise to make him do better." They were quiet with half smiles when Jane said, "Listen!" She had heard the first warning: a distant whistle. Next, white smoke appeared over the tops of the farthest trees, followed by an increasing vibration of air and earth that seemed to enter one's very being. It happened at last: the arrival of the awful, beautiful monster as it braked into the station, pouring smoke and a brief scalding spout of water before coming to a full grinding halt.

Jane said, "If God himself were to step off it, it would only just about be enough!"

Roman laughed.

As they watched, one passenger descended from a coach, and farther along, the side of a boxcar opened and two trunks were slid onto the backs of waiting porters. The man who now stood looking about, not as a stranger might, yet not as one expecting to be met either, was dressed in the Northeastern fashion of gentlemen, Roman noted, and he was a Negro. He was a young man who seemed a little too large for his clothes, although they were well cut. His face was grainy, with heavy lips and nose. His blue eyes looked and saw, but they seemed to ask nothing and they gave nothing. The impression he made was one of intelligence and intense homeliness.

"Who can he be?" Jane whispered.

The stranger saw that they were looking at him and approached them. At this, the white loungers froze in tableau. Not even the engine and its driver and fireman could match their new interest. Stopping a few feet away, the man bowed. "It is a long time," he said, "but am I wrong in thinking I recognize Miss Jane Davis?"

Surprised, Jane said, "Yes, I am Miss Davis." She stared at him as realization grew. "It is a very long time ago. You came to Beulah Land one night to warn us."

"Roscoe Elk," he said.

"My grandmother has spoken of you more than once in a grateful way."

"Has she?" The knowledge appeared to please him; he smiled broadly. Then as he became aware of the staring white men, he bowed again and left them to find the freight office to claim his trunks.

5.

"Grandma, my dog's turned sick. What must I do?"

"What's wrong with her?"

"Sits there; won't bark or growl; not an idea in her head. Used to take the end of a rope if I dangled it and hold on like a turtle, but now she sits there like she expects Casey to come take her picture. Not like herself, Delilah."

"Have you looked inside her ears for ticks? I don't know why, but when they nest thick inside, that dog's a goner. If you take a little lard and turpentine—"

"Her ears are clean as mine," Benjamin said.

"What about around her tail near her butt?"

"Clean as her teeth."

"Maybe she's just old. How old is she?"

"Nine."

"Every year for her is like ten for us."

"Hell's fire, Grandma! I remember when I was a lot older than *her* and now you're saying she's as old as Aunt Nell. Why do dogs have to get old faster than we do?"

"Ask God. I don't know. Chick, chick, chick! Here, chick!" It was late afternoon; they were in the chicken run next to the smaller barn. "Ben, move along there quiet. See that Plymouth Rock rooster, spurs long as your thumbs?"

"Yes'm."

"If you get close enough, give him a kick. Mean devil. Saw him this morning crouched over one of my best hens, pecking her comb like it was popcorn."

Ben moved as quietly as he and Daniel moved when they went hunting. The Plymouth Rock rooster hesitated. Ben grabbed. The bird squawked but was caught. "Got him!" Benjamin said.

"Wring his neck," Sarah directed.

Ben did so with his eyes closed. Feathers flew and floated in the air about their faces, so that they had to blow their breath out to keep them away. The other fowls scattered, then stood and looked on interestedly.

"You haven't broken his neck, you're just tiring him out," Sarah said as Ben continued to revolve his hand holding the rooster. "Give him to me." Benjamin did so. Sarah took the big bird, gave her hand one expert twist, breaking his neck and dropping him to the ground to flop his life out. "I'll have Josephine boil him all day tomorrow, for he's bound to be tough, but he'll make a good stew for us, and you know how your Aunt Nell—"

"Dearly loves a good chicken stew with a little sage and dumplings!" they chanted together, laughing.

Leaving the chicken run, they headed toward the house. "Remind me to send Josephine to get him." Sarah stopped, and Benjamin stopped because she did, looking at her questioningly. Her look questioned him too, but more intently. She saw Benjamin every day without thinking about him, and now and then she remembered that. Absently removing a downy feather that stuck to his sideburns, she smoothed his hair back with her palm. So long had he acted the man she was apt to forget that he'd had little chance to be a boy after eleven. Sometimes when they were alone, he would behave younger than he was, as he had just done about his dog. It wasn't that his concern for Delilah was anything but true, but his way of expressing it had been a child's. "Is everything all right with you, Ben?" He smiled, enjoying her attention. She pinched the flesh of his chin briefly and hard before walking on. "One of these days I'm going to wring Annabel's neck," she said.

He gave a big laugh before following her.

"I am," she insisted, as if he had contradicted her. "They'll come to you and say, 'Your grandmother Sarah has wrung your Aunt Annabel's neck, and she's flopping around the yard like a chicken.'" Her face relaxed; the image pleased her.

"What's she up to?" Ben asked.

"Making me worry about things I shouldn't, as if there isn't plenty other! Have you thought about getting married?"

"Not much," he said, his lack of surprise at her question an indication that he had. "There's plenty of time."

"Mm." The murmur neither agreed nor disagreed. "You'll want to marry one day. You ought to give it some thought."

"It'll happen."

"Well now," she said perversely, "you don't want to drift into anything, or force yourself to do anything either. No. I don't want you or Jane to marry just anybody. I want the best for both of you, you hear me?"

"Grandma, don't fret about it."

After a moment she said, "Ben, you please me. Do you know you're a very good-looking man? I won't say 'boy'; you're a good-looking man."

Smiling, he said, "You're a good-looking woman, Grandma."

"I know it," she agreed simply. "That's important: to know it if you are. I want you to know it and remember it and not throw yourself away."

"I'm nothing special, Grandma."

"Indeed you are." Again she stopped abruptly. "Dear God." They had come to the sundial.

"What?" he asked gently.

"I was remembering a talk I had at this very spot a few years ago with your grandfather Bruce Davis. He reminded me there'd been ivy around that old dial. —What a lot is crowded into these few acres and these many years! Sometimes I think I can't stand it." They walked on slowly a few steps. "Ben, I want you to do something for me!" Sarah slapped her leg in affirmation. "When are you going to Savannah?"

"I hadn't thought to go till I have to sell our cotton. October?"

"A long time. Well, when you do, then or before, I want you to look for Nancy and find out how she is for me."

He felt his heart beating hard. After a few beats it slowed, becoming normal again. "I thought you heard from her. Doesn't she write?"

"Last time was when she got married two years ago." She nodded. "I want you to look for her and see how she is. I've dreamed about her two nights in a row. I don't remember what I dreamed, I almost never do, but Nancy was in it. Your Aunt Nell misses her, said so just the other day. Abraham ought to see her again before he forgets her. She took care of him till he was four years old, you know. A little mama to him she was, and he oughtn't to forget her." She considered, frowning. "Annabel mentioned her the other day too. Annabel, of all! It's as if something is trying to let me know something." They had come to her back doorsteps. She scraped the soles of her shoes on the bottom step.

"You can't tell me anything more to do for my dog?"

"No more than I have. You're not going, are you? Stay and eat supper with us. Casey will be home soon. You always enjoy talking to Casey."

"I thank you, but I better go eat with Aunt Doreen; otherwise she'll be by herself." He turned back after he'd started, to find her watching him. "Don't forget to tell Josephine!"

"About the rooster!" Her laughter admitted that she had forgotten. With no more farewell she went up the steps and into the house, calling "Josephine! I've killed him! Send Mabella to get him."

Benjamin heard Josephine scream, "Mercy, Miss Sarah!" Their voices mingled inaudibly as she explained, and then he heard the two women laugh.

He crossed the yard and followed a path alongside a field into the woods, eventually climbing up to the Glade. It was nearly dark when he got there. He did not go into the cabin but stood a while by the brook, squatting once to trail his hands in the cold water. His mind had said the name a hundred times in the last half hour, and now he spoke it aloud. "Nancy." The sound of his own voice made him feel lonelier than before.

When he reached home, Zadok was waiting to tell him that Delilah was dead. Benjamin wept so wildly that Doreen and Rosalie came from the kitchen to stand on the back porch and stare at him in wonder.

6.

"You lucky I let you live here," Roberta said to Geraldine. "If I told him to, he'd kick your ass straight down the road yonder, and than where'd you be? You act polite to me or I'll tell him to do it. When me and him is married, you watch out, woman."

Geraldine released her rage in spiteful laughter. "He'd never marry you, not if he had ten wives and eleven of them died. Why would he marry a stinking little hole like you?"

"To get chillun. You never gave him none."

"There wasn't no point with him tied. She's going to sit in that asylum in Savannah till you're dry as a beef cow."

"Takes an old beef cow to know about that, I reckon."

"Sass me, bitch, and I'll hang you on a hook in the smoke-house."

There was the sound of a slap and a cry and falling furniture, then of tears and running feet. The old mistress and the young one were sharpening their claws for the long day ahead.

On the columned porch Junior and Roscoe sat with second coffee, hearing it all. Junior grunted at the sudden quiet. "They've gone. Now we can hear ourselves."

Embarrassed, Roscoe said, "Do they do that often?"

"Once or twice a day," his father answered.

"Why don't you stop them?"

Junior shrugged. "A cat fight sounds worse than it is. If it's bad enough, they go to bed and lick their wounds, and sometimes each other's." He winked at his son. "Sometimes I join them."

"Why haven't you told them about Mama's dying?"

"I like to know and know they don't. It makes me laugh to hear them squabble about what they'll do when she dies. Don't you tell them better either. I'd have a mess on my hands and have to get rid of one, or both. Sometimes I wish they'd kill each other."

"Where did you find Roberta?"

"One of my tenant families. Might say they raised her for me. I watched her grow, and she saw me watching. I didn't have to do a thing. She and her ma planned a long time how to get ahead of Geraldine." He laughed as if proud of the girl's cunning.

"What if she had children?"

"I'd get rid of her and them. I don't want any more."

"Roberta said you did."

"Her notion." Junior took a deep pull on the cigar he had lighted from the live coal the house girl brought with the coffee tray. "You've been home two days. What do you think? And I don't mean about my women."

Roscoe looked about him. The porch they sat on was col-umned and high-roofed; the house behind it was large. "I don't remember ever seeing Oaks when I was a boy."

"It stopped being Oaks a long time ago."

"I do remember the old house at Beulah Land though. That's what you tried to copy here."

"My house is bigger."

"Why?"

"To show them."

"They'll never see it," Roscoe reminded him.

"Think they haven't been told? They know very well I did it to insult them."

Roscoe sighed, finishing his coffee and setting the cup down. "Does that give you satisfaction?"

"It does, but I did it for my papa more than me."

"He wouldn't have cared."

"You didn't know him if you think so. He hated everything Kendrick."

"I remember him as gentle," Roscoe said.

"Maybe with you he was. Not with anybody else."

"Did you care about him, Papa?"

"I was glad he made money, and I honored him by making more."

"The house is just a shell. Why didn't you go on and finish it? You walk through one room and it's overfurnished, too much of everything, then into the next and there's nothing, not even a rug on the floor or curtains at the window."

"That's for the women to take care of. I let them alone unless I want them to do something. I don't care how it looks inside."

They were quiet a moment. "Why did you send for me, Papa?"

"I thought you'd like to see us all." Roscoe shook his head. "Well, say I'd paid for the education to make a lawyer out of you and decided you ought to pay me back. Help me with the legal end of things, although using white lawyers, I've found nobody ever argues with me. But it's a smart notion having you here looking over what they do. Makes them pay attention and not go slack. Something else: you might run for something."

"In government, you mean?"

"It's been done."

"That's not for me, Papa. I'm not a politician."

"What are you then?" Junior asked.

"I was doing all right in Philadelphia with the firm that trained me."

"I saw you there last fall, don't forget. You were nothing but a clerk, less important than the office cat."

"I want to go back, Papa."

Holding his cigar between his teeth, Junior opened his hands. "Go ahead." Roscoe looked unhappy. Junior took another cigar from his pocket and gave it to his son. Roscoe accepted it and rolled it slowly between his palms. "Specially made for me in Cuba." He smiled at a joke he did not explain. "It's a good idea your settling down here. You can run for something in the government after they get used to you. Two big things in your favor: my money back of you and the fact that you're ugly. Almost as ugly as Abe Lincoln was. Being ugly can be as much advantage for a man as disadvantage for a woman; and an ugly nigger has a chance of getting by with a whole lot of things."

"I won't be a man on a string, and I *will* go back to Philadelphia. I don't belong here."

Junior held his cigar for his son to take a light for his own. When this was done, he said, "You're mighty full of 'will' and 'won't' for somebody with a taste for my cigars." Roscoe looked down at the burning tobacco in his hand without answering. "You worry too much. You make up your mind too fast. Take it easier. Look around you. Learn to go slow and wait. What do you think of Roberta?"

Roscoe jerked his head up. "How do you mean, sir?"

"Does she please you?"

Roscoe shifted his chair unnecessarily. "I don't know her."

"Don't put sugar on your lips for me, boy. You want her, try her out; maybe I'll give her to you the way my papa gave me Geraldine when he was through with her."

"I don't want her," Roscoe said.

"I've seen her watching you. She's got a hot hole and can rock you to a peaceful sleep."

Roscoe was shaking his head violently. "No, sir!"

After a moment Junior said calmly, "You've let it go out. Don't waste a good cigar." Roscoe laid the cigar across his empty cup on the table between them. His father's eyes left him to look over the land. "I saw you walking around yesterday. What do you think of what I've done?"

"When you bought the Davis place, you planned to cut it up and sell it as small farms."

"That's what I said, but it didn't turn out that way. Nobody had any money, so I had to think of something else. I don't like to see land lie wasting. So I tried an idea I'd heard about. This: give a family a house and a piece of land, and take a share of their crop."

"They get paid for working on a plantation like Beulah Land now."

"I give them something better. They have the feeling they own the place they live on."

"But they don't."

Junior shrugged. "If they work hard enough, they get rewarded."

"So do you," Roscoe said.

"Naturally." Junior smiled. "And my share comes first."

"What if that's all there is?"

"They still have a place to live and enough to fill their bellies."

"What's the difference between that and being slaves? I talked to some of them yesterday. They all owe you."

"I show them the figures. They're not slaves. They can go if they don't like it."

"Not while they owe you."

"I'd be crazy to give away what I've made, and what your grandfather got before me."

"There are two white families," Roscoe said.

"I let anybody work, but the whites ain't worth a damn and I've told them so. I won't have any more of them."

"They wouldn't have come to you if they'd been worth a damn; you know that. I think you wanted a couple of tame white slave families."

Junior did not deny it. "It's just as well for us to have this talk," he observed. "No misunderstandings. I like the way you speak up, but don't do it in front of anybody but me."

"Papa, let me go back to Philadelphia."

"I can't stop you."

Roscoe studied his father's face. "Yes, you can."

Finishing his cigar, Junior threw the stub into the yard. He stood and walked to the end of the porch and back again. "Think about it. You'll like it here after a while."

"You still haven't told me why you sent for me and why you're making me stay."

"Maybe I get lonesome. There's nothing as lonesome as a rich nigger."

Roscoe was so startled he believed him, until he looked into the smiling eyes.

7.

Junior Elk prospered in a time when failure was the general expectation. Benjamin had kept his farm and Sarah her Beulah Land, but to do so they'd worked early and late, and lived poor, and they had been in debt more often than out of it since the war. Many they knew had lost homes and land, unable to pay the high taxes that had been levied by often ignorant and vindictive legislatures.

However, people continued to draw first breath and to expel last, and there was usually some celebration of the milestones in between. Two weeks before Bonard Saxon was to be twenty-four years old, his mother decided for various reasons, none having to do with wanting to give pleasure, to mark the event. She began to talk about it at once, and so had the reward of feeling generous before spending a cent. There, indeed, was the rub: the expense of the thing. Of her circle Annabel was perhaps the least straitened by hard times, but parsimony encouraged her to announce that it would not be a general sort of party at all but only for particular friends roundabout Bonard's age. She considered a ball because it would show herself off as mistress of a new and grander house, but even a small ball would require musicians and substantial refreshments and the hiring of extra hands to dispense them graciously. No, she decided, a ball was out of the question. Besides, one gave them for young women, not young men.

A small party of friends to take a festive supper was her second thought. She was tempted by the idea, but reflection told her it would be as costly as a small ball, involve much tiring detail of planning and arrangement, and offend everyone not asked to attend.

She settled finally on having a picnic and—happy inspiration! —gave it the theme of "Catch the Bachelor." Taking the tack of airing the notion with four or five of the plainer unmarried daughters of friends, she could say almost honestly that she was overwhelmed by an avalanche of demands for just such an event. Two advantages were evident: it would be cheap, and it would sharpen the minds of everyone on the subject of matchmaking, which was one of her purposes in celebrating her son's birth. It was settled that each young woman attending—and there was no need now for list-paring—would prepare a batch of her culinary specialty, whether it was salads or pickles, cakes, candies or fancy breads, with a prize to be given to the one she referred to as "the most delicious wife-to-be." The girls were delighted and declared that it was quite the wittiest notion that had occurred to anyone in all their years of party-giving and party-going. Every one of them prided herself on cooking one thing better than anyone else, and Annabel was happy to turn that innocent vanity to her advantage at the same time she gave an opportunity of showing off.

The young men were commanded to provide transport for the party. It would be on the Saturday afternoon nearest the actual birthday, and therefore wagons and mules and horses ordinarily involved in farm labor might serve with no reasonable objection from anyone.

Annabel herself would provide—though no one objected, she protested that nothing was to keep her from it—entertainment and liquid refreshments. The latter was created by boiling up a barrel of weak tea and adding to it a gallon of cane syrup, a dozen sliced lemons, and a pound or two of dried raisins, seeds, stems, mold, and all. The punch was so nearly undrinkable, Bonard poured into it a bottle of his father's brandy, and several of the male guests added to it potions of fiery spirits they had brought to the picnic to drink privately in the bushes. The result was a tolerably tasty drink to wash down the fried chicken, pickled peaches, and potato salad, as well as a couple of dozen specialties unusual enough to entertain the more adventurous palates.

As to the setting for her rustic carnival, it required two visits with a variety of threats and importunings, including a reminder of his debt to the bank, for Annabel to obtain Benjamin's consent to their using the Glade. Her blackmail sent him storming off to see Sarah, who, seldom discreet in expressing her opinion of Annabel, cheered him with a number of epithets she had tried in her mind but had not had occasion to speak aloud. The end of it was that he had given his word and would keep it. His private

Glade would be Annabel's picnic grounds, but Sarah would attend. Annabel particularly desired that Sarah not be one of the guests; it was the reason she was inviting no older people. Reading Annabel's mind with fair accuracy, Sarah determined to go.

The day was overwarm, but the Glade was shady, and the thirty or so young people who gathered there were as extravagant in praising it as they were in praising their hostess. Doreen and Millie had gone early to hang cardboard lanterns and colored paper streamers at Annabel's direction and to make other decorative improvements on the natural but unrefined beauty of the place. Benjamin stood about awkwardly when he was not ordered to lift, reach, or fetch. He was relieved when the first guests arrived. Leaving their wagons in his barnyard, they were directed by Zadok to follow the narrow trail leading along fields until it joined the hill path to the Glade. The young people strolled about making themselves at home as Benjamin stared at them, resenting every broken twig and crushed blade of grass, and fit to be tied when he saw Tom Cooper tap burnt ash from his pipe into the brook. The food tables were set up in front of the cabin, which Annabel used as a sort of pantry and ladies' resting and primping room.

Bonard was perfect that day—and why should he not be? Having few opportunities to dominate a scene, he knew himself to be the center of attention. He wore his best, which was better than any other young man present afforded, and he wore it well. He was immaculately barbered, sober, and cheerful, which in the special circumstance allowed him to be thought elegant, wise, and happy. He knew his mother's mind concerning the party and, for once, was in no disagreement with her. While he had not made much headway in projecting himself as a prospective lover and husband to Jane Davis, he determined to do so this day. He was not in love, but he knew he must marry sometime to accommodate his family, and he saw the advantages of the match his mother proposed.

Benjamin had never in their recent closer acquaintance liked him so little. Bonard's charm was quick but vaporous. Concentrated upon oneself, it seemed intense. Spread over many, it was thin. Benjamin reckoned that since becoming friendly they had not been together among large numbers. Whereas in private Bonard had a wooing manner that seemed an appeal for friendship, in such a general gathering Benjamin found himself all but ignored. Bonard did not understand that friends sometimes require a warmer appreciation in public than in private. Benjamin remembered that soon after they had started going around together, he had asked himself if Bonard would bother with him if he could do better, and reminded himself that he had no reliable regard for his cousin.

In addition to hating the invasion of the Glade, Benjamin was suddenly bored in the overwhelming way it happens to the young; for early arrivals consisted mainly of the plainer females with brothers who resented being their escorts. As others came, however, he found himself smiling more and beginning to flirt and enjoy the company. He had all but forgotten Bonard's casual treatment when Jane arrived with their grandmother and Daniel Todd. Jane might have stepped from an embroidered sylvan idyll. Her frock was simple and becoming, and in one hand she carried a basket of ripe strawberries. Benjamin had never before been so conscious of her prettiness as he was seeing the beaux crowd around her. Sarah too had dressed simply and looked easy and elegant, as indeed she looked whether milking a cow or opening a ball. Between the woman and the girl Daniel scowled at the group as distrustfully as a dog might sniff a painted bone.

Seeing Annabel in the doorway of the cabin, Sarah made her way to her. Annabel made no effort to conceal her displeasure. "I am surprised to see you, I declare I am! Surely you understood this is a party just for the young."

"Benjamin said I might come."

"It isn't his occasion."

"No, but it's his land."

"I shouldn't think of going where I'd feel in the way."

"I don't feel at all in the way." Turning, she said, "You're looking well, Doreen."

"I am pretty well," Doreen admitted, "with God's grace upon me."

"Cousin Sarah!" Bonard had come up, smiling and bowing. "I am honored to see you on my birthday!"

"I wish you a happy one, Bonard."

Annabel withdrew, deciding that Bonard was receiving Sarah more wisely than she had done. They engaged in light talk as gracefully as if they liked each other, whereas Bonard had always been somewhat afraid of Sarah, and she had recently become afraid of him. When Benjamin and Daniel came up a few minutes later, appealing to Sarah to settle a point between them, Bonard looked on smiling before drifting away. Sarah watched him go directly to the group of young people of whom Jane was the center.

The party was for Bonard, but it might have been in Jane's honor too. Almost everyone there had known her all her life, but it sometimes happens on such occasions that people who take each other for granted become aware that a change has occurred. Jane was apprehended to be a beautiful young woman who up to now had been only a pretty-enough girl. Where the boys gathered, the girls followed. If they could not be the queen, they would be courtiers. They vied with each other in paying Jane the most flowery compliments on her dress and her complexion, making a bid for her regard and an appeal to her generosity.

Sarah saw it and was proud, but noting that Bonard saw it too, she trembled. She so forgot herself in turning over her thoughts, she was surprised to discover presently that she was not standing alone. Daniel was still beside her, Benjamin having left them; and Daniel had forgotten her too. In that unguarded moment for both of them she read his heart from his face. He hated Bonard Saxon. He hated Thomas Cooper and John Baxter and Hobart Kenning and Frederick Shields and all the other boys who stared and smiled at Jane and marveled at whatever she said. He even hated the simpering sycophantic females crowding close around her in hope of catching the secret of her new blooming. Daniel hated all of them, because he loved Jane.

Tears of sympathy came to Sarah's eyes. Why had she not seen it before? Of all things, it was the most natural to have happened. For a few moments she remembered the night he had tried to declare that he loved her and she would not let him, although she had certainly been ready to love him as well. How right this was to happen! She longed to tell him so. Instead, she did what she knew she must: she left him alone.

The party ebbed and flowed as such parties will. Jokes were told and laughed over excessively. Children's games were proposed, at first in jest as they remembered earlier birthday parties, and then played with intense, adult zest as they sang the old refrains they would never forget: "Go in and out our windows, go in and out our windows, go in and out our windows; for we have games today! I kneel before my lover, I kneel before my lover—"

An uphill, backward-hopping race was won by Bonard, who at the last, as a congratulatory cheer was raised, stumbled and fell at Jane's feet, which was winkingly said to be a sign. The young people made couples, some the result of attraction, and some only for convenience as they ate and drank and talked and played in the shady Glade, and the sun slipped ever farther down the dome of the cloudless May sky.

The prize of the day went safely to one of the plainest girls for her sugar-glazed jelly rolls, and no one begrudged her the white china teapot Annabel presented with a droll speech. Benjamin built a small fire on a shelf of slate overhanging the brook, and everyone came to stand near it and sing romantic songs, pretending to be lovers to heighten the yearning sadness of the verses they crooned. Annabel was delighted with the mood she credited herself with having created.

As the guests drifted down the path to the trail below it and on to the barnyard to claim their wagons and mules and horses, Sarah took another way she knew back to Beulah Land and Casey. Before going she whispered to Daniel, "Stay and bring Jane home."

Finally Benjamin was left alone with the dying fire and the trampled grass and weeds. The sun had set, the moon had risen. Day was gone, but it was not yet dark. His private place had been defiled, made common ground. He would spend tomorrow clearing it of the crushed lanterns and torn streamers, and he would scrub the cabin floor with sand. But not until next year would he be able to touch a leaf and know it fresh or bite a blade of grass no foot had touched. Sick of the day, he had turned to go when he heard his name called. "Ben? Is that you? Did everybody go?"

It was Bessie Marsh coming out of the cabin rubbing her eyes. "I must have gone to sleep. Is the picnic over? Oh! I've missed my ride home!" Bessie Marsh was twenty-five, the daughter of a farmer who lived two miles along the road away from Highboro. She was a plain woman who had no chance of marrying in such lean times. She would stay on the farm and take care of her father and mother when they grew old, for the rest of her life be a dutiful daughter and a reliable neighbor. People would praise her, and despise her a little. One kind of hope gone, she might now and again give herself to a desperate chance, as she did tonight.

Benjamin had never, he could swear, thought of her before, except as an amiable girl who helped fill a room at a party. He pretended that he believed all she told him of falling asleep and being forgotten. He said he would hitch up a mule and take her home, that it would be no trouble at all. But not yet? He would like to talk. Would she stay and talk to him? He told her he'd thought earlier in the day that her corn relish was the very best thing anyone had brought to the picnic, which pleased her. He had, he said, always felt that she understood him a little better than the others. Wasn't it chilly as night came on? After a while they went inside the cabin, where she revealed that she understood him very well.

8.

Casey Troy had bought a four-seat rockaway carriage, and everyone at Beulah Land admired its appearance and enjoyed its comfort. Even Nell had taken a jaunt in it. When Casey brought it home, she protested that she would never get into it, but one day Casey simply scooped her up in his arms and carried her off for an hour, which pleased her so she bragged about it to visitors for many months.

On the morning after the picnic the rockaway rolled smartly along the Highboro road to church. Sarah sat beside Casey, who held the reins. Behind them were Jane and Daniel.

Jane said, "I've been feeling sicky this morning."

"You ought to have eaten more breakfast," Daniel told her. "Josephine had to scrape your plate into the slops for me to give the hogs."

Sarah said, "Too many picnic victuals, I expect."

Jane protested weakly. "It all tasted so good to me when I ate it, and everybody said, 'Have some of this, you mustn't miss some of that.'"

"That's when you have to be careful," Daniel advised her sternly.

She said, "I didn't see you holding back."

"Well, I'm all right," he said reasonably. "I'm not the one feeling—'sicky,' as you call it."

"What's wrong with 'sicky' if that's the way I feel?"

"Casey could stop and let you stick your finger down your throat," Daniel suggested.

Frowning, Jane murmured, "How crude you are."

He shrugged. "You might feel better if you threw up."

"Don't keep on," Jane said. "Gentlemen don't mention things like that to ladies."

Sarah said briskly, "It's a perfectly sensible suggestion. And ladies don't complain of feeling unwell to gentlemen unless it comes upon them suddenly at an inconvenient time in an inconvenient place. Nor do they call themselves 'ladies.' If you are feeling nauseated, Casey will stop the rockaway and I'll accompany you into the bushes. Otherwise, spare us your indispositions."

"I'm sorry I spoke a word," Jane peeped pitifully. "I reckon I shouldn't expect any sympathy from my own family."

Casey, whose amusement had been growing, let out his laughter. "When a girl begins criticizing her family, it means she's thinking of joining another one." Sarah gave Casey a hard pinch. "What did you do that for?" Sarah shook her head warningly. "You *pinched* me!" he accused her. "I wouldn't be surprised if you broke the skin right through my sleeve."

Daniel had been brooding over Jane's reprimand. "Who are these fine gentlemen, I wonder, you're talking about that won't say a thing plainly?"

"Well, you could certainly take a lesson in good manners from Bonard Saxon, for one!"

"Your *cousin* Bonard," Daniel said.

She gazed at the blackberry bushes growing thick on either side of the road. "Those bushes are loaded with berries," she observed wistfully, "but they're still green."

"A pity," Sarah said drily. "The way you sound, we may lose you before they ripen."

"Everybody's so hateful," Jane said, upon which the other three began to talk cheerfully among themselves, ignoring her.

Arriving at the church, Casey slowed the horse to a walk and drove directly into the grove to find a place for the rockaway. As soon as he brought them to a halt, Jane jumped down and headed for the churchyard, Daniel following her.

Sarah, who had not confided the true substance of Annabel's last visit to Beulah Land to anyone, now did so to Casey. He was astonished. "Jane and Bonard? —Oh, he's a well-enough-looking fellow, but not for Jane."

"That's more or less what I said to Annabel, but she's working and scheming, and I'm afraid."

Casey loosened the bit from the horse's mouth. "Jane won't have him."

"You heard her on the way. He was very attentive at the picnic yesterday."

"Tell her not to be silly," Casey said, and slapped the horse's rump.

"That'll only make her think of him more."

"They're cousins, as Dan pointed out."

"That can be got around. Don't you know why Dan said it about cousins to her?"

He shook his head. She told him of her discovery at the picnic. "*Dan* and Jane?"

"Yes."

"You're moonstruck. I've never noticed a thing between them."

"I'm right. I know I am."

"Poor Dan."

"Why do you call him that?"

"He's the last man she'll think of, because he's always been there, hasn't he? Like an old brother or a young uncle."

"He doesn't think of her as sister or niece. He's in love with her."

"What a nice mess women make of things!"

"You've got to help," Sarah said.

"What can I do? I didn't even know about it until five minutes ago!"

A buggy came to a halt near the rockaway, and the two parties exchanged morning greetings. The couple from the buggy hesitated as if waiting for Sarah to join them. She smiled in friendly dismissal and began to fuss with her reticule. When they moved away, she continued, "Dan's so jealous of everyone he's bound to do and say the wrong things when he's with her. Couldn't you tell him to be careful?"

"Dan isn't like that. He couldn't calculate himself with her—or with anyone, for that matter."

"Surely you could give him a little hint? You always know exactly what to say and do."

He smiled. "Do I?"

"He continues to treat her like a child, in spite of the fact that his feeling about her has changed. And that's exactly the wrong way for him to behave. She's discovering how much boys are drawn to her, and he—" She couldn't help laughing. "*He* tells her to stick her finger down her throat!" Casey laughed with her. "And talks about feeding her breakfast to the hogs with the other slops!" They laughed harder, until Sarah suddenly controlled herself and said, "He's such a solemn, good man, and Jane's at a time she wants to be gay and giddy."

"He won't allow that."

"Nor should any man for long. But just now she wants to play the belle. I know her and I trust her. Next year she'll be as sensible as anyone, but this summer she's going to be a problem to us."

He took her hand. It was such a common gesture between them that she paid no attention, but presently she said, "What do you think you're doing?"

"You know perfectly well."

"Don't be absurd. Do remember that we're about to enter the house of the Lord."

"God is love."

"And the devil can quote Scripture. —Casey, stop! Anyone might come along."

"Do you really want me to stop?"

"You have no sense of time and place, Casey!"

He let her go slowly.

Possessed of herself again, she fluffed out the ruffles on the front of her dress which he had crushed and then touched her back hair to see that it was in place. "The idea. Let me remind you: I have grandchildren old enough to marry."

He said, "You wait till I get you home, Granny."

She took his arm and they walked through the grove to the church as sedately as any old couple with their minds on the next world rather than this. As they came to the steps, he put his lips to her ear and whispered, "You've got the prettiest titties of any woman here."

9.

Since Abraham had not come to him and was under no threat to do so until fall, Roman went to the boy. School was out anyway and he loved the long hot days of summer, so he often took himself to the fields and woods of Beulah Land to walk alone or with Sarah, sometimes with Abraham. Floyd's son was eight years old. He was skinny, although according to Josephine he ate like a Baptist preacher, and he was as shiny black as his Uncle Otis. He was not assigned jobs, but he worked harder than the paid field workers, his hands ever ready when another pair was needed to hoe or rake or pick. He was the third generation of his family at Beulah Land, and he seemed to have inherited the accumulated knowledge and love his grandfather Ezra and his father Floyd had felt for the place. This was as apparent to those who observed him as his large appetite for food and fun. Whenever laughter was heard, Abraham was likely to be there and the cause of it.

He and Sarah were devoted to each other in an easy, unsolemn way, and so he found it no punishment to walk with Roman when Roman came to see her, and gradually he began to learn a little without minding. "It's just the way," Roman said to Sarah, "you first taught me. We walked and talked, and you told me about things. So until you make him come to school, I'm going to walk and talk some learning into that boy."

But when it went on too long and he became bored, Abraham would run away. Without a word he'd take off, leaving Roman to frown and shake his head. One day in late June when this happened, Roman continued to walk, thinking his own thoughts and paying little attention to where his feet carried him. Presently he found himself in an opening in the woods and sitting there on a log reading a book was Roscoe Elk. Surprised, not considering his words. Roman said, "What are you doing on Beulah Land?"

Roscoe looked up from his book. "Have I strayed? I thought I was on Papa's land."

Roman glanced around. "To tell the truth, I don't know where we are."

Roscoe smiled. "Then it must be Papa's, for they say you know every foot of Beulah Land."

"We've not met—to say 'meet.'"

Roscoe closed his book. "We share blood."

The mask of Roman's smile denied connection. "You've surely been warned to keep away from me."

"Oh, yes. Sit down." The invitation was quietly given, and Roman made a bold gesture of straddling the log to face the young man, feeling foolish when the other smiled.

"What does your father tell you about me?"

"Nothing you couldn't guess," Roscoe said.

"That I killed my half brother Alonzo. Do you know why? And that I was Leon Kendrick's bastard, although your grandfather was legally my father."

"I heard other things about you when I lived in Philadelphia."

Roman's expression became less rigid. "I was forgetting that we share Philadelphia."

"We share many things," Roscoe said. "I have white blood too, from my mother."

"Hence the blue eyes and freckles."

"And we are the only educated Negroes in the county—if you count yourself a Negro."

"One drop of black makes you Negro in Dixie." They smiled, able to share the bitter joke of those with mixed blood. "I had two fathers, you might say, and none; for both of them hated me. I did not love them either, although I wanted to love Leon Kendrick."

"I loved my grandfather."

Roman's astonishment made him exclaim, "I can't imagine anyone's loving him!"

"Well, I did." Roscoe's tone was level but it carried a warning which Roman recognized.

"It's strange to learn that somebody you've hated can be loved by anyone. Have you come here to live?"

"I don't know."

"What is the book?" Roscoe held it so that Roman could read the title. "What do you make of Javert?"

"Mad."

The acquaintance begun, they continued to meet. The second

time was also by accident. Having walked from town one morning, Roman paused as he turned from the main road into the carriageway to Beulah Land. He removed his straw hat to wipe the sweatband and was fanning his face when he heard himself hailed from an approaching buggy. Its single occupant was Roscoe Elk, who stopped the horse when he was level with Roman. After a few generalities about the weather and each other's health, Roman said, "Come with me to see Mrs. Troy."

"I'm on my way to Papa's office in town. I've started sorting old business agreements. They go back a long way, to Grandpapa's time, in fact."

"She says you promised to pay her a visit when you came home and you haven't."

As Roscoe measured that observation, Roman climbed into the buggy. "Save me the rest of my walk. I'm burning up." Slowly, Roscoe turned the horse into the carriageway and they went along through the orchard without speaking until the road curved to reveal the avenue of oaks at the end of which stood the main house. "When I round that bend," Roman said, "I forget sometimes and expect to see the old place as it was. It was bigger and, I suppose, grander, although we didn't think of it that way then."

"I remember it," Roscoe said. "Have you seen the house Papa built on the Davis land?"

Roman laughed shortly. "I'm not likely to, am I?"

"He tried to make it look like Beulah Land."

Roman thought about it. "Your grandfather hated Beulah Land, but he wanted it. I suppose your father was trying to give it to him."

"It doesn't work," Roscoe said.

"It couldn't." They were near enough now to see Sarah sitting alone on one of the side porches. Hearing the wheels of the buggy, she turned her head and discovered them. "She's Beulah Land, and no one can make a replica of her."

Sarah did not call a greeting, but she left her chair and was waiting at the top of the side steps when they got down from the buggy and approached. "So you've finally come," she said to Roscoe, "after everyone has seen you except me. I knew you right away." Turning back to her rocker, she sat down without waiting for an answer. "Drag those chairs over, Roman." As they did so and settled themselves, Sarah let herself examine the younger man. "You're looking well," she told him. "Coming back to Georgia agrees with you."

"Well," Roscoe said, "it does and it doesn't."

"That is the sort of answer I must expect from a lawyer, I suppose, but I'll hope for better. I'm glad to see you. I remember your acting a friend to us before you went away." Seeing that he was shy of her, she turned her attention to Roman. "How is the great scholar?"

"Trying to figure out how a schoolroom not big enough to swing a cat in is going to hold twenty-five squirming first-graders, come October."

They talked about the school and its problems, with which Sarah was almost as familiar as Roman. Roscoe began to relax, and as he did so, Sarah directed an occasional observation to him until they were all part of the same conversation.

Presently Roman interrupted a story he was telling about Selma and Pauline to declare, "I shan't pretend any longer—that's gingerbread I smell, and I must have some!" The fragrance of common cake did indeed lie sweet and heavy on the morning air.

"You'll want buttermilk to go with it," Sarah said.

Roman gave her his happiest smile, which always reminded her of the way he had looked when he was a boy.

She craned her neck and raised her voice to call toward the kitchen wing, "Mabella! Come here a minute!" A barefoot Negro girl of eleven or so darted out wiping her hands on a dishrag. Sarah told her to fetch a plate of gingerbread and a pitcher of buttermilk with glasses. The girl's eyes opened wide when she saw who was sitting with her mistress, and she left them running.

Roscoe said he must go, and Sarah said he must not, beginning immediately to talk of the recent death of old Stewart Throckmorton, who had administered St. Thomas's in Highboro for so many years. She observed that she had never liked him, finding him vain and arrogant. "And the new man, Horace Quarterman, is no better," she added. "It's like having flu turn into pneumonia." Ten minutes later the three were eating second pieces of gingerbread from their hands when Nell appeared. The men rose to their feet.

"Well, well," she said, "we've certainly come a long way from Bull Run, entertaining darkies. Middle of the morning too. Lord knows what the rest of the day will bring. However, nothing surprises me after all I've seen." To Sarah she said, "Why couldn't you send Mabella to tell me you were having a tea party? I have restrained myself from going near the kitchen, though the smell of that ginger was enough to raise the appetite of a corpse." As she talked, Roman brought her rocking chair with its special quilting and pillows, and she allowed him to help her into it, although she needed no help and knew that his action was only polite mollification. She had scooped up a piece of gingerbread on her way by the table, and she now laid her cane on the floor beside her rocking chair to have a hand for the glass of buttermilk Sarah poured for her. She ate silently as Sarah gestured for the men to resume their seats, and they continued the conversation the old woman had interrupted. Nell appeared to listen, looking from one to another of the speakers, but when she had finished eating, she went fast asleep holding the empty glass between her hands on her lap.

Casey and Jane, coming in to rest from work they had shared in the kitchen garden, found the group. Roscoe now insisted that he must go. Casey shook his hand as they were introduced and told him he had heard his wife speak of him. Jane smiled and remembered aloud that she and Roman had met him at the depot, happening to be there, on the day he came home. Sarah urged Roscoe to stay, but he would go, and he did, almost as though fleeing. After watching him drive down the carriageway, they talked of him and his father a little. Nell waked and wandered away, taking with her the last piece of gingerbread from the plate Mabella had brought piled high. When Jane was ready to work again in the vegetable patch, Casey told her he was tired, and furthermore, he did not care what anybody said, "working in a garden is the most boring and backbreaking thing I can imagine."

"You enjoy the squash and tomatoes well enough when they come to the table," she reminded him.

Roman settled their nattering by offering to help Jane, and the two went off together. Alone with Casey, Sarah began to collect empty glasses, putting them on the tray to take to the kitchen. She brushed crumbs from the big plate into the yard, and sparrows came hopping to take them. When she picked up the tray and looked at Casey as she always did before leaving him in a room, she found him smiling at her. Thinking it was to tease her for the little party she had made, she said, "I never thought I'd like one of that family, but I like that boy."

"What would you say if he joined the other boys that come mooning after Jane every evening?"

"Don't talk foolishness."

He laughed.

"You can make fun of me," she said easily enough, "but I'm glad Aunt Nell isn't here to hear you."

He laughed again to tell her she had read his amusement wrong. "You with your quickness to see that Dan had fallen in love with Jane! Don't you see that young man is in love with her too?"

The tray slipped from her hands and crashed to the porch floor, breaking plate and pitcher and sending glasses rolling as she stared at him.

10.

"Now, Ben, you quit," Bessie Marsh said, slapping his hand as she buttoned her bodice.

"One more squeeze," he begged, fingering through the opening of her dress before she could protest. "So soft and warm." He had discovered that if he pressed his ardor just after being reprimanded for it, he could often win over. When she lay still under one hand, he used the other to undo the buttons she had just done. "Glory, glory," he whispered, "if you are not something fine, girl." His lips touched and kissed and briefly encircled a large brown nipple, and then he brushed her bare skin with nose and chin in a quick, caressing movement. Presently he knew she was to be his again, but he paid her the courtesy of asking, "Please, Bessie-Nessie, honey Bess, Nessie hon." He had not bothered to put on his trousers when she began to re-dress; he always waited to do that last in the hope of another session.

For a time he led, and then they surged together. They heaved and hunched. They held and held back. They hurried and slowed until at last she clutched him in a trap of arms and legs and mouth and loins that he had no wish to escape. He had already come again, but he never lost his fullness with a girl, and when she groaned with repletion, he stayed on her and in her until she disengaged and pulled away. She lay on her back looking up at the hot blue sky, her breast rising and falling ever more slowly until she was almost still.

It was a Sunday afternoon in July, and he had gone to the Marsh farm in his buggy after dinner at home with Doreen. He followed his usual form of talking to her mother and father more than he did to her, about their crops and his, only suggesting a buggy ride to Bessie as if it were a sudden thought when he had already spoken of going along home. He urged her to come as she was, and she did so, just fetching a hat against the sun. When they were out of sight of the farm, he turned the buggy into a woodland road and stopped near a branch of creek they knew, tying the reins loosely to a low limb. They strolled to the dry leafy bank they had settled upon the first time Bessie guided him here.

Her eyes were closed now, but he knew she had not gone to sleep. The air was almost sticky with the smell of resin. He watched her without touching her for a while, a smile of pleasure widening and parting his lips. When he did touch her, it was a light tracing of one thumb along the slope of a breast and down along her rib cage.

"Don't tickle," she said lazily.

"'Thy navel is like a round goblet, which wanteth not liquor: thy belly is like an heap of wheat set about with lilies—'"

"It's not nice to talk about navels to a girl, and I always connect bellies with sows."

"It's from the Bible."

"Oh."

"A verse from the Bible."

"I think that's dangerous on a Sunday with us how we are."

"I never saw anything like it," he said. "Even when you lie like that, they're round and solid as pomegranates. Not at all like—"

She turned her face to him, her eyes smiling as she pursed her lips and supplied, "Not like most girls. That what you were going to say?"

"You are just about the sweetest thing that ever happened to me, Bessie Marsh."

She laughed.

"I mean it," he protested. "Sometimes I think I verily love you. What do you say to that?"

"I think you do too," she agreed.

His tone cooled. "Do you?"

"I think you do while we're doing it."

He allowed his voice to become wistful and sulky to disguise his relief. "But you don't think I do other times."

"No, Ben, I don't. I wish you did, and maybe you would if you were as much older than me as I'm older than you. Or if I was real pretty. Or if—especially if I was a Miss Somebody that lived in town instead of Farmer Marsh's old maid daughter nobody asked to marry."

"You're pretty. I'm always telling you."

"You never thought so until after the picnic on Bonard's birthday."

He was quiet as she buttoned her dress again; nor did he try to stop her. He reached for his trousers that lay beside them and drew them over his feet and legs. "I think you're picking on me," he said.

"You used to say you liked to talk afterwards," she reminded him.

"Well, not the way you're talking." He stood and turned away from her as he adjusted his trousers. She knelt and tidied her dress with her back to him. So did they always resume polite separateness after being physically joined.

He went to the buggy and waited for her. When she came a few minutes later, she said, "What would you say, Ben, if I told you I was going to have a baby?"

"My God."

"That's what I thought you'd say."

"Are you?"

"Going to have a baby? Mm. I think so but I'm not certain."

"You, you—think it could be mine?"

"It couldn't be anybody else's."

"You told me after you stayed with me the first time I wasn't the first one."

"You knew. I didn't have to tell you." He did not deny it. "You're the one I've been with most and the only one I've been with since we started. —Oh, Ben, you look like the sun's turned over. Is that how you feel?"

"You've taken me by surprise, I can tell you."

"I don't know why," she said. "You know how they get babies. You grew up on a farm same as I did. Hasn't it ever happened before?"

"No, it hasn't!" he declared.

"Then you're plain lucky, if half what they say about you is so."

"Well, it's the first time it's happened."

"You must have thought about it."

"I thought—girls did something afterwards. I don't know what I thought."

She sighed. "Well, Ben, you better take me home now." She stepped into the buggy and sat down. He got up beside her, having already retrieved the reins.

"What must we do?" Ben asked her.

"Wait and see what happens," she said.

"Just wait?"

"I don't hear you mention getting married."

"Bessie, you know we can't get married!"

"I wish you wanted to."

"I don't see what good that'd do us," Ben said.

"Maybe not you, but it would me."

"Now look a-here, Bessie: be fair. We didn't ever talk about being in love and getting married. We just said we liked each other and felt things the same way."

"You made me no promises, Ben. I'm not saying you did, like some who do it to get what they're after. You just went ahead like the bull in the barn thinking about your own self, didn't you?" She began to cry, and when he noticed, she cried louder. He was startled and embarrassed, but watching her and listening to her, he began to feel sorry for her and put his arm around her shoulders to offer comfort. Even as he did, he thought how plain she looked, marveled that touching her had so recently given him pleasure and now was only a bother.

"I wish you wouldn't cry, Bessie," he told her. "Please stop it, Bessie! You don't want your folks wondering what happened between us, do you? You don't want to worry them?"

"No!" She wailed more loudly for a minute or two, but gradually her emotion subsided and she got out of the buggy and went to the stream to wash her face. He remained where he sat, and when she returned, she stepped up and took her place beside him again, looking tolerably composed and telling him she was all right.

Encouraged by her calm, he said, "Maybe you're wrong, Bessie. You said you weren't certain about it."

"Nor am I," she agreed. "From what I know it's so, but I have to wait another month and see then."

"Well!" he said as if that were the solution. "By that time we'll have thought of something if it turns out it is so. You surprised me, you surely did, and I haven't had time to go over it in my head; but I promise you I will, and if you say I'm responsible, then I'll do whatever I can."

She knew the answer, but she had to ask the question. "You don't want to get married, do you?"

"No." The truth strengthened him, but he did not look at her. "No, I don't."

He slapped the horse lightly with the reins and made a busier thing than was necessary of backing and turning the buggy on the narrow road-trail. He wanted to trot the horse. He wanted to strike him with the braided whip he carried for show but never used. He wanted to race the buggy all the way to the Marsh farm and leave Bessie without another word. But he kept the horse at a walk, even when they reached the main clay road, only allowing him the slightest jog after five minutes.

She had not spoken again as they left the woods, although she did turn once in the seat the way a girl will to look a sentimental farewell at a place where she's been happy. They came to the farmhouse to find the old parents waiting in chairs they had set in the front yard. Bessie's mother said, "Get down, Ben, and stay for supper. There's plenty."

Bessie jumped to the ground before it could look impolite for Ben not to get out and help her. She was suddenly like someone else. "No, Mama!" she called gaily. "Ben has to get on home and feed his stock. We didn't think how late it was till a little while ago, but just look at the sun!"

"Surely your hands can take care of the stock," the mother said.

"He likes to do it himself," Bessie told her.

"I understand that," her father said in a quiet voice that carried. "Well, Ben, come back. Come and visit again."

"Yes, sir!" Ben answered, the older man's simplicity shaming him into over-hearty response. "Sure will! Bye, Mrs. Marsh! Bye, Bessie!"

Able to show a little haste now, he flipped the reins and made the clicking lip sound that signaled "hurry" to the horse. Off they went, but not home. Wanting to talk to Bonard, Ben drove directly into Highboro.

Annabel welcomed him and pressed him to stay for supper, which she said was being put on the table. During the meal she talked of little other than her amazement at how pretty Jane was turning out, and how industrious, and how sweet and virtuous. Few things will interest a man Ben's age less than praise of his sister, and as soon as supper was over, he drew Bonard outdoors on the excuse that he wanted to smoke his pipe. When he presented his cousin with his news and problem, Bonard congratulated him.

"What must I do?" Ben implored.

"I'd say you've already done it!" Bonard laughed so hard he had to bend forward.

"Be serious, Bonnie. Has it ever happened to you?"

"A dozen times."

"What did you do?"

"Told the girl goodbye. Figure this way: if she's letting you have it, she's letting others. So how do you know who found the spring? Besides, all women are harlots, except the ones we marry—" Bonard winked at him. "And our sisters."

When he left them to go home, Annabel gave him an armful of roses she said she had just cut and asked him to stop at Beulah Land and give them to "precious Jane" with her love. He put them on the seat beside him and rode away. Although he had pretended to take cheer from Bonard's advice, he was more unhappy with himself than he had been before going to Highboro. If there was a child—by now he had decided there surely would be—it was of his begetting. But he wouldn't, couldn't marry Bessie Marsh. It occurred to him that if it came to that, his grandmother would not permit it, no matter what his Aunt Doreen might say about right and wrong and chickens coming home to roost and the Lord smiting the ungodly. His grandmother had told him not to waste himself, and he would not. He was a Davis, as well as the last man in the family with Kendrick blood. Everyone knew the Davises and Kendricks were the best people in the county. Bessie could not expect him to marry her. Indeed, she had not seemed to expect any such thing that afternoon before they parted.

But she had wanted it, his conscience reminded him. He remembered with clear, cold shame the ways in which he had played up to the girl. At the very time he smiled and coaxed and flattered, another part of him had seen her for what she was, a plain daughter of a common family, an amiable spinster six years older than he who had given herself to him (and not to him first) because she had no hope of a proposal of marriage. He had played the cavorting monkey for a Miss Nobody. She had as much as said so herself. He had known all the time what he was doing. For the first time in his life Benjamin considered his sex a humiliating burden.

11.

Lightning flirted on the horizon and thunder grumbled, but it would not rain, although everyone had said it must. The air was as sulphurous as the devil's breath, and the falling of night did nothing to temper it. One of the barn cats crept into the open. Her rough fur smelled of cottonseed and mice, but when she attained the sunflower bed that screened the privies, she stood regally, a goddess commanding Egypt to worship her. Dogs whimpered as if they saw ghosts, and chickens tucked heads under wings, but would not go to roost. A single dove mourned like a soul in purgatory, and earthworms burrowed backward. It was what Sarah called end-of-the-world weather, a time to conjure spells and rhyme riddles for tombstones. Standing under the oak trees, she knew that if her nerves tightened another fraction, she would scream or laugh, and stride about like a prima donna in Italian opera. That was why she had left her guests.

Prudence and Blair Saxon had received a visitor from Savannah, whose name was Frankie-Julia Dollard. It was not uncommon for Southern girls to be named for both father and mother and to be called by the father's name if he had wanted his firstborn to be a son. Frankie was seventeen, and her mother was a first cousin of Margaret-Ella and Ann-Elizabeth. In January when Blair and Prudence were on a business trip to Savannah, Prudence invited the girl to spend a few weeks with her in Highboro, come summer. Everyone was doing something to entertain her, and it had been natural enough for Sarah to offer the hospitality of Beulah Land.

Forgetting that she was a goddess, the cat left the sunflower bed and rubbed her head against Sarah's shoe.

"Boo." Casey stepped from behind the nearest tree.

The cat vanished as Sarah twined her arms tightly around Casey's middle, dropping her head to his chest for comfort. "Madness, now sanity." She lifted her face, and he kissed her inquiringly.

"Don't you think you should go in?" he said. "Aunt Nell can't listen to Annabel five minutes without wanting to run swords through her."

"If only she would. They'd never hang her." He touched her forehead with his as they smiled. Drawing away, she said, "All right, I'm ready. James and Maggie haven't been to see us for ages, and I mustn't neglect them, or Annabel is certain to say I'm still jealous for Rachel. I like Maggie, I really do."

"I might believe you if you didn't protest."

"James has been good for her. But thank goodness they left those horrible children at home with Tenah."

Laughing, they walked arm in arm. "Do you think she's stopped having them?"

"She's forty-two, I know for a fact. Of course that doesn't— She and James are very loving, wouldn't you say?"

"I would. Still, three young ones would seem enough for a second family."

"More than enough to infuriate Annabel and Ann-Elizabeth," Sarah replied.

When they came nearer the house, they heard singing. Four male voices were taking separate parts in Stephen Foster's "Sweetly She Sleeps, My Alice Fair."

"Jane's troubadors," Casey said.

"Not hers alone tonight."

"Jane has been the belle this summer," Casey said. "I wonder how she feels about sharing her beaux."

"It will do her good," Sarah asserted.

"What do you think of her?"

"Frankie?" Sarah considered. "She is the prettiest creature I've ever laid eyes on."

Arriving at the porch, they paused at the steps for the song to finish. "'Let her sleep, I pray, while her dreams are bright, and a smile is about her lips.'"

As the melody died, Sarah applauded and mounted the steps. Jane and Frankie sat together at the end of the porch on a wooden swing. In front of them in a half circle stood Thomas Cooper, Hobart Kenning, Frederick Shields, and John Baxter. A little farther down the porch James and Maggie Davis sat alone holding hands. Daniel had excused himself from the company after supper. Prudence and Blair were crowded by Annabel, who had come to sit between them on the wicker settee. Nell slept through the recital in her own rocking chair. She woke at the sound of hand-clapping, which had been taken up generally, and Sarah went to her side, knowing the old lady was sometimes confused when waked suddenly.

Jane smiled at the guest of honor as Frankie exclaimed that she had never heard anything so delightful and begged the young men to sing again. "Only something not sad."

"I like the sad ones," Jane said in her first challenge of the evening. "It makes Tom and Hobart look so funny."

Nevertheless, after whispering briefly, the quartet burst out with the rollicking "Glendy Burk," which soon had Frankie clapping her hands in time with them. Jane smiled as if she had never been so happy.

Catching Sarah's eye, Annabel asked in a loud whisper, "Where did Bonard and Benjamin go?" Sarah shrugged and shook her head to indicate that she did not know. "I asked Bonard *particularly* to stay close," Annabel continued. "If he won't join the singing, he could at least *be here!*"

Nell leaned forward. "I am trying to enjoy the singing," she said primly.

"You've been dead to the world ever since supper," Annabel told her.

"The Glendy Burk" finished with a shout, the boys breaking harmony at the last, and during the appreciative applause and comments that followed, Sarah suggested that the older members of the party retire indoors for tea or something stronger, as they wished. Rising instantly, Annabel led the way, saying that she had been about to suggest it, "For the mosquitoes are eating me up. I'm always their first choice."

"How flattering for you," Nell said, adding that she would stay where she was for a while, for she wanted to hear more singing and now might have the silence to better appreciate it.

The four obliged her with "Molly Dear, Goodnight" and "Uncle Ned," after which Frankie said with a sigh that she supposed the loyalty and devotion of their former slaves was a source of unending gratification to them. The observation was received quietly, broken by Nell's laughter as her hands bore down on the arms of her rocker to raise her fat little body to her feet. "Worthless coons," she said. Seeing Frankie's shock, she added, "I am going inside. I just thought of something I mean to say to Annabel."

With a bewildered look, Frankie turned to Jane, who squeezed her hand briefly. "Most of the servants work for a fixed wage, which is only the law, you know."

"I was told that those belonging to you-all stayed."

"Some did," Jane agreed, "but they are paid now in money and not simply their keep."

Frankie smiled brilliantly. "I'm certain they'd stay even if you paid them nothing!"

No one answered until Hobart Kenning said, "Ah, there's nothing now to equal the old-timey days."

"With the darkies singing in the fields?" Frankie suggested.

Jane answered temperately. "Actually, Stephen Foster was a Yankee and didn't know very much about the South."

"Oh, I think he knows us better than we know ourselves. I just love his songs."

"So do I," Jane agreed, willing to let it go at that.

"So do we all," John Baxter added as a bolstering note.

Frankie looked around the circle of faces, her eyes coming back to Jane. "I believe you were trying to disillusion me," she said, archly.

"None of us would want to do that, Miss Frankie!" Thomas Cooper's voice vibrated with sincerity.

The other young men offered their assurances, and Jane looked at her lap.

"Well," Frankie said doubtingly and then smiled to indicate that her trust in them was restored.

"Another song?" Jane suggested.

"Something *cheerful*," Frankie demanded.

"Camptown Races?" Frederick Shields proposed.

Frankie clapped her hands. "It's my very favorite!"

They embarked immediately on the singing of the song, but after it apparently decided to make amends to Jane, for the next two songs were sad ones. Their third plaint was "Gentle Annie," but they had come only to the beginning of the chorus, "Shall we never more behold thee," when the air was rent by a series of quick explosions. Frankie first shrieked and then fainted. Although startled and trembling herself, Jane had enough presence of mind to attend her guest. The four young men ran in four directions into the darkness challenging whoever was there. Sarah and Casey appeared, and Casey gathered the fair Frankie into his arms and carried her into the house so that she might be revived and consoled in lamplight. Nell had exclaimed, "Yankees!" and grabbed her cane, and was waving it over her head as she joined the confusion on the porch. Annabel demanded repeatedly to be told what had happened. Blair and Prudence stood about in the way, contributing nothing beyond anxious looks, while James and Maggie sensibly remained in the living room.

Very soon the plot was revealed, when Bonard and Benjamin came out of the dark where they had been discovered by John Baxter and merrily admitted that they were the creators of the clamor. They were astonished that their setting off fireworks did not meet with approval and admiration. They had, they explained, waited patiently for the older folk to go indoors and set the crackers alight only when the singers embarked on a selection of the most tedious and lugubrious of ballads. Annabel marched directly to her son and slapped him, then burst into a fit of hysterical weeping. When Sarah offered to help her, she fought her off as if Sarah were one of the conspirators.

Everyone presently found himself inside making a protective frame around the sofa where the shocked girl lay recovering. Her eyes were open, but she did not appear to recognize any of her audience. Prudence and Jane knelt beside her murmuring reassurances and waving sal volatile. It was only when Nell recommended the burning of feathers as the surest means of revival that the girl quavered, "Am I alive?" There was a collective sigh of relief. All manner of comfort was then offered, and Sarah tendered regret for the prank. Annabel led Bonard and Benjamin to the sofa, where both of them, by now considerably abashed, made their own apologies. The four troubadours begged to be commanded. When Frankie looked up and saw them, she braved a smile and whispered, "You are all so kind to me," which brought tears to the eyes of the young men, although the women managed to remain tolerably composed.

For a quarter hour voices were as hushed as those in a room of death. Then Annabel decided they were all to go home and proceeded to organize the exodus until she was rather sharply relieved of her authority by Sarah.

Frankie was promised the most comfortable transportation available, which was in Annabel's carriage. She vowed that she loved them all for being so patient and good, and even achieved a languid wave of the hand as the carriage rolled away. Soberly, the others then made their own departures, and Josephine helped Nell to bed.

Benjamin remained with Sarah and Jane when even Casey had gone to his room. He was genuinely contrite, and it became clear that the fireworks and the idea of using them had been supplied by Bonard. Benjamin was his accomplice, but only after he had been persuaded that everyone would be amused. After again apologizing at the door as he left, he said, "I hate myself, I truly do, for doing anything to agitate that dear, beautiful girl. Grandma, don't you think she is the prettiest thing you ever saw?" Sarah agreed that she was abundantly favored, and Benjamin departed, shaking his head over his wickedness and hoping Miss Frankie would not despise him but give him a chance to atone for his crude behavior.

As soon as they were alone Jane said, "What a horrid creature!"

Sarah said mildly, "I do think he's sorry."

"I mean Frankie, not Ben. I could kiss Bonard for thinking of the fireworks."

12.

The rain that would not come on the evening of Sarah's supper party arrived early next morning. Despite its sultry prologue, it began softly and proceeded by fits and starts for an hour; but by daybreak there was a steady downpouring, enough to soak the corn and swell the kernels of its ripened ears, yet not so heavy as to beat down the cotton. There followed a gentling but no true letup, and those who had to go outdoors got wet. By midmorning the earth had absorbed all that it readily could, and water collected in the gutters between rows of planting. Although it had just turned August, the cool damp smells penetrated barn and house with a suggestion of autumn.

In the kitchen Josphine said aloud, but to herself rather than Mabella, "I know what I feel like. Ham." Unless Sarah gave her orders, Josephine cooked what she pleased. She took a cloth and went into the storeroom next to the kitchen where the last whole ham hung from a rafter. After wiping mold away with the cloth, she held her nose to the cured meat and sniffed appreciatively. "Fried ham and roast'n' ears. Tomatoes sliced thick and sprinkled with pepper. What else? Boil some potatoes, somebody'll eat them. Boil some string beans with a piece of fat. Squashes, three, four. One of my big, deep peach pies." She raised her voice. "Mabella! Come here, gal." The girl came. "I want you to take something and go gather me some peaches. Enough for all of us a pie, some good and ripe and some not so, you hear me?"

"Go out in this rain?" the girl wailed.

"Black don't wash off." Josephine lifted the big ham from its hook. "Now move your tail before I put a broom to it."

By eleven o'clock the rain had almost stopped, and Sarah and Jane carried their sewing from Sarah's office to the porch. Nell arrived after a visit to the kitchen to recite a list of the things Josephine was cooking, the fragrance of which had particularly enticed her that wet morning. When they heard a buggy coming up the carriageway, Nell broke off her inventory and went indoors, declaring that she could not tolerate company so soon again.

Prudence and Frankie were the visitors, the latter having so far recovered from her nervous indisposition that nothing, Prudence said, would do but that they come directly and thank their hostesses of the evening before. Sarah and Jane protested that they should not have exposed themselves to the weather and the hazard of slippery clay roads. Frankie vowed that she would have been very ill indeed not to hasten expression of her gratitude for the special notice taken of her and the hope that they should henceforth consider her home theirs when occasion required their journeying to Savannah.

To Sarah she said that she had never seen a place as beautiful as Beulah Land. She begged to be allowed on the first fine day to walk over its entire acreage: pastures, fields, and woods. To Jane she said that she would be eternally obliged if Jane were kind enough to let her draw a pattern of the muslin frock she had worn last night, for she herself had nothing half so sweet. Perhaps Jane would not mind her wearing a copy of the dress in Savannah if she promised never to put it on in Highboro. Jane assured her that she might copy the dress and wear it anywhere she pleased. Then as if Jane and Sarah were not present, Frankie turned to Prudence and proclaimed her admiration for the way Jane arranged her hair, the grace of her walk, the lilt of her voice, the excellence of her figure, the perfection of her face.

Later, Jane reported to Sarah that she had never felt so absurd or witnessed such flaming hypocrisy, but at the time she smiled, and Sarah invited them to stay to noon dinner.

—No, they mustn't!

Sarah would hear no refusal, although she knew Nell would be displeased.

The visit continued with Frankie's questioning her companions about the young men who had been guests last night. She must be told their ages, background, family circumstance, and attachments. They quickly exhausted all the details they were willing to reveal about Benjamin. ("How queer you look, dear Jane, to know that a friend finds your brother interesting! Now admit that you have never thought of him except as a brother!") Frankie drew from them particulars concerning John Baxter, Hobart Kenning, Thomas Cooper, and Frederick Shields.

"And what," she then said, "of the mysterious other gentleman? A trifle older than these, but unusually handsome, to my mind."

Jane looked at her blankly. "Can you mean Mr. Troy? He is certainly handsome, but—"

"I believe," Sarah said quietly, "Miss Dollard is referring to Mr. Todd."

Frankie nodded eagerly. "He is your overseer, is he not?"

"He is our cousin," Jane said shortly, and for the first time Sarah entertained a hope for Daniel.

"He is, in fact, our overseer too," Sarah said agreeably, "although here we don't much think about titles and divisions of authority."

"Beulah Land is to be his home forever?" Frankie inquired.

"It has been since the war," Sarah said, "and I am glad to observe that he no longer speaks of leaving us."

"Who could want to? You are all so close and contented," Frankie said with a flattering sigh. "Mr. Benjamin Davis with his own farm just next to you."

Sarah fixed her eyes on the needlework on her lap. It was a piece of crochet to go under a candlestick. She did not enjoy any kind of sewing, but she must always be busy and she understood its uses, not the least of which was social. Shading her voice to vagueness, she said as if she hardly considered the words, "Benjamin will one day have all of Beulah Land too." She did not need to lift her eyes from the crochet hook to register Frankie's alertness at this information.

"You will live to be a hundred, Auntie Sarah," Prudence promised her.

"I hope so, Pru dear," Sarah replied, but sighed as if she feared she would not. She did not like Prudence, suspecting slyness and deceit in her calculations, even as Annabel had suspected her mother. She praised Prudence to Annabel merely to annoy her. Nor did Sarah like being called "Auntie Sarah," which had for long been Annabel's way of addressing her. Therefore, she had taken to calling Prudence "Pru dear" when they were together in a small group to disguise her lack of regard.

"Mister Benjamin will be an important man," Frankie said.

"To us he is already important," Sarah said in what was almost a parody of the real pride she felt in her grandson. When Jane giggled, Sarah looked at her sternly before fixing a smile on Pru-

dence. "Now Blair," she said, "may be said to be *really* important,
for he will come into control of the bank one day."

"Yes!" said Frankie.

"We don't, of course, anticipate any such thing," Prudence said
modestly.

Sarah amused herself by imagining Annabel's face if she could
have heard them. "Not in this century, perhaps," she said. She
paused to allow them to stretch their minds into the future.
"Only consider," she said. "When I am Aunt Nell's present age, it
will be 1901! Yet I was born only a dozen years after General
Washington died."

"How quickly time passes," Prudence observed. "I sometimes
think of all history as a very personal thing."

"What a profound insight," Sarah said, slowly enough for any
other than Jane to believe her serious. To turn the mood and to
check the smile she saw in Jane's eyes, she said to Frankie, "Are
you homesick for Savannah?"

"Oh, no ma'am, for I love it here!"

"My sister and I grew up there, but I expect that everyone we
knew is buried and decayed."

Frankie laughed to comfort her. "Surely not, ma'am!" She then
proceeded to tell them about the important people she and her
family were on terms of intimacy with in Savannah.

By late afternoon when she and Prudence left Beulah Land,
Frankie claimed Jane as her dearest friend and vowed to deserve
her love. As they waved goodbye to the departing buggy, Jane
said to Sarah, "That girl is a fool."

"You will make a mistake," Sarah answered, "if you treat her
like one."

"She asked everything about everyone but Bonard. Can she
know no better? I suppose she will not forgive Bonard for last
night, and that only makes me think the better of him."

In this, however, she misjudged Frankie, who had avoided
mention of Bonard from no feeling of rancor but because Prudence had warned her that "Aunt Annabel" was determined to
effect marriage between him and Jane. She knew that if she
wanted Jane's support, she must not be tempted in that quarter.

Within a week, so potent is the power of a few words repeated
a few times, it was everywhere acknowledged that the two most
superior young ladies in town were specially dear to each other.
When they now met, as they often did, for parties beget parties

and the sun seldom set without an entertainment's being got up for the pretty visitor, Frankie must be beside Jane with her arm about Jane's waist. She must touch her hair, her cheek, and compliment her on a dress, a ribbon, sometimes no more than the stitching of a handkerchief. Jane could not refuse these attentions without rudeness; she was aware that any sign of coolness on her side would be taken for jealousy by observers.

Although August was one of the busiest months of the year for the county, the young people had the energy and found the time to dance and flirt part of each night after each day's work. Little parties evolved naturally. Refreshments need be no more elaborate than those at hand: watermelon, peaches and cream, cake and tea. Sarah listened every morning to Jane's account of the night before, and no day went by without her seeing her grandson. Their main concern was the picking and ginning of cotton, but it was plain to Sarah that Benjamin's mind was also full of Miss Frankie-Julia Dollard. He was so far along in his infatuation he did not notice that Sarah neither smiled nor had anything to add to his praise. She was begged to agree that Frankie was the prettiest girl she had ever seen, and in that she obliged him, reflecting that innocence may give beauty to a young girl and character may provide it for an older woman, but for those Frankie's age, prettiness suffices; there are only degrees in its perfection. Sarah allowed Frankie's to be triumphant.

Her manner in company was amiable, but no one could repeat anything she said, only marvel on the appearance she made. Much and nothing is spoken in the course of dancing, and although every young man in the county considered her a prize, none could know much about her qualities beyond the physical. She was said to enjoy music and to be artistically inclined, but only in the vague way such things were always said. There was not much grumbling or backbiting among girls her age. They were generous and guileless in their acceptance of her popularity. They were even grateful to her for providing a reason for the constant get-togethers.

It was soon apparent that Benjamin Davis was the front runner among those who competed for her favor. He was certainly the boldest. However unsure he felt, he had learned as a boy working with men not to show it, developing as a result a kind of poise some considered arrogance. He would one day be master of Beulah Land, and to be so was still conceded, in spite of hard times, a position of power and distinction second to none in the county. He was robustly good-looking, possessing a strong, tall body. His countenance was open, with features irregular enough to make his face interesting. A further asset he was said to possess was the friendship between his sister and Miss Dollard. However, Benjamin had still never been alone with Frankie, and the difference between two people alone together and with others is almost as remarkable as the difference between one and two.

Frankie had not accomplished her ambition of walking over all the acres of Beulah Land, but she had learned from Prudence how many there were, and she teased Jane into occasional excursions into Ben's fields. He was too diligent a farmer to abandon his work, but he would leave a row and idle in the shade with them for as long as it took his sweat to dry. As if that were his signal, he would then urge them to go to his house and visit with his Aunt Doreen while he returned to the job they had interrupted so charmingly.

The power of suggestion had begun to work in another quarter. Having opened her mind to the possibility of admiring her cousin, Jane now began to enjoy his courtship, and there was no interpreting his little gifts and special attentions any other way. No longer queen bee, she was the more sensitive to the pleasures of being favored. They danced well together; they looked well together. They engaged in a comical kind of talk they assumed they had invented, unaware that lovers have done the same since language began. Although the young may boast of their freedom from prejudice about position and advantage, they are acutely conscious of it. Not least were Jane and Bonard. Bonard's two grandfathers were the founder of the town's bank and the owner of what had been a great plantation. Jane was Miss Davis of Beulah Land whose brother would inherit that plantation and whose father owned the lucrative sawmill. The intimacy encouraged itself, needing Annabel's nudges no longer.

In a town as small as Highboro, there was no particular strictness about chaperons; the entire community was guardian to its young. Manners were free and trust given more easily than sometimes deserved. There was no questioning the propriety of a foursome that had quickly formed during the month of Frankie's stay with the Saxons. Jane and Bonard in his buggy, Frankie and Benjamin in his, but the four always together, they went on out-

ings of their own as well as to parties. One such occurred on a
Sunday afternoon when the junior Blair Saxons and their guest
were invited after church services to return to Ben's farm along
with Bonard and Jane. After dinner, while the others took chairs
into the yard and set them under the chinaberry trees to catch
the breeze, the two courting couples decided to sally forth to
Ben's Glade.

Frankie and Benjamin walked ahead. Although often together,
Frankie and Bonard never had much to exchange, seeming not
to have recovered from the episode of the firecrackers. Considering the general ease of manners, they even appeared to be over-
formal in the way they spoke and behaved to each other. Observing this, Jane was not displeased.

Frankie had been promised that she would see something special, but she considered this merely a ploy for the foursome to
get away from the others. When they came to the Glade, Jane
led Bonard directly to the brook, where they seated themselves
on the rocks. Frankie skipped eagerly about making exclamations, but she had nothing to say beyond words she used to
describe everything from a kitten to a carpet. It was "too sweet
for words." She had never seen "anything so dear." Then she
looked around in an inquiring way, as if now she was ready to
be shown the special thing she had been brought to see. When
nothing was offered, she asked what Benjamin intended to do
with the Glade.

Benjamin, who considered that it was already what he wanted
it to be, was surprised into answering that he hadn't yet made up
his mind and perhaps she'd suggest something to him. She observed that it didn't look good for much. It was so out of the
way, and who would want to climb the hill to reach it more than
once? Looking at it through her eyes, Benjamin began to feel an
embarrassed dissatisfaction, but it was with himself rather than
the girl whose opinion he had just heard. It wasn't anything after
all, he decided. He had known it for so long, had as a boy valued
it so greenly, he expected others to see in it things that had been
there only for him. In truth it was only a collection of rocks and
trees with a stream running through it; there was nothing to
brag about in all of that.

Noting his uncertainty, she was encouraged to plunge on. "I
shall have to put my mind to it before deciding what you are to
make of it. Let me see." She folded her arms and frowned to sim-

ulate thought. "I declare it's downright *spooky*. Maybe you could start a little cemetery." She laughed. "They're often on hills in the country, because hills are good for nothing but graveyards. Look at this." She stooped to pick a feather from the grass. "Anywhere else I'd take it for a bird's, but my first thought up here is that it's fallen loose from an angel's wing!"

Overhearing, Jane said, "You are fanciful, but don't imagine Benjamin will follow your advice. It means too much to him for that. No one is allowed to come here without his permission."

"Oh?" Deciding that if she had made a miscalculation she could use it coquettishly, she continued, "Well, he can just keep it all to himself, because it gives me the shivers and quivers. Ghosts, that's what I feel about this place."

Hastily, Benjamin found and played his part. "Miss Frankie, you have shown it to me in a new light. I do believe you're right." He laughed and pretended the place meant nothing to him.

Smiling, she said, "Maybe you could get a herd of goats. They'd surely find it suitable. They like rocks, don't they?"

"That's the very thing," Benjamin agreed.

Frankie protested that he must not forsake it on her account. He said there could be no better reason. She wondered if it might not strike her differently another day. "No place looks like itself on Sunday except the inside of a church." As the two vied to accommodate each other, Bonard winked solemnly at Jane.

13.

Annabel Saxon congratulated herself on the way life was going. The bank would weather the money panic, she had been assured by her husband and elder son—"my two Blairs," she called them when she found occasion to be pleased with them. Prudence had recently discovered that she was pregnant, and Annabel looked forward to many months of bullying her as she watched her become gross and afraid. She had already told her that she must send Miss Dollard back to Savannah, for it was unsuitable that an unmarried girl not her close relative be her companion during such a time. The match she was hatching between Bonard and Jane Davis gave every sign of progressing satisfactorily. She enjoyed going to church even in the stifling heat of September for the pleasure of smiling at Sarah and knowing that Sarah understood why she smiled. How good it was to best "Auntie Sarah!" She reckoned her to be unhappy on two scores. Not only had she failed to discourage Jane's attachment to Bonard, but she was now plainly worried about the likelihood of Benjamin's wanting to marry Frankie Dollard, the pretty nobody.

Had she been anyone, she'd have felt no need to attach herself so mosslike to dull Prudence; nor should she have turned her long summer visit into what was obviously a hunt for a husband. She could have no people of consequence or they would not allow her to take such a protracted leave from them and her home prospects.

There was a time Annabel had vowed to do her best for Benjamin in the way of finding him a proper wife, but when she tried to set his attention on Priscilla Oglethorpe, he had laughingly and firmly refused to listen. Miss Oglethorpe might be no beauty, but she was a modest and steady creature such as Annabel might have considered as wife for a third son, had she one. Very well; let Benjamin and his grandmother find the way out of their rabbit trap. They would get no further help from her. Frankie Dollard was no better than they deserved. Her beauty was praised to the skies, and might continue to be for another year, and the legend of it a few years longer. But Annabel knew all about that kind of fame. Had she not been the great beauty of her generation? She went into the dining room and gazed at the portrait Casey Troy had painted of her when she was hardly more than a girl. She had got beyond feeling mocked when looking upon her earlier face and now took courage and nourishment from it. The only person ever to ask the identity of the portrait was that same Miss Dollard!—which suggested impertinence or stupidity. In another year she would move the likeness of her father-in-law from its prominence over the drawing room mantel and put her own in its stead. She had been far prettier than Frankie Dollard, and she would like to tell her so. Let her marry Benjamin if she could. She would have to work fast, for her departure was now set three days hence. Business matters to do with the bank and the sawmill required her sons being sent to

Savannah, and they were to be her escorts—another sign that her family cared nothing about her or they should have dispatched a servant to fetch her, or an old aunt at the very least. Beyond prettiness Annabel could see nothing in Miss Dollard.

Annabel thought perhaps to stir herself on behalf of Daniel Todd. He was not bad-looking in an all-weather farmer sort of way, and his shyness and mystery made him interesting to the girls of the county, but he had never appeared to be interested in them. Still, there would be an amusing game in marrying him away from Beulah Land, because Sarah so obviously depended upon him and wanted him to remain her tame-hawk overseer.

Annabel mistook Daniel Todd's reticence for lack of will. Anyone who did not speak up for himself lacked spirit, she surmised; and she was always surprised when she discovered herself to be wrong. She would have been astonished to learn the ideas Daniel had about his future; for without knowing how he was to get her, he was determined to have Jane Davis for his wife. When, near the end of the war, he had come to Beulah Land half starved and with nothing to hope, Sarah Kendrick had taken him in and made him well. In the process he had come to love her as well as Beulah Land. Knowing he could not and should not aspire to her, he had nevertheless yearned for her. He loved her still, but now he yearned for Jane. Once he admitted the way he felt about Jane, he allowed himself no doubts. She must be his. She might enjoy a season of being a belle and having the county boys sing to her, but that would end; and when it did, he would become her husband. She would see that Bonard Saxon was not good enough for her, and if she did not, he would tell her so. Meantime, he gave himself to the hard work Beulah Land provided.

He had seen little of Jane during the summer months. Josephine gave him early breakfast two hours before Sarah and Nell and Jane had theirs, and theirs was at seven o'clock. He ate his noon dinner from a basket Abraham brought to him wherever he was working. Full of devilment as he was, Abraham took no one seriously except Daniel, and he loved Daniel like a father. Floyd, his own father, and Daniel had not been friends, but Daniel had learned a vast deal about Beulah Land from Floyd. Instinct told Abraham this, and he wanted to cull his father's knowledge from Daniel. But in addition to that, he liked the quiet, serious white man who never laughed at him but who sometimes touched him with awkward kindness when they talked, as if in this late way he was trying to make amends for undervaluing Floyd. Whatever feelings against Negroes Daniel had brought to Beulah Land had been fragmented. Some of his prejudice remained, transmuted into the other thing Southerners felt about Negroes and that no true name could be put to because it was such a compound of knowledge and ignorance, acceptance and fear. But Abraham was nothing to do with that. Daniel simply loved the boy as the boy loved him, and only Sarah understood it.

By the middle of September Benjamin's harvesting was all but done. There was some corn left to pull and some scattered cotton to pick, but Otis needed no assistance at the gin, and Benjamin brought his hired men daily to help finish the harvest at Beulah Land. Then there would be nothing to do but to cut and grind the sugarcane and make the winter's syrup.

At the end of a workday he and Daniel always, even when it was raining, refreshed themselves by bathing in the creek, after which Benjamin usually returned to his farm to take his supper with Doreen. Tonight, however, they would go together to the big house at Beulah Land. They had carried their best clothes with them to the creek, which would, they trusted, transform them from field hands into something like gentlemen when they had washed themselves. The occasion was a supper party for Miss Dollard to mark her leaving.

As they waded heavy-stepping and clean from the creek, Benjamin said, "Dan, how'd you like to marry Bessie Marsh for me?"

Daniel's eyes cut quickly to Benjamin's face and away again. His words had been frivolous but not their tone. "I don't think I would, Ben." Having nothing with which to dry their bodies, they shook themselves as dogs will emerging from water, and then walked back and forth, loosely swinging arms and legs to let the warm air dry them. "Does she need marrying?"

"People will say so."

"Your doing?"

"Yes."

"When did it happen?"

"Lord knows," Benjamin said. "The first time was after Bonard's birthday picnic in my Glade."

"I remember that well enough," Daniel said grimly.

"I was with her some during the month after."

"You're sure she's pregnant?" Shy in the ordinary ways of talking about sexual matters, Daniel had a farmer's matter-of-factness when conception had occurred, it becoming then simply a question of breeding.

"She told me this morning." Benjamin groaned, and slapped the trunk of a tree. "Ever since I heard she was leaving, I've been making up my mind to ask Miss Frankie to marry me. Last night before I went to sleep I made it up good and proper. This morning first thing I rode out to the Marsh place and asked Bessie how we stood."

"You didn't know before?"

"She told me back in July she thought so; but then I didn't see her for a while. It's not the kind of thing you're in a hurry to confirm. And she didn't come or send after me to tell me. It was during then I got to know Miss Frankie. I reckon you could say I wanted to forget about Bessie."

"Anyhow, you did."

They began to dress slowly, as if clothes were strange gear they must study how to use.

"The more I thought about Miss Frankie, the less I thought about Bessie. But this morning when I knew what I was going to do tonight, I decided I'd better clear up the other first." Daniel nodded. "Bessie made no bones about it. There's nothing sly or hateful about Bessie. I reckon I wasn't altogether joking while ago when I asked if you wanted to marry her for me." Benjamin smiled, deciding to tease his friend a little. "You'll want to get yourself a wife one day, and Bessie's better than a lot of girls I could name. And there's the advantage of she's already got a youngun started and you wouldn't have to bother. It ought to be a real good baby the way we worked at it." He waited for Daniel to smile, knowing he would not. "So I asked her this morning and she told me. She'd already let her mama and daddy know; and when they claimed to be brokenhearted, she said they were just to hush up, for she was a grown woman, and it was her baby, and she was going to have it."

"Do they know whose it is?" Daniel asked.

"Good idea, I expect, but she admitted to them she'd been with several. She didn't want to say which of us until she asked me."

Carefully, Daniel said, "Was there any talk about you and her getting married?"

"She would if I offered, but I don't see how I can do that. I told her so. She understood it. It's not like either one of us said we loved the other. We were just doing it together because we liked doing it." That was the nearest Daniel came to being shocked. He understood well enough what Benjamin was saying, and he knew from observation how undiscriminating the urge to mate can be, but he did not accept it in terms of human behavior.

"So," Daniel said after a moment, "it looks to me like you're in a situation." His voice was thoughtful, innocent of irony.

"That's the way I see it," Benjamin said. "Well, Daniel, what must I do?"

"Let me see," Daniel said slowly. "You've got one girl freshened and you're figuring to ask another one to marry you."

"That's it."

"Well." Dressed but still barefoot, Daniel sat on a log and began to put on stockings and shoes. "If I were you and I'm not, I'd go straight in and have a talk with the Lady." In private Daniel called her "Sarah," in company "Miss Sarah," and when he mentioned her to others sometimes designated her "the Lady."

Beside him on the log, Benjamin worked his feet into his shoes. He offered no demur to Daniel's suggestion. It was as if he had known it was the course he must take and only needed confirmation. "I dread it."

"I don't wonder," Daniel said drily.

14.

It was, Sarah thought, no different from a thousand and one other nights at Beulah Land, except that it was altogether different, since its outcome might change their lives forever. There had been abundant talk and some laughter as they ate the good supper Josephine had prepared and served. Now they rested on the long, wide porch, their chairs strung out so that there were several conversations instead of one, which made it easy for Benjamin to slip away with Miss Dollard for a stroll of the grounds, only Sarah noting their departure.

Annabel sat once again on the settee between her son and Prudence. She was telling them of the difficulties she had endured bringing both Blair and Bonard into the world, and she spoke as if she still nurtured a strong grievance. It was not the first time Sarah had observed that a woman hitherto reticent with a son on the functions of the sexes will, once he has begot a child, treat him to the most intimate details she knows or imagines about herself and other women.

Casey and Nell had drawn their rockers together, and he must have been whispering a silly story to her—he knew so many—for the old lady interrupted him now by gripping his arm to make him stop until she finished laughing. Farther down the porch sat Jane and Bonard and Daniel. When Bonard led Jane away from the others, Daniel accompanied them as if ignorant of Bonard's design. Good for Daniel, Sarah thought. She was standing alone, wanting to feel as much air and silence around her as possible. Leaning on a pillar, she looked into the twilight. Lightning bugs hovered and darted, dimming their fire only to let it glow again a moment later.

Sarah could still think of nothing but the revelations Benjamin had made in her office before the guests arrived. She wondered how she had attended to anyone since. She had not sorted it yet; her mind would jump from one point to another. Bessie Marsh— she knew the girl, of course, but had never thought about her— seemed to be taking a sensible attitude, making her decisions, assuming her responsibilities without hypocrisy or hysteria. And that Bessie Marsh whose features she found it difficult to assemble in her mind was going to bear a child, *her* first great-grandchild! What a thought. It quite dwarfed any present threat of Miss Dollard's entering the family as Mrs. Benjamin Davis. For all that she had followed day by day the course of Benjamin's involvement with the girl, she could hardly accept that he might at this moment be proposing marriage to her and that five minutes from now they would come to her together to tell her so. —Why, he did not know her. And what was there to know? For all her malice, Annabel was right in her aside before supper: behind the pretty face there was nothing but wet cotton.

She had listened to her grandson without trying to make it easy or hard for him, and when he had done, she had thanked him formally for confiding in her. It was the first formal moment they had shared. As she grew older, Sarah began to see the need for such. The only directive she allowed herself to make was that if he proposed marriage to Miss Dollard and she accepted him, he must then, in honor, tell her about Bessie Marsh and his intentions toward his unborn child. "Grandma," he had said at the last, "you can say I'm crazy. I know I ought to be miserable about it; but, Grandma, I'm going to be a father." She had kissed him then, and Jane had knocked at the office door to say she saw the Saxon carriage in the distance.

Sarah did not go with Benjamin and Jane to the front of the house; she wanted a moment to herself. She had never felt closer to Benjamin, as she remembered the one time in her life she had conceived. She had not been allowed to bear the child because it was not her husband's. It could only have been the result of the rape by Alonzo Elk or her one infidelity that preceded it—with Casey Troy. She had never in later years told Casey about it, and the only two people who had certain knowledge at the time, the doctor and Felix Kendrick, were dead. She recalled her bitterness on agreeing to abortion. And she relived the joy she had known, so briefly, when she first discovered that she had conceived. Yes, she understood Benjamin.

Nor was that all of it. Benjamin had worshipped his father when he was a boy, but their closeness had come to a sudden end. It was when James decided to sell Oaks plantation to Junior Elk. She put their subsequent estrangement to that, but she had also wondered if it could be the result of his somehow discovering that Adam and not James Davis was his true father. If he knew, it had made him feel fatherless, and no wonder that he found himself peculiarly sensitive to learning that he was to be a father.

Although she was waiting, not knowing for what, she was not prepared for the burst of weeping that suddenly made all of them on the porch go still. It had not the sound of grief, but was like the crying of a child who falls and hurts himself: alarmed and demanding. It stopped before anyone could move from his place, and Benjamin appeared almost immediately to ask his grandmother to come with him. Annabel and Prudence set up a racket in the guise of concern, insisting that they be told what had happened to "poor Frankie-Julia" and where she was. Ordinarily deferential with all females, Benjamin spoke in the voice he used only to command workers in his fields. "No one is to come but Grandma!" Sarah hardly heard the chittering of outrage and speculation behind her as she hurried after Benjamin to the side porch and into her office. "It seemed the best place to bring her," he explained, closing the door behind them.

Eyes closed, Frankie reclined on an old chaise longue, the only feminine piece of furniture the office boasted, and Sarah's first thought was that she had screamed and fainted again just as she had done with the fireworks on the night of her first supper at Beulah Land. But hearing the door close, Frankie opened her eyes and raised herself to a sitting position, placing her feet on the floor. "I asked Benjamin to bring you, Mrs. Troy." Although emotional, her tone was firm and controlled.

"Are you all right?" Sarah asked. "Can I get you anything? I keep brandy in here. Perhaps a small glass—"

"Thank you. I have collected myself, I hope."

Benjamin murmured sympathetically until the look in her eyes silenced him. He remained standing as Sarah drew a chair near the chaise and sat down. The face was the same, but the manner was not that of the young woman she had seen before; there was no smile, no attempt at ingratiation. Whatever her feelings, she had indeed composed herself. When Sarah sat, Frankie said, "Benjamin has made me an offer of marriage, Mrs. Troy." She said it deliberately, as if it was a fact she wanted to establish. Sarah nodded once. "May I believe it was with your knowledge and approval?"

Sarah answered mildly, "My grandson does not need my permission to marry, Miss Dollard, although he told me earlier this evening that he was going to ask you."

Frankie weighed the reply. "I accepted him—subject, of course, to the approval of my mother and father, which I cannot think they will withhold when they know your family as I have come to know it. Benjamin has for some time appeared open in his regard. This could only make me happy, for I had begun to recognize certain evidences of tenderness in my own heart toward him. I accepted. And then he, he has just now—" she found handkerchief and pressed it to her lips.

"Miss Dollard, if it will make it easier, let me say that Benjamin has told me about Miss Marsh."

"I was distressed."

"Naturally," Sarah said. "I am sorry."

"Beloved—" Benjamin began.

"No, Benjamin," Frankie said. She seemed on the verge of losing her composure when she bit her lip and continued with moderate calm. "I found myself ashamed of the feelings I had been encouraged to confess."

"My love!"

"I cannot say that I understand a gentleman's involving himself in such a situation with a common farm girl."

"Miss Marsh's people are respectable," Sarah said.

"Apparently Miss Marsh, as you call her, is not. I do not call her Miss Marsh. I do not excuse her. She is lost. Nor do I condone Benjamin's behavior as you seem to. However—"

"One does not condone a fact, Miss Dollard. One recognizes it."

"However, I am not a child, and Benjamin pleaded that what had happened was already finished before we met. There is some justice in his reasoning, but I cannot, I repeat, *condone* his behavior. What I do not understand, what I cannot accept—indeed what made me cry out while ago—is Benjamin's willingness to take the blame."

"Blame, Miss Dollard?" Sarah spoke as carefully as if she were in a court of law.

"Yes. That is why I sent for you. Surely you will tell Benjamin he must deny that he is the father of any child."

"I don't see how I can do that," Sarah said slowly. "I am sympathetic to the distress you feel, but my grandson knows better than you or I whether he is the father."

"He tells me she has been with others."

"Not during the time she was with me," Benjamin said.

"How do you know?"

"She said so."

"Do you believe her?"

"She wouldn't lie," Benjamin said.

"That is exactly what I think she has done and will continue to do."

"Why would she?"

"Because it's better to claim you as the father than some farm hand she might persuade to marry her. You have been gullible, Benjamin."

Gradually, it was coming to Sarah that here perhaps was salvation.

"She prefers a bastard acknowledged by the master of Beulah Land as his to legitimacy with a poor man. She will expect you to give her money and favors, not only for the child, but for her father and mother and, who knows, even the poor piece of earth she will eventually coax into marrying her. Once you begin, you are in it forever."

"Bessie isn't like that," Benjamin objected.

Frankie looked at him coolly before turning to Sarah. "Perhaps you will tell him, Mrs. Troy, that a woman who puts no value on her virtue is unlikely to choke on a lie, especially one that assures her future. She would think it a small price." Sarah lowered her eyes, and Frankie took the gesture for agreement. Although she had called upon Sarah, she plainly needed no one to put her case. "One day when Beulah Land is yours, Benjamin, another claim may be put forward." Sarah and Benjamin stared at her, but for different reasons. Sarah marveled that the girl could think so clearly and not realize how calculating she sounded. Benjamin merely waited for another blow. "If you and your wife, whoever she may be, are blessed, will your legitimate children have to be told of their father's shame in order that they may fight for their own rights? Have you not thought that the very property itself might be challenged if you acknowledge her child?" She paused for them to reflect on the possibilities. "I hope you see, Benjamin, why you must deny the woman's charge and admit nothing. If she is bold enough to carry it further, swear that she lies. Who can know beyond the two of you if what you say is true? Who can know but she?"

Benjamin finally broke the silence. "No." For the first time since he and Sarah had come into the room, his voice sounded like his own.

"You have not thought it through," Frankie said. "I beg you to do so, for the sake of your own future. I do not say mine."

"Frankie," he begged, "only trust me. I know this will be all right in time. You don't understand a girl like Bessie and you've wronged her. She'd never set out to do anything underhanded. Why, I've known—"

"Mrs. Troy?" Frankie looked at Sarah again. "I think you cannot blame me?"

Sarah wanted to talk for an hour, but she made do with "No."

"Nor fault my reasoning?"

"No, I cannot."

"Grandma!" Benjamin exclaimed as if the ground were crumbling beneath his feet.

Ignoring Benjamin, Frankie continued. "Then you must tell him that I am right and persuade him for his own good to wash his hands of the entire degrading episode."

"No!" Benjamin declared. "The child will be mine, and I'll say he's mine."

Frankie continued to look at Sarah and wait.

"I cannot advise my grandson to do anything that goes against his conscience, Miss Dollard." Sarah rose. "I'll leave you. I hope you will remain here and discuss these matters further, for they are important. I shall tell the others there has been a misunderstanding and that it is being sorted out. Impossible to say nothing to answer their concern, for they know something has happened. The only advice I give tonight will be for them. I shall forbid them to speak of their concern to either of you, unless you choose to speak."

Replacing her chair in its former position beside the desk, Sarah moved to the door. A glance as she opened it showed her that Benjamin had taken Frankie's hand and that she let him keep it. There would now, she guessed, be bargaining.

Nell had retired from the party, but the others gathered around her when Sarah came out on the porch. Before anyone could ask questions, she made a quick explanation of her absence and urged the most considerate discretion. Although her eyes glittered with curiosity, Annabel protested that she required no instruction in deportment. Sarah opened her mouth to answer and then closed it again, deciding to follow her own counsel.

Taking Jane's arm, Bonard steered her down the steps and into the front yard. Daniel promptly took Jane's other arm, and the three proceeded together, to Jane's amusement, although not Bonard's. Annabel, in a thorough bad temper, elected to drill Blair in the various commissions she had already given him to execute for her in Savannah once he and Bonard had delivered Miss Frankie-Julia to her family. Sarah joined Casey and quietly told him everything she had withheld from the others.

It was an hour before the missing couple returned. When they did so, Benjamin was silent for the remainder of the evening unless directly addressed, but Frankie was her usual self, a little subdued perhaps, a touch more thoughtful than she ordinarily appeared, but easy and amiable. Benjamin did not leave her side until she left his to step into the carriage, after Annabel but before Prudence, when it was brought around by Abraham to carry the visitors home.

As soon as they were out of sight, Jane turned on Daniel and accused him of behaving clownishly all evening. He answered that he had no notion of what she meant. Obliged to specify, she said that he had been unforgivably rude to Bonard, having had no civil word to say to him. Daniel denied it, and they found themselves in something like a children's spat in which nothing more edifying is exchanged than "Did so!" and "Did not!" She said she was going to bed, but before she could slam the door behind her, Daniel had set off whistling toward his own little house. Casey said good night, leaving Benjamin to Sarah.

"Did you make her understand you?" Sarah asked.

"Even tonight," he said, "with things as crossed as the top of a tepee, she was so pretty I didn't care what I was saying."

"How is it left between you?"

"I love her and swore I'd do nothing to hurt her."

"That doesn't tell me."

"I said I'd bide my time about things here, making no promises, until she writes to me. Then I'm to go to Savannah and meet her family. We're engaged but not to tell it until I've settled it with Bessie. She won't let me say I'm its father." Bending his head, he kissed Sarah on the cheek. "Good night, Grandma. I wish I was ten years old again." He went down the steps and into the darkness. She thought he was gone, but a few moments later he called back softly: "When I go to Savannah, I'll look for Nancy for you."

15.

On Friday morning the loungers at the depot did not have it all to themselves when the eleven o'clock train stopped at Highboro to pick up mail and passengers for Savannah. Miss Dollard and her trunk were there and waiting, as were Blair and Bonard Saxon. Annabel had come to remind her sons of the personal commissions assigned them beyond the business they were to transact for the bank and the sawmill. Prudence was at her husband's side, neither of them appearing much agitated at the prospect of a week's separation. Benjamin and Jane had come early to town in Benjamin's buggy, and he had already spent a private half hour with his ladylove at the old Saxon house before they all transferred themselves to the station.

During that time Jane joined the girls, who had made so much of Frankie's visit and would not miss her departure. They were drawn by a further incentive than friendship: the possibility of a marriage engagement's being made known, and maybe even two, since it is known that one may sometimes start an epidemic. Everyone said that Frankie and Benjamin were engaged to one another; everyone assumed that Jane and Bonard were about to be. Yet the principals behaved with such a cruel discretion, no one could vouch for a single fact. The splintery planks of the station platform were in a constant thundery tremble as members of the farewell party paraded about, faces shining from the heat of morning and eyes bright with anticipation.

Abraham had come to town with Jane and Benjamin, riding on the hay box at the back of the buggy and under Sarah's orders to spend the day with Roman. School would open in a week, with the main harvest in and the children's help in the fields no longer needed. Roman wanted a day with the boy to initiate him to the books and rooms that would soon become his familiars, and it had been his notion to win Abraham to the school by making him a part of its operation. To that end he told Abraham that he was to keep the fires in all the classrooms during the winter and, before that, to teach the beginning pupils how to use the swings and seesaws and spinning jenny Otis had set up for their recreation during periods of recess. At midmorning Roscoe Elk stopped at the school to tell Roman he was going to Savannah on business for his father and to ask if he could do anything for him while there. Roman and Abraham decided to accompany Roscoe to the station. The only link between them and the larger party they found was Abraham, who sometimes strutted and made faces when he caught Jane's or Benjamin's eye on him.

The depot always gave Jane a sense of heightened expectancy, going back to the days her grandfather Leon brought her there and held her up to watch the train come and go. Annabel removed her gloves—no one else wore them—and then put them on again, making the effort of straightening fabric over fingers a gesture to emphasize the words of command she repeated to her sons. Benjamin and Frankie walked together as far away as the platform allowed. Her face was pale, her lips set in a wistful twist. His face was flushed, his mouth grim as an ax.

"You will write to me soon," he said.

Frankie bobbed her head. "And when you come, you will be able to tell me all is settled about—the painful matter."

"I pray you will forget it," he said.

"I cannot until I know how it is arranged."

"You must not worry yourself."

"Easy to say, but I cannot command my dreams, however much I make myself think of flowers and music before sleeping."

Her hand trembled near his. He took it and pressed it to his lips, causing a pause in several conversations on the platform.

"I love you. I will do everything you ask."

Withdrawing her hand, she patted his briefly. "We shall be so happy. How I long for the day I can come back to this dear town as a bride!"

"Say you love me," he asked.

She smiled sadly. "Would we be speaking of marriage if I did not?"

"Say it, Frankie," he begged. "I want to remember the way you look saying it, until I see you again."

"It would not be right until the other thing is done."

"Damn the other thing! I've told you—"

Tears came into her eyes. "Shall my last image of you be with a curse on your lips?"

"My darling!"

Wanting to escape his mother, Bonard took a cue from the strolling lovers. Turning to Jane, he touched her arm to guide her down the platform in the direction opposite her brother and friend. Expecting a light confidence or a joke, Jane went readily enough. But he said, "I tried to talk to you privately at Beulah Land the other night, but your hired man would not understand and leave us alone. I sometimes think Auntie Sarah is too democratic!"

"Daniel is not anyone's hired man," Jane said. "You know well he is our cousin."

Bonard laughed. "And you know better that he is not."

"He's been with us so long, we think of him that way now."

"How do you think of me, Jane?"

"Good morning, Miss Davis," Roscoe Elk said. He spoke because he thought she was looking at him, and so she was, but she had not actually seen him.

"Good morning," Jane said to him.

"Good morning, Miss Davis!" Roman said a little mockingly.

Again she smiled.

"Good morning, Miss Davis!" Abraham affected a curtsey and pretended to lose his balance, falling to the platform. Jane quickly folded her parasol and smacked it on his behind. "Ow!" he hollered. "I'll tell Miss Sarah on you, see if I don't!"

Jane said, "Roman, when school starts, I hope you beat him every day, for he surely needs it. I gave him a pair of shoes to clean yesterday, and when I looked out in the yard, there he was with them on, sashaying back and forth, mocking me!" As the boy giggled and the two men smiled, Jane said to Roscoe, "Are you taking the train to Savannah, for I know Roman is not?"

He nodded. "A few days for my father."

"Jane?" Bonard said quietly and guided her away. When they were well beyond the Negroes, he said, "You didn't answer my question, and it's time for the train."

"What was it?"

"I asked how you thought of me."

"Yes," Jane said. "We were talking about Daniel and being cousins. Well then, I think of you as—my cousin and my brother's friend."

"I have wasted my breath if you think no more of me than that." He squeezed her hand, and she took it away from him.

"If I must own the truth, I think of you as a young man who dances better than anyone and who laughs easily, one who knows how to judge a horse and a cigar and a glass of wine. One who spends more time ordering his clothes than he does helping my father run the sawmill."

"That's unfair!" he complained, smiling broadly. "Am I not going now on your father's business to Savannah when I want so much more to stay here with you? —But at least you are thinking about me when you say it."

"Would you like me to continue?"

"Only if it's something nice and affectionate."

"I hope I have a proper regard for all my relatives."

"Ah!" he said, affecting disappointment. "I've been pining for your improper regard! —Although it's not improper, you know, even if some believe it is. And what care we?"

She stood back to examine him. "No," she decided. "You are too light a fellow for more than a quip and a reel. I shall never go beyond that."

"What if I promise not to joke again and to give away my dancing slippers? If I drudge from sunup to sundown at the blasted sawmill? Will that persuade you to think of me as a serious and worthy fellow?"

"I should only say you were making a more elaborate joke than ever and waiting the chance to surprise those who had been taken in by such uncharacteristic behavior."

"I'm serious, pretty Jane. Won't you be?"

"Let's go back to the others. It isn't polite to leave them for so long. I must pretend a little warmth for Miss Frankie if I cannot feel it."

"Jane, I love you," he said quickly. "I've wanted to say it forever."

"Even when Benjamin and I fought you and Blair with our Bibles after the Sunday school?"

"Don't make fun of me."

"You're not serious, Bonard; you know it."

"I want you to say you'll marry me."

"Funnier and funnier!"

"Say you love me too."

"You are distracted by the adventure of going away from Highboro for a week."

"Give me some hope or I'll go shouting along the platform as loud as I can: I love Jane Davis!"

"You're already saying it far too loud. Roman and Roscoe are looking at us. As for Abraham, there's no telling what that imp will do if he hears."

"Say you don't dislike me, Jane!"

"Of course I don't dislike you," she said uncomfortably.

He took her hand again. This time she allowed him to keep it, because he held it so firmly she knew that removing it would be more noticed than her acquiescence. "I mean everything I say, Jane. It's you who are joking now and being irresponsible."

"If what you say is so, then it's an awkward place and surely the wrong time."

"I'm a dunce." He let her go. "Wait until I come home. I'll take you out in the moonlight. I'll even hire those country troubadours to follow at a distance and serenade you with the sad songs you love. I'll tell you again all the things I've said this morning, but ever so much more prettily. In rhyming couplets with each line ending in o-v-e."

At the sound of the train whistle, she turned them toward the main group and walked back quickly. All of the party were now coming together, each girl insisting that she must kiss Frankie on the cheek and a couple of them managing a few sweet tears. Benjamin kissed her hand. Bonard squeezed Jane's meaningfully. Frankie's trunk and the luggage of the Saxon men were taken on board. Blair helped Frankie up the steps, Bonard following them. When they found seats, the party moved along the platform to talk and grimace at them through the window Blair had opened. Everyone chattered; everyone had some last thing to say except Benjamin, who stood behind them alone, staring at Frankie. He did not wave or speak as the train drew out of the station, only looked at her for as long as he could.

The party dispersed quickly then. It was as if their morning's allotment of energy and emotion had been expended in the leave-taking. Seeing Roman and Abraham walking away, Jane called, "Aren't you coming home with us, Abraham?"

Roman answered. "Tell your grandma I'll bring him this evening."

"Bye-bye-bye, Missy Davis!" Abraham smirked and smacked his lips.

She stuck out her tongue at him and followed Benjamin to the buggy. Getting into it, they took the road silently to Beulah Land, where Benjamin had earlier promised to return for noon dinner.

The depot was left to its regulars, one of whom said, "Come day, go day, and God save Sunday!"

16.

During the week that followed Sarah was of excellent cheer. Ten times a day she wanted to exclaim how delighted she was not to be threatened by the presence of Frankie-Julia and Bonard. All of her tact was needed to put on a long face when Benjamin mourned that Highboro without his love was as forsaken as Crusoe's island. Jane wandered about looking troubled and irresolute. Neither confided in her, for which she was not sorry. More than tact was required for her to hide her antipathy to Miss Dollard and the younger Saxon. If Benjamin received a letter, she did not know it.

On Wednesday after the great Friday leave-taking, Sarah was enjoying the solitariness of her side porch when she saw Annabel driving up the carriageway. Suppressing an urge to flee, she reminded herself that, at least with Annabel, she did not have to pretend. Annabel knew her fears. It turned out that she had come to play on them.

Hardly had they swapped routine salutations when she announced, with eyes showing more than a mother's love, that she'd had a letter that morning from Bonard in Savannah. "Poor Auntie Sarah!" Annabel said. "Bonard confesses that he was quite shocked on seeing the meanness of the Dollard household. No remark of Prudence's, or Blair's had prepared him for it. Do you remember the old ice dispensary on the corner of Drayton Street and Broughton Street Lane? They live close by, with no proper trees and only a low hedge to separate home from street. Not at all up to the airs and graces Miss Frankie-Julia affected with us. It's no wonder she set her cap in what we all thought such an obvious way for Benjamin, is it? And Benjamin has only had experience of our local girls whom everyone knows everything about. She has a pretty face, I grant, and must evidently make the most of it. Bonard said he should have laughed were he not afraid of offending. He describes the mother as vulgar, in addition to being plain as a pot of rice. But then, I'd expect no distinction of Prudence's connections."

There was more. The young beauty's father—well no one appeared to know, or at any rate be willing to say, exactly what he did, where his money came from, or indeed if he had any. Bonard suspected that he had not. Although it did not quite come to the point, Bonard had the distinct impression one evening—he and Blair had been invited for supper another day after delivering the Dollards' treasure—that Mr. Dollard was on the point of asking for a loan of money and would have done so had they not been suddenly interrupted by the entrance into the room of an aunt. As for the aunt! —Annabel had to stop and laugh. —She went barefoot about the house and was said to be a little strange, even writing poetry!

"Annabel," Sarah said coldly, "if I liked the girl, I shouldn't care if her father sold patent medicine, her aunt wrote bawdy songs, and her mother dipped snuff in the middle of South Broad Street. It's the girl who concerns me, and I won't pretend that I'm happy about Benjamin's asking her to be his wife. However, I'll stand by him, no matter what."

"Of course!" Annabel said. "If only he had tried to take an interest in Priscilla Oglethorpe, as I suggested. I don't understand young people nowadays. They set such store on romantic attachment. When I was a girl, we thought of character. I don't mind saying, Auntie Sarah, that I feel sorry for you. However, while you may have lost all hope of anything by way of Benjamin, there is still Jane to think of. I can promise you better luck there!"

"You know my feelings on the subject, Annabel, and there is no need to review them."

"Jane!"

Jane had chosen that moment to come onto the porch.

"Come here, you pretty child," Annabel crooned invitingly.

"Good afternoon, Aunt Annabel," Jane said.

Opening her reticule, Annabel took from it a letter which she merely waved in the air before returning it to its carrier. "If you knew some of the things said about you in this letter from Bonard, you would blush."

"Oh!" Jane said, and blushed. "Have you had a letter from Bonard?"

Sarah felt like slapping both of them.

"Pages and pages. He sends his most eager and affectionate remembrances." She laughed proudly. "I have always said that once he decided to apply himself, Bonard would leave his older brother behind. He appears to be doing just that. I am immensely pleased with his report on the lumber business he is transacting."

"How does James feel about it?" Sarah asked.

Ignoring her, Annabel continued her insinuations to Jane. "He asks me most pointedly at the end of his letter whether I should much mind welcoming a new daughter to our family! What am I to tell him when I write to him tonight?"

Jane was a study in confusion.

"Jane," Sarah said to save her own feelings as much as those of her granddaughter, "will you make some tea and bring it?"

The girl ran. Annabel might have looked upon Sarah the way a gladiator surveyed a mortally wounded beast in the arena. Instead, she gazed into the air as contentedly as a cow will contemplate clover.

On Friday afternoon, a week after his leaving, Roscoe Elk returned from Savannah on the train. No one met him. He carried his luggage to the livery stable, where he claimed the rig and horse his father kept there for town use. On the way home he slowed the horse, then made him go faster, and finally stopped him altogether. This play of indecision having occurred on the road approaching Beulah Land, Roscoe suddenly made up his mind and turned into the carriageway. He was not bold enough to go alone to the front door, but drove his rig around the house where by chance he encountered Sarah returning from the barns.

He asked her if he might speak to her privately, and she led him further into the yard to a seat built around the whitewashed trunk of the oldest oak. As soon as they sat, he said, "Forgive me if I am presumptuous, but what I have to say may bring pain to you and to those you love." Her eyes looked alarm. "On the day I went to Savannah I saw Miss Davis at the depot."

"Yes," Sarah said. "She and a party of friends were saying goodbye to a visitor returning to Savannah."

"Miss Dollard."

Sarah nodded.

Roscoe stared at her unhappily. "Have you heard nothing?" The blank look she returned was his answer. "I am glad I came," he said.

"Please tell me."

"I saw them this morning aboard the packet for Charleston at Rice Mill Wharf. My father's business placed me there. Mr. Saxon remembered me from the bank, where I often go with my father. He hailed me and said I must congratulate him, for he and Miss Dollard had just been married. I saw them sail for Charleston."

"You are *certain?*"

"I saw them." He interpreted the sound she made as one of grief and shock. "Mrs. Troy, are you all right, or may I call someone to you?" He touched her hand.

She clutched his as her laughter burst forth. "Oh, my friend! —Thank you!"

17.

Remembering that the bearer of bad news is often blamed for it, Sarah was in no hurry to acquaint Jane and Benjamin with what Roscoe Elk had told her. Benjamin had been at Beulah Land for more than an hour in the morning, and he did not return. Rare for her, Jane spent most of her day working at a dress she thought to wear to the Kenning farm next evening. The dress was two years old and had done hard service, but she liked its easy fit for dancing. She dyed it the color of mulberries and after supper worked yellow ribbon in and out at the cuffs and neck to provide fresh interest. Tomorrow the Kennings were to grind their sugarcane and make syrup, the cooking of which would go on far into the night, and county people were invited to stop as they pleased to sample cane juice. The juice was sweet and frothy and the color of clean creek water.

Those who came would stroll and gossip as they drank, at some point reminding each other that the juice always made one want to pee. So common became the activity that dignity went by the board, few waiting to use the formal facilities after nightfall but merely repairing to the nearest dark field for the minute or two necessary to relieve themselves before going back to drink more of the cold sweet juice and so begin the process again. A fiddler would appear, knowing he'd be wanted, and perhaps someone with a flute or banjo; and then dancing would commence on the hard-packed dirt yard. By midnight everybody was tired enough to go home. The gathering had come to be one of the gayest of the casual county traditions. Watching Jane thread ribbon, Sarah wondered how it would be this year, or if they'd go at all; for surely before another sun rose and set Jane and Benjamin would know from the general source what had happened to those who professed to love them.

Indeed, they knew by noon Saturday. The town knew, and the county, for Annabel Saxon was no oak to fall in the forest without a sound. For her, Apocalypse.

Arriving in Highboro alone, Blair Junior left his luggage at the depot and went directly to the bank, where he knew he would find his father working behind closed doors. The two Blairs had grown enough alike to make communication of the few details simple and quick. Bonard and Frankie-Julia Dollard had married and eloped. Blair knew nothing about it until he read the letter Bonard left for him with the hotel manager, who had been instructed to hand it over only after the sailing of the packet boat. In rough scribbling Bonard asked that he go first to the Dollard family and tell them what had happened, then to Highboro to tell his mother and father. They were to be in Charleston for only a week. Bonard had barely enough money for that, and owned freely that he would use a part of the sawmill's funds entrusted to him, promising to pay it back to his Uncle James within a month of his return.

The Blairs understood each other, but how were they to tell the new bridegroom's mother? (The bride's mother had seemed little wrenched by the defection of her daughter, merely chuckling and allowing that she knew the clever girl was up to something, for she had seen her pack a carpetbag). The Blairs stared at each other soberly as they considered the task ahead. Neither would agree to conduct the interview alone. Finally, both marched off to the Saxon house like men headed for a hanging tree.

Annabel looked up with surprise from household accounts on which she was working at her desk in the dining room. Since her last intelligence was that her sons were not to return until Tuesday next, her first words were "It's Saturday."

"Yes, Mama," the son said, turning to his father. "You will want to tell her, sir."

"On the contrary," the husband said, "you were there, and a firsthand report in these matters is always best."

"For God's sake, stop talking to each other and tell me immediately what is going on! Where is Bonard?"

"Ah." The son cleared his throat, which took a little time. "That's it, Mama. He didn't come home with me."

"I can see that, you simpleton."

As quickly as he could, he told her; but unlike his father, Annabel interrupted to challenge every statement. Blair was hardly able to answer one question before answers were demanded to a dozen others. She refused to believe it. She did not suspect him of anything as dangerous and heartless, she said, as playing a joke on her; but he had got it wrong, he had misunderstood, he had misjudged his brother's intentions.

He handed her the letter. She read it twice before she screamed. Had she a dagger and her younger son before her, Medea might have called her sister. "Base!" — "Betrayed!" — "Treachery" were the milder cries that rang through the house. When she found breath for longer accusations, "scheming wanton hussy" was one of them that seemed to afford her some satisfaction. The faithful Fox and Millie listened from the kitchen in a state of ecstasy which heavenly hosts might have envied, for they did not, in truth, much love their mistress, and to hear her suffering did not wring their hearts. She called for them loudly, but they did not come, having suffered often enough in the past Annabel's wrath when it should have been directed elsewhere. Blair was dispatched to find them and did so, after looking everywhere else, in the smokehouse deep in the back yard.

Soon the tidings were spread, and Annabel's friends began to arrive to wish her joy in her new daughter.

Prudence came to Jane, who at first and in a gentler way shared her aunt's disinclination to credit the news.

"It cannot be," Jane said. "They seldom had a word for one another in company."

"We were all of us deceived," Prudence said sadly, although in her heart she rejoiced at the notion of having Frankie-Julia as a sister instead of Jane, whose snubbing when her mother married Jane's father Prudence had not forgotten. She had learned to admire Miss Dollard's cool self-possession on their first acquaintance in Savannah, and the elopement was not as great an astonishment to her as it had been to others. "I hope earnestly the surprise of it is the severest emotion you feel, but I fear that Bonard has paid you such particular attentions everyone was led to assume an understanding between you which for reasons of your own you chose not to disclose."

Jane only looked grave a moment before answering. She did not herself know if simply her pride was afflicted or if she had begun to feel a true tenderness for Bonard. "There was none, I assure you. My cousin is a *gallant*, attentive to ladies; and then our manners have been free toward one another from childhood because of the family connection." Jane was determined that whatever Prudence expected to carry away as an interesting tale should be given no substance by her. She knew, though, that it would be too studied an evasion if she did not acknowledge the possibility of her brother's being more closely affected. "I imagine my brother will be as surprised as I, but whether he is more than surprised is not in my power to say. We are affectionate in everything, but not confiding in everything."

This exchange was conducted on a side porch at Beulah Land in early afternoon. Nell was asleep in her room. Casey had ridden into town after dinner to photograph a dead baby. It was the kind of assignment he deplored and generally refused, but the young father had made a special plea on behalf of his heartbroken wife. Sarah had hastened to her office and closed the door on hearing wheels of an approaching buggy, without waiting to see whom it brought.

Prudence's service as messenger was not to go altogether unrewarded, little as she got for her trouble from Jane. Not encouraged to linger, she used the unexpectedness of her visit to excuse a quick departure. "There are so many who will want to know, but I came to you first. You have reassured me that your heart is whole, and I am so glad." She smiled at Jane even as she looked at her keenly. Jane walked with her to the buggy, but before Prudence could drive away, she had the satisfaction of witnessing Benjamin's arrival.

He did not see her. Galloping into the grounds the back way through the fields, he jumped from his horse and stamped up the steps to Sarah's office shouting, "Grandma! Do you know what Bonard has done? I'll find him and kill him, see if I don't!"

That was all the young women understood, for Sarah had

drawn him into the office, closing the door and warning him that they did not enjoy privacy. Prudence took up her reins, giving Jane a distressed look. "Poor boy, he has heard. You must try to comfort him."

Jane made no answer, nor was one necessary, for Prudence turned horse and buggy in a rapid circle and was gone down the carriageway.

Benjamin meant all he said, and he said a great deal, Sarah remaining silent, until he exhausted some of his anger. She then said, "Bonard has been unwise."

"Unwise! Is that what you said?"

"Yes. Bonard has been unwise, but that is no less than can be expected, considering his mother and his own lack of the commonest sense."

"He is the luckiest of men!"

"I doubt that he will agree with you a year hence. Thank God he did not secure Jane's love."

"What has Jane to do with it?"

"You are blind if you do not know how Bonard has pursued her these last two months on his mother's instructions."

"Then she is safe, but I have not come to talk of Jane. Have you no pity for Frankie, who is his prey?"

"If she is his prey, then so is the eagle the rabbit's."

"He *stole* her! He surely must have deceived her to accomplish that."

"Nonsense. She merely considered Bonard a better risk than you are, with other claims on you."

"You wrong her."

"I doubt that would be possible."

"You adored her!"

"I never granted more than that she was pretty, and she is certainly that. She is also two-faced and self-seeking. I'd as soon trust a Yankee peddler."

"How can you say so? She loved *me*, and I had nothing to offer her."

"She saw in you the future master of Beulah Land, and she saw herself in my position."

"I don't believe such a thing entered her head. You make Frankie sound a monster," he said, but his tone was becoming more thoughtful than challenging. "She is nothing like that."

"I remember your saying something to the same effect to Miss Dollard about Bessie Marsh."

"But Frankie is a lady. Bessie's a farm girl."

"I'd rather see you marry an honest limb of Satan like one of Crawford's trollops. At least they do not deceive."

It was the first time the Crawfords had been mentioned between them, and Benjamin blushed, guessing that his grandmother knew of his visits to them. "I don't see how you can speak of them in the same hour you speak a name as pure as Frankie's."

"She is unlikely to have remained pure until this hour, let me remind you."

Benjamin winced. She knew she was hurting him, and she meant to, for she also knew that realization of betrayal is the quickest cure for misplaced love. "I loved her, Grandma. I always will." The pity in Sarah's eyes released his tears. She pulled him to her and held him hard.

18.

"I'm glad she isn't going to marry Bonard," Nell said. "Children of first cousins turn up peculiar. Webbed toes or eleven fingers or albinos. Always a mule, neither horse nor jackass."

Not knowing what Nell noticed and overheard—sometimes much, sometimes nothing, depending more upon her degree of interest than the state of her wits—Sarah had thought it prudent to speak to her of what had happened before all of them came together for supper. She'd tried to make Benjamin stay, but he'd ridden off without saying where he was going, not toward home but the main road, still angry and unreconciled to his loss of Frankie.

When she knocked on Jane's door before supper, Sarah found her wearing the mulberry-dyed dress. She turned to show it off before sitting at her dressing table, where she had curling irons heating over the oil lamp.

"It does you credit," Sarah said approvingly, with a shade of added meaning.

"It looks new and feels old," Jane said. "No bad thing." She took the iron from the heat, wiped it with a cloth, and rolled hair into it. "There'll be a crowd at the Kennings'."

Sarah said, "No more than usual, I suppose."

It was their first meeting since the afternoon visits of Prudence and Benjamin. Jane smiled deliberately at Sarah's image in the mirror. "Oh, I think everyone will come. They'll have to see what each other knows about the elopement." Sarah's eyes questioned Jane's in the glass, but she did not speak. Removing the iron from her hair, Jane set it again to heat and fluffed the curl it had made. "And they'll want to see how Ben is taking it."

"And you?" Sarah ventured.

Jane licked a finger to test the heat of the tongs, deciding they were not yet ready. It gave her time to decide to drop her guard. "When she left, Prudence was glad, she said, to have found me 'heart whole'—the opposite, naturally, of her true feeling."

"Are you?"

The girl and the woman looked frankly at each other in the glass. "I've been thinking about the last few months. I don't say I don't care. My pride is hurt, and I'm embarrassed. If *you* asked me, I'd admit that I might have been about to wade into deep water. That would have been a mistake. Have I been a worry to you?"

"Yes!" Sarah said. "The thing that scared me most, I think, was your no longer making jokes about Annabel."

Jane laughed. "Prudence reports Aunt Annabel as completely devastated."

"If only one could believe her," Sarah said. "You're letting that get too hot."

Jane quickly removed the tongs from the lamp chimney and wiped soot from them before testing again with a wet fingertip. "Aunt Annabel cares so much about everything." She set hair between the tongs and deftly rolled them.

"And so little about anyone," Sarah said. "I'm glad you've dressed up so to go to the Kennings'."

"I shall be gay, but not so much as to rouse suspicion," Jane said with self-mockery. "I only hope Dan doesn't try to joke about Bonard."

Sarah smoothed the back of Jane's dress. "I don't think he will."

Jane sighed, frowning at herself in the mirror glass. "He likes to tease."

"I've never heard him say anything mean," Sarah stated.

More curling and thoughtful mirror-gazing ensued. "Frankie thought him handsome. Do you remember?"

"Mm."

"Do you think he is?"

"I've known him too long and too well to think him ugly."

Jane's face cleared, and when she finished the hair-curling a few minutes later, they left the room arm in arm, pleased with each other. Casey rose from his chair on the porch as they joined him and Nell. "Come and be cheerful. That poor father had to keep fanning flies from his child so that I might make the photograph. It was a wretched afternoon, and the mother crying in the next room." Daniel joined them, looking neat and clean for the evening. Sarah was glad to see that after a glance at Jane he went to Nell's side. Drawing up a chair, he began to talk to her about a new trap he was making to catch fish, because he had little time now for hook and line. She had taken one of his hands as he talked and held on to it in the anxious, clawlike way the young and the old hold any life they grasp.

By the time the rockaway rolled into the Kenning farmyard it was getting dark, and other people were already there. Hobart came to greet them and stayed with Jane and Daniel when Sarah and Casey went to find his father and mother and to taste the first cane juice of the evening. As time went on and the party increased, Daniel was never far from Jane, although he did not hover grimly as he'd used to do when Bonard was with her. He even smiled at her when he was standing at the side and she was dancing a sassy, strutting movement, copied from Negroes, with Rupert Hammett. And did he?—yes, he lifted the gourd cup from which he was drinking cane juice, as if to congratulate her.

Again Jane was queen bee.

When Blair and Prudence Saxon arrived, they were hailed and questioned eagerly about the elopement, but Blair could furnish few details not already known to them. Prudence assured them that "dear Mama Annabel" was recovering from her first shock and beginning to talk of welcoming her younger son and his wife when they came home. They had no place of their own to go;

there had been no time to plan for it. She would insist on their living at the old Saxon house until something suitable might be arranged.

All evening there was talk of Bonard and Frankie, most of it reflecting amusement and surprise that they had been so success-ful in hiding their attachment. It was easy enough because Ben-jamin was not there and Jane appeared to be as carefree as any-one, as little affected by the news in a personal way. Only the doctor's daughter, Celia Platt, who had always been envious of her, essayed a tentative spite by saying, "We all thought you were to be the one, Jane. You certainly acted like sweethearts. Are we to suppose you were in on the secret and helping them fool the rest of us?"

Jane colored, but before she could think how to answer, Pris-cilla Oglethorpe took her hand and swung it playfully. "Pshaw," she said. "All of them try to be Jane's swain. Look at them now: it's like a roll call in school. Johnnie Baxter, Tom Cooper, Rudy Heffernan, Hobart Kenning, Fred Shields—" The moment passed in laughter.

"Celia's jealous," Rupert Hammett declared, "because I've been dancing with Jane." There was more laughter, for Rupert was the youngest of the boys dancing and the only one with an honest claim to being ugly. Most of them were what was called average and equal in appearance, in spite of physical variations and any lack of resemblance except the general sectional one. But young Hammett's ugliness went beyond plainness and would have gone charitably unremarked did he not himself comment on it as freely as farmers speak of sun and rain.

Daniel claimed Jane for the next dance, and Jane felt that she had never loved her friends as dearly as she did now. They were good, generous souls. They had opened their ranks to the stranger, Frankie-Julia Dollard; she had taken their admiration as her due and got off with one of their prize young men. Yet they bore her no grudge and would welcome her as his wife when he brought her back among them. She tried to say some of this to Daniel as they danced, and all the time he was smiling at her as if he was listening but having thoughts of his own, and all he said when she paused for his comment was "Yes."

There was much coming and going. Guests were in and out of the house as freely as if they lived there. Mrs. Kenning, noticing that some of the youngest and oldest girls lacked partners, invited them to the kitchen to make candy from some of the new batch of syrup. There was always a group at the cane-grinding, watching hypnotically the blind mule go round and round, and Hobart's father used his gourd dipper constantly to fill the cups held out by his guests. The fiddler never flagged, the banjoist danced with the dancers. The older couples had gone to sit indoors to escape the chill of evening, and some were talking of leaving as soon as they could persuade their children it was time, when Benjamin arrived. He was in fair command of himself, but his eyes were bright and his cheeks flushed, and Jane knew he had been drinking. She asked him to dance with her. Shaking his head, he said, "My girl's left me, so I won't dance with anybody."

There was some uneasy laughter, but the banjo and the fiddle continued, and so did those who kept time to them. The dancers were as flushed as Benjamin, and only those nearest guessed him to be a little drunk and sorry for himself. Daniel talked to him in a low voice, and when Hobart led Jane into a reel, Benjamin went with Daniel toward the knot of men watching the cane-grinding. Daniel had no experience of overdrinking, but he seemed to remember hearing that other fluids were supposed to have a sobering effect, so he plied Benjamin with cane juice. Benjamin was thirsty and cooperative.

"How are you, Mr. Kenning?" he said to Hobart's father.

"Very well, Benjamin. I understand you've got your crops in."

"Yes, sir," Benjamin said. "I'm going to Savannah next week to see what I can sell for me and Grandma."

"Beulah Land had a good year," Kenning said.

"Better than some, I'm told."

"I hope you do good in Savannah."

Benjamin held out his cup.

The older man said, "I don't think I'd have any more right now, Ben."

"If you say, Mr. Kenning."

The farmer turned to fill another cup.

Daniel said, "You all right, Ben?"

Benjamin was frowning. "I don't want to go to Savannah. That's where Frankie went and where I lost her."

"You don't want to think too much on that, Ben."

"You ever feel like: 'Where did everybody go?' One girl left, and for me it was like everybody. I went over to Crawford's. You know Crawford's?"

"Heard of it."

"God bless you, Dan. You're one of the cold brothers that needs no fire to warm you. But I'm not like you, so there's Crawford's. I drank a lot of his bad liquor and I took all five of his daughters, one by one, to the barn." He held up his hand with fingers splayed apart and counted them off. "Alvina, Alma, Annie, Abbie, and Adeline. I had every one of them, but I couldn't come. I'm done, Dan. I'll never be able to come again."

"Ben, don't talk so."

Benjamin's face appeared to age ten years as Daniel looked at him. "I think I'd rather die right now than ever sober up." He walked back into the yard clapping his hands loudly until he stopped the musicians. "Hey, all my friends! Have you heard how Farmer Ben lost his girl?" He clapped his hands again "Most beautiful girl—gone! All alone is lonesome Ben! Will any girl dance with me?"

There was sience, then: "I'll dance with you, Ben." The still couples shifted to allow a girl to walk thorugh. It was Priscilla Oglethorpe. She stopped before Benjamin and held her arms up in position. After a moment the musicians began to play, but as if they expected to be stopped again. Benjamin glared at Priscilla, suspecting an insult or a joke, but as she returned his look with a steady, grave one of her own, he took her hands and they began to dance together. The musicians recovered their courage and their volume, and the other dancers resumed. Benjamin and Priscilla did not look at each other, and they did not dance easily together. Abruptly, Benjamin halted them and bowed as stiffly as a marionette. "Excuse me." He left her and went quickly to the side of the yard, where Daniel met him and held him as he vomited.

Jane had gone to fetch Sarah, and they were ready with Benjamin when Casey drove the rockaway around to them. Casey drove with Jane beside him. Benjamin slept with his head in Sarah's lap behind them. Daniel followed the rockaway on Benjamin's horse and took Benjamin into his own house and bed for the rest of the night.

They woke and dressed and went for breakfast at Daniel's usual early time. Only Nell joined them. She accepted Benjamin's presence with a nod, saying, "I dreamed there was a woman at a window reading a letter. What do you reckon it means?" Since neither could say, she talked to Daniel about his new fishing trap. "I dearly love a sweet pike, or a bream, for that matter." Josephine brought them fried white meat and succulently greasy griddle cakes. Over them they poured fresh syrup from the gallon Hobart Kenning had given Jane as they left his party last night. "The Kennings have always made the best syrup in the county," Nell anounced approvingly. Benjamin found himself in good appetite and realized ruefully when he started his second stack of cakes that he had not thought of Frankie since waking until that moment. "Woman at window," Nell murmured. "Reading a letter. Now who do you suppose it could be?"

19.

Opening announcements had been made and the first hymn begun when Doreen and Benjamin slipped into the church and made their way quickly down the aisle to the old Davis pew. Knowing the words, Doreen started singing as she walked, for she hated to miss any fraction of a church meeting. They were late because a wheel of the buggy had gone wobbly on the way into Highboro. Hoping to avoid acquaintances whose interest in yesterday's events must still be lively, Benjamin exaggerated the seriousness of the trouble and made a thorough repair instead of using a twist of wire to render the wheel safe for the day. It was not until after church services, therefore, that Doreen was able to catch up with her sister.

Annabel had looked upon church attendance that day as a challenge, and she had met it triumphantly, talking to all who approached her, and everyone did so, of her joy at her younger son's marriage. But the effort exhausted her, and she now hoped to escape with her husband without lengthy encounters.

"Annabel, wait," Doreen said. "I have not seen you since the news. I know your new daughter is beautiful, but is she a true Christian? The least of us may be considered beautiful in the sight of the Lord if we be righteous and praise his name."

Annabel felt that she had done quite enough that morning in the way of making the best of things, and Doreen was only a sister. Firmly removing the hand from her shoulder, she said, "I believe she has admitted Jesus to be her Savior."

"Admission is not enough; only the full embrace suffices."

"She is a Presbyterian, and that will have to satisfy you. At this stage of affairs I can't see how it would matter if she were a Hottentot who worshipped a waterfall and subsisted on human flesh."

Doreen gasped. "Oh, my poor sister, I can see your heart is heavy-laden. I shall pray for you."

Annabel turned to greet Eloise Kilmer, who was bearing down on her from another side. Since Miss Kilmer was a choir member, she'd had no earlier contact with the congregation that morning. Without being asked Annabel declared, "Ever so pleased! Yes, delighted. Blair Junior has given me a full report with expressions of the tenderest regard from both. They are to come to us as soon as they return from Charleston and her own family can spare them. I expect a letter tomorrow and shall be much surprised if you do not see us all together here next Sunday!"

Miss Kilmer screeched and cooed her surprise and congratulations. Over her shoulder Annabel apprehended Sarah and Jane. They had only smiled at a little distance before. Now they came face to face, as both sides knew they must, and braced themselves to observe the proprieties. Greetings were exchanged and happiness wished.

Sarah said, "How very gratifying for you, Annabel, to have your hopes fulfilled of Bonard's marrying. His wife will continue the tradition of beauty in your family." It was only then, and then only for a moment, that Annabel's guard fell, and she looked at Sarah with fury. Sarah patted her cheek before turning to Casey, who had come to claim her.

Benjamin had recovered his self-possession and even managed to make mild jokes against himself with friends, as he waited for Doreen, who was in conversation with Miss Kilmer. Presently he caught sight of Priscilla Oglethorpe, who was talking to Jane and Daniel on the steps. He had not remembered her until that moment. Going directly to her, he said, "Good morning, Priscilla. Thank you for your kindness last night. I'm sorry I was boorish and hope you forgive me."

She smiled. "We'll dance another time, Ben."

"If you'll honor me."

"When do you go to Savannah?"

The four talked of Savannah until they were joined by Priscilla's mother. Jane and Daniel moved on to join Sarah and Casey, who now appeared ready and eager to leave. Benjamin remained talking with Priscilla and Mrs. Oglethorpe until Doreen had finished the round of Christian admonitions that had become part of her ritual after Sunday service. Because she was one of them, acquaintances accepted her impertinence as mere Davis eccentricity.

Benjamin had long ago learned how to attend his aunt minimally while thinking his own thoughts, so during their buggy ride home and dinner together, he gave her automatic responses, which was all that she required, while reviewing what Daniel had called his "situation." The affair with Frankie-Julia Dollard was done, and although her face and voice in his mind caused him pain and would continue to do so at least until he had seen her as Mrs. Bonard Saxon, he had begun to believe himself well out of a scratchy patch of briars. He'd put off doing anything about Bessie Marsh, reluctant to honor his promise to Frankie by lying. The promise was canceled by her marriage, and he would instead offer Bessie protection in every way short of marriage.

This he imparted to Sarah an hour after dinner. She approved his resolution and asked if he'd like her to accompany him to the Marsh farm that afternoon. Since it was just what he'd hoped but not liked to ask of her, they set off immediately. The Marshes were surprised and pleased to see them. The exchanges were frank and friendly.

On the way to the Marsh farm they passed the land that had been the Davis plantation and was now Junior Elk's. Although they said nothing to each other, Sarah thought of her daughter Rachel, whose home it had been, and of her friend Edna, whose very heart it had been. It was curious, she mused, how literal was the word "heartache." Her own was sore for her old friend. Benjamin remembered the day his grandfather was murdered and the house burned and relived the moments the blind James had been the object of soldiers' jeers in their game of blind man's buff.

Inside the Elk house, Roscoe Elk lay sleeping. Geraldine had supervised the preparation of a Sunday dinner that was itself an enlarged imitation of those served at Beulah Land in days gone by, even as the house was a copy of the old house there. Roscoe was a young man of great appetite and had enjoyed the meal. The main reason he stayed on in Highboro was a growing fascination with sorting his father's and grandfather's business papers. The family history became real and clear to him for the first time as he read. But another lure was the luxury of food and wine and cigars in his father's house. Junior understood his son's greed and used it to keep him there without himself knowing exactly why he wanted him to stay. Large minds are frequently partnered with large physical appetites, the bribe the body takes for providing superiority. Roscoe Elk's was such. He was a little ashamed of it even as he accepted it as true, only endeavoring to check his desire for his father's young mistress. He despised her, and she knew it; but he wanted her, and she knew that too. When she was present, he could not help watching her.

After feeding from a thick slab of beef with rich flour gravy generously spooned over rice and sweet potatoes, Roscoe retired to his room. Removing his outer clothing, always uncomfortably binding after one of Geraldine's meals, he lay on his back in his drawers. For a time he considered the latest bills and agreements he'd gone over at the office. However wide of the truth, rumor is seldom without some basis, and rumor had consistently linked his father with the Yankees. Junior Elk had been given special consideration by the early forces of occupation and later by the military rulers who replaced civil administrators on act of Congress in 1867. While there had been rumors about him, he had been more feared than resented, and rumors died or were replaced by new ones. No evidence of his exploitation of others was revealed.

Much of the Elk property had been accumulated before the war, and it did not seem peculiar to people that the property and power continued to grow. Few questioned the respectability of property and power handed down by their fathers. Every day now Roscoe discovered fresh evidence of Junior's complicity with the conquerors, and of his manipulation of others to profit himself. The very cigars that arrived regularly from Cuba were made by some of those Junior Elk had sold from their brief freedom into new slavery. The tenants of his farms would never pay their debts to him. It would not be possible if they lived and worked by present agreements for a thousand years. Given maximum yield from the land they tilled, their indebtedness could only increase. The taxes Junior paid on property during the years after the war were infinitesimal compared to those levied on white plantation owners, many of whom, too poor to meet the demands, lost their land, which was subsequently bought by Junior Elk at a fraction of its evaluation for taxes. Everything was there in the bundles of papers. The question in Roscoe's mind was: why had his father wanted him to see those papers?

Roscoe went to sleep. He dreamed, he snored, lying on his back with his mouth open. The snoring woke him at one point, and he closed his mouth until it was moist again. He slept and dreamed. For a long time he slept deeply, and then less so, finally surfacing to that dim area where he dreamed that he was dreaming. A moment came when he knew the dream had been made flesh. Opening his eyes, he saw Roberta naked before him. She had tickled him to erection and was astride him taking his penis into her body. She stared at him as she settled upon him like a hen setting eggs, and then she rode him. It was no more than masturbation, but it was an act in which he acquiesced. When it was finished, she lifted herself off him, ran her hands between her legs and smeared moisture over his chest and neck. "You don't have to watch me no more like a hungry dog." Without clothes she went out the door, leaving it open. He heard her run laughing down the hallway as if it did not concern her who saw or heard her. Rising, he cleaned himself at the washstand, dressed, and went out to walk.

When she returned to Beulah Land late in the afternoon, Sarah made Benjamin leave her at the main road because she wanted to walk alone for a little time. She strolled contentedly along her road through the orchard and into the avenue of oaks leading to the main house. The birds were making a great thing of their twilight singing, and she paused to listen to one song that seemed to her a miracle of invention in the way it maintained the same character through infinite variations. She didn't know what bird sang, nor did she want to know. She had no desire for knowledge beyond her requirements and even liked to hold certain mysteries by ignorance. She would not have thanked anyone who tried to explain a rainbow to her.

She was surprised to find Roscoe Elk on the side porch in a chair beside Casey when she came to the house. Both rose to greet her, and Roscoe quickly explained his presence. "I was walking this afternoon on one of Papa's tenant farms and found

Miss Doreen Davis. She had a shovel with her and was digging up the ground. She asked me who I was but didn't understand when I told her. She then asked me what I'd done with Pharaoh. I saw she wasn't herself and persuaded her to walk home, walking with her. She never stopped talking about Pharaoh."

"Where is she now?"

"I left her with their house woman—"

"Rosalie."

Casey said, "Daniel and Jane went over as soon as we heard."

"I must go," Roscoe said.

"Pharaoh was her horse," Sarah said. "She loved him more than anything." Following Roscoe to the steps, she added, "I seem always to be thanking you. I thank you again. You are a kind man."

"No thanks are due to me, Mrs. Troy." He started down the steps, then paused but without turning his head. "What happened to her horse?"

"He's buried on your land. The Yankees tried to ride him, and when they couldn't, they killed him before her eyes and mutilated him."

20.

Doreen was puzzled by the attention she suddenly received. James and Maggie came to see her on Monday morning, apparently for no reason, as they only sat looking apprehensive and grave for an hour. Later, Annabel arrived and seemed to be at crosses with her, putting sharp, fretful questions in much the same way she had done when they were girls. Dr. Platt, whose attendance surprised her most of all, hummed and ummed and asked her about her bowels, for which she thanked him to mind his own business. After a few further hints and nudges, he suggested paregoric at bedtime and went his way.

There was a family conference in Sarah's office late that afternoon which included everyone but its subject. Annabel declared that she was there because she knew her duty, but that whatever they decided must be implemented without her help, for she had her hands full with Bonard's marrying, etc. Dr. Platt said that Doreen was rational, or as rational as he'd ever known her except for her sudden preoccupation with the horse. Benjamin revealed that this was not the first breakaway she had made from everyday realities but that he was accustomed to her milder vagaries and never thought them of any moment. He would, he said, postpone going to Savannah. James offered to make the trip for him, but Annabel pointed out that, being blind, he could not do so alone, that he was not familiar with the business of Beulah Land, and that even if he were he could not be expected to conduct it effectively, for with strangers he should be quite lost, however capable he considered himself in dealing with town acquaintances. Maggie interrupted Annabel to say that in any case James must remain in Highboro in order to make a strict accounting with Bonard of sawmill funds when and if the runaways decided to come home. Sarah brought them back to the business at hand. Casey offered himself as courier to Savannah only because he knew his offer would be refused. Sarah allowed that Abraham knew more about Beulah Land then he did, which provided the only laughter of the meeting. Dr. Platt added that Doreen would doubtless do very well with no one but the servants; but none of them was happy to leave it at that. They separated, having made no decision.

The solution came simply from an unexpected quarter. The following morning Annabel waited at the post office to see if the Savannah train brought her a letter from Bonard. It did. She opened and read it. "Ah, Miss Kilmer!" she called, wanting an audience and spying that lady buying a postage stamp. "You will be pleased to know my son and his wife return on Saturday; so you are sure of seeing us all together in church on Sunday, just as I predicted!"

Miss Kilmer was gratified at being the first to share the important news, and they fell into conversation, in the course of which the problem about Doreen was disclosed. Miss Kilmer's response was immediate. "She must come and stay with me in town. It will be a change for Miss Doreen and company for me and my two pussies. The dear soul needs to lift her mind from the past. T'other day in the church she spoke of her Pharaoh, but I fancied she had the name confused with Jehovah's and so did not take it up. With me she will be near the church and the work she loves. It is the very thing."

Annabel agreed and went to tell James and Maggie that she had, in spite of her own pressing concerns, found a moment to resolve the matter of what to do with Doreen during Benjamin's absence. Miss Kilmer begged a ride on a wagon that took her to Ben's farm, where she gave Doreen her invitation. Doreen was delighted, accepting on the spot. During a talk with Sarah that evening, Benjamin decided to proceed to Savannah—only not, Sarah suggested, until after Bonard and Frankie had come home, for otherwise the timing of his departure would furnish gossip. He would take the Monday train.

That meant church on Sunday and a public confrontation with Bonard and Frankie. He dreaded it but knew that it must come, so better soon than late. In the event he could congratulate himself on having behaved properly with no embarrassment, for Frankie did not attend church on Sunday, pleading fatigue from her journey. She therefore made a liar of her mother-in-law, which Annabel did not hesitate to tell her. After church Benjamin delivered Doreen and her little trunk to Miss Kilmer's house, where the two cats, each with a velvet ribbon about her neck to celebrate the event, waited on the steps to welcome the guest.

It was sunny and cool on Monday when Daniel and Jane brought Benjamin to the depot in one of the farm wagons. Daniel insisted on shouldering Benjamin's trunk aboard the train, and Jane stood outside his window to tell him she wished she were going somewhere too, and that they would miss him. The brother and sister seldom had occasion to think how they felt about each other, but as the train pulled out of the station, they watched each other disappear with a sudden awareness of their love.

Daniel then asked Jane if she had any commissions to fill in town while he took the wagon to the general store to pick up the barrel of flour Josephine needed. "No," she said, so he helped her into the wagon and they proceeded along the street. Jane was wearing an old merino wool dress, once her party pride but now relegated to everyday, a homely shawl around her shoulders, and a loose bonnet to guard her face from the sun. Daniel was in his usual coarse work clothes. As they drew up and stopped in front of the big store, Bonard and Frankie came out of it. The two couples looked at each other dumbly for a moment. Then Bonard and Frankie exchanged a glance and burst out laughing. Daniel jumped down from the wagon and helped Jane to the ground.

Her face burning, Jane went directly to Frankie with her hand out. "Welcome back to Highboro," she said. "I think I must congratulate you both on making a perfect match." Daniel followed and stood quietly beside her.

"Thank you," Frankie said, shaking her hand. "You must forgive our laughing, but everything and everyone amuses us this morning!"

"It's not what you *think*," Bonard said archly, "but only that you looked so—like any farm couple coming to town on the family wagon."

"And so we are," Jane said.

"How are you, Dan?" Bonard asked heartily, as if Daniel were hard of hearing.

"Very well, Bonard." Daniel bowed stiffly to Frankie. "I'll go get the flour." He left them and entered the store.

"'I'll go get the flour!'" Bonard repeated. "What a comical fellow."

Jane made herself smile as she said, "I wonder why you say so. I remember it was you, Frankie, who early in your visiting days pointed out how handsome he is."

"Old Dan handsome?" Bonard laughed, looking first at Frankie and then Jane, expecting them to share his merriment.

Frankie had collected herself. Her tone was gently concerned. "How is your brother, Jane?"

"On his way to Savannah. Dan and I have come from the depot, where we saw him leave on the eleven o'clock train."

Bonard said, "Not too angry with me, I hope?" Jane looked at him. "Truth is: I thought it a good joke putting one over old Benjamin, who always thinks of himself as the biggest buck in the county." Bonard snapped his fingers. "Stole his girl right away from him, didn't I, my love?" Bonard had appealed to his wife in order to avoid Jane's cold gaze, but Frankie had enough sense of the moment to give him no audible support.

She said to Jane almost as if they were alone, "Our decision to marry was a surprise even to ourselves, and there was no opportunity to let friends know."

Jane said, "As long as your families were considered and con-

sulted, friends can feel no offense at being left in temporary ignorance."

"You are good to say so," Frankie said meekly.

"See here, Jane," Bonard said, "I hope you're going to be all
right about Frankie and me. It happened pretty quickly, and
well—" He paused, smiling confidently. "You had treated me like
the joker in a deck of cards that day at the depot when Blair and
I were leaving with Frankie and I told you I was—well, perhaps
I gave you the idea that I—" He stopped, looking from one pair
of cold eyes to another. "I reckon I stepped on the gator's tail
that time! We'd best get along, Frankie. Plenty of things to do."
He took out his watch, snapped it open, closed it, and put it
back in its pocket. "Due at your father's in a little while. He and
Miss Maggie kindly asked us to dinner."

Jane held out her hand again to Frankie. "You'll be very busy,
but we shall surely be meeting everywhere."

"I long for a quiet hour with only the two of us," Frankie said.

Jane smiled, but firmly enough to make it appear an answer.

It was over. She had done it. The first encounter was now a
part of her private history, of no interest or concern to anyone
else. She saw them being stopped a few paces away by Miss
Lucy Goldthwaite and her mother, both still in black for the father and husband who had died of consumption in March. Jane
turned quickly into the dry-goods store next door and walked
about in studied aimlessness for a few minutes, pretending casual interest in this and that pattern of partially unfurled bolts of
cheap dress materials on the counter. When she returned to the
street, neither the Saxons nor the Goldthwaites were in sight. She
went back to the wagon, and the mule perked his ears in recognition. She scratched the angle of his jaw. Daniel and a stout
Negro man came out of the general store bearing between them
the barrel of flour, which they hoisted onto the back of the
wagon. As it settled, flour dust rose in the air and clung to their
faces.

Jane climbed up to the seat. Daniel stepped over the back of
the seat after securing the barrel and took the reins. Shortening
one and loosening the other, he turned the mule and wagon into
the street. Jane took off her sunbonnet and held it in her lap as
they went through the town and joined the road to Beulah Land.
The last house behind them, they came to a crossroads. Jane
said, "I remember riding in one day with Grandma. Just here we

stopped. Soldiers were camped over there and one of the officers crossed the road. He'd been down to the spring to shave and still carried a shaving cup and the folded razor in his hand."

The mule kept a regular pace, the wagon wheels turned over the hard clay road, and tears came into Jane's eyes. Daniel appeared not to notice. But after an interval, when the road turned, he reached into a breast pocket and drew out a brown paper sack containing sticks of peppermint candy, red-striped like a barber's pole. She accepted one. He took another, breaking off a piece with his teeth and crunching it fiercely.

She had just learned two things: she loved Daniel, and he loved her. The knowledge was sudden, and it overwhelmed her. It was not a quiet realization; it was thunder and lightning, the sea roaring a revelation. She wanted to cry his name. She wanted to take his hand with its coating of flour dust on the back hairs and hold it forever. She had forgotten him as she flirted with Bonard Davis and sighed to the sad ballads of Thomas Cooper, Frederick Shields, Hobart Kenning, and John Baxter. She turned her head so that she might watch him without seeming to. There he sat, looking angry and chewing hard candy as he held the reins over the mule. She would wait no longer. "Dan," she said, "we are going to get married."

It was as though she had never seen him smile before. He halted the mule with one pull of the reins. She was always to remember and to tell her grandchildren that their first kiss tasted of flour dust and peppermint.

21.

How was he to find someone whose name he did not know? Benjamin smiled at the absurdity of not knowing her name—it was Nancy! But Nancy what? Her mother was called February, but if she'd had another name than Kendrick, Benjamin did not remember. He asked everywhere, but no one had heard of a Nancy Kendrick. He reminded himself that she had married, but he had never been told her husband's name; so he began to rely on description. That didn't help him much either. "Well, suh, there's many a Nancy, most of them colored, and several about as old as you say and tall as that. They all laugh—sometimes. They all have their pride and can show a temper. I'd like to help you, but I just don't seem to know her." Heads were scratched as eyes turned thoughtful, because everyone in Savannah, black and white, had a courtesy as distinctive as the Savannah walk, said to have taken its original character from the citizens walking on sand.

Benjamin stayed in a boardinghouse because it was cheaper than a hotel, but it was clean and respectable. It was also close to Bull Street and Bay Street, the junction of these forming the central axis of the city. The boardinghouse was therefore convenient, whatever the weather. He had been taken to Savannah first when he was seven by his grandfather Bruce, and only an occasional year had passed since without his returning. After the war he had gone each autumn with Sarah and Zadok, but the last two Octobers he had come alone to do the business of Beulah Land and his own farm and to buy the special whims and needs his family's women were not able to find in Highboro for Christmas.

After a day of selling and buying and business gossip, he liked wandering the old city, stopping perhaps at a street stand to sample the pickled oysters, in spite of having eaten well at his boardinghouse. The grid pattern of the streets appealed powerfully to his farmer's love of order, as the squares with their lush planting satisfied his hunger for luxuriance. For the rest of his life he would measure other cities against Savannah, and while admitting them to be richer in this or that if measured by numbers and amounts, still they were poorer in his mind than Savannah.

He had been there for a week. His business was all but done. There were only two more calls to make at banks and a last visit or so to the cotton market. He had written to Sarah that he would return Friday after giving himself a little diversion. He continued to ask about Nancy wherever he went, although he had by now very nearly given up hope. It is at such times that hope may be fulfilled. He was lolling on the wharf with a cotton clerk about his own age late one afternoon. Colley Burns was a joking, exuberant fellow he always found amusing for half an hour. The man knew of Benjamin's quest and suddenly said, "Have you tried the whorehouses?"

"No!" Benjamin declared. "Nancy wouldn't be in one. I told you she grew up on our place as part of the family. When she wanted to leave, my grandma helped her come here, where she found work and then married somebody, and then we lost track of her."

"Well," Colley insisted, smiling, "she might have got married and her man might have up and left her. Happens all the time. Some of the darkies have seven wives, one for every day of the week. They think it was part of the Emancipation Proclamation. You hear them talk about 'my Monday wife and my Tuesday wife' and so on. Fact. However good a girl she was, she may be just somebody's Wednesday wife. A lot can happen to them when they come to the city. She could even have moved on somewhere else."

"Maybe," Benjamin agreed.

Colley studied it over. "The whorehouses are worth trying, if she's all you say. Wouldn't that be something, and no hardship either, fucking your way through every whorehouse in this city to find one nigger gal! Lordy-mighty!"

He laughed, and then Benjamin left Colley Burns and began to consider what he'd said. He decided to try the houses. He knew two and went to them first, enjoying a glass of wine and bed pleasure before questioning the madams about other houses. The second one he talked to said, "I know of a girl that might be the one. At Miss Maysie's. —Bet you a dollar! She took this new girl six months ago, not so young, about the age you say, and name of Nancy. Supposed to be a humdinger, gentle*mens*ir! You go ask Miss Maysie and say I sent you."

Miss Maysie's was a large, commodious house near the City Hall, from which it was said to enjoy both custom and protection. It was off a discreet alley, surrounded by a wall seven feet high and boasting its own brick courtyard with a gas lamp, a well, two chinaberry trees, and a stone bench. Miss Maysie was white and in her fifties and was said to hail from New Orleans, which may have been true, for her house, although not furnished richly or flamboyantly, was well run. Her girls were all dark, which was one reason she was let alone, unlike another madam who mixed the races. Her clientele were all white. Several of the girls came from Cuba, but most of them were Georgia-born, and none was nearer white than a quadroon. Their sleeping quarters were separate from the working bedrooms. They enjoyed good food, a fair share of their earnings, and even a private sitting room into which gentlemen were not allowed. Her girls were carefully chosen and usually remained with her for a long time. Two had been there for more than twelve years and were much favored by fathers who felt that a mature woman was the best introduction their sons might have to the privileges of manhood. They were free to leave whenever they chose, but each agreed on joining Miss Maysie not to set up a house in Savannah, although several had done so successfully in other cities.

A grizzled, crippled, very black man was porter of this house of pleasure, and it was of him Benjamin asked if he might see Miss Maysie. Uncle Aaron, as he was known, inquired into the nature of his business, which Benjamin told him, giving his name. Benjamin knew then that he had come to the right place, for the old man drew back his head to study him, and presently his eyes and mouth relaxed and he smiled a little. "Miss Nancy said you'd come one day, sure did. Come in, sir." Opening the door, he ushered Benjamin into a small, square reception room and asked him to wait. Not long after, Miss Maysie came in. She was a plump, pretty woman with a bright, cheerful face and a bustling manner. Benjamin felt comfortable with her at once. Two minutes later he found himself in a small office where he was presently joined by Nancy.

Coming in, she closed the door behind her. They looked at each other intently for a moment or two and then simultaneously began to laugh, opening their arms and coming together. Their delight in meeting was that of old friends long apart; and they exclaimed joy and admiration without hearing what each other said, only knowing they were lovingly welcomed.

Then came questions.

Nancy: "How is Abraham? How is Miss Sarah? Miss Nell? Miss Jane? She married yet? *You* married yet? Tell me everything about Beulah Land! Sometimes I get so *homesick*. Does Miss Lauretta write y'all from Maryland? Is Miss Eloise still living? Does Miss Doreen still have the birdcage she gave us after we were burnt out? Tell me everything, you Ben—talk to me!"

She was pleased to hear about Sarah and Casey and happy when he told her that Sarah had dreamed about her twice ("Did she? What was I doing?") and made him promise to find her on this trip because she was worried about her. She wept to know that Nell missed her. "Sweet old soul, I'll never see her again in this life. Tell her I love her and will remember her till I die. Never forget the day the soldiers came, what me and her went through together. She tried to fight them off me. Cried and hit at them till they had to hold her back and told her they'd kill Miss Jane if she wouldn't let them be. Ah, Ben, those times. How did we live through them? And then you rode off, just a little boy, to kill that Yankee. When you came back, I met you where the road turns in and said you'd done it to revenge my honor!"

Benjamin took her hand quickly. "And so I did. Do you remember what happened later the same night?"

She laughed. "It was the only way I knew how to say thank you. I was a bad old girl!"

"You're the best I ever knew. Why did you make us stop, later on?"

"Don't you know?" she said. "I was getting to like you too much."

"Don't you know I—liked you too?"

"That's why I made us stop. I could see trouble."

"Have you ever been sorry?"

"Have you?" she said.

"Every day."

They looked at each other quietly. A little later she said, "No, stop. I said stop. Ben, don't. Oh, my good boy!" Another minute and she pushed him firmly away and said matter-of-factly, "Not in here we can't. This is Miss Maysie's office."

"Where?"

"I don't know."

"Think of something. You must know where we can. The old man said you were expecting me to come."

"Uncle Aaron tells too much."

"He didn't strike me that way."

"You know what Miss Maysie tells the gentlemen that come here? 'Just you be as much of a gentleman as Uncle Aaron and we'll have no trouble.'" She straightened her dress. "There's a little house back of this big one Miss Maysie calls her hospital. It's just one room, but pretty-furnished, where a girl is sent when she gets a bad cold or anything Miss Maysie don't want the rest of us to catch. Nobody's there now, and nobody's been coughing. I'll go ask her."

"Does she know about me the way Uncle Aaron did?"

She looked at him from the door. "Oh, yeah. All of us have one from before we came we brag about."

Miss Maysie let Nancy use the little house for two days, excusing her from her usual work. Benjamin was in and out. When he tried to pay Miss Maysie, she looked stern and shook her head. Next time he came he brought her a light lacy shawl which pleased her. Discovering that Uncle Aaron had a preference for a certain dark, rich chewing tobacco, he brought him a little wooden box of it on his last visit. And between the first and the last Nancy and Benjamin were let alone. They were seldom fully dressed, except when they came and went, and they rarely left the bed, although often they simply lay talking. They talked about everything that had happened since Nancy left Beulah Land.

Nancy's life had been close to what Colley Burns suggested. She'd done housework for a year after coming to Savannah, but everyone was poor and the pay was low. Then she married. He rode racing horses for sporting men, and she knew when she took him she shouldn't, she said. He stayed with her a month and went off, she didn't know where, or care where. Before leaving he told her he'd already married three girls before he met her and she needn't wait around for him. That was that. She made up her mind she was done with marrying. She liked men, always had and always would, but she'd found she didn't like living with one, because it was more "wash my shirt" than "kiss me." She was lucky not to be pregnant. She thought maybe she couldn't be as a result of what the soldiers had done to her. She didn't know, and what did it matter? The world didn't need any more Nancys.

She got housework again, but she hated it. She'd never cared for it, but at Beulah Land it was different because it was home, and the Kendricks belonged to her as much as she had belonged to them. She discovered that housework for strangers left her angry as well as worn out at the end of a day. They wanted every minute of work they could get from a girl. And she didn't like being called "girl"; didn't she have a name?

She thought over carefully the idea of selling herself. Negroes had been sold by others, why not by themselves? She gave it a try in a cheap house, finding she didn't mind it as long as the trade was with gentlemen who were clean and not too drunk.

Hearing about Miss Maysie's, she came to see her, and they liked each other. Miss Maysie agreed to try her, and here she was. It was a good business, they got the best; and she'd keep on as long as she could, saving her money, and one day she might move to another town and have her own place. She had regulars now and seldom took a stray.

What about Benjamin?

He told her about Bessie Marsh, and she giggled at the prospect of his being a father, pounding him on the back to punish and congratulate him. He told her about Frankie-Julia Dollard.

"Don't care how pretty she is, sounds like a mean little bitch-belle and you're better off without her. Still, you ought to marry one of these days, not wait too long."

"Nancy," he said, "I been thinking about this, so don't you say anything till you hear me out. You remember the Glade. Why don't I tear down the shack and build a real house there for you? It's the prettiest place on all our land. You could leave Savannah and come live with me."

"You want me to?"

"More than anything."

They made love enthusiastically, and when they rested, Benjamin said, "Well, that's settled."

"What you mean what's settled?" she said.

"You coming home to Beulah Land."

"No such a thing."

"You promised."

"Bed promises, be they death or otherwise, are not binding on people."

"Who said so?"

"Me. I made it up."

"Nancy, you *know* you promised me!"

She tried to sound disgusted. "And me thinking you'd grown up."

"What's wrong with my idea?"

"Everything."

"What?" he insisted.

She turned on her side and looked at him. "We going to live outside this world? You found a door how to get out?"

"Nobody need know."

"Everybody'd know. They'd start up the Ku Klux Klan again just for us. —You want me to sit there and never go anywhere and never see anybody? For nobody would come to me, they'd be scared to. I'd get to hate you."

"No, Nancy!"

"I tell you, some mistakes I don't have to make. You know it's so as well as I do. I got too much respect for me and too much for you to think of doing any such thing. What do you think Miss Sarah would say? Uh-uh. Bad idea."

"If you were white, we'd get married."

"Well, I'm not." She held her arm alongside his. "But thank you for offering, since you know it's safe. Bessie Marsh would envy me."

"I wish I was colored."

"No, you don't. There can't be anything for us but like this."

"Can't we find some better way?"

She laughed, or tried to. She laughed again, and it came out better. She shoved him playfully as one child does another, careful not to offend. "Need me, do you? Well then, how come all the time you're needing me, you're making babies throughout the countryside, tell me that! And what about your Miss Frankie-Pinkie, hey? Bet you sure was needing me when you asked her to marry you!"

"I'll bet you I was! And listen to you talking about me! Look what all *you've* been up to."

"Only for money," she said airily.

He reached for his trousers on the back of a chair, overturning the chair but finding a dollar in his pocket. "Here!" he said, dropping it on her breast.

She brushed it aside. "Can't take it; you keep it. You're my fancy man. All us whores have one fancy man we don't take money from. Keeps us self-respecting. You're mine."

"Nancy!" he cried warningly, grabbing her arms and pinning her down. She made no struggle, and he let her go. "I hate to hear you talk like that. I hate to think of you with another man. You wouldn't have to live in the Glade the way I said. You could live anywhere you want to. Have a little house in Highboro and I'd come see you in it." She lay quietly, not looking at him, and after a moment he raised his eyes to look at her. "Will you think about that, Nancy?"

"No, Ben."

He turned his head away, and she knew he was crying. She stroked his back for a minute and then pulled him down beside her. She touched one of his nipples with the tip of her tongue, feeling him come erect as he held her more urgently. They made love until sated and happy, then rested on their backs again.

She reached to a low table on her side of the bed and picked up a book. "See what I was reading before you came?"

"Mm," he said without looking.

"You want me to read you some from it?"

"No."

"I read real good. I read better than I talk. You wouldn't know me from Queen Victoria if you heard me read."

"Tomorrow."

"You gentlemen ought to be more interested in us ladies' achievements of the mind and not just think of us as something to hide your ugly old peters in."

He raised his head resentfully. "What do you mean 'ugly'?"

She cackled. "Never seen it fail. Quickest way to hurt a man's feelings is throw off on his do-whacky. Call him a liar and a scoundrel and he just smiles at you, but say his thing ain't pretty and he doubles up his fists."

He said lazily, "You smell real niggery when we've been doing it."

"No more niggery than you."

"Do I smell niggery?" He sniffed himself. "Not niggery, just fucky."

"I told you not to talk dirty. Us whores don't like it, even from our fancy man." She yawned and slept and woke only a few minutes later, feeling the warm breath of his laughter against her breast.

"Am I really your fancy man?"

"The fanciest ever lived," she assured him.

22.

There was no formal announcement that Jane and Daniel were to marry; they simply told people. The only one to express no astonishment was Daniel himself. Beulah Land was first to have the news, but on the same day Jane and Daniel went into High-boro to see James. His reception foreshadowed the town's: surprise that Jane was marrying so soon and amazement that Daniel was her choice.

That he was a decade older than she was naught. That his station was not lofty was considered of small consequence in a time of humbled pride and with the ranks of young men still thin from the war. But that he was an outsider mattered, for no one had ever believed him a cousin. From his arrival he was judged to be a Yankee who had deserted the Army. His quiet ways had over the years gained him acceptance, although few would have said they liked or disliked him. There was too little to go on. He was not one to dally and talk about himself. If a question was put, the question was answered, but without the seasonings that give flavor to a man. His virtues were thought of as negative: he was not forward, he never presumed; he was not a drunkard or a gambler; he was no trifler with women.

But suddenly Daniel showed himself another man. If he had appeared shy and retiring, he did so no longer. Never was a prouder bridegroom-to-be. Jane was without a flaw; he shouted her praises like a crazed prophet proclaiming a new heaven and earth. The sidewalk would hardly hold him; he walked so big he needed the street. He smiled upon everyone; he called a greeting even to mules he recognized. Friend and foe, native and passing stranger—all were one to him. To say the world loves a lover is a lie, but in Daniel's case it was nearly true, for his face was a mirror of his love, and to look upon it was to comprehend some of its miracle. It was discovered that he was handsome, agreed that he was a knowledgeable farmer, and at last allowed that he might now become one of them.

The first and only outspoken critic of the engagement was Annabel Saxon, Maggie having given her word of the matter minutes after her stepdaughter left the house. (Typically sly, Annabel thought, even as she gobbled the tidbit in one snap of the jaws.) Driving her own horse and buggy, she came to Beulah Land an hour after the return there of the announcement party. Seeing no one, she proceeded to Sarah's office, shouting for her.

"Auntie Sarah, how terrible for you! —At last you have my sympathy! —Such a betrayal of your trust and generosity in taking in the outcasts of the world! —Let it be a lesson, for no one is to be trusted; that is the surest truth I know!"

Shutting the door behind her, Sarah said, "Stop raving and sit down. What ails you anyhow? If it were the dog days, I'd say you'd been bitten by a mad stray."

Shaking her head and looking upon her with relentless pity, Annabel repeated, "Poor Auntie Sarah! So brave! I should know you'd try to brazen it out, for what else can you do if they are determined? But admit your heartbreak to me!"

"I suppose you've heard about Jane and Daniel," Sarah said, taking a chair beside her.

"We must persuade James to forbid it."

"I couldn't be happier about anything."

"Save your nobility for others—I know better. Did you not look with disfavor on even *my* son when I thought he fancied the child? Anyone who sniffs at a Saxon has something more royal in mind than a hired hand."

"Daniel is not a hired hand, he is Beulah Land's overseer."

Annabel waved the distinction aside. "Call him what you will." Her eyes showed a new glint. "Of course!" she said as if she suddenly understood. "You need him what with Floyd dead and you getting old, and with a husband who hardly knows which end of a hoe cuts, and apparently unwilling to learn."

"Daniel is a friend and family member," Sarah said grimly, "and I am ecstatic at their wanting to marry."

"Even your perversity can hardly stretch so far. He is an ignorant Yankee who could still be sent to prison, if some of us told what we know."

"If you do, Annabel, I shall take you by the hair of the head and march you to the chopping block in the back yard and wield the ax myself."

Annabel blinked at her. "There's no reason to take it out on me that your hopes for Jane are disappointed."

"Annabel!" As her voice rose warningly, so did Sarah.

Annabel smiled and patted her hand. "What a peculiar woman you are. I'll never understand you. I swanee, you'd do anything for Beulah Land, and not even a blood Kendrick. You need Daniel and see the marriage as the best way to hold him; but why can't you say so? Jane, naturally, has done the whole thing from wounded vanity, to show Bonard she doesn't care. That's what people will say."

Sarah resumed her seat. "How is your new daughter?" she said with measured calm.

Annabel blinked again, more thoughtfully. "Busy. I'll say this for her: not a lazy bone in her body. I think she'll be good for Bonard. It's a match far exceeding her expectations, you'll agree, seeing that she was willing a short time ago to settle for Benjamin, who has nothing but connections. Having caught Bonard, I expect she'll try to make him more—" She studied for a word. "—serious." She nodded. "She doesn't let him alone a minute. There's more to her than a pretty face."

"I never doubted it," Sarah conceded so pacifically Annabel glanced at her with suspicion.

"She was particularly interested in the silver at supper last night, handling it as if it were pearls. I've caught her lips moving a time or two; I think she's counting. This afternoon they've gone out to look at houses."

"Are there vacant ones in town?"

"Two or three families want to sell." She shrugged. "Hard times."

"They won't be staying with you, then."

Annabel caught her breath in what might have been the beginning of a sigh or a shudder, Sarah could not tell. "No."

People enjoy surprises if they are not directly affected by them, and Annabel's reaction to the coming marriage was the least charitable and the most suspicious it received. Jane was generally popular, and never more so than when she removed herself from the list of "eligible unmarried young women." Parties were given, including a ball at Beulah Land. Two rooms were cleared for dancing, and Josephine prepared a supper tasty enough to delight Nell and modest enough to afford Annabel a comfortable sneer with Ann-Elizabeth. As the first substantial entertainment to be held after her marriage, it was seen by Frankie as an opportunity to show herself off in her new role. But Jane triumphed by generosity and the fact that no woman who is married can be as interesting as one who is about to be. It was remarked behind more than one hand that Daniel showed a good deal more devotion in his attendance than did Bonard to his wife. Quick to see how the land lay, Frankie assumed the airs of the wise young matron, offering the friendliest counsel to Jane, who thanked her almost as if she meant it.

For a few hours everyone was gay and said how like it was to Beulah Land in the old days. Of the more venerable ladies present, Nell was the only one to avoid being led into a dance, the others needing little persuasion by a grandson or their host. Few of their husbands survived to ask the honor, and those who did were firm in their determination "not to shake up old bones." Nell enjoyed herself hugely and managed to say two things to Annabel—she had spent all day thinking of them—as cutting as they were hilarious to those who overheard them. Selma attended with Pauline, they keeping to their usual quiet corner, but visited by those having a friendly interest in the school. They had long ago established precedent for Pauline's social presence, and there was no comment on a Negro woman's taking her seat with other guests, for she never left her friend and sponsor. Roman was there to play his flute, and when Sarah opened the dancing with Casey, James led his daughter to the first bars of a waltz before relinquishing her to Daniel Todd. Daniel took her hand eagerly, and Jane leaned forward to whisper, "Do you remember when I was a child and taught you to dance? You see it has come in handy." Abraham was there because he had begged to be, to tend the first fires of autumn and to pass among the assembly with glasses of wine on a tray. Offered places in James's carriage, Doreen had come with Eloise Kilmer. She had twice postponed going home since Benjamin's return and, indeed, she and Miss Kilmer had that very evening clasped each other in a conspiratorial hug after announcing to the cats that she was *never* going back to the farm to live. Each had found her heart's companion and vowed to serve God together until death should part them.

Benjamin danced every dance, remembering his claim to Priscilla Oglethorpe and taking her for the first round. He was relaxed and affable with Frankie and Bonard, too relaxed to please the vanity of his former sweetheart; and Bonard treated his cousin with an irritability suggesting that Benjamin, not he, had got the best of the upset proposals. Benjamin's homecoming had been an altogether happy one, graced with the pleasure of his sister's engagement, at which he was perhaps more surprised than anyone. He had conducted his and Sarah's business affairs shrewdly in Savannah, and they both looked to do well in a year their neighbors considered a near disaster. He had managed to procure everything of his various shopping assignments, or substitutes considered satisfactory by those who had commissioned him to make purchases for them. In addition, he brought presents for Sarah and Nell and Jane and Doreen which charmed them, and a baby bed with its own fittings including a small pillow which made Bessie Marsh laugh when he delivered it to her.

He gave Sarah a mostly truthful report of Nancy, leaving her to pass along what she would to Nell and others. Sarah noted that he appeared to feel easier in his own skin after this trip than he had been for a long time before it. He was becoming the man he had been forced to act. When the first fuss of his welcome subsided and they had an hour alone in her office, she asked, "Are you all right, Ben?"

His eyes acknowledged the reach of her question, and she had never heard his voice so gentle. "Yes'm. I've been and I've come back."

Of those in the county who had any special feeling for Jane, the only one absent from the ball at Beulah Land was Roscoe Elk, who could not be asked, and who would not have been able to attend in good heart had the social laws been differently ordered. He knew about it, for Abraham, who had developed a strong hero worship for him, had chattered of little else for the past week.

Thomas Cooper, Frederick Shields, Hobart Kenning, and John Baxter, Jane's faithful summer beaux, were there, and although at first they tried to look jealous and pining, they were having too jolly a time to hold the pose for very long. Less eager than they had once been to delight Frankie, they sang one lugubrious ballad after another for Jane until she begged them, with tears of laughter, to stop.

On the day after the ball Sarah and Jane were up early to go into Highboro and do the autumn turn of their twice-yearly cemetery drill. Since she'd first begun it with Edna Davis, Sarah had kept to it, and Jane now found as much satisfaction in the physical labor as her grandmother. It was, they agreed, exactly the thing to do the day after a party. As they weeded and hoed, as they cleaned and reset fallen bricks, they had a thorough gossip about the evening before, and they paused in their work at noon to share a bottle of blackberry wine and leftover party victuals Josephine had packed for them in a basket. Late in the day when they were done, they cleaned and put away tools in the back of the buggy, and then returned to the Kendrick and Davis graves to survey what they had accomplished and to speculate on what might be done next time.

Sarah's fingers trembled suddenly as they traced the letters of her daughter's name: R A C H E L   D A V I S . Jane saw the tears on her face and made no move to comfort her. Grief was a natural thing, a tangent of memory, not something to be denied as if it were unclean. Jane had no abiding love for her mother, but she knew that Sarah did. Presently Sarah turned to her. "I'd forgotten something until this moment, a little thing. It was one day when Rachel was four or five; she was wearing a new dress and bonnet, both starched stiff as bone, and she was so proud. She took Leon's hand and said, 'Come on, Grandpa, let's go!' They were both so happy. I don't know what the occasion was, I only remember that." Her lips moved without words before she added, "How quickly it goes."

Late in November the cold weather they hoped for came. They killed hogs, and after glutting themselves on fresh pork, the smokehouse was still crowded with tins of lard and hams and great loops of sausage. For days afterward Nell enjoyed her favorite crackling bread and was finally heard to observe to Daniel that she wouldn't mind if he went hunting and brought some squirrels home, for she'd "just about had a bate of backbone."

Jane was busy in what they called the little house, which had been built for Floyd and lived in for several years by Daniel. Soon, on her insistence, it was to be Jane's home too. Although Sarah had offered to build a wing on the big house for her and Daniel, Jane wanted to live there. But she must have new curtains and wallpaper and a new carpet for her sitting room. Daniel went into Highboro one day with a wagon and came back with a big, handsome bed he'd bought because, he explained, they must have one none had ever lain on before. Jane stopped short of demanding her own kitchen. When Annabel came for an inspection a week before the wedding, she declared that such a bed for such a small room was shocking. She added with acid resignation that "no one knows the sins of greed in a woman until she begins to furnish a house."

The bank had bought the house that once had belonged to Nell and Felix Kendrick, who sold it to old Roscoe Elk after Felix became ill and they went to live at Beulah Land. Roscoe lived in it until he died, but Junior had left it empty after building his mansion on the Davis land he acquired from James. He now sold it to Blair Saxon, whom Frankie had coquettishly bullied into presenting it to her as a wedding present. Frankie was directing repairs and revisions, certain that her father-in-law meant them as part of the gift. She had been to Savannah twice to order furnishings, the stores in Highboro not suiting her taste. Bonard was working hard at the sawmill. James had no negligence to complain of, Annabel said.

Jane and Daniel were married on the second Thursday of December 1873, at St. Thomas's Church. Lauretta sent her a silver tray in the shape of a heart.

23.

Abraham Kendrick's mind was too lively to be satisfied by the everyday life of Beulah Land, and he needed no further persuasion to attend school; but it was Roscoe Elk who settled his commitment to learning. He'd seen Roscoe and Junior in town, and over the years he'd picked up the history of Elk and Kendrick enmity. He knew that Roman was, curiously, both Elk and Kendrick. But he had not met Roscoe until that day he stopped at the school and they walked with him to the depot, where Roscoe was taking the train to Savannah.

Their acquaintance was at first through Roman. For all his plainness and reserve, Roscoe was a romantic figure to Abraham because he'd lived in a big city far away north. He had been to a college and was a lawyer, as any white man might have been. To see Roscoe's respect for Roman and his interest in the school increased his own, and before they were a month into the winter term, he was the school's most eager pupil. His only problem was impatience; he wanted to hurry ahead, no matter that he was sometimes not ready. No attempt was made to check him. His special relationship to the teachers assured him encouragement, and only necessary discipline. Pauline was his aunt, and Selma had loved his grandfather Ezra more than anyone in the world before she loved Pauline. But the three teachers were to Abraham *old*, whereas Roscoe Elk was an age Abraham could believe he might one day achieve.

When Roscoe visited Roman, Abraham stared at him as if he intended to draw him later. He was the first Negro Abraham had seen to have blue eyes and skin light enough to freckle. He was also the first person Abraham felt shy with. To overcome that, he began to show off, but stopped when he saw that it only made Roscoe frown. He began to copy Roscoe in the way he spoke and walked and, as far as possible, dressed. He begged for the kind of wool hat Roscoe wore until Sarah bought him one, and he wore it every day to school, not minding that his appearance made the other boys laugh. He knew their laughter was envious.

Soon, seeing his idol by chance was not enough. He began to follow him in town when he could, and he often slipped over the boundaries that separated Beulah Land from Elk property. With his easy ways he struck acquaintance with several of Junior's tenant families as an excuse to ask them about Roscoe. Every scrap he learned fascinated him; nothing was forgotten.

The first time he ventured onto Elk land he felt daring, but three or four excursions made it seem natural to be there, and he went about openly, only avoiding the owner and his son. But one afternoon when he turned a path in the woods he came face to face with Roscoe and Junior. As Junior glowered at him, the old tales of Elk perfidy sent fear through him, and he turned to run, but Junior caught him roughly by the shoulder and spun him around.

"You, boy! You're from Beulah!"

"Yes, sir," Abraham whispered.

"Abraham." Roscoe helped him up from the ground and turned to his father. "I know him; I see him at the school." To Abraham he said, "You've crossed over. Didn't you know?"

"Yes, sir, but I meant nothing. I better get."

"Who sent you?" Junior demanded. "Don't say nobody, because my people tell me you've been hanging around a lot and asking questions."

Abraham was shaking his head in nervous denial. "No, sir, nobody sent me, I just come like, for nothing else to do."

"Never mind," Roscoe said calmingly. "You'd better go home now though, before they miss you and wonder where you got to."

"Yes, sir. I was about to do that very thing." Abraham wiped his palms on his trouser legs.

"Another time I'll show you around," Roscoe offered.

"Not today," Abraham declared firmly. "I'm in a flying hurry. I be seeing you!" He turned and fled.

"The little bastard is spying. They've sent him, and I'll find out why."

"He's not a bastard," Roscoe said. "He's Floyd Kendrick's son." He looked at his father and waited for what he would say. Junior walked ahead.

When Roscoe caught up with him, he said, "You're too much around that school. I've told you to stop going."

"I like Roman's company."

"You want people to think you're a sapsucker too?"

"I never heard anyone call him that but you," Roscoe said.

Junior stopped and looked directly at his son. "Maybe you knew people like him in Philadelphia. The old white-mammy tutor of the Davises took him there, you know, right after he killed Alonzo."

"When I lived in Philadelphia, the 'old white mammy' was spoken of with respect as Professor Proctor who'd started a school for Negro children."

"Runaway slaves. He was nothing but a sapsucker. Both of them: sapsuckers."

"Nothing to do with us, is it?"

"Roman killed your uncle."

"Roman *is* my uncle," Roscoe said.

Junior shook his head. "It's one thing I'll say for him: he doesn't claim kin. We had the same ma and that's all. The same brood sow. It's the boar that matters."

"You had Floyd Kendrick killed, didn't you?"

"Who said so?" The answer was as unemphatic as the question had been.

Roscoe said, "I've gone through the office papers."

"There's nothing in them about Floyd Kendrick."

"Roman talks about Floyd, and I remember him when I was a boy. I know how much he meant to Beulah Land. Many believed it couldn't last without him. When I saw his son at the school, I felt uneasy without knowing why. When the boy took to me, I felt worse; so I started thinking about it. Asked myself: who hated Floyd? Floyd had no enemies, he was a good man. Asked myself: who hated Beulah Land? Grandpapa and you. Abraham never knew Floyd, but he misses him. In spite of everybody at Beulah Land spoiling him, he needs a pa, and he's latched on to me because I'm a Negro. I tried to ignore him and couldn't. I couldn't shake away a feeling I owed him something." Junior spat to show contempt and walked on, Roscoe beside him, not letting him get ahead. "I've found out everything I could about the day Floyd was killed."

Junior stopped and waited.

"It all comes back to you. You and Grandpapa kept every single paper that had to do with business, even the ones that might have hanged you. There's one that notes payment by you of fifty dollars to an ex-slave named Jubah Jackson 'for personal service.' Same day Floyd died, Jubah left for Savannah, promised a job there by you. Nobody here ever heard of him again."

"A lot of men go and don't come back."

"There's another paper dated a month after Jubah left. It says: 'Received nine hundred dollars for J.J., Felipe Santores, Havana.'" Roscoe took a cigar from his breast pocket and held it up. "That's the man sends you these."

Junior smiled. With the anger in his eyes was a flash of commendation. "We'd better look at those papers together."

"Why do you want me to know everything?"

Junior appeared to study the question. "What use is it if nobody appreciates how smart I am? And who to tell but my son? You're not the son I wanted, but you're the one I've got. Those papers are part of what you'll inherit one day, if I don't kill you first. You like my cigars and my wine and my big house, and you like my woman. I know all about you and Roberta, and I don't give a shit what you do with her. You can fuck her up the ass or nose, or feed her to the hogs, if that's your pleasure." He smiled carefully at the shock on his son's face. "Do you close your eyes and call her Jane?" He slapped the arm Roscoe raised. "Don't make a fist to me, and don't talk about me hanging, you hear? That'll never be. You want the good things; oh, yes, certainly. I'll give them to you, but you have to take it all. I won't let you pick out the pieces that please you, like a plate of fried chicken. You looked up to your Grandpa and down on me. What I am and know, I learned from him. I'm proud of the old Indian. Learn from me the way I learned from him. You think he cared anything about you? You were nothing but a toy in his sick old age. A hand-licking hound dog would have done as well. He hated Kendricks, and so do I, and so will you."

"Why?" Roscoe asked.

"Because they're white."

"No. It's because you're not."

"Don't think you're smart because you take my words and pull them inside out. Oh, I like your being smart about the papers." He hit him hard on the shoulder, a mockery of congratulation. "Be smart. I hate a dumb nigger. You've read through the papers and found out some things, and guessed some things. Find out more; and remember everything you find out is your legacy, just as much as the land and the people I own—one day, when I get through with them. Give me that cigar."

Roscoe reached into his pocket and presented the cigar. Junior took it, rolled it carefully between his palms, sniffed it, bit off an end, and licked it lightly all over. They had come to one of the tenant shacks. Seeing them, a girl looked frightened and ran. Junior looked the way she had gone before walking into the shack, and Roscoe followed him to stand at the door. There was a Negro woman inside who might have been forty, although she looked older, sitting on a rickety hide-bottomed chair in front of the glowing hearth fire. "Callie!" Junior called, a command to attention rather than a greeting.

The woman had been nodding, and he so surprised her she fell sideways off the chair to the floor before scrambling to her feet and gripping her hands in a have-mercy attitude.

"Save your praying," Junior said, "and light my cigar."

"Yassah!" The woman sprang to the hearth and scratched in the coals for a small live ash. Taking it into bare hands, shifting it from one to the other to keep it from burning through the rough skin, she held it up until Junior drew fire into his tobacco. At first smoke, she dropped the coal and began to suck her fingers, bowing again. "Thank you, sah! Thank you, sah!"

Junior reached into his trouser pocket, felt through his coins until he found a silver quarter-dollar, and put it into the woman's hand. "Bring the girl tonight. Scrub her clean and dress her in white."

The woman's hand closed over the coin as she continued to bob and bow. "Yassah, I thankee. Claribell will come. That do take the burn outen my old hand!"

Junior walked from the cabin, and Roscoe followed him across a field toward the big house.

"Do you know who she is?" Junior said.

"Roberta's mama."

"Roberta beats her if she comes to the house, so I didn't imagine you'd seen her."

"At the woodpile one day picking up pine knots. She wouldn't talk to me, so I asked about her. I thought maybe she was deaf and dumb."

"Scared of Roberta," Junior said. "Roberta's a wildcat. That's why I gave her to you. I'm breaking in her sister Claribell. The ma brings her when I say. She thinks it's a good joke on Roberta. The quarter I gave her was for tonight, not for lighting my cigar."

Roscoe said slowly, "Is Claribell the child that ran away?"

"She's thirteen. Roberta isn't to know, so keep your mouth shut. I told Claribell she'd kill her if she finds out, and that keeps her tolerably quiet."

There was a quarrel that night during supper between Geraldine and Roberta. Junior allowed neither to share the dining table with him and his son; they took their meals in the kitchen. But Roberta resented being put aside and still made herself heard when she felt like it. She had too long and too recently been the master's mistress to consider her old position quite lost. When she started going to the son's room, she thought herself clever until Geraldine let her know in one of their running quarrels that she went to Roscoe with Junior's knowledge. She still offered herself to Junior. She learned that she could no longer tease him and the only way he'd lie with her was for her to be silent and submissive. She pretended to be so, only to attack him with claws and teeth when he was well along in his action. Now he would not touch her, or even allow her into his room.

On nights she could get the liquor from Geraldine, she drank herself unconscious, and Geraldine saw that she had it when Callie was bringing Claribell. Denied intimacy with the master, Roberta tried to win over Roscoe, only to have him finally bolt his door against her when he retired at night. She knocked and kicked and yelled through it, but he would not let her in. More than once when Callie dragged the younger girl to the master's bedroom, they passed within inches of Roberta, asleep on the bare wooden floor of the upper hallway, her arms cradling her head as if from expected blows.

Roscoe sat bolt upright and listened for the sound that had broken his sleep. It came again, a whimper like that of a dog. Leaving his bed, he crept to the closed door and put his head against it. Hearing nothing in the immediate hallway area, he unbolted the door and went out. The crying came again, and he followed it to his father's room. Outside it he found Callie. "Was that you?" he said.

"Nassah."

The cry came from inside the room, and he reached for the knob, but Callie braced herself in his way.

"Master say let nobody come!"

"He's hurting the girl!"

"Go to your bed, sah, love of God!"

Her fear turned him away. When he returned to his room, he heard in his head what was like another child's crying and slowly realized that he was making the noise. He remembered the time he had cried, hearing his father whip his mother. His throat thickened, and stuff came up the back way into his mouth. He managed to get to the washbowl before he vomited. Then he washed the bowl into the slop jar set underneath his bed and drank a glass of water from the pitcher. In bed he told himself: think of night and nothing. Some time later he heard the dry shuffle of bare feet in the hallway and a closing door. Then there was silence. Sleep would not come, though he closed his eyes and begged God for it.

24.

Casey posed and photographed them on the wide, shallow steps that followed the porch on three sides of the big house at Beulah Land. First he required the principal group: Nell, Sarah, Benjamin, Jane, Daniel. Then there were separate posings of Casey and Sarah, Sarah and Benjamin, Jane and Daniel, Nell and Daniel, Sarah and Abraham, Sarah and Josephine and Mabella. Mabella wept that her soul was being stolen, but when Josephine cuffed her and gave her the choice of staying or going, she stayed. Last, Sarah asked Casey to make a portrait of Benjamin alone. Benjamin stood for it, serious and still, and when Casey spoke the words of release, a large smile broke over Benjamin's face. "Happy New Year, everybody!"

It was a bright, overcast day, and they drifted indoors, marveling that it was 1874 and making vocal lists of who had died and who had married and who been born in the old year finished. When they went their separate ways a little later, Benjamin mounted his horse and rode to Highboro to make New Year's Day calls. The first was on James and Maggie Davis. The second was at the little house shared by Miss Eloise Kilmer and his Aunt Doreen, where he allowed one of the cats to crouch on his lap, making it difficult for him to drink his tea, while the other sat directly in front of him on the carpet, gazing at him with total disbelief that such a thing as a man existed, and that if one did, he should have penetrated that tiny, tidy parlor.

Bonard and Frankie Saxon had taken residence in their own house two days after Christmas, leaving, as Annabel said, "their Christmas clutter in *mine.*" Benjamin's call on them was brief, although he submitted to a tour during which he praised the taste and richness of the renovation and furnishings, which gratified Frankie and made Bonard look glum. It was no wonder that he had, as everyone declared, "turned over a new leaf" and set to work earnestly on the business of the sawmill. To do anything else would have been to sink under his all but overpowering indebtedness to the bank. The sportiest buck of the county was learning the awful meaning of a hard day's work. As for Frankie, she was everything a first-year bride may correctly be, including pregnant. A woman does not feel that a man is lost to her when he gets another woman with child; but a man's heart abandons a woman who becomes pregnant by another man. Benjamin was whole again; he looked upon Frankie with an even pulse.

He returned to Beulah Land for supper, and the meal was the traditional one for the day of cured hog's head cooked with dried black-eyed peas, served with chopped onions and green tomato relish. After supper Jane and Daniel said good night and went to their house across the yard. Nell was there one minute, and then she was not. When she came to clear used coffee cups and glasses, Mabella said that Josephine was helping her to bed. Casey decided to work on the photographs he had executed that afternoon, leaving Sarah and Benjamin alone.

"Everybody seems to be getting married," Benjamin said.

"Oh?" Sarah said. "Who?"

"Bonard and Frankie. Jane and Daniel. And pretty soon everybody'll be having babies. Frankie's going to. And Prudence is well along."

"And Bessie."

"Yes'm. Well—"

"No 'well.' Bessie was first."

"I wonder if I ought to get married."

"Certainly not because 'everybody else is,' according to you, although I could name you twenty times as many single people who aren't getting married as who are."

He sighed, as if to drop the subject. "One thing. I'm finally going to build me a house in the Glade."

"Are you?"

"Do you reckon Aunt Doreen will ever come back?"

"No," Sarah said. "I truly think not."

"Not much work till plowing starts later this month; even then not enough to keep me and Zadok and the others busy. Seems a good time."

"Mm. What about those repairs we say all summer we'll do when winter comes?"

"Done."

"You're ahead of us."

"I could offer to help Daniel."

"Imagine the answer you'd get. He's been spacing the work so it'll last and not leave the men idle. All right. Maybe you've found the right time to build your house. Are you positive about wanting it at the Glade?"

"Yes'm."

"Why?"

He shifted in his chair, stretched his legs in front of him, crossing them at the ankles. "I hate the house I've lived in since Oaks. The floors are cold, never get warm all winter. Not a one of the fireplaces draws proper. It's not mine. Other people, no kin to me, have lived and died in it."

Sarah recollected the dramas there and the actors who played them. "Yes."

"I want a place that's home, the way I felt about Oaks."

"Why not give the house to Zadok and Rosalie and move in here? They need more space for those children."

He shook his head. "Mine."

"This will be yours."

"Now," he said quietly.

She thought about it and suddenly nodded approval. "Then build."

"I know what I want. I've talked it over with Zadok. We've got Joffee Tompkins coming Monday to help lay it out."

"You *have* decided."

They sat a little while in easy silence. "Grandma, do you think Priscilla Oglethorpe is plain?"

"I don't think her beautiful, athough she may be in time. You never know until it happens."

"I mean now."

"You're full of 'now' tonight. Ben, if you didn't know your own mind, you wouldn't be asking. You're contrary the way your great-grandma Edna was. You never ask anybody anything when you're uncertain."

"I don't think her plain, but I don't want others to."

"That sounds more a matter of your pride than hers."

"Do you think Aunt Annabel is a fool?"

"I should be lying if I said anything but yes."

"Always?"

She considered the qualification. "Yes."

"She might be right sometimes."

"She's right frequently," Sarah conceded. "That isn't what we said. One may be both right and a fool. Annabel is walking testimony."

"What do you know about the Oglethorpes?"

"Daughters: two. Priscilla, nineteen; Elizabeth, called Betty, eleven. Two sons killed in the war. Father Philip lost his left arm up to here at Shiloh. Mother Ann small, proud, good but not amusing."

"I don't think Priscilla is plain."

"Then neither do I. Thank goodness we've settled that."

"Well!" He stood and stretched. "Her mama was serving banana pudding to callers this afternoon."

"Extravagant."

"No'm. Betty said she wouldn't let anybody eat them at Christmas until they got so ripe nobody would. So she made banana pudding."

"A thrifty woman."

"I don't think she likes me."

"Why?"

"She gave me such a little dab of pudding. And hit the serving spoon hard on the plate."

Benjamin's building a house in the Glade was considered a

folly by most of those who delivered themselves of an opinion. Annabel spoke her mind on the church porch the first Sunday after construction was begun. She pointed out that he had no wife, that his other aunt had removed herself from his roof, and that the old farmhouse would certainly do for a young bachelor, and besides he couldn't afford it and would be in debt. He reminded her that he had paid off his long-standing debt to the bank last November. She said that she was only thinking of what was good for him and she reckoned that being his aunt she was entitled to say what she thought. He thanked her for her concern and turned to pay his Sunday respects to Priscilla Oglethorpe, her mother, father, and sister, who were just emerging from the church. Flushing with annoyance, Annabel went directly to Prudence, who was in conversation with Frankie, and told her that she was looking more like a haystack every day. Without appearing to, Sarah observed Benjamin's exchange with the Oglethorpes. Priscilla was unaffectedly pleased at his attention. For the first time Sarah thought that she wasn't so very plain. There was nothing wrong with her features save a certain pallor and lack of animation. She had clear, intelligent eyes, but her brown hair was dull and dressed severely, making her appear a decade older than she was until one looked her straight in the face and saw her youth. The younger sister was shy at an age most girls begin to embroider their girlishness with silliness. The elder Oglethorpes were grave and correct, certainly not warm in their reception of her grandson. She wondered if there was something in Benjamin's feeling that Mrs. Oglethorpe did not like him. She had never paid much attention to her, considering her a strait and crabbed woman. And then Doreen and Miss Kilmer made a pounce on Benjamin and drew him away to tell them about the building of his new house.

Sarah had put by her qualms before she lost them, but now she counted herself an enthusiastic ally of her grandson. She had loved the Glade before Benjamin was born. To know that he loved it gave her a deepened sense of the continuity of life at Beulah Land which Benjamin increasingly provided. He was her son and heir and she was his mother, without any regard to their tenuous blood relationship. True kinship becomes evident only with time and is little to do with the entries in family Bibles and the carvings of family tombstones.

After listening to what Benjamin said of his needs and hopes

of it, Joffee Tompkins planned the house on the land itself, be-
before he laid it out on paper. Soon after, Sarah was invited to the
Glade to "walk" the plan as Benjamin explained it to her.
Carried along by his vision, she soon appreciated the logic
behind it. She approved his leaving the place as it was. Only two
trees would have to be cut; there would be no changing the
course of the brook, no shifting of rock and shelves of slate. The
house would follow the site, not be imposed on it. There were to
be no farm buildings, only a covered stall for a milk cow. The
barns, pigpens, and chicken yards would remain below at the old
farmhouse, which Zadok and Rosalie and their five children
would find none too large. A well was already sunk to provide
water. A road between the Glade house above and the farmhouse below was being laid out, following and widening the old
pathway.

Once the project became definite, others visited, skeptical on
arrival, believers on departure. Roman and Roscoe were brought
by Abraham on a warm afternoon in February when school was
over. Sarah and Jane were there without Benjamin's invitation or
encouragement, Jane having decided that it was time to think of
flowers. The natural setting was all very well, but a place was
not civilized to Jane's mind until seeds were planted, cuttings
set, and vines trained. They would do nothing, she assured him,
that could not be changed or abandoned if it did not suit the
taste of the occupants of the house.

Spying the three as they came up the hill and into the clearing, Sarah called, "You, Abraham! Come here to me and hold
this stake! —Afternoon, Roman, Roscoe. You come help too."
Roscoe had not been to Beulah Land since Jane's marriage, and
it gave him as much pain as pleasure to see how blooming a wife
she made. But as they worked together, they were united in their
teasing of Abraham and easy in their other talk, and the tension
in Roscoe faded.

Most of them had some past connection with the Glade, unknown to each other, unknown even to one of themselves, for
Benjamin had been conceived there. Sarah remembered the time
—so very long ago, it seemed to her now—Casey asked her there
so that he might make sketches for the portrait he had been commissioned by Leon to paint. It was there they had become lovers.
It was there she'd had the encounter with Alonzo Elk that
resulted in Roman's killing his half brother. Roman remembered

his meetings in the Glade with the Davis tutor, Driscoll Proctor. Benjamin had his own memories, of Nancy and of Bessie Marsh.

Rosalie arrived swinging a lidded basket. Before starting supper, she said, she'd fried a batch of apple tarts, to use up the dried apples she was afraid would go moldy. Were they hungry? Everybody accepted one, eating it from their hands as they walked about discussing the progress of the building.

Another day Doreen came with Miss Kilmer, and they stood watching with their hands behind their backs as if to emphasize that they were town ladies, reluctant to touch country things. But they gathered a few pine cones before leaving, as toys, they said, for the dear pussies, Jessie and Jezebel. They told Benjamin that it was not too soon to train a cat for the house and leave her there to watch the rats. Annabel sent word that she might find an hour to come out if Benjamin required her advice. She remembered the Glade as a quaint little place and said that it had served very well as the site of Bonard's birthday picnic. Bonard, however, did not come; nor did Frankie.

25.

Benjamin had his visitors at the Glade; while among hers at Beulah Land, Sarah received one of some importance to Benjamin's future. On a cloudy, drizzly afternoon in late February, she lighted the fire in her office, where she sat sewing for Bessie Marsh. She and Bessie had become friendly. There was no embarrassment between them any more than there was pretense of affectionate ties when they talked of the coming child. Each looked upon it in a practical way, leaving the poetry of its birth for Benjamin to ponder. Bessie worked hard on her family's farm and was grateful to Sarah for making the baby clothes, which she had little time to do and her mother was too nearly blind to manage. When Mabella knocked at the door to say Mrs. Oglethorpe was there and asked to see her, Sarah laid down her work and went to welcome her guest.

"I hope you won't mind sitting in the office, ma'am. There is a fire, and it is the place I spend much of my time."

Entering, Ann Oglethorpe shook her head impatiently, as if to ward off civilities. She accepted a chair without observing the room. "I can say what I have come for anywhere."

Sarah sat. "And what is that, since you put it so? —Let me just tell the girl to bring us tea."

"No, I thank you. I never take it."

Sarah waited. However wanting in manner she considered her guest, she could see that she was preoccupied and troubled. For a few moments her eyes held on the sewing Sarah had put aside, without seeming to see what they looked at. "There is a habit of second marriages in your family, madam."

Sarah stared at her. "I fail to understand—?"

"Yourself. You are now Mrs. Troy. However, I knew you first as Mrs. Leon Kendrick."

"I was a widow for several years, ma'am, before Mr. Troy and I were married."

"Benjamin Davis will be your heir?"

"Yes!"

"His father, Mr. James Davis, married twice."

"My daughter died."

"Threw herself out of a window. Brain fever, they said. However that may be, Mr. Davis's second wife, too, was marrying for the second time."

"The war made many widows."

"Your sister, Mrs.—I believe her name is now Mrs. Colonel Ward Varnedoe, but she did marry more than once—at any rate, I hope she did."

Sarah suppressed a smile. "She did, ma'am."

Mrs. Oglethorpe appeared to struggle with her feelings. "These second marriages are common among you and show a certain—adaptability that I cannot find sympathetic."

"I'm afraid I do not understand what you mean to say to me, Mrs. Oglethorpe."

"This: I do not consider your grandson suitable."

"I am in the dark. You were speaking of second marriages and then my grandson. He has not married once!"

"Exactly! And he must not look to us!"

Sarah required a few moments to collect her thoughts and to order her temper before she spoke. "Mrs. Oglethorpe, do you mean to tell me that Benjamin has made a proposal of marriage to your daughter Priscilla?"

The visitor looked much agitated. "No, and he shall not!"

"Let us try to speak as calmly as we can about this. I am not aware that my grandson's attachment is serious enough to indicate marriage."

"Ah, so you admit it!" cried the lady in horror. "Then what can he intend but seduction and our ruination?"

"Mrs. Oglethorpe! I must say that your words shock and offend me. I have the highest regard and respect for my grandson, and it is fully deserved."

"Why, *why* does he look to her?"

"I ask you to tell me if my grandson has behaved improperly to any of your family, ma'am."

"No, he has not," said the lady in despair. "Oh, Mrs. Troy! My daughter is a plain girl. When I understood that she was to be so, I rejoiced, seeing protection in it of her virtue. But now see what has happened! She is singled out for particular attention—she is 'courted,' if you will—by the acknowledged libertine of the county!"

"My good Mrs. Oglethorpe, I cannot allow you to say—"

"Was he not engaged to be married to the Savannah traveler who is now Mrs. Bonard Saxon?"

"He was not." Seeing the incredulity in the other's face, she went on. "I do not say he was indifferent to her. He was, in fact —infatuated, if you allow me the word."

"Any you please, so long as you keep to the truth!"

"They were not, however, engaged to marry."

"His sister! Was she not meant to marry that same Mr. Saxon before he changed his mind, or she hers, or both together, and she became Mrs. Todd?"

"She was most certainly not engaged to Mr. Saxon. My grandson often and properly keeps his own counsel. My granddaughter is good enough to confide in me. She never loved Mr. Saxon, and her marriage to Mr. Todd, although it may have appeared sudden to you, was the fulfillment of a long hope of mine and others in the family who knew them both. —However! What has any of this to do with—?"

"What an unruly family you are!"

"Mrs. Oglethorpe!"

"Is it true that Benjamin Davis has got Bessie Marsh with child?"

"Why, yes."

"He acknowledges it, I am told, so you would have to say so."

"Madam, I am being lenient with you because I see your agitation, but I must warn you that—"

"I need no warning, I have it already! Can one hope for constancy in a young man who proudly acknowledges unborn bastards his begotten, while he freely pays attention to respectable young women?"

"It may be unusual, ma'am, but no matter for alarm, I pray you will believe."

"A veritable license for immorality. Is that what you ask for your grandson?"

"I do not at this moment, ma'am, see how the behavior of any of my family should be your concern. I will speak no more of it. I am sorry, but you have—" She paused, her head trembling, her bosom rising and falling rapidly. "I must apologize for allowing myself to become as overwrought as you evidently are."

Ann Oglethorpe's eyes suddenly glistened in the firelight. "I have offended you. I apologize. I am truly sorry. But I would risk offending you a thousand times over to save my daughter."

Striving for a calmer tone, Sarah said, "Perhaps your daughter is not in such danger as you suppose. I will say, although I do not like to speak of the feelings of one of my family to any outside it: I am not—I have not been told by Benjamin of any strong feeling he may have for Priscilla. If he should ever develop such, he will speak for himself. I assure you that he will speak truly. He is in everything honorable."

Mrs. Oglethorpe dried her eyes angrily. "I have done this badly. If I had only asked what I came to ask and nothing else!"

"What was that, ma'am?"

"That you tell your grandson he is unwelcome in our house, that his attentions, whether serious or light, are unwelcome to my daughter."

"I take your request, ma'am, as a command. I shall speak to Benjamin this day."

"You will have my gratitude." Mrs. Oglethorpe rose from her chair jerkily, as if she had been sitting longer than she had been. Her eyes went again to the bundle of sewing that had given

Sarah employment before the intrusion of the visit, and this time she saw what her eyes looked upon. "Baby clothes. Whose?"

"I am making them for Bessie Marsh."

A shudder passed through the slight, straight frame of the woman. "Then you condone her behavior."

"Oh, Mrs. Oglethorpe, if only you could be less solemn about it all!"

"Nothing you have said, madam, shocks me more than that. I do not ask you to understand us—only to leave us alone!"

Sarah bowed her head in anger and humiliation as her caller hurried from the room.

She returned to her sewing, but after twice pricking her fingers deeply enough to draw blood, she put it down again. Setting a screen around the fireplace, she found a shawl on the chaise longue and left the house. The drizzle had stopped, but it was still chilly and the ground was wet, and her shoes were muddy by the time she climbed to the Glade. Benjamin was high in the rafters, but she called him to come down and together they went into the cabin he had built earlier, and now used as a workshop, and would tear down when the new house was finished. Quickly, as quietly as she could, she told him of the interview with Mrs. Oglethorpe. He did not interrupt except to ask now and then that she repeat a direct quotation so that he might be certain he had it right in his mind. When she finished, he said, "Damnation," but not as if he had been surprised by her recital of the event. "Did she come with Priscilla's knowledge?"

"She did not say so, nor did I ask; but I cannot conceive her taking such a step without her husband's consent and without having first told her daughter what they had agreed."

"So." He rose from the side of the bunk where he had sat as she talked, and walked to the doorway, moving as if he were tired after a long day's labor. She followed him and took his hand. He would not hold hers, but shook it playfully and let it go. "Not going to be so easy to marry me off, is it, Grandma?"

"Ben, I don't interfere with you, but don't go to Crawford's tonight."

He smiled dimly. "No, ma'am, I won't be doing that. I did because of Frankie, but this is different. I'm going to build my house. Maybe I'll live in it alone."

26.

The most reliable thing at "Big Beulah," as Junior Elk sarcastically called his house, was the food. Geraldine knew what was good and how to make it, and Roscoe considered that it was the only thing he would mind leaving when he went away. On a blowy March morning he and Junior paraded the front portico smoking cigars after a bountiful breakfast of fried beef steaks smothered in onion-flour gravy, grits and eggs, biscuits and watermelon-rind preserves. They walked back and forth, not together, passing each other with awareness but no acknowledgment of look or remark until the mesmeric spell of wind-sound was broken by a scream of pain from the kitchen quarters at the back of the house. Junior continued his walking as if he had not heard. Roscoe stopped, looked at his father, and waited. The scream was followed by a chattering of voices, then a wail and the hard bouncing of metal. Watching his father, Roscoe observed that he frowned and then drew more deeply on his cigar, but his pacing was not interrupted until two women came running through the center breezeway and onto the portico. They were Geraldine and the plain cook, Roxanne.

"You got to do something!" Geraldine implored furiously. "That Roberta, she crazy! Went to lift the coffeepot from the stove to pour her a cup and it shook in her hand so, she splashed herself. Threw it down on the floor! Coffee everwhere! That not enough, she grabbed the kettle full of boiling water—"

"I was fixing to wash my dishes!" Roxanne wailed in explanation.

"You hush and let me tell it! —Chunked it down! Right on the floor! Scalding water everwhere!"

Roxanne was nodding rapidly and lifted her skirt to show a bleached and blistered patch of thigh. "Scalded me! *Scalded* me! Help mercy!"

"Get back where you belong, both of you," Junior commanded.

"I've told you never to be here unless you come to serve or clean. Now, move!"

"You got to make *her* move!" Geraldine said.

"Where is she?"

"Went running out—God knows—off cross the yard."

"You get on back where you belong." The women looked at him doubtingly but retreated to the breezeway. Junior recommenced his pacing in deliberate calm. After a moment he addressed himself to the air. "I'll put her away."

"The way you did Mama?" Roscoe said.

Junior turned as if surprised to find him there. "Your ma went crazy. She had every care in the asylum. I paid for it."

"You saw she never left it till she died, too. I went to look it over, one of my Savannah trips."

"I like you knowing things," Junior said, "but I don't like you snooping. Your ma is lucky I didn't kill her when I found her with that Yankee officer. Nobody would have charged me."

"Captain Ponder burned Beulah Land and Oaks for you, and you paid him back in your fashion. Do you think because I was a boy I couldn't see and hear? If I didn't understand it then, I did later. You got rid of him and Mama when you were through with them."

Junior looked at him a long moment before pointing his cigar at him. "You be careful I don't get rid of you too, if it suits me."

"You won't have to do that. I'm leaving."

"You move when I say. You've got no money."

"I've enough to get me to Philadelphia. I wrote them a month ago, and they'll take me on again. I was a little more than the office cat, in spite of what you think."

"Have you been stealing money from me?"

"Only what I want for the trip and to keep me a month."

"You'll go if and when I say and not otherwise."

"No, sir. I'll go when I say."

Junior closed his eyes. His lips moved as if he were adding. "Today. I want you out of here today, you blue-eyed son of a near-white bitch. Take nothing but your clothes and your appetite. If I miss a cigar, I'll have you arrested at the wharf in Savannah."

Junior threw his lighted cigar into the front yard and went into the house and through the breezeway. In the kitchen Geraldine and Roxanne heard him coming. Stepping to the door, they saw him stop on the back porch and take down the whip coiled on a nail there. He often carried it when he walked his land; but today the watching women smirked at each other, and Roxanne whispered, "Him gone find that Berta and beat shit outen her."

"He can do it," Geraldine assured her. "I seen him one time go for Roscoe's mu-dear. It was a sight."

Others saw him too. Hoeing grass from a field so that young plants might survive, four men watched him without appearing to watch. By nightfall the wife of one of the two white tenants was to relate a hundred times that she'd been in the yard with her terrier bitch turning the woodpile upside down to find a rats' nest they knew was there, when he passed without speaking, which was not unusual, walking with his head down and the whip coiled loosely at his side.

As he came to Callie's cabin, he stepped on the drooping wing of a sick hen drowsing in the dirt by the single doorstep. The chicken gave the alarm to those inside, and when Junior entered, he caught the mother and two daughters in attitudes of fear and threat. Claribell cowered on the floor. Roberta stood over her with a switch she had broken from a peach tree on her way down from the big house. Callie was flattened against the wall as though to beg pardon.

"What are you doing now?" Junior said.

Roberta said, "You're just in time to watch a whipping."

"Let her up."

As if the command to Roberta was one also to her, Claribell crawled quickly beyond her sister's reach, raised herself to a crouch, and ran in that posture out the back door of the one-room cabin.

Callie was looking at her master in terror. "I didn't tell her! Swear 'fore God I didn't tell her, sah! Not me!"

"Did she?" Junior said to Roberta.

"Tell me you been fucking Claribell?" She shook her head. "Geraldine told me."

"After I teach you a lesson, I'll tend to her," Junior promised.

"You say it's so?" Roberta was astounded. "You think you smart! Nobody told me nothing till you just now. I was beating that child for stealing my blue beads."

As he looked at Callie, Roberta laughed. "What kind of man you be, want to prong a youngun like her? Let me tell you: you ain't messing with her no more. I'm more woman than you can fuck, you remember that. I been letting you by easy, but no more. You going to take me to town and us get married. Roberta and Roberta alone is to be Missus Junior from now on."

"What about the missus I've got?"

"She locked-up-crazy, don't count no more. You get rid of her, you hear? You know how. Oh yeah, you know how. Ain't you bragged when half of you was up my hole how you done this one and that one? You had the ride, time now to pay me."

Junior's lips drew apart; his eyes crinkled. He appeared to be laughing but without making any sound until he spoke. "There's no missus; she's dead. I could marry you this minute if I was minded to. —Marry you? By God, look at you. You stink like a privy. Your hair's full of lard and lice. You haven't changed your dress for a week. No wonder my fat boy locks his door to keep you out at night."

Roberta's hand had gone to her hair, but her eyes had gone to the wooden table in the center of the room. There was knife on it, old and tarnished, its blade nicked in so many places it might have served as a saw. Callie kept it sharp with spit and whetstone. She called it her everything knife, and indeed it was used for everything from gutting fish and fowl to hacking through salted sow belly. Roberta moved to the table, her hand edging along its surface until Junior lifted his foot and threw the table on its side, dropping the knife to the wooden floor, where it stuck point first.

"You hear what I told you?" Junior said.

"Who's dead?" Roberta said.

"My wife."

"When she die?"

"Long time ago."

"How come you never say to me?"

"How come I ought to say to you?" He mocked her voice and question.

"You promised me!"

"I don't promise sluts; sluts promise me."

"You tricked me," she said, sounding more sullen and tired than angry.

"You and your bitch ma tricked each other."

Callie cried, "Nawsah! I didn't tell her nothing!"

Roberta said, "Is she dead sure enough?"

"Dead as rainwater," Junior told her.

"Me waiting to be told." Roberta's voice strove for wounded dignity.

Callie edged her way along the wall.

"Mama." Roberta's voice stopped her. "Is he telling me the truth?"

Callie slid wordless to the floor, abject as a dog seeking to apologize for bad behavior.

"Roscoe's leaving," Junior said.

"Where to?" Roberta looked at Junior in panic. "Make him take me!"

"Maybe I will. I told him to get his big belly out of my house. It's a good morning's work, getting rid of you and him. You're a good pair."

Roberta had begun to weep. "Mama, what he say? You remember he promised me —You tell him so, he got to! Listen, Mama, listen good. You been taking Claribell to him? —You, Big Man, tell me true now, your missy die?"

"Ask Roscoe. He knows all about it."

"Knows and never cried? His mama?"

Junior looked at Roberta for the last time before turning to Callie. "You see to her going by night, or you go too. I'll let you both starve before I let you suck a shuck of my corn." He turned and left.

Roberta caught Junior as he stepped down from cabin to ground. She leapt on his back like the wildcat he had sometimes called her, slashing the knife into his neck and face and eyes and nose and cheeks. He bellowed, but she clung. He could not shake her, and she rode him as he sank to his knees and crumpled on the ground, blood pulsing from a dozen cuts.

When they heard his first roar of surprise, the four field hands dropped their hoes, and the white woman and her bitch terrier left their rats' nest prize. But when they got there, Junior Elk was beyond rescue, perhaps already dead; or if not, his life flowed out of him as they gaped, spreading over and into the bare earth. Roberta was still on him, and she did not stop using the knife until they grabbed and pulled her away, kicking her further into the yard as others, hearing the clamor, came running. One of the men turned Junior over so that he lay on his back. Both eyes were out of their sockets, and lips and nose were sliced away, his teeth exposed in a bloody death's head grin. From the doorway of the cabin Callie laughed.

27.

Both Benjamin and Sarah were keeping mainly to home and work, because home suited them and work on the land required their attention. They went into Highboro for church on Sunday, but for common errands relied on others. Benjamin's house in the Glade was up: topped and bottomed, roofed and sided. He would take his time finishing it, for the plowing and planting now consumed a large part of every day. The chimneys had lifted their first smoke, but only to test the fireplaces. They would have all summer to dry and settle. A few times Benjamin spent the night there, sleeping in a quilt on rough floorboards merely to see what it felt like. But however known and familiar and *his* it had become by day, darkness made him an intruder on the Glade's night privacy.

Benjamin had not, of course, called at the Oglethorpe house since Mrs. Oglethorpe's visit to Sarah. He saw Priscilla at church, but she was always flanked by mother and father. Aware of her plainness—had not her mother rejoiced in it all her life?—she had never learned the ways a pretty girl takes to tell a young man without words that she finds him interesting. Benjamin on his side appeared to interpret her shyness as coolness and kept his distance. One missed or awkward encounter prepares the participants for the next, and Benjamin's and Priscilla's diffidence matched and encouraged each other's.

Sarah studied them to discover the true nature of their sentiments, and could not. She had not forgotten her own feeling of inadequacy as a girl competing with her older, prettier sister, but she decided that Priscilla accepted her parents' dictates with no complaint. As for Benjamin, he made no display of regard as he had done when Frankie was Miss Dollard. Late one afternoon as she worked beside him smoothing the surface of a windowsill, she asked, "Why did you decide to build now? You never answered when I put the question early on."

"It just seemed right."

"I've seen too many birds build their nests to take that as anything but evasion."

"All right, Grandma," he said, "I'm building a nest."

"For whom? Or do you know?"

"Yes'm."

She sighed with impatience. "You make me tired."

He smiled, more for himself than her. "I have to wait."

"Are you thinking about Priscilla Oglethorpe, or have you got your bee-nose in another flower?"

"It's Priscilla."

"You're sure you want her?"

"Yes'm." He hesitated. "She's not a girl I used to think about. I might not have at all but for Aunt Annabel's mentioning her, and then I put it aside. But Priscilla got into my mind, and there she stayed." He shook his head to indicate that he could not express what he meant. "She's—good."

"Young men seldom love girls because they are good."

"Oh, ma'am, that's not all of it."

He said no more, and she felt that she had intruded enough.

It was not until a morning in March when Sarah and Casey drove into town to meet the Savannah train that Sarah saw Priscilla alone. After they watched the train come and go, Casey strolled to the dry-goods store, through which he now ordered certain supplies for his cameras, while Sarah made her way to the post office to wait for the sorting of mail and exchange gossip with others doing the same. She claimed a letter from Lauretta and opened and read it as she walked back to the buggy.

Lauretta and Colonel Varnedoe had spent a month in New York in late winter, returning only two weeks before to their house on the Maryland shore. Lauretta gave minute descriptions of new dresses and hats, shoes and a corset. She referred cursorily to her anticipation of the delights of coming spring. She gave it as her opinion that she had not expected to see another year begin with Aunt Nell still enrolled among the living inhabitants of this world, and asked to be remembered affectionately to all who loved her. She reported that the recent stay in New York had seen the successful conclusion of several business matters for her husband. "In spite of the Panic last year, our fortunes remain serene. Should anything—Heaven forbid!—happen to remove the dear Colonel from the marital embrace, I shall not have to tread the boards again to earn my bread."

Musing that she quite enjoyed Lauretta as long as she did not have to see her, Sarah folded the letter and dropped it into her reticule. Still thinking of her older sister, she looked up to find herself back at the buggy and facing Priscilla Oglethorpe and her younger sister.

"Good morning, Mrs. Troy," Priscilla said quietly.

"Good morning, Priscilla. Good morning, Elizabeth. How pretty you both look!"

Unused to such address, the girls were startled, but Priscilla said at once, "And so do you, Mrs. Troy."

"Betty, I wonder if you'll do me a favor? I seem to have lost a small oblong package wrapped in blue paper. I was at the post office last. If you'll look there—I must have dropped it. And if you don't find it, just step along to Mr. Pilbeam's and ask if I left it on his counter. We'll wait for you here."

The young girl skipped away, happy to be given an unexpected errand.

Sarah then said, "Are you keeping busy this spring, Priscilla?"

"Only the usual things with Mama and some church work."

"Ah!" Sarah smiled benevolently, as people do at the mention of church work. "We have so much to do out our way, it seems. You'll have heard that my grandson is finally building a house for himself in what he calls the Glade. —But you were there for Bonard Saxon's birthday picnic, I remember. Almost a year ago! So quickly does a year pass."

"Benjamin has been very busy then," Priscilla said slowly, as if the information might have special significance for her.

"Yes, but then that's always so."

"He hasn't come into town often."

"No," Sarah agreed, "but he might if there were a particular encouragement."

"I understand that Miss Doreen will be staying on at Miss Eloise's."

"She seems happier in town."

"I trust Benjamin doesn't find himself too much alone because of it." She hesitated. "But perhaps he—if he is building a new house for himself, he has plans for the future."

"Hope, I think. Not yet plans."

"I shan't be sly and try to tease you into telling me who she may be."

"You know her very well, I assure you. But perhaps you don't really care?"

"Oh, I do, ma'am." She blushed and checked the sudden movement she had begun to reach to Sarah. "Here is my sister."

Sarah said with vexation, "There, Betty, you must have run all the way. You mustn't, you know. The streets of town are getting so crowded, you never know when a cart will suddenly be wheeled in front of you."

"I didn't find it either place, Mrs. Troy."

"Then will you just inquire at Mrs. Bascom's candy shop? And here's a penny for your trouble. Buy yourself something sweet to suck. And don't run! A girl's heart is a delicate thing."

Betty left them again.

"As a fact, Priscilla, I tell you Benjamin *is* lonely. I think he would be particularly pleased if you stopped to see him one day —finding yourself in the country and passing."

"If Benjamin wanted to see me, Mrs. Troy, I think he would come to visit the way he used occasionally to do."

Sarah had discovered what she'd set out to learn. "That is just what he may not do, my dear. He has been asked by your mother to stay away from the Oglethorpe house."

"My mother!"

"I thought you knew, and so did he."

"Please tell me what you mean, Mrs. Troy."

As briefly as she could, and with as little resentment of Mrs. Oglethorpe as she could manage, Sarah related what had transpired, finishing with: "I am certain that she did so only because of her concern for you. But I know my grandson, and there is no better young man in the world. —Here is your sister again!" To the younger girl she said, "Betty, you would verily outstrip the messenger of the gods! What have you there?"

In each cheek Betty held a boiled candy, one green and the other yellow, but they were not the subject of Sarah's question. The child carried a box. It was oblong, and it was wrapped in shiny blue paper. Perhaps Sarah had herself seen it somewhere that morning and its description had come handily to mind when she found herself inventing.

"Isn't it yours?" Betty found it difficult to form the words around the two candies in her mouth.

Sarah stared at the box. "No, dear. You must take it right back where you found it before Sheriff Byrne comes and puts you in jail." As the girl began to run, Sarah called after her. "Never mind looking further! I left it right here in the buggy all the time!"

"Mrs. Troy," Priscilla said. "Thank you for telling me what you have. I did not know. I honor my mother, but I am not a child, and if Benjamin wants to see me, then he shall!"

"It would be wicked of me to advise disobedience, but if you did not know, then you have not been forbidden to see him, have you?"

"No! I have not." For the first time that morning, a real smile softened her face. "You follow the letter of the law and not the spirit, ma'am."

"Always when it is to my advantage." Sarah, who had been watching her throughout their exchange except for the seconds she'd had to spare to Betty Oglethorpe, said softly, "Priscilla, I meant what I said when we met. You are pretty."

The girl looked at her eagerly. Sarah knew that she was not pretty, but seeing her then, she thought she might one day become beautiful. "Another thing: whatever your mother may advise, you have nothing to fear from Benjamin."

"I know that, Mrs. Troy. I have always known it. He is— good."

There was the word again, Sarah observed to herself. She had no more idea now what the girl meant by it than she'd had when Benjamin used it. Her eye catching movement in the distance, she exclaimed, "Here comes that child again! Help me—I've run out of things to say to her. There was never a package, blue or otherwise."

Priscilla's laughter leapt to exhilaration. "She hasn't enjoyed herself so much since her rabbit died!" She explained: "Mama let her plan a whole funeral. She said it would be good training for the future, for people are always dying!"

"Mrs. Troy," said the honest Betty, not even breathing hard, "I don't think I should have spent your penny before finding your package, but I did. I'll give the sweets back. They're only a little used and they'll last ever so long."

"Keep them, my dear." Sarah patted her shouder. "You're a good girl. Good morning to both of you!"

The Oglethorpe sisters went on their way, each happier than she had been before meeting Sarah on their morning walk into town. Sarah got into the buggy to wait for Casey. She reread

Lauretta's letter and put it away again. Casey had not returned. An occasional acquaintance passed along the sidewalk with whom she exchanged greetings, but no one paused to talk for more than a few seconds. She reached down for the horse's tail and held it on her lap. The horse looked around at her inquiringly as she took a handful of his tail bristles and idly began to plait them. Glancing up presently, she saw Casey hurrying toward the buggy. She shook out the plait and wiped her hands together. When Casey was close enough for her to see his eyes, she knew something had happened and got down to meet him. "What is the matter?" she asked before he reached her.

He took her hands. "They are saying that Junior Elk has been killed."

He felt the hard shudder go through her as she said, "How?"

"I don't know. Roscoe is with the sheriff."

"Let's go to him."

When they arrived at the jail, which also served as Sheriff Byrne's office, there was a little crowd in front of it made up of more than the usual town loungers and drifters. Sarah did not pause to speak to them but instead marched directly in, Casey after her. She found the sheriff and Roscoe Elk seated, with the sheriff's desk between them. "Is it true?" she said to Roscoe, ignoring Byrne. The sheriff kept his seat, but Roscoe came to her and Casey and told them what had happened.

Junior Elk was dead, and a woman named Roberta was being held in jail. She admitted, even boasted of having wielded the knife against the dead man. Her mother Callie had agreed with everything anyone said, which had caused confusion for a time, but something like a true account of events had been collected and given substance by the field hands working nearby and by Mrs. Mullins, who had with her terrier been expelling rats from a woodpile in the vicinity of the attack.

"What can we do to help you?" Casey said.

"Nothing," Roscoe answered.

"When you are done here, come to us," Sarah suggested.

"I'd better go home," Roscoe said. "The people will want to know everything."

"Of course," Sarah agreed.

"Are you going back to Beulah Land?" Roscoe asked. Casey nodded. "Will you stop at the school and tell Roman and ask him to come? I'd like him to be here, as he and Papa were half brothers."

Casey promised that they would. The sheriff glared balefully as they left. There had never been friendly relations between the old man who had for so long been sheriff of Highboro and those who lived at Beulah Land. Quickly, Sarah and Casey went through the crowd of the curious and reached the buggy. As they drove toward the school, Sarah said in a voice of wonder, "For the first time since I came here as a girl, there is no Roscoe Elk I must hate and fear."

Casey said, "That boy is now the richest man in the county."

28.

Alive, Junior Elk had been one of the most important men in the county. Dead, he was a dead Negro.

His murder provided sensation enough, but it was an excitement devoid of personal involvement for those who enjoyed it. Junior had no friend, and his only acknowledged family was his son, who claimed a larger share of the general interest than his father because he was his heir. Then too, victim and executor of the crime were colored, and it was assumed to be a matter of primitive passions, remarkable only in that no one had ever considered Junior Elk vulnerable to such. The possibility of sustained interest in the case by way of a trial was annulled the next morning when Sheriff Byrne arrived at the jailhouse to find the naked body of Roberta swinging from the rope and noose she had made of her dress. It was published that she had taken her life in a fit of fearful remorse, which satisfied the public conscience if not private truth, which was that Byrne had told her she would surely hang at the end of her trial, and she had anticipated the hangman in despair that was close to madness. Roscoe gave her proper burial early on the day his father received more ceremonial disposal. Attendance at both was substantial.

During the week following his father's death Roscoe came often to Beulah Land to ask Sarah's advice, or merely to sit with

her in her office to talk over whatever was on his mind; and there
was much. Several times she went with him to the Elk house.
When she first saw it, she stared with a recognition she could
scarce credit, observing after he showed her around that although
she'd heard that his father held the original house at Beulah
Land in mind when he built, she had not imagined how it would
look. She decided that it was more a freehand drawing than a
copy. "For nothing is accurate, everything a little wrong or off-
scale."

Her first visit was to decide Geraldine's fate. Sarah asked Roscoe to let her talk to the housekeeper alone, and the two women
sat together for half an hour in the replica of the office at the old
Beulah Land. Afterwards, Sarah told Roscoe she thought Geraldine's days of causing trouble were done. She was growing old,
and her great fear was that she was now to be abandoned. On
Sarah's departure, Roscoe was able to reassure Geraldine,
thereby winning her loyalty; and the fact that she had been
approved by the mistress of Beulah Land enhanced her authority
over the remaining servants.

The tenants were told to go on as they had done until further
orders were given. Since Roscoe knew little of farming, Sarah
asked Daniel to accompany him once a week on a tour of the
tenants' fields that once had been the Davis plantation and now
comprised the Elk estate. Although he had a good understanding
of local law, Roscoe kept on the white lawyer his father had employed, thus providing continuity to business dealings in Savannah as well as the area of Highboro.

One revelation came as a thunderbolt: Claribell was pregnant.
Roscoe made the discovery when he caught Callie beating her
daughter; he took the problem to Roman, who took it to Pauline
and Selma. The consultants moved that the girl be separated
once and forevermore from her mother. She was put into the
care of Josephine at Beulah Land until her future could be decided, since it was deemed urgent to get her right away from
those she had known at the Elk house.

Although Sarah followed these developments closely, she still
had a mind to consider the affairs of Benjamin and Priscilla
Oglethorpe. On the Sunday after her chance meeting with Sarah,
Priscilla gave particular attention to Benjamin at the church as
he went about among acquaintances. She noted that he was, as
always in town, clean and dressed in good, sober clothes. His

smile with those who sought his attention was gentle, yet generous. His attitude toward his father and stepmother and his Aunt Annabel was carefully reserved, she thought. She was delighted to see him appear surprised to meet Frankie and Bonard Saxon, as if he had forgotten their existence. His manners with his grandmother and his sister were easy and fond and proud—and, oh, she envied him that, as she glanced at her own prim mother and dour father. Except for Betty, who was at an age and stage to bore everyone including herself, Priscilla was thoroughly sick of her family. There were even moments when she wondered if it were Benjamin she cared about or his family. Sarah and Casey Troy, Jane and Daniel Todd—all who lived at Beulah Land seemed to her blessed with a confidence in themselves and an affability toward each other beyond anything she had known in families.

She watched Benjamin turn his eyes gradually in her direction, and then he was looking directly at her; but she guessed that he was uncertain of his reception, for he smiled quickly and moved away, evidently not wanting to approach her as she stood with her parents. She heard little of the sermon that day and did not think of it at all until she sat with her family over their cold noon dinner of boiled potatoes and fat, sinewy beef. Mrs. Oglethorpe vowed that nothing would ever persuade her to offend the Lord by cooking food on His Day. Since she was a poor cook at best, it mattered little to her family. Presently she announced that she considered the morning sermon lacking in substance. No one answered her until Priscilla, pressed for an opinion, said that she had not attended to it and could not remember two consecutive words of it. After frowning at her, Mrs. Oglethorpe discovered that her husband, with only one arm, was having trouble with his beef. She took his plate from him and sawed the meat into small pieces, a service he received with indifference, although when she handed his plate back to him, he began to masticate steadily and glumly. Betty said she wished she'd saved one of the candies Mrs. Troy had given her for running an errand the other day and suddenly remembered to ask Priscilla what she and Mrs. Troy had been talking about that made her look so funny when she came back the second time. Mrs. Oglethorpe stared at Priscilla as her older daughter murmured vaguely about a blue package and turned a potato on her plate, sighing to find the other side of the moon very like that previously visible.

Monday morning it was raining. Priscilla made her way as usual to the church to help Miss Kilmer and Miss Davis with the cleaning and tidying after yesterday's services. She lingered at the pew where Benjamin had sat with those she considered his real family from Beulah Land, touching the song books and prayer books with dreaming hands. In the course of conversation she discovered that next day her companions were to go on a delivery wagon from the dry-goods store to Benjamin's farm, because Doreen wanted to fetch more of her personal belongings to town. It was easy enough to wish a place for herself in the wagon, and she told her mother only that she was going on a country outing with the two ladies.

Soon after the wagon put them down at the farm, Priscilla learned from Rosalie that Benjamin and Zadok were at work on the new house because the ground was too wet from yesterday's rain for them to go to the fields. She set off for the Glade without excuse or explanation. For two as diffident as they, Benjamin and Priscilla greeted each other with an open gladness that dispelled any shyness that might have attended their first private hour. Each felt himself accepted, and that is enough and all. As they walked about, she made no sensitive exclamations and no interesting suggestions; but he liked her plain comments, and he knew that she was saying only what she meant when she told him, "It is a perfect place for you to live. You've loved it all your life."

"Will you live here with me, Priscilla?"

He had surprised her, but not very much. She nodded, and so it was settled.

He laughed. "Great God," he said softly, and repeated it as a shout: "Great God-A-mighty!" Priscilla found that she was laughing with him, and both sensed that their laughter joined them together, even as it separated them from everyone else in the world. Then they found words racing to their lips as they tried to say what neither had ever said to another living soul. That might have gone on longer but that they were practical young people and knew the problems they faced. The main ones were the child Bessie Marsh was about to yield and the bias against their connection by Mrs. Oglethorpe.

Priscilla listened gravely but not reprovingly as Benjamin told of his approaching parenthood and what he intended to do about it. At the end of it she said, "I am sorry for Bessie Marsh, but her child's father cannot be her husband if he is to be mine. I am sorry for you, Ben, because although you are right to admit to him, you cannot treat your first child as entirely yours. I am not sorry for me, for I shall have you and your other children."

They would not yet, they decided, tell anyone the state of their feelings and intentions. Benjamin understood that she would have to maneuver carefully the rapids of her mother's disapproval unless they were to resign themselves to a lasting estrangement. Her father was of less concern. He would agree to whatever her mother recommended. He was a man who had believed in the Southern cause and fought hard for it as a professional soldier. His spirit was lost when his sons and their cause were lost; and his disappointment was aggravated by living with three females, from whose affairs he had schooled himself to be relatively detached.

As soon as Priscilla returned home she found her mother and informed her of her visit to Benjamin's farm, for she had no talent or taste for deception. Although a pious woman, Mrs. Oglethorpe was possessed of a powerful battery of invective, which she trained upon her daughter, bolstered in her militancy by the conviction that she was saving that daughter's soul. Priscilla took the fire with bowed head; but when Mrs. Oglethorpe paused to accept the white flag of defeat, Priscilla instead announced that she was unvanquished. Mrs. Oglethorpe trained her guns again and fired away for another quarter hour only to find when the smoke cleared no weeping penitent but a rebel standing rock firm. No command, no threat of annihilation moved her. She was her mother's daughter. She might stand pale, but she stood without wavering.

The only weapon left was physical force. Mrs. Oglethorpe grasped her by the wrist and led her roughly to her room, in which, she declared, she would be held prisoner until she begged her mother's pardon and pledged obedience and submission.

"If you keep me here," Priscilla replied, "I shall open the windows and scream."

"You have never screamed in your life."

"It is not, I believe, something one has to learn like needlework."

"How dare you be impertinent!"

"I am sorry, but if I were not, I fear I should do worse."

There was more: the resort to calm reason, reminders of the

family's honor and the father's infirmities, and one or two cowardly forays into self-pity. But in the end it was the mother who gave ground. Yet still she persisted. "You will promise not to see him if I leave you free?"

"No, Mama, I will not."

"Then if I allow you to see him in the ordinary ways, and solely for the sake of what others may think, for there must never be gossip about you, you will promise not to marry him."

"No, Mama."

"I say you will! For I shall never *allow* you to marry him!"

"We shall marry finally; that is all I will promise."

When Mrs. Oglethorpe said that she would have to speak to Mr. Oglethorpe, both knew the meaninglessness of the ploy; it was mere playing for time. At the door the mother turned back. "Will you promise not to become engaged to him *now?* It would be a scandal to do so when he is owning up to a child that will be born of sin at any hour. Will you promise to speak to no one of an engagement until I say that it is proper to do so?"

Priscilla thought about it. "I am to see him in the meantime as I will, and he is free to call on me here?"

Hors de combat, Mrs. Oglethorpe opened her hands and bowed her head.

"Very well, Mama. We'll not say that we are engaged to marry until you agree it is a proper time to do so."

Head still bowed, but now to hide the victory she felt she had finally won, Mrs. Oglethorpe left her daughter, and she did not lock the door behind her.

29.

Bessie Marsh's son was born on April 8, a few days before his father's twentieth birthday. As soon as they received the news, Benjamin and Sarah went to the Marsh farm to see the child. Asked what she would name him, Bessie said to Sarah, "I'm hoping you'll let me call him Leon. Mr. Kendrick was always good to us. Gave Ma meal and Pa fodder more than once when we were low, and lent him a plow when ours broke, and other things. He used to bring me a sack of candy from town when he came by. I looked up to him, Mrs. Troy, I sure did. You've been good too, making the baby clothes; and I'd like to."

"I think it will be a good name for him," Sarah said. "Leon Marsh."

Bessie looked down at the infant nursing from her big breast. "Not much milk yet, but there will be, so you go to it, boy. Funny-looking little red thing, but one day you'll take over and run this farm for me."

Benjamin returned often, and on one of his visits brought Priscilla. Bessie was glad to see her and allowed her to hold the baby. The two women ignored Benjamin until Bessie noticed him fidgeting and scooped the baby from Priscilla's lap, giving him to his father. The child gratified her by crying, and Bessie took him back. Holding him against her to quiet him, she smiled at the two who had drawn together to watch her. "I'm glad you're the one," Bessie said. "I'd have minded if it was anybody else."

They did not deny her assumption, only claiming that nothing was definite yet. "Well, don't you wait on my account. I've already got me a fellow coming courting. Talbot Cass, you know him, Ben. Widow man in his thirties bought the farm two miles over after the war. Funny how they start coming when the heifer's freshened. Sits talking to Pa and looking at me. One of these days he's going to make up his mind to speak to me, don't you reckon?" She winked at them, and they laughed.

Bessie was, then, the first to know how Benjamin and Priscilla stood to each other, after Sarah and Mrs. Oglethorpe. But very soon everyone in Highboro was taking for granted a match between Miss Oglethorpe and Benjamin Davis. Benjamin called on her at the Oglethorpe house regularly. The first time after his banishment, Mrs. Oglethorpe sat mournfully with the couple, although Mr. Oglethorpe retired to his study after observing the amenities, and Betty had been bribed to keep to her room with a penny's worth of candy. However, Priscilla and Benjamin ignored her and talked so cheerfully to each other Mrs. Oglethorpe was obliged for the sake of her own dignity to find other occupation in the house, only coming into the sitting room now and then to look at them sternly. Townspeople spoke openly of the courtship, and the bolder ones began to ask Mrs. Oglethorpe when an engagement was to be announced. Mrs. Oglethorpe denied that any such thing would occur. Everyone except Mrs. Oglethorpe was pleased at the pairing. Priscilla was such a good girl, they said; how delightful that it was she who tamed the young rascal!

In late April Sarah paid a rare call on Blair and Prudence Saxon after the arrival of their daughter, and found Annabel puzzling over the fact that the child had been born with flaming red hair, since no one on either side of the family had been so afflicted. Annabel paused in her wonderment long enough to congratulate Sarah on Benjamin's having followed her advice in pursuing Miss Oglethorpe.

Priscilla made frequent visits to Beulah Land, with and without Benjamin, finding herself welcomed with genuine interest by his sister and his grandmother. Even Frankie Saxon remarked that she was amused at Benjamin's getting over his "unhappy disappointment" so quickly, and added that, although Priscilla Oglethorpe might not be everyone's idea of a fair prize, she was a perfectly respectable young woman against whom nobody could place a word.

Mrs. Oglethorpe held stubbornly to her position until she realized that Priscilla and Benjamin were not urging her to change her mind and let them make an announcement. She then began to see, or imagine she saw, "funny looks," as she called them to Mr. Oglethorpe, and ventured to fear that people were misconstruing the companionship between their daughter and Mr. Davis as "highly improper" if it were not leading them to the church door. The long-tormented Mr. Oglethorpe turned on his wife and shouted, "For the love of God, woman, put an end to it and stop bothering me with your female affairs!" The middle of May, Mrs. Oglethorpe lowered her flag. She told Priscilla that Mr. Oglethorpe and she were ready "reluctantly and with gravest doubts to consider the idea of a formal engagement, although the question of a wedding date is not yet to be talked of." Priscilla replied that she and Benjamin looked upon a long engagement as a most agreeable prospect. Thinking this over suspiciously, Mrs. Oglethorpe said she would allow a date to be set. Priscilla pointed out that Benjamin was a farmer and likely to be busy the rest of the year. "Everything is over by October," Mrs. Oglethorpe offered. Priscilla said she would ask Benjamin,

and she did, and so it was agreed: the wedding to take place at
St. Thomas's in October.

Roscoe Elk had worked hard at his father's—now his own—
affairs, and toward the end of May he asked Sarah and Benjamin
to meet with him and Roman at the business office in town. He
wanted them to know what he had done and what he planned to
do, as far as plans had been made; and he wanted to ask their
advice. When they gathered, they sat on the four sides of a
square table. First, Roscoe told them of the new agreements he'd
made with his tenants. They were to have greater freedom in
running their farms and a fairer share of what they produced,
but at the same time he was going to hold them fully accountable for what they did. Any man was free to move his family
away now with his debt canceled. If he stayed, he must make his
farm productive within three years or hand it back for Roscoe to
sell or let out to another family.

Roscoe had drawn a long-term agreement with Mr. James
Davis for his sawmill to take timber from his thousand woodland
acres. There were business properties in Savannah producing
regular rents, as well as a few in Highboro; and added together,
a small tract here, another there, there were more than two thousand acres of farmland aside from what had been Oaks plantation.

Although they listened with interest, Benjamin and Sarah exchanged an occasional puzzled glance as they wondered why
Roscoe was telling them what was properly his own business. If
he had been anyone else, they might have suspected him of bragging, but they knew him too well to imagine that. Sarah began to
listen more carefully, and presently Roscoe explained some of
the ways the large property had come under the Elk name.
Without passing the papers before him, he referred now and
then to one. Nothing illegal had been done, but hard lines had
been followed, and on no occasion had hardship to others been a
consideration.

"The history is long and tangled," Roscoe said, "and there is no
practical way to make restitution where I think there was wrong-
doing. But I want to clear my grandfather's name as far as I can,
and I've considered something else. The last of the Elk adventures—Grandpapa had nothing to do with it, but he would have
approved of it—was to build a house on the Davis place that

outdid the one at Beulah Land where he'd been in the position of a servant, although not a slave. I don't need that house or want it, and nobody is likely to buy it from me. There are four hundred good acres around it Papa saved for himself when he cut the big property into small farms. I'm going to keep a few of them to build me a house. Like you, Ben, I want my own, not one other people have tainted with their living. So, now—" Roscoe paused and looked at the faces of his three listeners, all of whom shifted in their chairs with a sudden alertness as they realized that he had come to the point of their meeting. "What am I going to do with that big house? —Big Beulah, Papa used to call it." He looked at Sarah, then Benjamin, and last at Roman.

Roman began to speak as he began to understand. "You're going to—give it to me for the school."

"Roscoe!" Sarah exclaimed. "Are you?"

His face relaxed. "It was you who started it," he said to Sarah, "the day you first said a-b-c to Roman."

Sarah reached to find Roman's hand. It was trembling, and it grasped hers quickly.

Roscoe took the papers before him and straightened their edges, putting them into a cardboard box and closing the top. "You can bring all your books and slates and maps and chalk, all your rules and children; and you can make that house anything you want it to be, you and Miss Selma and Miss Pauline. It's big enough so you won't have to complain again for a while about not having enough room. When you need more teachers, find them and bring them here. You won't have to worry about money. Except for the few acres I keep for my house, the farms on what was Oaks plantation will be worked for the school. The money they make is the school's."

As Roscoe continued to talk, the others joined in, and soon there were a dozen conversations, all part of the same conversation. They wondered whether the school should be kept for Negroes or opened to whites. After discussion, they decided to keep it entirely for Negroes. The school was a fact. To build on what was there would be acceptable to the community, however apprehensive they might feel about its growth and prosperity. They would employ white teachers when they could not find Negro teachers who were well enough qualified. Roman had a strong voice that had grown stronger through years of teaching, and he began to do what Sarah called speechifying as he unrolled his dreams. They let him preach and rave, enjoying his visions, until he speechified himself into tears; and then they laughed him to laughter again.

It was Benjamin who brought him back to earth. "Confound it, Roman, think as big as you want to, but you better talk smaller, lest they stop you before you start."

"He's right," Roscoe said to Roman. "As soon as they stop feeling sorry for you, you're in trouble. We'll all have to walk slow and carry our hats in our hands. Miss Sarah, do you think you can teach that Abraham a little humility, for Roman can't."

"It won't be easy," she said, shaking her head. "Let's give it a name."

"Oaks Academy," Roman suggested promptly.

"Not Oaks," Benjamin said. "Oaks was something else, and is no more.

"Elk Academy," Sarah said.

"Not Academy," Roscoe said. "That sounds too aping-white, the way Papa tried to copy Beulah Land. Let us have something businesslike and plain."

"Elk Institute," Roman said. Each of them pronounced it a few times and found it sounded like a name that already existed. "Elk Institute." In the fire of the hour they pledged themselves to work together. And so was the family founder, the first Roscoe Elk, finally betrayed.

Yet what is a dream of power such as his but ambition for a place in the sun? In a hundred years the Kendrick name might be forgotten, save in family annals; but because of his grandson, the name of Roscoe Elk would endure with honor as long as there was the Institute—and such places, once started, have a way of lasting. Its head would be the bastard of his wife Clovis and Leon Kendrick, both of whom he had destroyed. Thief and murderer, Roscoe Elk would not be the first such, or the last, to be praised for benefactions he would not have approved. In a living memorial he would have hated as much as ever he hated Kendricks and Beulah Land, his dream of a place in the sun would come true.

30.

By and by, came October and two events that were to matter in the life of the county for a long time.

The first was the opening of Elk Institute. Roman and Roscoe had been busy during the summer. Roscoe built a new house for himself, with Geraldine installed as housekeeper and Roxanne as cook. Roman went to Philadelphia to renew acquaintance with the school he had spent most of his early life working in, and to solicit the interest of Miss Eliza Truman's friends in the Institute. He persuaded a Negro couple, both teachers, to return with him to Highboro and the Institute. Carl Boland was proficient in mathematics and draftsmanship; he would start a workshop in addition to teaching. His wife Mathilda was primarily a grammarian. She was also a religious woman who hoped to take a strong part in the spiritual instruction of the school's pupils. Selma and Pauline would continue to teach, but both were in their middle sixties and insisted on leaving administration entirely to Roman.

Big Beulah—everyone quickly adopted the nickname for the school—was set up for classrooms and the necessary offices. The wide center hallway would serve for assemblies with folding chairs to be stacked along the walls when its function was that of passageway. Only Roman would live in Big Beulah; the Bolands were assigned one of the tenant houses and Selma and Pauline another, alterations and improvements made to suit.

Early on, Sarah had the idea of enlisting Annabel Saxon in the cause of the school. Annabel, when approached in a deferential way by Roscoe and Roman, was all eager condescension. She lacked a cause, and her only summer entertainment was to watch Frankie grow fat and uncomfortable as July sweated into August, and no one believed a cool day would ever dawn again. Sarah had thought carefully about asking Annabel's help before she suggested it. She knew that Annabel bullied and offended people with her causes, but she saw in this effect the advantage of drawing away any poison of public feeling from the school to Annabel.

Confiding her participation to Sarah, Annabel said, "It is, of course, on the very site of my birthplace and old home, so it was proper for Roscoe Elk to come to me. He truly is a genteel darky; rich, but knows his place. My two Blairs tell me he provides a considerable business for the bank. Oh yes, quite respectable. He speaks well of you, Auntie Sarah. You must try to be polite to him, however prejudiced you feel against his father and grandfather." She sighed. "It is hard for the aging to forget the past, but those younger have learned to move with the times and understand that life cannot be again as it was."

Although not asked to do much, the fact that she associated herself vocally with the Institute was helpful in exactly the way Sarah hoped it would be. Annabel saw herself as the Institute's counselor and clarion. "I hope never to be laggard in a worthy cause," she declared. She was present on the day the bell rang a beginning for the new school, although there was no great ceremony to mark the occasion. A general assembly in the wide hallway with all the pupils and the five teachers was attended by Roscoe Elk; and Sarah came with Casey, who had offered to make commemorative photographs. Mathilda opened the brief proceedings with a prayer Doreen might have envied her. Roman gave a speech that would have been longer if Abraham had not been sitting in the front row crossing his eyes at him. Annabel was introduced as the Institute's first patron. Pauline closed the meeting with a brusque exhortation to all to work hard. As the gathering dissolved, the children filing in orderly lines to the classrooms, Annabel said to Sarah, "Bonard's little boy is to be called Blair, they have at last decided. I told them to feel free to use the name since Prudence produced only a girl as her first, and with red hair at that. He is to be Blair Saxon, the Third." She laughed. "Like a dynasty of kings!"

"Or the Roscoe Elks," Sarah observed mildly.

"Really," Annabel said sharply, "you are getting peculiar, Auntie Sarah."

The other event of October was the wedding of Priscilla Oglethorpe and Benjamin Davis at St. Thomas's Church.

A part of the gallery was reserved for the Negroes who had been asked to attend. Zadok and Rosalie came early, leaving their children at home in the charge of the eldest. Abraham sat beside Josephine. Tenah was there, and Millie and Fox. Roman was with Pauline and Selma in the row behind Abraham, on whose back all three now and then fixed a watchful eye. Roscoe Elk had been invited but did not come. Elsewhere in the gallery and crowding the pews downstairs was a substantial portion of the population of Highboro and the surrounding county. Benjamin and Priscilla enjoyed a wide regard, but it was not that which made the wedding an occasion; it was the consciousness that Beulah Land was marrying. The last such marriage was Sarah's to Leon Kendrick, and it had taken place in 1828 in Savannah, another October. Highboro had not seen a wedding of such importance to Beulah Land since that of Leon Kendrick's parents, Arnold and Deborah in 1800. Deborah and Nell Singleton, sisters, had married Arnold and Felix Kendrick, brothers. Today people came to bear witness to yesterday and to be able to boast tomorrow that they had been there.

Benjamin's best man was Daniel Todd. Priscilla's attendants were her sister Elizabeth and Jane Todd. Nell made an exception to her rule of not leaving Beulah Land. She appeared to be interested for a time, but the music and the long sitting made her sleepy, and she nodded as she nibbled a square of sugary fudge from the napkinful Josephine had provided her. All the Saxons were present except the youngest, who were at home in the care of their mammies. James and Maggie Davis sat close to each other holding hands, as was their wont. Doreen helped Miss Kilmer with her music sheets, although Miss Kilmer did not refer to them at all, so well had she prepared her two songs.

Casey Troy was handsomely genial to all, making it seem a happier event than did Sarah, who looked sometimes sad and distracted, and then startled and a little angry, as if she were just realizing the import of the day.

At the later gathering at the Oglethorpe house, Casey made photographs of the couple in the wedding clothes. There was the customary milling about, and Nell, disappointed at the spartan table refreshments, pled fatigue and asked Jane and Daniel to take her home.

Sarah and Casey's trunks were at the depot, for they were going to Savannah on the train. Daniel would join them in a few days for his further initiation into the autumn selling of crops, a matter attended to in recent years by Benjamin alone. Priscilla and Benjamin were to go directly to their house at the Glade following the reception. Priscilla wanted it so, and Benjamin was happy not to be going to Savannah this October. Annabel called it most odd that there should be no wedding trip and asked why he had not combined one with his regular business sojourn in the coastal city. Receiving no answer, she shrugged. "No one will be surprised, I suppose, for no one expects normal behavior from those who live at Beulah Land."

While Priscilla changed her wedding dress, Benjamin drove Sarah and Casey to the depot. Casey crossed the street to buy cigars, and Sarah and Benjamin walked on the platform arm in arm.

"Grandma, if you see Nancy—" Benjamin began after a short silence.

"Oh, I shall see her. You told me where to find her."

"I don't reckon you ought to go there by yourself."

"I am certainly not going to take Casey." When he did not smile, she continued. "All females are curious about such places. I intend to have a thorough chat with your friend Miss Maysie. Anyway, I want to see Nancy."

"Tell her," Benjamin said after another pause. "Tell Nancy about me so she'll understand." He did not look at her as he said it, but she looked at him, and her hand tightened on his arm.

"I expect she will understand well enough," Sarah said. "I reckon she'll tell me what I came for before I say it."

The train arrived, and so did Casey.

Talking through the window when they were aboard, Benjamin said with the stranger's smile people always assume for leave-takings, "Now you won't forget anything, will you?"

As the train started, Sarah said, "Who taught you, Big Britches?"

The October sun was hot, and Roscoe carried his book to the shady end of the porch of his new house. It was shady because Jane had planted cuttings from Beulah Land and trained the vines when they grew. The wedding would be over by now and Sarah and Casey Troy on their way to Savannah. Roscoe felt lonely, remembering his last meeting with Sarah the evening before. Mathilda Boland had taken an interest in Claribell when she heard her story and asked if she might take her into her house and care, at least until the child was born, and longer if it proved a satisfactory arrangement. Sarah knew Mathilda to be a trustworthy woman and was no longer startled at her greeting when they had not seen each other for a few days: "How is the state of your immortal soul, Mrs. Troy?" Sarah had decided that it was not an accusation but the anxious question of a friend. Claribell had now been with the Bolands for a week, and Roscoe reported her as satisfactorily settling in. Sarah said to Roscoe, "I wish you'd forget your turkey-tail pride and come to the wedding tomorrow." He shook his head. Sarah said to Roman, "I'll miss you both in Savannah."

Pleased, Roman pretended to scoff. "Listen to her. Everything is the way she wants it, but she'll miss *us*."

"Well, I will," Sarah protested.

"You want everything."

"Yes, I'm greedy. I want it all."

Shifting in his chair, Roscoe saw a face peering at him through the vine leaves. As soon as she knew herself discovered, Claribell turned and ran. "Wait!" Roscoe commanded.

She stopped and faced his direction, but she did not come back.

"Will you like living with Mrs. Boland?" he said to keep her.

She stared without answering.

"You must mind her, and she will do her best for you."

She looked down at the ground and inched away, as if he would not see her go a little at a time.

"You can come and sit on the porch if you want to," he said. "It's all right."

She looked up at him with comprehension, but she did not move.

"Nobody's going to hurt you, little sister."

On the Marsh farm, as day waned, the old mother, nearly blind, started a fire in the kitchen stove, her hands sure where her eyes were not. Bessie in the next room crooned her baby to sleep with an old lullaby her mother had sung to her. "When you wake, I'll bake you a cake; so go to sleepy, little ba-by."

The Glade waited for its new tenants. The house was finished and furnished. The milk cow was in her stall. Cold ham and chicken waited in the mesh-fronted food safe. Autumn flowers gave their scent to air already pungent with resin from the pine trees. A Jesus bug with long whiskery legs stood on the still water of a pool at the side of the brook. The cat named Ptolemy, gift of Miss Kilmer a month ago, found and ate a moth, licking his paws with as much pride as a lion that has dined on antelope. The Glade waited; and presently they came up the hill.